A Peculiar Connection

JAN HAHN

A *Pride & Prejudice* ALTERNATE PATH

Meryton Press
Oysterville, WA

Also by Jan Hahn

An Arranged Marriage

The Journey

A Secret Betrothal

A PECULIAR CONNECTION

Copyright © 2015 by Jan Hahn

ISBN: 978-1-936009-40-4

Layout and design by Ellen Pickels
Cover art by Janet Taylor
Original paintings of the children on the front cover by Jean Baptiste Greuze

Acknowledgments

With heart-felt gratitude, I would like to thank—

Jakki Leatherberry, my more than able editor, whose efforts made my story read so much better;

Janet Taylor, whose talent and skill created the front and back covers from my glimmer of an idea;

Michele Reed, Ellen Pickels, and all the staff at Meryton Press who once again turned my little narrative into a book;

Debbie Styne, L.E. Smith, and Ellen Gelerman, for being the first to give their reviews and suggestions when this work was a story entitled Sins of the Fathers;

Ali from A Happy Assembly for sharing her knowledge of Ireland;

My dearest family and friends who continue to support my endeavors;

My readers who hold a special place in my heart; and, of course,

The incomparable Jane Austen who continues to inspire me each time I read her words.

Prologue

Before I begin my tale,
I must share with you what I have been told.

Some one and twenty years earlier, on a night turned darker than usual in early springtime, a man ran through the wood of Pemberley as though chased by Satan himself. A storm had broken at the exact moment he learned that she was dead. He had staggered backward down the stone steps, so stunned he did not see lightning strike a tree beside the great house. He was unable to comprehend what he had heard, unable to think what he must do, unable to breathe.

Like a blind man, he turned in the direction of the wood with his hands outstretched. The wood had been sacred, the place where they first met, their haven against the world. Rain and wind lashed his body without mercy while thorn-covered branches reached out to tear at his clothing and skin. Heedless of injuries, he stumbled through the brush and lurched from tree to tree. Unspeakable sorrow pierced his heart.

Nature's outburst endured throughout the night as did the man's sojourn in the forest. With the first touch of dawn, the storm's rage abated at last, and the man found himself outside the only place of comfort he could find. A single candle glowed within the old church, and he knew the door would be unlocked. He burst into the sanctuary. Throwing himself on the floor, prostrate before the altar, he cried one word over and over.

"Why?"

The noise interrupted the man of God's prayers, and he hastened to minister to the man lying in misery. "My son, what has happened to cause such anguish?"

He attempted to brush back the mass of wet curls from the young man's forehead and pulled him to a seated position on the floor. "You must tell me," he demanded.

"All is lost. She is dead."

"Dead? No, she is far too young! How can this be?"

"A fall. Her brother said—oh God—he said she fell from the head of the stairs to the bottom!"

He collapsed back onto the floor and beat the stones with his fist, unaware that blood flowed from his hand into the crevices in the rocks until they were stained crimson. "Oh God, oh God," he cried again and again.

"I grieve with you, my son." He reached out to bind the man's hand with his handkerchief. "But let us pray. God will hear you."

The man jerked his hand away. "You ask me to pray? How can I? There are no words. There is nothing I can— This is above what I can bear!"

"There is nothing you cannot abide with God's help."

The grieving man rose to his feet with difficulty, as though a massive millstone pressed upon his back.

"Why must it be her, and why now when God knows she is my life?" His voice rose louder and louder until he was shouting. "It is not fair!"

The old man shook his head. "Life rarely is, a conclusion all of us reach eventually."

"I have nothing left."

"Come now. You have suffered great tragedy, but you have your family, your future."

"They mean nothing without her—nothing. What am I to do?" His voice cracked, and he began to sob anew.

"We are all in God's hands. I have watched you fight for the life you desired, but now it has been taken from you. It is time, my son—"

"Time? Time for what?"

The man of God's hand trembled as he placed it on the young man's head. "Time to allow Him to work His will in your life."

Chapter One

There was a time in my life when I expected an ordinary day to be just that. I have since discovered that expectations are fragile whether they pertain to a solitary day or to life itself. Circumstances can shatter expectations as easily as dropping a china cup upon a slate floor splinters its beauty into misshapen shards of pottery.

I no longer depend upon childish assumptions. In truth, the fates have taught me to fear an ordinary day. I have learned that, when one anticipates reason and routine, one may receive neither. I am now painfully aware that my life never was or ever shall be as I once envisioned.

That day—the day my life deviated with a vengeance from the commonplace—began like any other, lit with the shimmering golden haze with which autumn paints Hertfordshire. The good people of Longbourn village went about their lives as always. Rising early, they milked cows, gathered eggs, baked bread, and churned butter.

My family, who dwelt at the manor house for which the village was named, engaged in the usual activities to which they were accustomed. My father suffered through my mother's harangues at the breakfast table until he escaped into his study. Mary applied herself to the pianoforte with zeal unappreciated by her sisters. Kitty set herself the task of answering Mrs. Wickham's latest letter. Jane anticipated her intended's visit by selecting a gown in his favourite shade of blue while I offered my opinion on which style the maid should do her hair. All in all, it could be accurately deemed the beginning of an ordinary day.

When I think back, I do recall a certain nervous anticipation, a feeling I had entertained for more than a week. Ever since Mr. Bingley had returned to the county and arrived at our door accompanied by Mr. Darcy, I longed to see the latter gentleman once again. Alas, on the day Mr. Bingley proposed to Jane, Mr. Darcy left for Town, but Mr. Bingley expected him to return, and I lived on that prospect.

I awoke each day in hopes I would see him. We had known each other for almost a twelve-month—an eventful year that commenced in misunderstanding born of prejudice and pride on both our parts. Now, however, I harboured the expectation that our disagreements lay buried in the past and dared to dream of a new beginning.

I recalled how Mr. Darcy had proposed to me the previous spring and how I refused him with unbecoming resentment. At the time, I had believed Mr. Wickham's lies and did not comprehend the truth of Mr. Darcy's character. Eventually, events transpired to reveal how mistaken I had been. I now knew him to be a gentleman of the highest integrity, a man I could respect, a man perfect for me. I longed to thank him for uniting my sister Lydia in marriage with Mr. Wickham. Although my family did not know the generous part Mr. Darcy played in the affair, I did, and I understood the gratitude we owed him.

And I yearned—oh, I yearned with all my heart—for him to renew his addresses to me, for by that time, I had fallen in love with Mr. Darcy…deeply in love. When we had parted in Derbyshire, I had given up all prospects of seeing him again because of the scandal caused by my sister's foolish elopement with Mr. Wickham. Some time later, upon gaining knowledge that Mr. Darcy had thereafter travelled to London and toiled day and night to find my sister, I had allowed my heart leave to anticipate that he might still harbour warm feelings for me.

He had given no hint that tenderness toward me remained. Since Mr. Bingley's return to his estate in Hertfordshire, Mr. Darcy had called upon us but once, and the visit had proved awkward. My mother had snubbed him most conspicuously, and I was shamed by her behaviour. Not a word passed between us, but I felt his eyes upon me more than once. I had no other cause for hope, but still, I began each day wondering whether Mr. Darcy would return.

And so, although I termed the beginning of that day ordinary, my feelings were not. Still, my familiar surroundings concealed any cause for undue anxiety…until she arrived.

Lady Catherine de Bourgh refused to wait to be announced but swept into our parlour like a bitter north wind. She barely acknowledged my mother and sisters before she summoned me to accompany her out of doors to the portion of our lawn she termed a *prettyish kind of little wilderness.* I scarce had time to grab my pelisse before she sailed out the door. Silence reigned between us until we reached our destination, whereupon she turned and fixed her stare upon my person.

Using her cane for emphasis, she paced back and forth, all the while accusing me of entering into an engagement with her nephew Mr. Darcy, an engagement she affirmed impossible. I was at a loss as to what had brought about the unexpected declaration, for I knew it to be untrue, but I would not give her the satisfaction of an outright denial until she asked me point-blank.

"Tell me, once for all, are you engaged to him?"

"I am not," I had to admit.

She gave a great sigh of relief. "And will you promise me never to enter into such an engagement?"

"I will make no promise of the kind."

"Miss Bennet, I am shocked and astonished. I expected to find a more reasonable young woman. But do not deceive yourself into a belief that I will ever recede. I shall not go away till you have given me the assurance I require."

I refused to yield, and we continued to argue the horror of such a union. At last, she insulted my family and me to an extent that I could bear it no longer.

"Lady Catherine, I must beg to return to the house. I have nothing further to say. You know my sentiments." I turned my back on her and took steps toward the iron gate.

"You refuse to oblige me? You refuse to obey the claims of duty, honour, and gratitude? You are determined to ruin him in the opinion of all his friends and make him the contempt of the world."

"Duty, honour, and gratitude have no claims on me in the present instance. None of those principles would be violated by my marriage with Mr. Darcy."

"Very well. I shall now know how to act. Do not imagine, Miss Bennet, that your ambition will ever be gratified. I came to try you. I hoped to find you reasonable, but depend upon it: I will carry my point. You err grievously to think you may pollute the shades of Pemberley with such a union. I will not allow it."

I stopped short. My colour was high but not as florid as hers. "And how might you exercise this power of prevention upon either your nephew or myself?"

She reached inside her reticule and pulled forth a folded square of paper, creased and yellowed by time. "I hoped to avoid this, but you leave me no choice. You cannot marry my nephew. It would not only be despicable in my eyes and that of the world, but it would be a sin against Heaven itself!"

"A sin against Heaven?" I could not help but laugh. "Surely, even you cannot give voice to that claim. Mr. Darcy is a gentleman. I am a gentleman's daughter. So far, we are equal."

"You speak the truth. You are the daughter of a gentleman, but not the gentleman in whose house you have been reared."

I blinked. *Has she lost her senses? Of what is she speaking?*

"You are not Elizabeth Bennet. In truth, you possess only your Christian name. You are the natural daughter of George Darcy. You and my nephew are brother and sister."

My knees gave way, and I reached out to the nearby stone wall. A loud racket buzzed in my head, and I could not comprehend her conversation. She must have led me back to the bench, but I do not remember it. Evidently, several moments passed before my faintness subsided and I understood her words once more.

"Shall I call for a servant? Your countenance is uncommonly pale."

I shook my head and attempted to focus my eyes. At last, the trees ceased to whirl in their contorted dance. Lady Catherine sat beside me, and I became aware that she held my hand. I stiffened and withdrew from her touch.

"No, do not call anyone. I am well."

We said nothing for a moment or two while I tried to make sense of her statement. "I do not believe you," I said at last.

"Whether you believe me or not does not change the truth of the matter."

"How? How can I be the daughter of George Darcy? Do my parents know?"

"I have no idea what knowledge Mr. and Mrs. Bennet possess other than the fact that you were not born to them."

"What…what proof do you have to make such a claim?"

She handed me the parchment, but I could not read the words, for they would not remain still. Instead, they leaped up and down like demons around a witch's cauldron.

"My father…I must speak to my father."

"Miss Bennet—"

I heard Lady Catherine's voice, but I forgot all manners. Rising from the bench, I ran from the park, across the wide expanse of green yard, and back to the house where I burst into my father's study. "Papá!"

He looked over his glasses and placed a marker in his book. "Lizzy, child, what ails you? All colour is drained from your countenance."

"I have told her the truth." I heard Lady Catherine's voice behind me and watched my father rise from the chair, a frown covering his face.

"I beg your pardon," he said.

"I have told this young woman that you are not her natural father, sir. I assume you are the man who fostered her."

His face paled as he rounded the desk and took hold of my hands. "Lizzy, will you grant me the favour of an introduction to this lady."

I opened my mouth, but before I could speak, Lady Catherine continued. "I am Lady Catherine de Bourgh of Rosings Park, aunt to Fitzwilliam Darcy, the son of my late sister. I know George Darcy fathered a girl child and that you raised her as your own. I insisted my husband tell me the truth of the matter before he died, and I have confirmed it with Fawcett. I would never have revealed the scandal but for the fact that this girl believes herself entitled to marry my nephew. She has drawn him in with her arts and allurements, but I shall not allow this travesty to occur."

"Lizzy, are you engaged to Mr. Darcy?"

"No, Father, but what Lady Catherine says… Is it true? Tell me, I pray you, am I not your daughter?"

By that time, my mother and Jane had heard the uproar and entered the room, hearing only my last query. Mamá gasped and began to wave her hands about.

"I knew this would happen. Did I not warn you time and again, Mr. Bennet, that this day would come?"

My father signalled for Jane to close the door to his study. "Calm yourself, Mrs. Bennet."

"What does she mean, Papá?" I demanded. "I must have the whole of it."

"Sit down, Lizzy. Jane, ring for some tea," my father answered.

"I do not want tea. I want to know who my real father is!"

He winced at my words but turned to our visitor. "Madam, might I prevail upon you to grant us privacy?"

"Yes, I see you have a significant explanation before you. Very well. I shall be on my way, but be assured, sir, the pretence is over. The girl must know who and what she is." She stalked toward the door, which Jane immediately opened for her. "Do not dare to entertain the foolish fancy of destroying that letter. It is merely a copy made many years ago. My barrister has the original safely locked away. If you wish to discuss this further, I shall be in residence at the home of my nephew's friend, Mr. Bingley."

Upon her leave-taking, Mamá resumed her hysterics while Jane attempted to quiet her. Papá took the wrinkled paper from my hand and sank down upon a chair. The line between his brows deepened the longer he read.

"Did you know about that note, Papá?"

"No, my dear."

"Is it true? You must tell me."

He kept his head lowered, raised his hand to his forehead, and began to rub the furrow back and forth as though he might somehow erase the ugly revelation.

"Tell her," my mother cried. "Tell her once and for all."

My breathing grew shallow, and a knot rose up in my throat until I could scarce draw breath at all.

"Lizzy," Papá began, his voice sounding defeated.

"If you do not, I will," Mamá declared. "But first, you must explain why Lady Catherine was here. Is Lizzy of possible kin to that great house?"

Of a sudden, a new fear gripped me. If my mother suspected I had connections with aristocracy, she would not wait to spread the news. Frantically, I searched my mind for some disclosure that would satisfy her. Fortunately, my father spoke for me.

"Of course not, Fanny."

"Then what was the purpose of her visit?"

"If you would grant me a moment, Mrs. Bennet, I shall explain. And pray, quiet yourself. There is no need for Mary and Kitty to hear, much less the servants." He rose and paced back and forth as though he were purchasing time to think up a plausible explanation for Lady Catherine's revelation.

"It all happened so long ago. Lizzy, your mother and I—we never—I never thought it necessary to tell you. You have always been our daughter. I believe I almost forgot your mother did not give birth to you."

"I never forgot," Mamá cried. "I told you from the beginning someone would find out someday, but no, you would not listen, and now it appears we have a fine mess on our hands and all of it your creation."

I began to cry quietly. I had never felt as close to my mother as I did my father, and now I knew why. She did not consider me her daughter, and, in truth, she was right. Immediately, I felt Jane's arms around me as she sat down on the settee and pulled my head onto her breast.

"Lizzy," Papá said. "You must believe me when I tell you I never knew the name of your parents until this day. I simply knew you were orphaned and in need of a good home."

"And now you know the identity of Lizzy's parents? Then out with it, Mr. Bennet, even though I am quite certain they are long dead. Do not keep us in suspense any longer," Mamá cried.

"It…seems our Elizabeth is a distant relation of the Darcys."

Distant relation? My eyes grew wide in wonder at my father's falsehood.

"The Darcys?" Mamá grabbed her throat and sank down upon a chair. "Well! But why should Lady Catherine come to tell us that? Why did not Mr. Darcy come?"

"Mamá," I began, sitting up and pulling away from Jane.

"What else did Lady Catherine say? How close is the connection?"

"Not close," Papá said quickly, "not close at all. In truth, my dear, she was born to Mr. Darcy's poorest relations. The lady has only recently become privy to the knowledge, and she came to warn Elizabeth not to prevail upon it."

My mother frowned as did Jane. "But, Papá," my sister asked, "why should she think Lizzy would do such a thing?"

"Hmph! Lizzy has no use for Mr. Darcy and makes no bones about it," Mamá said. "As for Lady Catherine… Now, Lizzy, it might be wise if you were to cultivate a friendship with her. Curb your saucy manners, and flatter the great lady. If you are admitted into her inner circle, think of the advantages she might offer."

I sighed deeply. "That is highly improbable. If you had heard our conversation, you would know Lady Catherine has not the slightest interest in any future entertainment of my company."

"And, my dear," my father added, "if you listened closely, you might recall that I said the connection is with the Darcys, not the de Bourghs."

Just then, Hill entered the room with a tea tray and placed it on the desk.

My mother refused the tea, calling for her salts instead. She left the room with Hill, declaring she must lie down, for she had much to think about, a statement that filled me with dread. She called for Jane to assist her, and although I wished my sister might stay, my father dismissed her with a nod. The moment they closed the door, I rose and whirled around to face him.

"How could you tell such a tale? You know Mamá will take delight in spreading what she believes a fortunate turn of events throughout the community."

"I thought it the lesser of two evils."

"Do you think Lady Catherine will rejoice when news reaches her that I am Mr. Darcy's poor relation?"

"She will prefer my story to the fact that you are Mr. Darcy's illegitimate sister. According to a letter I received from Mr. Collins this morning, she plans for Mr. Darcy to marry her daughter."

The word *illegitimate* slammed into me like a hard fist in the pit of my stomach. Once again, I was forced to sit down to keep from falling. "Oh, Papá, why did you not tell me the circumstances of my birth long ago? How could you let me grow up thinking I was your daughter?"

"You are my daughter."

"And Mr. Darcy… Even after he came to Hertfordshire, you still did not think it necessary that I know he is my—" My voice broke, for I could not utter the word.

"I did not know. Lizzy, believe me. Until moments ago, I did not know the name of your natural father."

He rose and walked to the window, his shoulders slumped. Suddenly, he appeared old, his vigour and liveliness dimmed. At length, he returned to sit across from me, leaned forward, and took my hand in his. "Lizzy, allow me to tell you how it happened."

He then laid out the entire sordid tale. One night, almost one and twenty years earlier, the vicar of Longbourn Church had sent a messenger requesting Mr. Bennet's presence. The hour was late. The knock at the door sounded just as my father had picked up the candle in his office and headed for the stairs. The message urgently requested his assistance, and so he complied without delay. Some months earlier, Mrs. Bennet had taken Jane, who was but a toddler, to London to visit her brother and his new wife, so there was no one else at home save the servants.

At the vicarage, the parson met him with a worried look. A well-dressed gentleman stood within the parlour, but no introductions were made, a curious occurrence made even stranger when Mr. Bennet heard the faint cries of an infant. Within moments, the gentleman made his departure.

"What is all this, Mr. Fawcett?" Mr. Bennet asked.

Closing the door behind the gentleman, the vicar drew close and spoke in a low voice. "I am beset with a strange task, Mr. Bennet. I call upon you as squire of the village for guidance."

He led him toward a basket from whence the soft sounds emanated. There, wrapped in blankets, lay a tiny dark-haired baby.

"She was the prettiest little thing I had seen next to my Janey," my father said. "Where my own babe had golden curls, this little one had a mass of dark tresses and the sweetest pout of a tiny pink mouth."

The clergyman explained that the child was the natural daughter of a gentleman from the North Country. Her mother had died giving birth two days earlier, and she had been brought to him because of an old friendship from earlier times. It would cause a scandal for the gentleman's family unless the child was raised in a distant county. He would provide funds for her upbringing but wanted all other contact with her severed. She was never to know his name.

"Which family in the village shall I call upon to take her, sir?" the vicar asked.

Mr. Bennet shook his head sadly. How could a man turn his back on such a child? She was beautiful and appeared to possess a good constitution. He searched his mind for a suitable house, and the two men discussed several families who might be prevailed upon to take in the baby. They, at last, settled upon the Pratt household. The mother had lost an infant to the fever the year before, and she might look favourably upon the substitution. It was determined that the vicar would call upon them with the morning light, and he would awaken his housekeeper to tend the infant through the night.

Mr. Bennet took one last look at the little bundle; the baby had ceased whimpering. He pushed the blanket back and softly caressed the tiny pink cheek. Instinctively, the baby girl's little fingers curled around his large forefinger and held on for dear life. Her dark eyes sparkled, and a diminutive smile flashed across her sweet countenance for a second. At that moment, she not only snatched hold of Mr. Bennet's finger but his heart as well.

"I could not let you go, Lizzy." He covered my hand with both of his. "From that moment, you were my child, my daughter. I never looked back. I never again thought of you belonging to another man. Oh, I had some convincing to do when your mother returned a few days later, but for all her bluster, she took to you as one of her own. The vicar and I agreed we would never reveal your parentage. Your mother's visit had been lengthy because of her sister Gardiner's difficult confinement that resulted in a stillbirth. When Fanny returned, we told everyone she, too, had given birth while in Town. Your mother was of a sweeter, more compliant nature at the time and, with a little persuasion, willing to keep the secret even though it went against her better judgment. No one questioned us, and I never thought it necessary to say otherwise. The servants were bribed and sworn to secrecy, and, in fact, Hill is the only one remaining from that time."

He had stared at the floor or around the room during much of his recital, rarely meeting my eyes. He now did so, and I saw the mist therein threatening to spill. "I am sorry, my dear, so very, very sorry. I am guilty of a grievous error in judgment. I should have told you. I see that now. I pray you will forgive me."

I SPENT THE REMAINDER OF that day wandering the back lanes and countryside of Hertfordshire on foot. I could bear neither the closeness of the house nor my sisters' solicitude. My father decided to tell Mary and Kitty his altered version of my birth and connection with the Darcys, adding that my real parents had been killed in an accident shortly after I was born. Naturally shocked, they each declared their love for me. Each expression of sympathy simply renewed my grief, and I desired solitude in which to grasp the enormity of the morning's revelation.

Where I walked, I could not tell you. My mind raced from shock to anger to anguish while my body instinctively plodded on, placing one foot before the other. How could I accept the knowledge that my life would never be the same again…that I was not the person I always knew myself to be…that the family I loved as my own was nothing of the sort…and worst of all… that secretly I must now think of Mr. Darcy as my brother?

Hope no longer existed. He could never renew his addresses. Even the idea was abhorrent now. Most likely, he would flee the county to avoid facing the scandalous consequence his own father created, unaware of the fabrication Papá had invented. I should never be allowed to express my gratitude for his part in saving Lydia, for I knew in my heart that I would not see his face again.

Twilight had descended by the time I returned to Longbourn. Unaware of the lateness of the hour, I was surprised when of a sudden I could barely make out the road before me. I hastened my steps toward the lights shining in the windows of the house in which I had grown up. My heart ached to think I did not truly belong there. If my real father had wanted me, I would never have known Papá or Jane. I would never have slept in the bed I had crawled into every night all these years or shared the laughter and comfort of growing up one of five Bennet sisters.

Once more, tears trickled down my cheeks, and instead of entering the house, I stood back and remained in the shadows until I could wipe my face clean with the sleeve of my pelisse and swallow the emotions that choked me. At last, I opened the front door, hoping the family sat in the parlour so that I might make my escape above stairs.

"Miss Elizabeth!" Hill cried. "You must go into the family directly. They have been sorely troubled."

"No, pray tell them I am tired and have gone to my room."

"But you must, miss. The gentlemen callers are most anxious to see you as well."

"Gentlemen callers?"

Just then, Kitty emerged from the parlour, and seeing me, she called back to my family that I had returned. With a great sigh, I straightened my shoulders before I was ushered into the room. The entire family was present along with Mr. Bingley, and to my utter dismay, I saw Mr. Darcy standing at the window.

"Lizzy, where have you been?" Mamá cried. "We have been worried nigh to death. Have you no compassion on my poor nerves?"

"Come in, my dear," Papá said as he rose and crossed the room to my side.

I could feel my cheeks burn as I curtseyed briefly to Mr. Bingley and in the general direction of Mr. Darcy. I could not lift my eyes to meet his but chose to study the pineapple design in the carpet at my feet, a pattern as familiar as the wallpaper in my chamber. Never in my life had I felt such shame, not even at the news of Lydia's elopement. Why was *he* here? How could he possess so little understanding?

"Shall you not answer me?" my mother asked again. "We feared you had been snatched by the gypsies, staying out this late in the evening."

"Forgive me. I strayed too far and did not notice the passage of time." I quickly crossed the room and sat beside Jane.

Mamá threw her hands in the air. "Did not notice—head in the clouds again, I suppose! And Mr. Darcy here has waited several hours—"

"It is of little importance," Mr. Darcy interrupted, "as long as you are well."

I raised my head then, feeling his gaze upon me. The expression in his eyes was pained, the natural dark-brown colour now almost black. We looked straight into each other's eyes, and I was shocked to see neither disdain nor anger, but what appeared to be a reflection of sympathy.

"Mr. Darcy," my father said, "I am in need of serious libation, and since it is obvious Mr. Bingley desires naught but the nectar of love, would you care to join me in the library?"

Jane blushed at Papá's words, but they did not seem to deter Mr. Bingley's steadfast attention.

As the men reached the doorway, my father turned back and inclined his head toward me. "And, Lizzy, I would speak with you."

"Oh, yes," Mamá said, rising quickly. "That is an excellent idea, Mr. Bennet. Let us repair to your study immediately."

I saw consternation flicker across Mr. Darcy's face, but Papá intervened. "My dear, you must not neglect our other guest. Think what Mr. Bingley should suffer in your absence. I am sure Mr. Darcy will make do with the sacrifice, for he is a generous man."

My mother looked somewhat torn between the choices, but when Mr. Bingley bestowed one of his beatific smiles upon her, she happily sat down and gave him her full attention.

Inside my father's study, I sat on the chaise at his insistence while Mr. Darcy remained standing.

"Lizzy, Mr. Darcy and I have talked at length. He agrees that no one must know the true nature of your relationship, not even Mr. Bingley, Jane, or his younger sister. He is perfectly willing to abide by the story that you are a distant cousin, and he has returned from Town this very day to make you a handsome offer."

I frowned, baffled at the suggestion.

"He desires to bestow a generous settlement upon you."

"I do not understand." I turned to look at him. "Why should you do that, sir?"

Mr. Darcy took a few steps nearer. "I have the entirety of the matter from Lady Catherine. I mean to give you your inheritance, Elizabeth—secretly of course, but your rightful inheritance."

"I still do not comprehend your meaning. Did your father name me in his will?"

He looked away, and I could see the embarrassment this entire scene caused him. Oh, I could not bear to be the reason for his shame.

"There was no mention in his will, except that a certain sum was to be sent to his solicitor in London every year in payment of a private debt. When I took over as master of Pemberley, my father's attorney simply told me it was a *personal* matter. I now assume the money has been sent to the vicar of Longbourn Church, who then handed it over to Mr. Bennet."

"That is correct," my father said.

"The will provided Georgiana an ample fortune but left the bulk of his estate and the property, of course, to me. I propose to share a goodly portion with you. It shall be accomplished discreetly. No one need ever know, not even Georgiana. If Lady Catherine is your concern, be assured that she will remain silent, for she fears the taint of scandal. "

I was mortified. How could he think I would accept such a gift? "Mr. Darcy, there is no need for you to make such a gesture. I thank you, but I shall not allow it."

"But why not? It is your right. You are"—he swallowed—"my sister just as Georgiana is."

"No, I am not." I rose and walked to the window where I fingered the drapery and peered out into the darkness. "I am your half-sister, sir, born on the wrong side of the blanket, a fact that must be kept secret so as not to sully your good name. Your father did not want me, and I do not want anything that is his. If the only father I have ever known will allow me to remain in his house, then this is where I shall stay." I turned my gaze upon Papá and saw him nod in agreement.

"Good night, Mr. Darcy. I do not think we should ever meet again." I walked across the room, out the door, and up the stairs.

Chapter Two

In our bed that night, Jane allowed me to weep on her shoulder until, spent, I at last drifted into troubled slumber.

Upon awakening, I saw the rumple of sheets I had created. My sister had already risen and dressed. One look in the mirror told me I did not wish to encounter anyone before somehow repairing my wild tangle of hair. Restoring my swollen, red eyelids was another matter.

A slight tap at the door announced the maid bearing a tray containing mugs of hot, steaming tea.

"Taste it, Lizzy," Jane said, "while I attack your curls."

"Mmm, a hopeless task I fear." I sipped the comforting drink and closed my eyes as my sister gently worked at the snarled locks streaming down my back.

"I hope you feel better today."

I squinted at the sunshine beaming through the window and, for Jane's sake, decided I would attempt a cheerful tone. "'Tis difficult to remain sad on a day deprived of morning fog. Not a cloud appears in the sky."

"After I have worked wonders on your hair and we have breakfasted, shall we not go for a long tramp in the woods?"

I shook my head. "You forget Mamá has claimed you for the dressmaker's this morning. Another fitting for your wedding gown awaits." She frowned and opened her mouth to protest, but I was quicker than she. "Go along, Jane. I shall be well."

"Shall you not come with us? You know I treasure your opinion above that of Mamá."

"I fear I would be a gloomy impediment on what should be a joyful excursion. Let me remain here for today."

"But, Lizzy…"

I rose from the chair and took the brush from her hand. "I insist, Jane. From the looks of that bed, I have already spoilt your night. I shall not spoil your day. Forget this mop of hair as well. I shall pin it up in a simple knot, and it will do perfectly well. After all, it is not as though there is anyone of importance who will wish to see me."

She caught my hand and pulled me around to face her. "Now, Lizzy, you must conquer this. I know the secret you learned yesterday is shocking. It pains all of us that you were orphaned as an infant and not born a Bennet, but it does not change who you are: my sister, my dearest sister, who is lovely and lively and brings joy to any room she enters. I pray you will not let this accident of birth alter that essential."

I closed my eyes, but she would not let go of my hand. How I longed to tell her the truth, but I could not bring myself to inflict more pain upon her. I did not wish anything to interfere with the happy anticipation of her coming marriage.

"Very well, I shall try, but only for you, Jane." She hugged me and helped me shed my gown and don a morning dress of pale yellow and white. "That does not mean I shall go to Meryton with you, though."

"But, Lizzy…"

"No, Jane, not today. Do not ask more than I can give."

That afternoon, when the house had emptied of my mother and sisters and Papá had been called to the stable to inspect a recent wound in the ear of one of the cows, I found myself increasingly restless. After wandering about the parlour, upstairs and down again, I found nothing with which to occupy my mind. At last, I grabbed my bonnet and left for a walk. Throughout the morning, I had tried my best to remain cheerful with both family and servants, ignoring the strain the effort played upon my emotions. Relief abounded in the freedom of a solitary trek through the woods. There, I no longer needed to offer pretence of any sort.

I had no particular destination in mind but soon found myself nearing the stream that meandered through the deepest part of the forest. Sounds of water rushing over the rocks caused me to hasten my steps, for of a sudden, a longing to sit beside its clean, untroubled flow washed over me.

I stopped short, however, when I heard the sound of a man's voice.

Cursing! Harsh, angry words spewed from his mouth as fast as the spring bubbled below. Quickly, I stepped behind a tree, but not before he saw me. Mr. Darcy looked up and halted both his pacing and his swearing.

"Miss Bennet—Elizabeth!" He threw the hat he held in his hand to the ground and took a step toward me.

I turned away, wishing nothing more than to flee from the scene with all haste.

"Pray, do not go." Within moments, he stood beside me and then moved to bar my escape. "Forgive me. I should never have used that language had I known you were present."

"I did not mean to intrude, sir. If you will excuse me." I attempted to brush by him, but he took my hand in his. My skin tingled at the warmth of his touch.

"You did not intrude. Come now." In spite of every inclination to leave, I allowed him to lead me down the bank to the stream. He dropped my hand and picked up his hat. "You must think you happened upon a madman."

"One can see you are angry."

"Angry...that does not begin to describe my feelings."

"I thought you would return directly to Town or to Derbyshire," I said, floundering about for some way to change the subject. I felt quite sure I was the cause of his anger, and I did not wish to argue my decision of the night before.

"No...not yet. Will you sit?" He indicated a large grouping of rocks near the water.

I picked my way through the stones and found a smooth place. "I have whiled away many an afternoon on this old stone. It is an excellent perch not only for soaking one's feet but for contemplation as well. The calm I find in this setting has never yet failed to ease my soul. I consider it much like a familiar friend."

He smiled slightly, picked up a stone, and skipped it across the pond. When I commended his skill, he repeated the action. "If you had grown up at Pemberley, no doubt you would have discovered all the creeks and rills hidden within the wood, for I know you delight in nature's beauty."

"Mr. Darcy—"

He raised his hand as though he would brace himself against my words. "I know what you will say. I shall not add to your woes by painting a picture of a past that can never be. You have enough with which to make peace. I can see it is far too early to expect you to wish to learn more of the heritage that should have been yours."

"Thank you," I murmured.

We said nothing for a few moments. He picked up a stick and began working it between the small stones along the bank as though he might forcibly dig up an answer to our dilemma with his endeavour.

"I just do not understand it," he said.

"Sir?"

"My father—*our* father—was a most excellent man. For him to have engaged in irresponsible behaviour is utterly out of character. If I had not been in London when Lady Catherine told me of what had transpired, and if I had not gone immediately with her to the solicitor's office and read the words written in his own hand, I would never believe it."

"I confess I do not even recall what the note said."

"Assailed by the shock of it all, how could you? Mr. Bennet gave the copy to me…if you care to read it now." He reached inside his coat pocket and retrieved the worn, crinkled paper. My hand trembled slightly as I reached for it.

6 December 1791
Lewis,

Tonight I must beg leave to call in all favours you owe me. After you receive this letter, take the child somewhere safe. Find an honest, discreet soul who will provide for her. Inform Barnesdale in London where to send her yearly support. If at all possible, keep this from Catherine so that my dearest Anne will never know. As you are well aware, her constitution is delicate, and I cannot bear to witness her disappointment.
—George Darcy

A hastily scrawled postscript was added below:

9 December 1791
Delivered the girl child to Fawcett in Hertfordshire this date.
—Lewis de Bourgh

I swallowed the lump in my throat and still found it hard to draw breath. The first date was the day I was born, the birthday I had celebrated for not quite one and twenty years, never knowing I had made a perilous journey that same night or shortly thereafter, hastily scurried away from Derbyshire to be hidden miles away in Hertfordshire. I thrust the paper toward him. "Do you think your mother ever knew?"

"Dear God, I hope not!" Mr. Darcy began to pace again.

I stood up and turned to leave. The disgust in his voice pierced my heart. I could feel the stricture in my throat begin anew and the sting of tears about to fall. I would not let him see me cry.

"Excuse me," I managed to whisper and began to climb the bank.

"Elizabeth, wait!"

I did not heed his command but hurried all the more as I heard his steps follow mine.

"Why must you run away?" He caught my hand and attempted to halt my progress, but this time, I flung my wrist clear, shook my head, and walked even faster. Relentless and quicker than I, he soon blocked my path.

"Mr. Darcy—" I attempted to push my way past, but he would not let me go. He placed his hands on my shoulders, and cupping his hand beneath my chin, he forced me to raise my face to his. I could no longer hide the tears.

"Elizabeth, forgive me. Pray, do not cry. Come back, and let us talk."

I could not resist his strength or the kindness in his voice and once again allowed him to lead me to the rocks beside the water. There, he sat me down and knelt before me. No matter how I turned my face, he would not permit my escape from his persistent stare. His voice was soft and conciliatory. "Speak to me. Tell me what you are thinking."

"Why? What difference does it make? You cannot undo the past."

He shook his head slightly. "True, but with your consent, I can give you a more prosperous future."

"I told you last night that I did not want your father's money, sir, nor do I want yours."

"Can you not see it belongs to you? Imagine what you could do and who you could be with the inheritance that rightfully belongs to Elizabeth Darcy."

Elizabeth Darcy. I closed my eyes when he said the words. I had dreamt of wearing that name as his wife, not his sister. Had he so easily put away his former feelings for me? My mind raced, searching for some way to turn our conversation to another matter and thus conceal my strong emotion.

"Mr. Darcy, you must allow me to thank you for what you have done for my poor sister Lydia. My family would thank you if they knew, but because they do not, allow me to do so on their behalf."

He stiffened at my words and rose. He remained quiet while I explained that my youngest sister had let the story slip. I went on to assure him of my family's gratitude and that of myself for not only the money his aid had cost him but also the humiliation he must have borne in securing my foolish sister's marriage to George Wickham. "You must not feel you owe me anything more, sir, for I could never repay what you have already done for my family."

"Your family does not owe me anything, nor do you. I did what I did for…because…well, because it was my fault entirely. If I had warned Mr. Bennet of Wickham's character, the elopement would never have occurred. The fault was mine; thus, the remedy was mine to make."

"I cannot agree with that."

"Whether you agree or not, let us speak no further on the matter. What is of concern now is *your* future, Elizabeth. I cannot allow you to remain hidden away in this country burg when the fortune and society you deserve are yours for the taking. With the settlement I propose, you shall have whatever you wish."

I raised my eyes to his. "I shall never have what I wish."

He immediately turned away, but not before I heard his quick intake of breath.

Mr. Darcy left Netherfield the next day, and once more, I assumed I would not see him again.

Life went on; somehow, it does, no matter what. The story of my birth, subsequent fostering by the Bennets, and distant relation to the Darcys soon spread throughout the county. With servants at Netherfield and Longbourn knowledgeable of the circumstances, one could hardly expect to keep it quiet. Although surprised and curious, of course, our friends and neighbours rallied around my family. They continued to treat me with warmth and friendship; however, I could not help but detect a slight difference in their manners. I was not a lady of substance, but they knew full well I had been born to parents connected to a wealthy family. I was not Miss Darcy, but in their minds, I would never again be just Lizzy Bennet.

Within our own abode, the shock of my birth eventually faded. Jane's wedding took precedence, for which I was thankful. Mamá gradually overcame her pique that I had refused to better my situation by accepting a settlement from Mr. Darcy when preparations for the long-awaited event between Jane and Mr. Bingley began to consume her.

The wedding date was set for early January. With the holiday season and the Gardiners arriving from Town to stay through Christmas and until after the wedding, our house was a beehive of activity. Jane and I took every opportunity to perform our tasks together. I rejoiced that she was to marry a man she loved, but I felt our looming separation most acutely. I treasured every moment I spent with her and particularly those when we were alone.

"Lizzy," she said one night before bed, "do you ever regret your decision to forego taking advantage of your kinship with the Darcys?"

"Why do you ask me that, Jane?"

"At times, I detect an expression about your eyes, as though you yearn for something you do not have."

I rose from the dressing table and smoothed back the coverlet on the bed although the maid had already turned it down. "I do not know what you mean."

"I think you do. Lizzy, be honest. You would like to visit Pemberley again, would you not?"

"Visit?" I nodded. "Perhaps a short visit would be nice, but you know I do not wear the mantle of poor relation well."

"I do not believe Mr. Darcy or his sister would treat you shabbily. Besides, what is there to keep you here?"

"For one thing, you will live nearby. I can tramp through the fields to Netherfield whenever I like."

She smiled. "Yes, you may, but you know that Charles and I shall travel to London with the start of the Season. That will not be long after we return from our marriage tour. I am afraid I will not be here for some months."

I shrugged my shoulders. "Perhaps I shall visit Charlotte and our cousin again. Rosings Park is lovely at Easter…" My voice trailed off with those last words as I recalled the Easter before when Mr. Darcy had proposed.

"Would you truly entertain the idea of abiding Lady Catherine's presence on a daily basis? Surely not, Lizzy."

I pulled a face. "You are right. I do not care ever to see her again. Oh, do not worry about me, dearest Jane. I shall find ample activities with which to occupy my time until you return."

She placed the brush on the dresser and gathered her robe close before kissing my cheek. "Lizzy, do you still dislike Mr. Darcy?"

I hugged her and, in so doing, hid my expression. "I now think Mr. Darcy as good a man as I shall ever know. I just do not feel comfortable in his presence."

"Of course! I almost forgot he once asked for your hand in marriage. That was so long ago, but I suppose it is awkward if he still harbours feelings for you."

I held my breath for a moment, afraid of revealing the truth even to Jane. "I am certain his feelings were conquered the moment I refused him in such an abominable way. It would be impossible for him ever to think of me in that manner again."

"Then what is it? Are you afraid his sister has changed her opinion of you? You said she was most agreeable when you met at Pemberley."

"She was, but last summer, she had only to acknowledge me as an acquaintance, not as a distant relation possibly hoping to better her situation."

Jane looked thoughtful as she walked around the other side of the bed. "I believe you are mistaken. You told me how protective Mr. Darcy is of his sister. He would not have offered to render a settlement if he thought it might disturb Miss Darcy."

"It does not signify now. I have refused his offer, and that is the last we shall ever see of him. Good night, Jane."

"Good night, Lizzy, but do not make statements you cannot support. I have it on good authority that Mr. Darcy will attend my wedding." With a smile, she climbed into the bed and blew out the candle on the table beside her.

Oh, no! Why had I not thought of that? My head began to pound as I crawled into bed. So I would have to face him again after all.

THE HOLIDAY SEASON CAME AND went in a jolly blur. Our house brimmed over with children, merriment, and amusement. My mother suffered frequent bouts of nerves, and my father often retreated behind the closed doors of his library, but I welcomed the diversion. With Christmastide and Jane's wedding to occupy our days, I could bury the longing that threatened to overwhelm me at times. And yet, without warning and at the most inopportune moments, a sudden image of Mr. Darcy's beloved face would flash before me, and it was all I could do to retain control of my emotions. How could I ever think of him as my brother? I dreaded seeing him again, but even so, I yearned for a glimpse of his countenance just once more.

It did not help that my aunt Gardiner happened upon me all alone one day in the stillroom, whereupon she broached the subject for the first time. Having heard the entire altered version of the story of Lady Catherine's visit from Mamá, she seemed surprised I had not accepted Mr. Darcy's offer. She repeated the measure of esteem in which she and Mr. Gardiner held the gentleman. She believed he was a man of honour and would do his best for me.

"Lizzy, think of the society and privilege your connection would bring. And surely, you cannot have forgotten the splendours of Pemberley! Can you not imagine what pleasure the possibility of a future visit to that great house might afford you? I should think any connection with a family like the Darcys bears merit."

I shrugged and tried to change the subject, but she would not relent. "My dear, I think you should reconsider. It is an opportunity not granted to everyone. You should be grateful."

"I am grateful, Aunt, but at the same time, I am angry."

"Angry? Surely not with Mr. Darcy."

I shook my head. "No, no, not with him. I am angry with his—with *our* father."

My aunt looked up quickly. "*Our* father? I do not understand."

"He did not want me. He sent me as far from Pemberley as possible."

Without restraint, I confessed the true story of my birth to my aunt, the woman I had always trusted with all my heart. Throughout my childhood and beyond, I had considered her more of a mother than Mamá. Like a flooded river breaking through a dam, the words gushed forth. When finished with the tale, I gasped, shocked that I had blurted out the truth and yet strangely relieved, as though a tight rope had been loosened from around my neck.

Obviously shocked, she did not react in hysterics as Mamá would have done but kept her voice soft while attempting to use words that were sensible and comforting. "What else could he do, Lizzy? You have lived a sheltered life here in the country, but be assured these sorts of things are all too common. Mr. George Darcy might have disavowed any responsibility for you—many gentlemen do—but at least he provided for you."

"And that makes it right?" My voice rose in spite of my best efforts to curb my disapprobation. "A gentleman may betray his wife and desert the poor woman he takes as mistress as long as he provides for the result and keeps the good name of his family free from scandal?"

She reached out and held my hand. "Dearest, your anger has made you distraught. I hope you will come to peace with it in time."

"I have known of it but a brief time, Aunt."

"Yes, and 'tis true that the sins of the fathers are visited upon the children."

"How apt that the word '*fathers*' is plural in Scripture, for when I allow myself, I find I also am somewhat angry with the father who reared me."

"Thomas should have told you."

"Did you know, Aunt? Were you privy to the secret all these years?"

"I knew that you were an orphan and passed off as your mother's babe, for she stayed with us in London during the very time she supposedly gave birth to you. Naturally, Thomas had to take your uncle and me into his confidence to support the story, and Fanny also needed someone in whom she might confide her fears and misgivings. Thank God it was your uncle and I who shared her confidence and not my sister Philips."

I closed my eyes at the thought of my aunt Philips's loose tongue, but when I considered it, I changed my opinion. "Perhaps it would have been better had Aunt Philips known the truth, for then I would have been told at a much earlier age, and this entire situation could have been avoided."

"Why would you say that, Lizzy? Neither Thomas nor Fanny knew your real father was the late Mr. Darcy. In truth, if Lady Catherine had not felt it necessary to inform you, none of us would know it to this day. I still do not understand why she revealed such a tale. Surely, she knew it would only bring scandal upon her nephew's name. Why did she tell you?"

I felt my face grow warm. I did not wish my aunt to ask me that question, for what was I to answer?

"I...I do not know." I fumbled about for words. "She seemed to fear an association between our family and that of Mr. Darcy...perhaps because his close friend is marrying Jane."

"Surely, she did not think you had designs on Mr. Darcy. Everyone knows your account of the man, although I did observe a softening of your attitude toward him when we visited at Pemberley. But you never cared for him, did you, Lizzy?"

"Of course not," I said quickly. I turned away and busied myself with a basket of dried blooms. Carrying them across the small room, I paid strict attention to sorting them into separate stacks by specie and colour.

"I assume your position toward him did change to one of gratitude when you learned of his assistance to Lydia."

"I have expressed my thankfulness to him on our family's behalf. At the same time, I do not wish to be further obliged to the man, so you see, it is best that I refuse his offer and remain as I am."

I looked up to see whether my aunt believed my reasoning, but her expression appeared clouded. However, she agreed to share the true circumstances of my birth only with her husband and assured me he would not speak of it, a fact I trusted and for which I was grateful.

THE NIGHT BEFORE JANE'S WEDDING found me as nervous as the bride-to-be. My head ached anew at the thought of seeing Mr. Darcy again, so much so, that I could not swallow more than a few bites at dinner. My appetite had waned since I learned of the circumstances of my birth. Three times the dressmaker had altered the waistline of my dress for the wedding, and it still hung upon my frame. I could not sleep for dread of the coming day.

"This is insupportable!" I whispered to myself, rising from my bed. Walking to the window, I opened the shutter and stared at the full moon. I knew I must overcome the anxiety that dragged my presence down like an anchor thrown into the sea. The man was my brother; acceptance was the only answer. I would bury any other feelings I had ever felt for him and begin to think of him as I thought of Kitty or Mary.

"You can do this, Elizabeth Bennet," I said to myself. There, I had voiced my resolve, and I would carry through no matter what. From that day forward, Mr. Darcy would be of no more consequence than a distant familial connection, just as Papá had declared he was. I would be as I had ever been …before I loved him.

With a determined set to my shoulders, I turned and quietly crawled back into bed, hoping to avoid waking Jane. The only problem that remained was what to do with the pain in my heart.

Chapter Three

J ane's wedding was lovely, almost as lovely as the bride herself. Kitty and Mary had placed plentiful bouquets of dried arrangements at the altar, and their colours provided just the right contrast to Jane's white silk gown and Mr. Bingley's starched neckcloth.

I had attached myself to Jane's side before the ceremony and remained with her above stairs until time to walk to the church. Neither of us could eat, although for dissimilar reasons. Inside the sanctuary, I was conscious of a number of guests as we walked down the aisle, but I kept my eyes upon Jane. If Mr. Darcy stood among the crowd, I did not wish to see him and thus cause my countenance to alter.

Sunlight filtered through the stained glass windows as though God Himself beamed with joy at the union. As I listened to the bride and groom recite their vows, I fought the mist that filled my eyes. I was so happy for Jane—truly, I was—and yet, I could not help but wish I stood beside her, speaking those same words to the man I loved.

Stop it, Lizzy! I told myself. I dug my fingernails into my palms to distract my thoughts. *You have vowed to think of him as your brother. Do not forsake that vow.* Silently, I repeated the words before God. *Mr. Darcy and I are brother and sister. I renounce all prior feelings for him from this moment on.*

At the breakfast afterward, however, it proved impossible to avoid him. I felt his presence nearby rather than saw it, and with his greeting, I steeled myself to appear calm. Surprise overtook me when I turned and observed he was not alone. His sister stood beside him.

"Miss Bennet, I am so pleased to see you once again," she said with a curtsy.

I responded in kind and searched my brain for something to say. What must she think of me now? I must have mumbled something coherent, for she moved closer, and I found myself standing between her and Mr. Darcy.

"My sister has been anxious to speak to you," he said.

"Anxious?" I could not comprehend his meaning.

"Perhaps 'anxious' is an overstatement. 'Eager' might prove the better description."

"Oh yes," Georgiana said. "I have been eager to renew our acquaintance, especially in light of recent events."

"Recent events?" It seemed I could do nothing more than echo like an idiot.

She drew close and whispered in my ear, "We are now something like cousins, are we not? My brother has told me the whole of the story."

I straightened my shoulders, afraid of what she would say next.

"He says my aunt's revelation has overwhelmed you, and I can readily understand that. To learn that the parents you have always honoured are not truly your parents must be difficult to accept. To realize that your real parents died before you even knew them must grieve you anew."

"And do you not find it strange to accept that we are related, Miss Darcy?"

"I did find it shocking, but I am most pleased."

"Pleased?" Once again, I sounded like a parrot.

She smiled and touched my hand. "I liked you from the first time we met, and I can think of no one I would rather call cousin more than you."

How gracious her acceptance—it almost renewed my tears, and I took several steps backward to distance myself. Evidently, Mr. Darcy had told her the untruth my father created, and she, naturally, believed him. I wondered whether she would be as accepting of our relationship if she knew that we were sisters. I turned away slightly, hoping to spy Jane and thus escape the uneasiness of the situation, but Miss Darcy again laid a gentle hand on my arm.

"Miss Bennet, my brother and I would be honoured if you would consider visiting us at Pemberley. We leave Netherfield next week and hope you will make the journey with us."

I could not believe the words I heard. Visit Pemberley again? Had Mr. Darcy seriously encouraged Georgiana in this request? Was it I, alone, who imagined daily torture if I returned to Pemberley attempting to act the role of poor relation while, in truth, I was his sibling?

"Forgive me, I must attend Jane," I mumbled.

Forgetting my manners completely and without another glance in their direction, I fled the Darcys' presence and crossed the room to find Jane and Mr. Bingley surrounded by well-wishers. When I could not penetrate the throng, I hurried through the entryway and out the side door.

The sting of cold January air caused me to gasp, but it was not unwelcome. It had grown much too warm within the house filled with guests, and although I was surprised when snowflakes fluttered softly about my cheeks, I rejoiced that it would make a picturesque setting for the bride and groom's departure. Eventually growing cold, for I had not taken time to don a cloak, I stomped around and rubbed my hands up and down my arms to keep warm.

"Lizzy," Kitty cried as she ran out the door. "Will you come help us with the bridal wreath? Jane and Mr. Bingley shall depart at any moment."

I walked back into the house long enough to open the door while she and Maria Lucas carried the huge arch of beribboned flowers outside. Almost immediately, the throng of company followed them with much gaiety and cries of excitement. The crowd swept me out the door along with them, and before I could turn around, I heard my mother's voice calling out last-minute admonitions to Jane. And then, there they were—Mr. and Mrs. Bingley —running through the wedding arch and climbing in their carriage. I reached out and clasped Jane's hand for but a moment. She stopped and pressed her cheek to mine, and I could see joy shining in her eyes.

And then they were gone. What we had earnestly hoped and prayed for so long had now come to pass. My mother was thrilled that my sister married a rich man. I was thrilled that she married the man she loved. I knew for certain I would never be that fortunate.

Many of the guests began to take their leave while others stayed at my parents' urging. I caught a glimpse of Miss Darcy in conversation with Mary and knew her brother would not stray far from her side. They turned to re-enter the house while I walked in the opposite direction. I crossed the park and hurried up the lane. Snow began to fall in abundance, and once more, I regretted not having grabbed my coat. I passed the villagers' cottages and acknowledged several greetings. I knew I should return to my parents' house, but I did not wish to face Miss Darcy or her brother again until I thought of an excuse to refuse her invitation. My vow would be easier to keep if I never saw him again.

Before I knew it, I stood upon the threshold of the church building. The door remained open, and I could feel the warmth from within. Slowly, I walked into the deserted sanctuary and down the aisle Jane had trod a few hours earlier. I sank down upon a polished wooden pew close to the altar. Once again, I gazed at the stained glass window, but the sun no longer beamed in approval. Snow clouds darkened the coloured panes, and the old building suddenly seemed filled with shadows.

"Dear God," I prayed silently, "favour me with your grace. Help me honour the vow I made earlier. From this day forward, may I truly see Mr. Darcy as my brother and nothing more. Blot out those feelings I harbour for him. You know my thoughts, Lord; rid my mind of them. Oh, God, I entreat thee. Have mercy, I pray."

"Miss Elizabeth?"

I shuddered at the sound, aware that I was not alone. Turning, I saw the stooped figure of Mr. Fawcett standing in the aisle outside the pew. The old man had long ago retired as Longbourn's vicar, but he remained in his house, a legacy granted by my father for the years he had served the parish. He still looked after the church building as former habits could not be denied.

"I thought that was you," he said, "although my eyes are not as proficient as they once were. What causes you to seek refuge here, my child? I thought you would be a participant in the happy event."

"They made their departure a short while ago, Mr. Fawcett."

"And you tired of a house full of guests? I am surprised. For one my age, that would be natural, but you are a young woman, and do not the young enjoy a good party?"

I smiled. "I confess I strayed from the house without a wrap, and the warmth of the church drew me in."

"Do you miss your sister already?"

I nodded. "I am very happy for her, though."

"Yes, but not so happy for yourself. Am I right?"

"Sir?"

He sat down beside me, his eyes a cloudy blue beneath their overgrown brows. "Your father told me of the recent revelation, and you may recall I had a most unpleasant call from Lady Catherine. I trust you do not remain despondent."

I was surprised at his boldness until the knowledge came flooding back that he had been vicar when Lady Catherine's husband delivered me to the church at Hertfordshire twenty-one years earlier. "I hope I am not, sir."

"I always thought Mr. Bennet in error to keep the truth from you. But then, I do not have children, so it was not for me to say."

"How did you know Sir Lewis de Bourgh, Mr. Fawcett?"

He looked away with a grimace. "As a young curate, I served at Hunsford parish. Unfortunately, I incurred the disapproval of Lady Catherine, so much so that she insisted on my removal from the living. If not for Sir Lewis's intervention, I might have been forced from service to the church altogether. It was due to his kindness that I received the living here at Longbourn. He was a friend of a friend of Mr. Bennet's, so when the gentleman came calling in the middle of the night, asking for my assistance, I could do nothing less."

"Sir Lewis himself delivered me to Hertfordshire?"

"With the help of a serving woman who cared for you on the journey. 'Twas a difficult beginning, my dear, but one that turned out well after all, would you not agree?"

"Mmm...I am indebted to the Bennets for taking me in."

"Child, they did not just take you in. You are truly their daughter."

I shivered slightly.

With difficulty, he rose from the pew. "The fire has gone out. Perhaps you should return home."

I stood, but before stepping out into the aisle, I placed my hand on his arm. "Mr. Fawcett, did Sir Lewis ever tell you anything of my mother... my real mother?"

He shook his head. "Only that you were given her Christian name and that she died giving birth. He did not say who she was, but I sensed that your mother was not a servant, that she might have been of noble birth."

"Whatever gave you cause to think that?"

"Sir Lewis said neither family—that of your father nor your mother —could bear the disgrace. Common folk live with their sins; the gentry possess the means to hide theirs."

I closed my eyes and turned away. He patted my shoulder and then shuffled toward the side door. "Do not stay too long, my dear. The chill in the room will soon turn bitter."

I swallowed as I heard the door close behind him. *I shall not weep again. I refuse to give in to grief any longer.* I took a deep breath, squared my shoulders, and stepped out into the aisle to return to Longbourn. I was startled to see the form of a man standing beside the last pew at the rear of the building. The dim light was just enough for me to make out who stood privy to my conversation—Mr. Darcy.

He wore his great coat and held his hat in his hand, apparently ready to leave. "Elizabeth."

"Sir." I walked toward him, my head held high. "Is it your nature to listen in on private conversations?"

"Of course not. I did not mean to overhear."

"And what brings you to God's house—fervent need of prayer?"

He smiled slightly. "You did not respond to my sister's request, and Georgiana wished to bid you farewell. Someone said they saw you walk in the direction of the church."

"I see."

"Is that what drew you here—your need of prayer—or did you come to question the old vicar?"

"We are all in need of prayer, sir. And no, I did not seek Mr. Fawcett. He found me here by chance."

"I see."

"I assume you heard what he said. It was the strangest thing."

"About the woman who gave you birth? Yes, I heard."

"Do you have knowledge of her family, Mr. Darcy?"

He shook his head. "I cannot help but believe, though, that we might find the answer in Derbyshire."

"We?"

"Elizabeth, if you consent to return to Pemberley with Georgiana and me, perchance we could find some bit of information about your mother. The attics are filled with old trunks containing various papers, records, and journals. Surely, somewhere someone wrote of your birth. If you will come, I will brook no obstacle to solve the mystery."

I frowned at him. "I do not consider that a prudent idea."

"What would be the harm in a visit? Tell me that if you can. Mrs. Annesley, my sister's companion, travels with us, so everything would be in order. You would have a chaperone."

"Why must you insist on continuing your involvement in my life? I do believe you are the most stubborn man I have ever known." I walked toward the door, but stopped short at the sight before me: snow now covered the village.

"It seems we share the family trait, for you possess a stubbornness of your own. Here, take my coat; you cannot go out dressed as you are."

"No," I said quickly. "I shall wait here until it slackens. Pray, go and bid your sister farewell on my behalf. I will send her a note tomorrow expressing my regret that I must forego her gracious invitation."

I felt his eyes upon me, and when I turned to meet them, I was surprised at the fire I saw therein. "I shall not part from you until you tell me the truth. Here, in this sacred place, one must not lie. I want to hear the true reason you wish to sever all contact between us."

"I beg to differ. You have oft been told the truth, and you refuse to accept it."

"When last we met, you spoke in anger—justifiable—yet anger. You said you do not want any of that which belonged to my father, but there is more. I can see it in your eyes."

"Indeed? And what more do you see?"

"Mistrust. I believe you consider me faithless because of what occurred between us at Kent last Easter. You fear I cannot look upon you as a sister."

I caught my breath. *Was I that transparent?* My lip trembled, and I was afraid to move lest I confess to him more than I should.

Turning to stare out at the snow, he began twirling his hat round and round. "I wrote in my letter that you need have no fear of my renewing those addresses you found so disgusting."

"Please, do not remind me of that time, Mr. Darcy. I am quite ashamed of how I abused you."

"I shall never forget the turn of your countenance when you said I could not have acted in a more ungentlemanlike manner."

"My words were harsh and uncalled for. I pray you do not hold them against me."

"What did you say that I did not deserve? The manner of my declaration was abominable. When I think back on it, I cannot imagine myself uttering those insults toward your family and yourself. Make no mistake in thinking I still harbour those sentiments."

My stomach lurched at his declaration, but was it true? I knew him to be a man who abhorred deceit, but was I so in error? Of what sentiments did he speak—his disapproval of my connections or his declaration of love? Had I misunderstood his attentions at Pemberley or his kindness at Lambton when he discovered me grieving over Lydia?

I took a deep breath. "Then, sir, may I ask why Lady Catherine travelled to Longbourn with such haste in fear that you and I were soon to be engaged? What led her to reveal my true parentage if not in dread that an attachment between us loomed imminent?"

The hat twirling in his hand ceased as suddenly as it had begun.

"I cannot speak for my aunt or for her malice. Although directed at you, her anger was meant for me. She had called at my townhouse in London the day before and confronted me once again concerning a proposal for her daughter. I told her for the last time that I was not to marry Anne, and that my affections lay elsewhere. For whatever reason, she presumed you were the object. That is when she produced a copy of the note written by Sir Lewis. As I told you earlier, I went directly to her solicitor's office and examined the original. Unknown to me, the following day, she travelled to Longbourn. I returned to Netherfield where she found me after her visit with you. She appeared delighted with her Machiavellian efforts but became affronted when I informed her that I would share my inheritance with you."

His affections lay elsewhere. What does that mean?

"Elizabeth, ours is a peculiar connection, but a connection I will endure. You must not doubt me, for I possess the strongest of wills. When I set my mind to a task, it is accomplished. The moment I learned you were my sister, I determined to think of you in that manner. The past is now dead."

"As simply as that?" I whispered.

I saw the nerve in his cheek tighten as he pressed his lips together. "Since that day, you have been naught but my sister. You have my highest respect and regard. You need have no fear of me."

WITHIN A FORTNIGHT, I LEFT for Pemberley with Georgiana and Mr. Darcy. Even though I assured my father I was going for only a short visit, he still clung to my hand until the door closed on Mr. Darcy's carriage. My mother and sisters were breathless with excitement. Mamá had calculated how many men of fortune I might meet. I stressed that I did not go in quest of a husband, but she would not have it. At last, I gave up my attempts to convince her and left her to indulge her fancies.

One may well ask why I agreed at last to the Darcys' invitation after I had insisted I would not go. One might think it because of Mr. Darcy's renunciation of any feeling for me, other than that of a brother. Or one might consider the attraction of solving the mystery of my mother's identity compelling enough to alter my decision.

In truth, I grew bored and lonely at Longbourn without Jane. She had asked that I accompany her and Charles on their wedding trip, but I declined. I feared that being a daily witness to their devotion would simply reinforce my own loneliness. Within days, I wished with all my heart that I had accepted. Restricted to the house because of inclement weather, I quickly tired of my mother and younger sisters' company while Papá locked himself in his library with increasing regularity. A spirit of tedium and impatience began to plague me with uncommon consistency. The thought of spending the remainder of the winter in such dull surroundings filled me with annoyance. Since the prize of Pemberley had been paraded before me, I could no longer find contentment in the existence I had always known. It seemed I wished to experience what life with the Darcys might offer after all.

And if I were honest, I should admit I craved the excitement of Mr. Darcy's company. Even if he was but my brother, I felt more alive in his presence. His intelligence and wit matched mine, and I knew I would not tire of sparring with him. I also found Georgiana amiable, and I trusted that the time I spent with her would be agreeable. Besides, I longed to see the great house again, and anticipation of the beauty of Derbyshire's peaks and dales made my spirit soar.

I generally possess a hopeful outlook, and I soon tired of grieving over the circumstances of my birth and my disappointing prospects. I longed to return to the cheerfulness I had known before, and I determined it to be possible. Once I made the decision to travel to Pemberley, it somehow became easier to keep my resolution.

Mr. Darcy shared the carriage seat with his young sister on the journey while Mrs. Annesley sat beside me. She was an older woman, pleasant and quiet in the presence of her employer. As the miles rolled by, Georgiana chattered about all that awaited us. She made a verbal list of families in the area and urged her brother to plan a dinner or even a ball to welcome me.

"A ball? Surely not," I said. "For I know with what distaste your brother considers dancing."

"Ah, Wills," she said. "Could you not forego your displeasure for the sake of Miss Bennet?"

He raised one eyebrow but said nothing.

"We could ask the Whitbys and the Stones, and perchance Lord Darnley's nephew has not yet left for the Season in Town. Oh, Wills, could we not have a ball?"

"Let us give Miss Bennet time to settle in before we impose Derbyshire society upon her."

"That suits me perfectly," I replied. "Remember, I shall not stay long, Miss Darcy."

"But you must! It is such a distance from Longbourn. We may not have opportunity to visit for some time. Pray assure me you will stay for several months at least."

"Georgie, do not inflict your wishes upon her. We will not force Miss Bennet to remain at Pemberley unless she is content to do so."

Georgiana frowned, and I noted how pretty her countenance, even when pouting. "Oh, I am tired. Shall we never reach Derbyshire?"

Mr. Darcy took her hand. "Rest your head on my shoulder."

She gladly took advantage of his proposal and, within a short span, fell asleep. I was fascinated by their intimacy. If I were his legitimate sister, would I ever feel that comfortable with him? At ease enough to sleep on his shoulder? I could not imagine it.

Within moments, Mrs. Annesley's head began to fall forward as she, too, drifted into slumber. Mr. Darcy and I rode in silence for some time before I spoke again. I kept my voice low so that I might not disturb our companions.

"So you are 'Wills' to your little sister?"

He nodded. "And you are 'Lizzy' to yours, am I correct? To my mind, the diminutive does not suit you."

"Oh? And what would you have me called?"

"I do not think I could ever think of you by any name other than 'Elizabeth.'"

"And I cannot fathom calling you by any name other than 'Mr. Darcy.'"

"Is that not formal? Our close connection does not warrant addressing each other in that manner in private."

"Pray, sir! Mrs. Annesley might hear you."

"She is a sound sleeper; do not worry."

I leaned forward and peered closely at the woman. Assured that she truly was insensible to her surroundings, I felt easier and took up the conversation again. "What should I call you then? 'Wills' belongs to Georgiana, and I fear my tongue would trip over 'Fitzwilliam,' so what else other than 'Mr. Darcy'?"

"You are clever enough. I believe you will select a name for me."

"I suppose there is always 'Fitz' or 'Fitzy.'" I cut my eyes at him to see how he responded to my mockery.

"I call my cousin 'Fitz,' and no one shall ever call me 'Fitzy.' I forbid it."

"Forbid? Oh my. Then that leaves but one option. I shall have to call you 'Willie.'"

"Under no circumstances!" He spoke with such force that Georgiana stirred in her sleep.

"Shush," I whispered. "You will wake the child."

"Then soften the provocation."

I struggled to subdue my laughter. Silence ensued, and I turned my attention to the passing landscape. The farther north we travelled, the whiter the countryside appeared. I had rarely seen so great an amount of snow, and I loved the artistic purity of it. It was as though the woods and meadows had been washed clean, scrubbed with a generous helping of soapsuds.

"I have it!" I whispered at last. "The perfect name for you, sir—'Fitzwilly'!"

His left eyebrow shot up like a bullet. "Then I shall call you 'Bessie.' Shall that please you?"

"My father's cow is called 'Bessie.'"

A satisfied smirk settled about his mouth. "Then I suggest a compromise: I shall be 'William,' and you shall be 'Elizabeth.' Agreed?"

"Oh, very well…although I do think 'Fitzwilly' possesses a certain distinction."

"As does 'Bessie.'"

I could not help but laugh, and I was pleased to see the hint of a reluctant smile emerge upon his face at last.

Chapter Four

Although I imagined it to be impossible, Pemberley was as striking in mid-winter as in summer. The snow-draped grounds made a magnificent setting for the huge mansion. With the roof wrapped in white, icicles sparkled and glittered all along the eaves like jewelled pendants hang from a woman's ears. I caught my breath in wonder. Our journey had been long and tiring. The inns at which we had stopped on the way proved adequate but not memorable. Now, anticipation revived my spirit, and I looked forward with eagerness to entering the Darcys' beautiful house once again.

Mr. Darcy had written the housekeeper, Mrs. Reynolds, to expect us. He told her we had discovered that I was a distant relation, and thus, he and Georgiana invited me to spend some time with them. I was relieved to find a warm smile upon her face.

"Miss Bennet, I am most pleased to see you again," she said. Evidently, she believed our story; however, she was but a servant and asked no questions, of course. The test would come when I was introduced to Derbyshire society. Surely, some of them had lived in the county all those years ago and heard the rumours of my birth.

We entered the drawing room to be warmed by a roaring fire and steaming cups of tea. Later, I was established in a lovely bedchamber decorated in delicate shades of rose and green. The prospect from the windows took my breath away; slivers of the evening sunset's brilliant hues peeked through the parting snow clouds and danced upon the surface of the lake.

After dinner that night, while Georgiana played for us on the pianoforte with Mrs. Annesley nearby to turn the pages, I felt Mr. Darcy's eyes upon me. He sat in a large overstuffed chair, his head reclining against the back. I thought him asleep once or twice, for he closed his eyes during several refrains, but I was mistaken, for at the close of the song, he remarked upon his favourite movements in the music. He appeared truly at ease in his home. If ever a man belonged to a house, Mr. Darcy belonged to Pemberley. It fit him like a well-tailored coat. I wondered whether I would ever feel at home in such a great house. Even though we shared the same father, I knew I would never share his sense of birthright.

"Has the evening's refreshment relieved the strain of travel, Elizabeth?" He spoke softly so that he would not interrupt Georgiana's concert.

"The meal was delicious, and one could not ask for more pleasing entertainment."

"But you are weary, are you not? I see fatigue in your eyes. After she finishes this song, you must retire."

"I would not shorten Georgiana's enjoyment. Pray, do not ask her to stop on my behalf."

"There is always the morrow when she may play as long as she wishes while I show you the house in detail. I know Mrs. Reynolds gave you and the Gardiners a tour last summer, but I wish for you to see the house through my eyes. Shall we say after breakfast, around one o'clock?"

"If you wish." I was more than eager to explore the great house once again and especially with one who knew it intimately. Georgiana and I soon retired to our chambers, and I fell into the luxurious, soft bed with grateful surrender.

THE NEXT DAY, WE BEGAN our tour in the kitchen, a curious choice in my mind, but one I soon understood. Mr. Darcy knew each of the downstairs staff by name along with their responsibilities, including Mrs. Soffel, the cook, who ruled her domain with a sharp tongue. She barked orders to the lower servants like the best sergeant-at-arms before she realized the master had invaded her kitchen.

"Beggin' your pardon, Mr. Darcy," she said with a curtsy. "I didn't see you there, sir."

"Quite acceptable," he responded. "I recall as a lad you ordered me about in that same tone of voice."

She blushed bright red. "I never, sir. Well, perchance...but only when you snatched cookies before they cooled."

"And burnt my tongue as a result. They were well worth it, however."

"Aw, go on with you, sir."

As we walked from room to room, I could see in what esteem his servants held him. It was evident their deference was heartfelt and not prompted by duty alone. I recalled Mrs. Reynolds's words from last summer: "He is the best landlord and the best master that ever lived."

We worked our way up the floors, and I wondered anew at the splendour therein. Its understated elegance extended from the architecture to the perfectly selected furnishings. I could not find a single item I would change if I were mistress.

You shall never be mistress of Pemberley, I reminded myself.

"And I suppose Mrs. Reynolds showed you the gallery, did she not?" Mr. Darcy asked.

"She did, but I would welcome a closer view."

He led me up the grand staircase, pointing out paintings by Italian and Dutch artists that lined the wall. In the great hall, my eyes travelled immediately to his large portrait. I thought it exceptionally fine. The artist caught his face in a benign expression, and he smiled in a manner I had sometimes observed before when he looked at me. Mr. Darcy began naming various relations, but I confess I only half listened, for I could not tear my eyes from the only face whose features were known to me.

"I believe you will find this likeness of interest." He had walked a number of paces ahead while I lingered behind. "Elizabeth?"

I coloured, hoping he had not caught me out and hurriedly joined him. "And who did you say this gentleman is?"

"My...our father." He drew near and spoke softly, even though it appeared we were alone.

I raised my eyes to observe the subject of the painting. Mr. Darcy resembled him in many ways. They possessed the same chin and turn of countenance. Although the man's hair in the portrait had turned silver, it fell across his forehead in curls much like that of his son. *My* father—I searched his eyes attempting to recognize some part of me therein.

"I can see you, but I fail to find myself in his image," I murmured.

"His hair was dark like yours when he was younger."

"Dark hair is common enough. I confess I cannot see any connection." I cast my eyes on the full-length portrait of a woman hanging next to that of Mr. Darcy Sr. "Is that your mother?"

He nodded.

"She was a beautiful woman, much like Georgiana."

"Yes, my sister inherited her blue eyes and fair colouring."

"And you have her dimples."

"Do I?"

"When you smile. 'Tis one of your best features you might exhibit more often."

We walked on down the hall while he named grandparents and various relations on his mother's side of the family. Then he stopped in front of a portrait of a young man and woman.

"These were our father's parents—your grandparents, Elizabeth—James and Siobhan Darcy."

"Siobhan? Was she Irish?"

"To the core. As a young man, my grandfather sailed to County Cork and spent the summer there with friends from Cambridge. He fell in love with Siobhan MacAnally, the daughter of a landed family that harked back for generations. Her father forbade the marriage, but they eloped anyway. She gave up her entire family to marry my grandfather and return to Derbyshire with him."

I frowned. "Gave up her family? Did they never reconcile?"

Mr. Darcy shook his head. "It could not be done. Her choice was entirely insupportable."

"But surely, one would not disinherit a daughter simply because she loved an Englishman."

"It was not just nation but religion that separated them. Our grandmother was Catholic, and our grandfather, of course, was not. She was required to renounce her religion and rear her children as Protestant. In truth, Father said his parents attempted to hide all traces of her former faith once they settled in England."

"Of course. Her husband would have endured persecution if she did not. How difficult it must have been for her."

Mr. Darcy walked on a few paces, stared at the floor, and lowered his voice even more. "Few know this, but Grandmother continued to practice her faith in secret."

"In secret?"

"In public, she attended services with her husband and children at the village church, but whenever possible, she stole away to visit a priest who maintained a small Catholic church just past the edge of the wood. He tended a small flock that clung to the Papist belief. The church remains to this day."

"And did your grandfather know?"

He nodded and smiled. "My father said his father permitted it because he loved her. He found it hard to deny her anything even though his own family was not at all pleased that my grandfather married beneath him."

"Beneath him? I thought her family prosperous."

He shrugged his shoulders. "Irish and Catholic? 'Twas unacceptable. Besides, Grandfather married her without her father's consent. She came to him without a dowry. Yes, I would say he married below his station, but then, he married for love."

His eyes met mine, and for one unguarded moment, it was as though I caught a glimpse of his soul. Almost immediately, however, he cleared his throat and marched on ahead. "That is sufficient for today. I shall not bore you with more family history. Let us walk on to the opposite wing of the house. I want you to see the ballroom."

I had to hurry to catch up with his long stride, but not before I turned and looked into the green eyes of Siobhan Darcy once more. I felt a chill run down my spine when I recognized that they were mine.

By nightfall, Mr. Darcy had exhibited the entire great house, save the attics. We agreed to postpone those for a day when we had adequate time to devote to our quest. I was pleased to know he had not abandoned his offer to search for knowledge of my birth. I had feared it might have been simply a scheme to entice me to visit Pemberley.

A welcome break in the weather occurred on the morrow, and we enjoyed four glorious days of sunshine. Mr. Darcy took advantage of it to show me the grounds. Even covered in snow, I could see the gardens were outstanding and that I had experienced only the briefest of tours during my visit the previous summer. The stables were filled with thoroughbreds, and he took pride in naming each horse's forebears—all superior pedigrees, I am certain, had I known anything about breeds. He was surprised when I informed him that I was no horsewoman, and he assured me that riding lessons would commence as soon as the weather permitted. I met his declaration with the same enthusiasm I would have exhibited had he served me a beaker of pickle juice.

On what proved to be the final day of clear weather for some time, Mr. Darcy announced at the breakfast table that he would take Georgiana and me on a ride in his phaeton. She clapped her hands in delight, her eyes sparkling with anticipation.

"A phaeton?" I asked. "Will it not be rather crowded with three passengers and cold as well?"

"Oh no, Elizabeth," Georgiana declared. By that time, we had progressed to addressing each other by our first names. "The wind has disappeared, and the sun is out today. We can fit if we squeeze close together. Tucked under a rug, we shall be quite cosy."

Sipping my tea, I raised my eyes to observe Mr. Darcy's reaction. He appeared completely satisfied with the idea, unconcerned with any discomfort such intimacy might cause. Well, if he could sit close beside me without problem, I should do as well. *After all, he is your brother,* I reminded myself. I quickly swallowed the remains of my cup, but in so doing, I choked and coughed to the point that I was forced to excuse myself from the table.

A half hour later, I descended the stairs and saw the phaeton waiting at the side entrance. Attached to a beautiful white mare, the shiny green conveyance with its huge yellow wheels looked like something out of a painting, even down to the bells hanging around the horse's collar. My sister carried a white muff and wore a fur coat and hat. Mr. Darcy had swathed his neck with a flannel scarf, but he frowned when he saw my plain wool coat and bonnet.

"Do you have no fur?"

"My coat is adequate."

He shook his head and ran up the stairs two at a time, calling for a servant. I followed Georgiana outdoors. She climbed up into the vehicle with aid from a servant and urged me to join her, but before I could, Mr. Darcy returned with a fur hat and cape.

"Exchange that bonnet for this hat," he demanded. "I shall not have you catch your death."

When I hesitated, he untied the ribbons himself. Before I knew what had happened, he handed my bonnet to the maid, placed the warmer covering on my head, and then wrapped the cape around my shoulders.

"Whose garments are these?"

Georgiana smiled. "They are mine. Wills, we must see to a more suitable wardrobe for Elizabeth."

"Yes, we must."

"No," I protested. "I shall not accept—"

"'Tis better than coming down with a chill, is it not?" He raised one eyebrow while he completed tying the bow under my chin. I shivered slightly, uncertain whether it was caused by the weather or the intimate nature of Mr. Darcy's concern for me.

Stepping up into the carriage, he held out his hand to assist me. "Now, let us arrange the blanket, and we shall be off." He sat between Georgiana and me and securely tucked the warm throw around each of us. I held my breath as he leaned over me, his head so close that his hair brushed against my cheek. "Warm enough?" he asked.

"Perfectly," Georgiana announced. I could manage nothing more than a nod.

Not even a hair could have squeezed between us, and I became keenly aware of the warmth of his leg touching mine. *This is a mistake,* I thought. But how was I to escape? Before I could think of an excuse, Mr. Darcy flicked the reins, and the great horse picked up her heels and trotted off. The cold wind fanned my cheeks, and I gasped to catch my breath. How fortunate that I could blame the elements for the rosy colour of my countenance.

That day, I discovered Mr. Darcy had a passion for driving fast. We had scarce left the outskirts of the park before he urged the horse into a brisk gallop. Georgiana squealed as we rounded a corner and laughed gaily when I protested.

"Do not fear, Elizabeth," she cried. "Wills is an excellent driver. He will not allow us to spill."

I held on in terror, for I had not the confidence she possessed. Unknowingly, I grabbed the side of the phaeton with one hand and Mr. Darcy's arm with the other. Within moments, he turned the conveyance to the left as we rounded a sharp curve, consequently causing both my companions to swerve to my side. Once more, his face appeared alarmingly close to mine. I felt his breath warm on my cheek and heard him chuckle before we turned back onto a straighter path.

"You are welcome to hold on, Elizabeth, but when you clamp my arm that tightly, it does hinder my driving somewhat."

Immediately, I withdrew my hand from his arm, shocked that I had touched him unawares.

"Do take care," Georgiana cautioned. "I fear you frighten Elizabeth."

"Are you afraid?"

"Of course not," I lied, straightening my spine and sitting as tall as I might. Within moments, he rounded another curve, and I found myself clinging to him with both hands. I heard him laugh softly in spite of Georgiana's gleeful screams.

"You are incorrigible, sir," I declared. "You drive like Jehu!"

At last, to my great relief, he slowed the horse to a gentle trot. I reached for my hat to make certain it did not sit askew and pulled the cover back into place, for it had slipped loose in all the twists and turns. I felt my heart beating furiously and took a deep breath of the cold, frosty air. The remains of my breath hovered about like miniature clouds.

"Shall we drive by Lady Margaret Willoughby's house?" Georgiana asked. "It lies directly around the next bend in the road."

Within a few moments, we came upon a large manor house set far back from the road, surrounded by the forest. It almost appeared a part of the wood, for what park surrounded the house was untended, allowed to grow wild, obviously abandoned.

"That is Bridesgate Manor," Mr. Darcy said.

"Is her ladyship away, for it appears vacant?"

"Oh, Lady Margaret no longer lives there," said Georgiana. "She died years back before I was born, did she not, Wills?"

He nodded. "Since her son had died before her, the estate passed to her grandson, and he has let the house to a family named Denison. I hear they shall take possession by Lady Day."

"I do hope we shall like them," Georgiana said. "Perhaps they have a daughter near my age and sons to court Elizabeth. Would it not be lovely if she were to marry and live nearby? Then, we would not have to travel to Hertfordshire to visit her."

I swallowed at the thought. "Georgiana…"

"Do not speak nonsense," Mr. Darcy said.

"Is that not one reason we invited Elizabeth to Pemberley—to find her a husband?"

"I am in no hurry to find a husband."

"Of course not," Mr. Darcy agreed. "And I know little of the family other than Mr. Denison is a retired admiral in the King's Navy. They certainly do not dwell on Lady Margaret's level."

"Even though they shall now dwell in her house," I murmured.

"You may scoff, but the Willoughby family was the reigning aristocracy in the neighbourhood when I was a lad. I recall my parents often dined at the old lady's table. 'Tis a pity her grandson has not taken better care of the place."

He turned and drove the horse up the long path leading to the house. Brambles wound through the wild bushes that lined the drive. The beautiful old trees appeared almost bent under the weight of vines grown unchecked for years. It would take a prodigious amount of work to clean the grounds. One could only hope the inside of the house had been better preserved.

"Shall we walk for a bit?" Mr. Darcy asked. When Georgiana and I agreed, he stepped down and assisted us from the carriage. I missed the warmth of his body next to mine and shivered slightly as the wind came up.

We began to walk about the property, the paths covered in snow, and I could see the estate compared poorly to Pemberley. The house was about the size of Netherfield, but due to lack of maintenance, it appeared sad and bleak.

"A door is open here on the side," Mr. Darcy announced, having walked on ahead of us. "Do you wish to see inside?"

Georgiana and I readily followed him into the entrance that opened upon a great hall. It smelled musty and dank, but it did provide relief from the cold.

"Evidently, neither the workmen nor servants have arrived as of yet," Mr. Darcy said. "I should think Denison would have ordered preparations to commence long before now."

"Look where the portraits were removed." Georgiana pointed up to the wall lining the staircase. "The house is in sore need of fresh paint."

"And soap and water," I added as we followed Mr. Darcy above stairs.

The draperies in the drawing room were still hanging, and what furniture remained was covered in dust cloths. Georgiana spied the shape of a pianoforte beneath the coverings and pushed them back so that she might run her fingers over the keys.

"How sad. It is out of tune." She sat down on the stool and began to amuse herself with chords and scales. Mr. Darcy indicated that I follow him into the dining room, where a grand table and chairs were still in place.

"When did anyone last dwell in the house?" I asked.

"The family moved away from these parts when I was but a child. I could not have been more than seven or eight years. That is, all but the grandmother, Lady Margaret Willoughby."

"Do you mean she stayed here alone?"

"The grandson moved his mother and sisters to London, but his grandmother refused to accompany them. I still remember the night my father returned from a visit and told us, 'Lady Margaret said she came to Bridesgate as a bride, and she would not leave until she died.' Her family could not persuade her otherwise."

"And did she live out her declaration?"

"She did. If I am not mistaken, I believe she died that same year or soon thereafter. I recall my father attended her funeral although there had been some kind of break between her and my family. I do not know the particulars. I just recall my father ordered me to stay away from the place. 'Twas a command I found hard to obey. For some reason, the old house has always drawn me in as though some spirit called to me—a silly notion for a lad."

"How sad," I murmured, "to die all alone in this great old house."

"It was her choice."

"Perhaps…but then, she might have felt this was the only place she belonged."

"When her family sought her company in Town? My father said they did all they could to persuade Lady Margaret to move to London when they did."

I walked down the length of the table and gazed up at the massive stone fireplace on the far wall. "It was her home. She lived here almost all of her life. It is important to feel one belongs…to know where *you* belong."

Unbeknownst to me, Mr. Darcy had crossed the room and stood close behind me. "Do we still speak of Lady Margaret, Elizabeth?"

The nearness of his presence startled me. I blinked and shook my head slightly. "What? I…of course." I turned my face toward his, and the tenderness reflected in his eyes touched my heart. I could feel my defences slipping away, and I knew tears would prove my undoing.

Just then, Georgiana skipped into the room and exclaimed that the candelabra still held the remains of burnt candles. She claimed Mr. Darcy's attention, which allowed me the opportunity once again to swallow my emotion. We soon quit the house and climbed back into the phaeton, bent on driving around the next turn in the road.

I was surprised to see another great house built not far from Bridesgate, a structure much more modern. Mr. Darcy explained that none of the Willoughbys ever returned to live at the estate, and Lady Margaret's grandson had consistently sold off the land surrounding the old family home until the domain was now reduced to a fraction of its former glory. A family named Whitby had purchased some of the property and built the newer house.

"They have two suitable sons, Elizabeth," Georgiana announced. "I am sure one of them will please you."

I did not even bother to protest, for her brother growled enough for both of us. It did little to temper the young girl. She entreated Mr. Darcy to drive by the home of yet another family of young men in the area. He, instead, turned off the main road and onto a country lane that led us directly through the woods. When Georgiana questioned him as to our destination, he cautioned her to practice patience.

We rode for some time, allowing my mood to lighten. It proved insupportable to remain melancholy on such a beautiful day, in the company of a cheerful, chattering girl and nestled snugly against the warmth of the body next to mine.

"Here we are," Mr. Darcy announced as he pulled off the lane onto a narrow drive. I looked in the direction he indicated and saw a small, well-kept church hidden well back within a shady glen. No sign indicated its name without, but a solitary cross adorned the steeple.

"What church is this, Wills? I do not recall ever visiting here."

"It is not one of our persuasion."

"What do you mean?" Georgiana held out her arms for him to lift her down from our high perch.

"It is a Papist church, is it not?" I said, climbing out the other side, unaided.

"Papist? Here in Derbyshire?"

"The religion is not outlawed, Georgiana," Mr. Darcy said.

"Certainly not prevalent, though. We know no one of that faith, do we, Wills?"

His eyes met mine. Evidently, he had not shared the secret of our grandmother with his young sister.

I was surprised when we found the door unlocked. Inside, we were greeted by the smells of incense mingled with lemon oil and old wood. One would never guess the beauty of the interior from the simple stone structure without. Georgiana marvelled in awe at the statues of the Madonna and Child and another saint, whom I did not recognize. As she and I crept silently about the sanctuary, Mr. Darcy disappeared through a side door at the front of the room. It seemed such a reverent place that both Georgiana and I spoke in whispers.

"Is not the altar magnificent?"

I agreed as we approached the table covered with a lace cloth and containing various religious emblems, among which I saw the Celtic cross.

"Is it true they worship idols?" she asked.

"I doubt it," I said. "But I am not acquainted with their rituals other than I believe they confess their sins to the priest."

"All their sins?" Her eyes grew wide.

"Do you find that shocking?"

"I do. I should not like that to be a requirement of my faith."

I smiled. "I am certain you are a sick and wicked person."

Her lip trembled, and tears formed in her lovely eyes.

"Oh, Georgiana, I did not mean it. I am simply teasing you. Forgive me."

"You might be surprised to learn how wicked I have been. I fear you would no longer think highly of me if I were forced to confess it."

I assured her that nothing she did would ever lessen her reputation in my eyes, but I could see it did little to comfort her. Mr. Wickham's escapade with her had robbed her of her innocence. I put my arm around her and led her into the pews to sit beside me.

"Georgiana, I know what happened at Ramsgate." A look of horror covered her face. "It was not your fault. I know Mr. Wickham; he married my youngest sister, and he is a man who deserves to be branded wicked, but not you."

"I should never have entered into the alliance. I was such a fool."

"You were young. You are still young, much too young to recognize the man is a scoundrel."

"Your poor sister! How will she manage in a marriage to such a man?"

I looked away, a cloud descending over my expression. "It is sad, but there was nothing to be done. Her name would have been ruined had she not married him. Thank goodness he was made to do the right thing, and it is all due to the generous nature of your brother."

"Wills is a good man."

"I know."

We said nothing more for a while and simply sat back on the pew, absorbing the stillness of the place. A curious peace settled upon me. Although the religion was not mine, I found it satisfying to know my grandmother had been granted this lovely setting in which to practice her faith.

We were startled from our reverie when the door opened and Mr. Darcy reappeared. A priest robed in black stood within the doorway. They exchanged words we could not hear, and shortly thereafter, the older man disappeared behind the closed door. Mr. Darcy motioned for us to accompany him, and within moments, we were once again seated in the phaeton.

Mr. Darcy folded Georgiana's hand around his right arm and then tucked my hand around his left.

"Hold tight. We shall make haste and return to Pemberley before dusk."

With a jerk forward, we once again flew through the snow. Georgiana squealed with excitement, but I was content to hang on to Mr. Darcy's arm.

Chapter Five

I had spent little more than a month at Pemberley when an unexpected guest joined us: Colonel Fitzwilliam. He was a cousin of the Darcys on their mother's side of the family whom I had met in Kent the previous Easter. I was delighted to renew our acquaintance, for I thought well of the gentleman. His manner and general amiability made him an agreeable addition to our table.

I was surprised, however, to learn that the colonel already had knowledge of the altered version of my past. He explained that Lady Catherine had erupted in anger when she heard I had accepted Mr. Darcy's invitation to visit Pemberley. The great lady had travelled posthaste to Eden Park, the home of her brother who was the colonel's father. There, she spent no little time casting disparagement upon my character although, evidently, she did not tell the earl that I was sister to Mr. Darcy and Georgiana. She despaired of her nephew and declared he had lost his senses to offer me—a distant poor relation of no consequence—a portion of his inheritance.

"She insisted I visit you, Darcy," the colonel said with a twinkle in his eye, "and—let me recall precisely how she put it—oh yes, 'restore you to your former good sense.' According to my aunt, Miss Bennet is quite the little fortune hunter."

Mr. Darcy threw his napkin onto the table and immediately rose from his chair. "That is preposterous! Surely, you, of all people, do not believe such twaddle."

"Of course, I do not believe it. Sit down, Cousin."

"Wills and I invited Elizabeth to visit Pemberley," Georgiana said. "Since we are related, we wished to know her better."

"And Elizabeth has refused any offer of assistance, even so far as the thought of establishing a dowry for her," Mr. Darcy added.

The colonel reclined back in his chair, turned his face to the side, and looked me up and down with a bantering air.

"Come now, Miss Bennet, you must at least allow your cousin to provide you a dowry, for I have it on good authority that he has plenty to spare. 'Twill greatly increase your chances in the marriage market. Added to your green eyes and lovely smile, it shall prove you irresistible."

"Must you make love to my cousin at the dinner table, Fitzwilliam?" Darcy snapped.

I was embarrassed to be the centre of attention. "You forget, sir, that the remoteness of my connection to Mr. Darcy and my subsequent fostering by Mr. Bennet would never render me irresistible, whatever dowry I possess, so there is little reason for me to accept it."

"You are mistaken, my dear," the colonel responded. "A fortune can make one overlook a great number of things."

"Then I shall surely forego the gift, for I prefer a man who does not seek my hand for material gain."

By that time, Mr. Darcy's obvious annoyance had heightened, and he signalled the colonel to join him in his library for their after-dinner libations. Georgiana and I retired to the drawing room, where I took up my attempt at needlework and she returned to the novel she was reading. A short time later, the gentlemen joined us, whereupon the colonel persuaded me to play and sing. He insisted upon standing by my side and turning the pages of music. The only blight upon the evening was that Mr. Darcy's mood had turned dour, and neither my songs nor Georgiana's proved sufficient to lighten it.

During the following two weeks, I found Colonel Fitzwilliam's company diverting. He was always game for any activity that Georgiana or I suggested, and he often accompanied me on my turns about the park. The snow had melted at last, and the wind lifted on most days. Whenever the sun favoured us, I hurried outdoors, for I loved to walk, and Pemberley possessed a blissful provision of paths that turned and twisted enough even to please me.

On one such day, we strolled along the lake, and I silently recalled the previous summer when I had happened upon Mr. Darcy unexpectedly, neither of us aware of the other's presence in Derbyshire. I grew sombre thinking how much had changed since that time.

"Miss Bennet?"

"Pardon? Pray, excuse me, Colonel. What did you say?"

"Nothing of importance, but what draws you away? You appear to be in deep contemplation."

I shook my head slightly. "Just an old memory."

"Ah, memories haunt us at times, but I am surprised to see you so reflective out here where winter is about to give way and your beloved spring awaits, for I do remember how you loved the woods at Rosings last April."

"I did. I spent many a happy hour exploring the paths in Lady Catherine's park. Now, I am certain I shall never see them again."

"Do not worry on that account. I am sure my aunt will come around when Darcy marries Anne."

I was surprised to hear the colonel make the statement as though it were an inevitable event. "I thought Mr. Darcy did not wish to marry Miss de Bourgh."

"He is in no hurry, but in the end, Lady Catherine will have her way. She always does."

"How convenient for her. Then I should look forward to banishment to New South Wales, should I not, for I am sure that is her wish for me."

He laughed and tucked my hand within the crook of his arm. "My aunt is not all that bad, Miss Bennet. She simply looks after her daughter's interests. Is that so fierce? All of us look to our own interests, do we not?"

We said little more and soon returned to the house, but I did not care for the turn the conversation had taken or the tone of his voice.

A WEEK OR SO LATER, I stood in the gallery and gazed upon the portrait of Siobhan Darcy. Repeatedly, something drew me to my grandmother's painting and to Mr. Darcy's image. I found I could study either of them for some time without growing tired. Each viewing afforded me some detail I had overlooked before. On that particular afternoon, I heard heavy footsteps behind me and assumed it to be the colonel, for he had become my frequent companion. I turned and was surprised to see Mr. Darcy instead. Since the colonel arrived, Mr. Darcy had absented himself from my company except for meals and after dinner. I wondered at his actions, but supposed he had much business to attend concerning the estate.

"Studying your ancestors, Elizabeth?"

"Somewhat."

He remained silent for a while, clasping his hands behind his back. We walked a bit further while I gazed up at the enormous portraits.

"That lady in the white wig is my mother's mother, Lady Catherine Anne."

"She bears a strong resemblance to Lady Catherine de Bourgh, does she not?"

"I believe there is a similar expression of determination about their mouths. From what my mother told me, neither of them ever tolerated being crossed."

"Colonel Fitzwilliam tells me Lady Catherine always wins and that she will have you for a son-in-law eventually."

A frown wrinkled his brow. "Fitzwilliam talks out of turn, and just because he speaks a word, do not depend upon it."

"Would you have me doubt him? Surely, you do not cast aspersions upon your cousin's honour."

"You misunderstand. My cousin's honour is intact. He simply speaks rubbish at times. I shall never marry Anne."

I turned my face away to hide the smile upon my lips. Why did that please me? The bitter fact was that he would marry some day, a truth I was compelled to accept. Quickly, I walked ahead and feigned excessive interest in a portrait of three children, all boys. They sat upon a scarlet couch, their faces scrubbed and shining. The boys still wore their hair styled in curls, and all three were dressed in starched white collars and dark velvet jackets.

"Who are these children?"

"Father and his brothers."

"The two younger appear very close in age. Which is your father?"

He pointed to the older boy on the left, and when I looked closer, I could see the promise of the man whose likeness I had seen previously. "And did he have sisters as well?"

Mr. Darcy shook his head. "Only George, Peter, and Henry Darcy survived to carry on the family name."

"George has certainly done so, but what about the others?"

He shook his head again. "The youngest, Henry, went to sea, not necessarily by choice. At a tender age, he had already developed a somewhat questionable reputation here in Derbyshire. Even though I was a child, I was not unaware of the rows between my father and him."

"Over his behaviour, I assume."

"Father said Henry would never listen to reason, that he was determined to live life as he wished, and Father feared it would take a tragedy to bring him to his senses. My father's will reigned just as strong as his brother's, however, and at his insistence, Henry left Pemberley to make his way within His Majesty's service. He was already eighteen, almost too old to begin training, but my father prevailed and secured him a position. I assume my uncle eventually reformed his wild ways, for in time, he began to apply himself, and years later, he reached the rank of admiral. He even married a respectable woman of means some years his senior, but she never delivered a healthy child. She is a widow now and resides in Bath."

"His early days sound like those of Mr. Wickham."

Mr. Darcy grimaced. "I often wondered whether Father favoured Wickham because he reminded him of his young brother."

I did not wish to remain on the subject of Mr. Wickham. "And Peter, the middle child?"

"He was studious, quiet, and excelled in his studies at Cambridge. He chose another life altogether."

"And shall you tell me about it?"

He walked ahead until he reached the end of the great hall, whereupon he opened a door and indicated I should follow. He began to climb a narrow back staircase that lay just inside the landing, and I, of course, scampered after him.

"Sir? Will you answer my question and also tell me where we are going?"

"In good time, Elizabeth."

The attics proved to be Mr. Darcy's destination. An extravagant number of objects filled the room we entered, from boxes stacked to the ceiling to dressmakers' forms to countless trunks covered in dust and cobwebs. He pushed aside an assortment of rubbish from a chair, pulled a trunk close by, and indicated I should sit.

"I promised you a search for the woman who gave you birth, so let us commence."

He placed a valise on a small table nearby and motioned for me to have a seat and open it. When I hesitated, he grabbed an old rag and wiped down the chair. "Forgive me. I failed to allow for the dirt. I shall order a thorough cleaning first thing on the morrow."

I sat down and attempted to open the latch. "It seems this one is locked."

"A good sign. Perchance it contains secrets." He smiled before he grabbed a hammer and struck the lock until it popped open. I swallowed and leaned forward to begin the quest.

Hours later, our hands and clothing were coated in dirt. I had sneezed repeatedly and blown my nose until I felt certain it was now swollen to twice its normal size, yet we had found nothing to enlighten us. Both of us had combed through letters, journals, accounts, various mementos, and relics that meant nothing to us but must have been precious indeed to the Darcy ancestors.

I blew at a stray lock of hair that had loosened and persisted in falling over my left eye. Wiping my hands on the dirty cloth, I allowed a sigh to escape. It seemed an impossible task. Why had we ever thought to engage in this undertaking? Just then, I felt Mr. Darcy's hand under my chin.

"You look an absolute fright." He tucked the unruly curl behind my ear. After pulling forth his handkerchief, he began to rub my forehead. "What a great amount of dirt you have on your face! You could not look worse if you had swept the chimneys."

"Your own attire, sir, is nothing of which to boast. Are you turning prematurely grey or donning a wig made of cobwebs?" I began to squirm as he rubbed harder and playfully slapped away his hand. "Leave my dirt where it is, and see to your own."

He ignored my plea, turned my face upward, and attacked the smudges again. "Do not be impertinent. I am attempting to clean the mess you have made."

"I made? Who brought me up here, I might ask? And you, sir, really should look to your own interests. Your clothes are downright foul." I began to swipe at the dust on his shoulders but succeeded only in causing us both to sneeze.

"You are right, Elizabeth. We must leave this place. Why, your petticoats are six inches deep in dirt, at least." He spoke in a mocking tone, and we both began to laugh.

"Can you imagine the horror on Miss Bingley's face if she were privy to our soiled clothing?"

"Her reproof echoes in my ears: 'I am inclined to think that you would not wish to see your sister make such an exhibition.' How disgusting we are! Come, let us give up for today and repair to our chambers."

I continued to giggle as I followed him to the door, and we climbed down the stairs. It struck me that we had been more at ease with each other in the attic than at any time since we had been told we were brother and sister.

Upon opening the door to the gallery, we came face to face with Colonel Fitzwilliam. The shocked expression he wore made me laugh anew.

"So here you are! I thought you had left the county, for I have searched the grounds and the house. I did not think to check the attics. My word, Darcy, what have you two been up to?"

"I am training Elizabeth to be an upstairs maid," Mr. Darcy said with a straight face. "If she will not accept a dowry, she must earn her keep in some manner."

The colonel raised his eyebrows. "I have never before observed you instruct your servants with such detail."

"Nonsense. I always personally see to it that my servants know the correct procedures."

"Even upstairs maids?"

"Especially upstairs maids."

I could not refrain from laughing aloud.

"And how did Miss Bennet do? Did she take to instruction well?"

"Like she was born to it. You see for yourself that she can more than adequately cover herself in dirt."

"Indeed." Colonel Fitzwilliam walked back and forth, shaking his head at us.

Without even a glance in my direction, Mr. Darcy barked an order. "That will be all, Elizabeth. Tell my man to draw me a bath, and you may take time from your duties to change your frock."

"Yes, sir," I said as I curtseyed, then hurried down the hall. *Mr. Darcy can laugh at himself!* For some reason, the thought made me happy all over, and I felt my spirits begin to lift.

WITHIN A FEW DAYS, MY spirits tumbled down with a thud.

The time arrived for my first instruction in riding a horse. Of course, I had ridden before at Longbourn, but only as a child perched behind Jane upon the back of an old nag who would take barely a step or two before stopping. It took incessant urging from us to make the animal move more than a short distance. Thus, one could understand why I looked upon the art of riding with less than breathless anticipation. I sought to dissuade Mr. Darcy from the attempt, but he would not hear of it, and the colonel's encouragement spurred his efforts.

Thus, one morning, I found myself sitting gingerly upon the back of a beautiful chestnut mare while a young groom led the horse round and round the stable yard. All the while, Mr. Darcy and the colonel admonished me with more commands than I could comprehend, much less obey.

After numerous walks around and around, I thought I at last had achieved some dignity in my posture. I finally allowed my eyes to rise from the ground far below. I straightened my back, and I held my head up. Just as I congratulated myself on my progress, Colonel Fitzwilliam ordered the groom to have the animal trot. The horse, naturally, kicked up her heels and followed the boy's lead. I lurched forward, grabbed the horse's mane, and screamed.

"No, Fitzwilliam!" Mr. Darcy cried. "She is not yet ready."

"Nonsense! She will never learn until she is exposed. Sit up straight, Miss Bennet. Do not pull the horse's mane; hold the reins."

My screams must have alarmed the animal, for it seemed to me that she ran even faster. As for holding the reins, I could not find them, perhaps because I screwed my eyes shut upon first view of the ground rushing by at unbelievable speed. I remember not how long the horse trotted around the stable yard but only the relief I felt when she, at last, was slowed to a halt. I opened my eyes to see Mr. Darcy's outstretched arms, and without a moment's hesitation, I slipped down into his waiting embrace.

"You are trembling." He led me to a nearby bench and bade me sit. "Fetch the lady a glass of water." Within moments, a servant returned with a beaker.

As I sipped the cool water, I saw the colonel approach. He swished his riding crop back and forth in the air as he walked. "Darcy, do not coddle your cousin. She will never learn unless you are firm. As soon as she has had her drink, she must try again."

My heart rose up into my throat at the thought, and I swallowed the water with difficulty.

"A word, Richard," Mr. Darcy said.

The colonel followed him a distance away where I could no longer hear their conversation with clarity. I saw what appeared to be a heated argument with much flapping about of arms, pointing of fingers, and other animated gestures. At length, the colonel turned and stalked back to the house. Mr. Darcy called the groom to saddle his horse, a great beauty, black and sleek, but taller than a giraffe in my eyes. He then motioned for me to join him beside the animal. My mouth fell open in dismay, and the glass of water slipped from my hands and down the front of my dress.

"Oh!" I jumped up and began to dab at the cold, wet spots with my gloved hands.

"John, a towel." Mr. Darcy arrived at my side with the necessary cloth before I could even look up. "Now, see what you have done. Is there no hope for you, Elizabeth?"

He shook his head in dismay and began to wipe my dress with the towel. He stopped in mid-stride when he reached my bosom, as though he just then realized what he was doing. "You...finish the task."

I took the towel and turned away, wiping furiously at the dampness. My face burned, escape my only desire. Within moments, I threw the towel upon the bench and took steps to return to the house.

"Where do you go, Elizabeth?"

I did not answer but continued to walk straight ahead. Before I could reach my destination, however, I felt his hand on my arm, and the pressure was strong enough to detain me. "Elizabeth?"

"Inside to change, sir. Where else?" Irritation coloured my tone and knit my brows together.

"You cannot be that wet. Your gown will dry soon enough here in the sun. Come with me."

"Where?"

"Your riding lesson is not yet over."

"Oh no! I shall not climb on that horse again, and if you mean to frighten me with the suggestion that I ride your huge beast instead, I shall not hear of it. Nothing will induce me to change my mind."

He took my hand in his, placed his left hand at my back, and prodded me forward as he spoke in a voice low enough that only I could hear.

"Come now. I shall not have any sister of mine afraid of a horse. There is nothing to it once you learn the technique. You must not show fear, for the horse can sense it. I shall not let you ride alone."

"What do you mean?"

With more questions and exclamations, I protested his actions, but my objections would not persuade him. Within moments, he lifted me upon the back of his great horse, swung himself into the saddle, and placed himself close behind me. He encircled me with his arms, picked up the reins, and urged the horse into a gentle walk. I wanted to cry aloud, but one has to breathe in order to do so, and some time passed before I realized I had forgotten to take in air. I opened my mouth with a great gasp.

"There, now. It is not so fearsome, is it?"

I realized Mr. Darcy had one arm wrapped snugly about my waist. "As long as you do not let go," I whispered.

"I shall not let you go, Elizabeth. You may depend upon it."

CONVERSATION AT THE TABLE THAT night was somewhat strained. Neither Mr. Darcy nor Colonel Fitzwilliam spoke to each other during the entire course of the meal. If not for Georgiana's chatter, disquietude would have curdled the creamed soup. She appeared unaware of any distress between her brother and cousin and happily entertained us with news of the neighbourhood.

Restoration was well underway at Bridesgate, and the Denisons moved in a week earlier. The neighbour's housekeeper had told Mrs. Reynolds that the Whitbys were to hold a ball, and the Denisons were to be invited. At least four ladies and five gentlemen from Bridesgate would attend.

The colonel, who sat across the table from me, raised one eyebrow and smiled. "Too many gentlemen."

"Have you received an invitation, Wills?" Georgiana asked.

"It came in today's post."

"Wonderful! Now, Elizabeth, we shall find someone for you."

"Georgiana—" I began, but the colonel interrupted.

"For Miss Bennet? What is this? Are you in such a hurry to rid Pemberley of your new relation?"

"Oh no! I do not want her ever to leave, but she must marry sometime. If she marries a neighbour, then she will settle nearby, and we shall have the easy pleasure of her company."

"Ah, I see. Well, if the purpose of this ball is to find the lady a husband, then I must not attend, for if I did, I would insist upon securing her hand for the first two dances."

I smiled at the colonel. "There is no such purpose to this ball, and I should be happy to accept your invitation."

Mr. Darcy stood up somewhat abruptly, signalling the end of our meal. He and the colonel retired to the library and evidently settled their disagreement, for upon their return, the colonel appeared more at ease. The only mention of the day's earlier contention occurred when Colonel Fitzwilliam accompanied me to the pianoforte, drew a chair close by so that he might turn the pages of my music, and offered his apologies for his part in frightening me during the morning instruction. I, naturally, accepted his offering, and nothing more was said about the incident.

I did notice Mr. Darcy's steady perusal while his cousin and I remained at the instrument. In truth, I felt his eyes upon me much of the night, but he said not a word. Instead, he consumed a more than generous amount of brandy. Each time he refilled his glass, he grew quieter, and his look darkened.

It made me uneasy to see him drink heavily, and I could not dismiss the idea that something I had done displeased him.

Chapter Six

Sleep deserted me that night. I crawled between the sheets with an apprehensive mind, for thoughts of Mr. Darcy's dark mood nagged at me. From Colonel Fitzwilliam's expression and behaviour, the earlier disagreement between the two men had appeared resolved; so what demon prodded Mr. Darcy to drink such an unusual measure of brandy? I had not seen him in similar dark spirits since I happened upon him beside the stream at Longbourn.

I wrestled with the dilemma for some time. At last, I closed my eyes and vowed to banish all thoughts from my mind. Immediately, I felt his arms around me as we rode his great horse. Back and forth, our bodies swayed in unison to the natural rhythm of the stallion's gait. I grew warm at the memory and threw off the blanket from my shoulder.

"Do not do this, Lizzy!" I said aloud.

I would not allow myself to enter into the pleasure of that remembrance, for I knew it to be forbidden. Would I never be free of the former affection in which I held Mr. Darcy? Obviously, he had kept his resolution to think of me as his sibling. Could I not be strong enough to feel naught but a sister's love for him? I hated my weakness! I gritted my teeth, hoping to drive away thoughts that insisted upon having their way.

A good read will distract me, I thought.

I rose from the bed and lit a candle. As I scanned several novels in my collection, I sighed, for I had read half of a new book but could not find it in the stack. Then, I recalled I had it last in the drawing room. The clock on the mantel chimed the quarter hour past one. Would Mr. Darcy and the colonel have retired by now? Surely. I slipped a shawl over my shoulders, gathered it close about myself, picked up the candle, and stepped out into the hall.

Descending the stairs, I rounded the corner toward the drawing room when I saw lights issuing from within and heard the sound of men's voices. I shrank back into the shadows and blew out my candle. Sufficient illumination remained in the hall sconces to show the way. I had tiptoed lightly, my slippers making little sound on the walnut floor. I turned to retrace my steps when I realized the argument between the men would drown out any muffled sounds I might make.

"But you do not care for dancing, Darcy. Thus, I see no valid reason why I should not have secured Miss Bennet's hand for the first two dances."

"She is pretty enough. Plenty of men will seek her favour. You need not claim her attentions for the entire first hour."

"But she knows no one in Derbyshire. I fail to see why my invitation rouses your temper."

"Do not concern yourself with my temper; it is within check. And you are mistaken. Several neighbours have called since her arrival, and we have returned the visits. Elizabeth is acquainted with enough local gentlemen to attract an adequate number of partners."

"Then why in heaven's name are you in such a humour? I have not seen you drink this amount since we left Rosings last Easter. What is wrong with you, man?"

I could not hear an answer and quickly scurried across the hall until I stood right outside the door. I wished to hear Mr. Darcy's words more than I feared detection.

"The whole affair is troublesome," he said, his voice sounding defeated. "Elizabeth's connection with my family is obscure, to say the least. I would not draw undue attention upon her or raise questions that might cause talk."

"I do not understand your reasoning."

He sighed deeply. "I wonder just what my neighbours think of her. I cannot recall when the Whitbys moved here. Surely, there are others among my friends whose families lived here when it all happened."

"When what happened? Out with it, Darce. Of what do you speak?"

"What?" Mr. Darcy sounded as though he had been awakened from a private reverie and somehow been caught revealing more than he should.

"You said you wondered how many of your neighbours lived here 'when it all happened.' I do not understand to what you refer. Is Miss Bennet's birth the result of some sort of scandal?"

"Of course not, Fitzwilliam!"

Silence followed. I could hear my heart beating, and I began to tremble, holding my breath. I heard someone begin to pace back and forth within the room.

"It is just that her parents were killed in an unfortunate accident right after her birth, and she was left an orphan. To have been taken in by a family other than her own kindred may give rise to gossip, and I will not have talk about her!" His voice grew insistent. "Do you hear me? I will not tolerate it!"

I released my breath, reassured that Mr. Darcy had covered his blunder.

"Calm yourself," Colonel Fitzwilliam said. "I cannot help but hear you. I still fail to see cause for concern. According to Lady Catherine, your family lost touch with Miss Bennet's parents long ago, before the time of her birth. As you said, the connection between them was remote. It is most likely that no one even knew to bring her to your father's house. I think you have swallowed far too much tonight, and drink is duping your brain."

"Did your father know about Elizabeth, Fitzwilliam? What did he say when Lady Catherine descended upon Eden Park?"

"He did not know. He was surprised. We all were, naturally. Of course, you know the earl never totally approved of your father or his family, but he is devoted to you, Darce."

"Because of my mother."

"Yes, he loved his sister, but also because he genuinely loves you. He and Lady Catherine both do. Surely, you acknowledge that fact. With your father it was—well, you know—his Irish connections and the Papist church he allowed to be erected in the wood here at Pemberley."

"My grandfather authorized that building, Fitzwilliam, not my father."

"And my father knows why—because your grandmother never truly renounced her religion. Neither her husband nor her son forbade the church."

"How could they? They loved my grandmother, and that was her faith. I would not have denied her the right, either."

"My father says you allow the congregation to continue to meet on your property. Is that true?"

"It is. Only a handful of parishioners exist, and I see no reason to forbid it."

The conversation ceased at that point amid the sounds of tinkling crystal. The gentlemen, or at least one of them, refilled his glass. I heard the fire crackle and spit as though one man stirred the logs. And then, the colonel spoke in such a low tone that I could not distinguish the words. There was no mistaking Mr. Darcy's return, however. He was angry, and he lashed out, telling the colonel how much he drank was none of his business. I felt ashamed for Mr. Darcy and determined to return to my chamber. I had no business eavesdropping, especially when he was in such a state. I took but a step when I halted, struck by what I heard.

"Just what are your intentions toward Elizabeth?" Mr. Darcy slurred the words.

"My intentions?"

"Every time I look up, you either sit beside her, walk beside her, or remain by her side in some manner. You practically declare yourself if you are to claim her attentions for two dances."

The colonel's only response was a chuckle.

"I asked you a question, Fitzwilliam. What are your intentions?"

"You are drunk, Cousin. Come, let us retire for the night."

"No! I do not want to go to bed. I want an answer. I demand you answer my question."

"Very well, but I doubt you will remember this conversation in the morning. I find Elizabeth Bennet a handsome woman. She is lively and entertaining; but for the fact I am a younger son, I would pursue her in earnest. I am not in love with her, but I believe she possesses sufficient charms to tempt me into the state. You possess the means to help my quest."

"Help you? Why should I?"

"She must marry someone. Why not keep her in the family? Darcy, if you would convince her to accept a sizeable dowry, the impediment to our marriage would no longer exist."

My heart sank to the floor. I did not wait one moment more to return to my room. I could not climb the staircase quickly enough. Upon reaching the landing, I fled to my chamber and closed the door behind me.

Marry the colonel? I had thought of it only in passing when visiting Kent last spring. Upon meeting him, I acknowledged his pleasant conversation and agreeable manners, but he soon dashed any contemplation of a possible match by informing me of his position, of his need to secure a financially advantageous alliance. I had never entertained the thought again. And now, at the mere suggestion, gooseflesh crawled up my arms.

I KEPT TO MY CHAMBER most of the next day, pleading a headache. Georgiana checked on me and satisfied herself that my complaint was minor. She agreed to make my excuses to her brother and cousin, and thus, I avoided facing them. I feared that knowledge of the conversation I had overheard the night before might reflect in my expression, and I needed time to conceal my apprehension.

By late afternoon, however, I tired of my surroundings and stole quietly from my room. I climbed the staircase to the great gallery wherein the paintings of the Darcys and their ancestors hung. Once again, my grandmother's portrait drew my attention. I searched her face, wishing she could speak to me, that she could enlighten me on the mystery of my birth. Hers was the only personage with whom I felt a kinship. Why, I do not know.

At length, I walked on down the hall and stopped to gaze upon the portrait of Siobhan Darcy's three young sons. Their faces shone with innocence, and I wondered whether my grandmother had lived long enough to know of her oldest son's transgression. I made note to ask Mr. Darcy in what year she died to see whether it occurred before the year of my birth.

I walked back to the portrait of my father. I still could not find myself hidden within his features. Above his painting and to the left hung a portrait of a man in a naval uniform. I glanced from the man's face to that of one of the three young boys. Yes, I could see it was Henry Darcy, the youngest son. At even a young age, he had a mischievous gleam in his eye, as though he longed for adventure. It caused my heart to warm, and I smiled in return. There was something about him...

Someone cleared her throat. I startled somewhat, for I had been preoccupied and failed to notice Mrs. Reynolds's arrival.

"I beg your pardon, Miss Bennet. I did not mean to surprise you."

"No, no, I just did not see you, Mrs. Reynolds."

"I trust you are feeling better. Will you join the family at dinner?"

"No, please have a tray brought to my room. I confess I only left my chamber because of boredom and not because my headache has lifted."

"Very well, Miss Bennet." She turned to leave, but I stopped her with a question.

"Did you not tell me you have been at Pemberley since Mr. Darcy was a boy?"

"Yes, Miss Bennet, since he was four years old."

"Did you know either of his uncles, Messrs. Peter or Henry Darcy?"

"I did, ma'am. Admiral Henry had not yet joined the Navy."

"I see his portrait."

"It is very fine, is it not, ma'am?"

I nodded. "And which of these men is Mr. Peter Darcy? I confess I do not recognize him as an adult."

She cleared her throat before answering. "That gentleman's portrait was never painted as I recall, ma'am, because of the disgrace."

"Disgrace?"

She lowered her eyes and pressed her lips together.

"You do not wish to tell me, I take it."

"Begging your pardon, Miss Bennet, it is not my place to do so."

"Well, goodness, what could he have done to cause his memory to be banished from the family portraits? Even Mr. Wickham's likeness remains in the cabinet below stairs."

"Yes, ma'am, that is because Mr. Wickham was a favourite of Mr. George Darcy."

"But his own brother's likeness does not exist? Come now, Mrs. Reynolds, did he turn into a brigand?"

"Oh no, Miss Bennet, 'twas nothing like that." She stepped closer and spoke in a whisper. "You must not let anyone know I told you this: Mr. Peter Darcy immigrated to Ireland."

"To Ireland? Surely, that cannot be so shameful. Why, his own mother was born there."

"True, but 'twas the manner in which he left. Mr. Peter Darcy just disappeared."

"Disappeared?"

She nodded, her mouth drawn into a tight little line. "He up and vanished without a word to anyone. The family did not know his whereabouts for a long time. It caused Mr. George Darcy and my lady much anguish. Years later, they finally learned his destination, but he has never set foot on Pemberley since that time. 'Tis unfortunate that he ran away before his likeness could be taken."

I turned back to the portrait of the young brothers. How sad to lose one's place in a family, to simply give it up as though it did not matter. What had that done to his mother? I determined to ask Mr. Darcy the particulars. I would not discuss the family further with the housekeeper, but I found it all quite curious.

THE DATE OF THE WHITBYS' ball coincided with Pemberley's first crocus blooms. I know because I spent no little time awaiting their arrival in the gardens. Scattered throughout the vast beds, hidden in front of the hyacinth and daffodil bulbs, they emerged from the dark soil like soft, delicate treasures of pink, white, and lavender. The gardeners had planted them in abundance in the more prominent plots of ground, but I had discovered a hidden trove secured within a small alcove behind a brick wall at the rear of the house. It became my place of refuge.

Since overhearing Colonel Fitzwilliam's suggestion of marriage, I had done all in my power to avoid his presence. I practically threw Georgiana into his company, suggesting all kinds of outings and errands for which she might employ her cousin.

Even though I wished to satisfy my curiosity about the fate of my father's youngest brother, Mr. Darcy had not proved approachable. He continued his dreary silence and avoidance of me. Obviously, he had little desire for my companionship. No more riding lessons were broached, and no further forays into Pemberley's attics were suggested. In truth, Mr. Darcy said scarcely more than was necessary at the dinner table. And each evening after dinner, he sat on a corner of the sofa like a brooding wolf, a bottle of brandy claiming much of his attention.

I did not see him at breakfast even once during the days leading up to the ball. I assumed the effects of the previous evening's consumption of spirits diminished his enjoyment of the morning light.

We had entertained only one brief conversation during that time, and it led to harsh words. Georgiana prevailed upon him to order me a new gown for the ball, and when I refused, protesting that I would wear the gown I had brought from Longbourn, his temper flared.

"Will you not accept one paltry gown from me?" he demanded.

"Shall I shame you in the gown I wore to the Netherfield ball last year?"

"Of course not. You were lovely...but would you not like something new? It has been my experience that most women do."

"I do not."

We stared at each other as though waiting to see who would give in. "Very well. Attend the ball in the frock you have on, for all I care."

He turned and stalked from the room. I felt as though he had slapped me.

And so, I spent a great portion of each day in that hidden alcove awaiting the crocuses. A stone bench sat in the shade, and it proved an agreeable haven in which to read and to think. I could not account for the change in Mr. Darcy. I knew an excess of strong drink produced adverse effects on a person's behaviour, but what had precipitated this new habit? I had known him well over a year now and had never before seen him imbibe extravagantly. I could not rid myself of the fear that I was somehow to blame, that I had caused his aberrant conduct.

Only one other instance provided any sort of clue to the mystery. Three days before the ball, Georgiana and I walked into the hall from our social calls to hear an uproar coming from Mr. Darcy's study. Unmistakably, the colonel and his cousin were engaged in a disagreement once again. I quickly asked Georgiana to fetch a piece of music from a large stack of songs in the music room so that I might memorize the words for that evening's entertainment. A worried frown clouded her countenance, but she hastened to do my bidding.

I stood in the hallway where I could hear the argument without obvious eavesdropping. Indeed, the servants passing by were privy to the raised voices, reason enough to pardon my actions in my mind.

"I have told you, Fitzwilliam, Elizabeth will not accept a dowry from me. Why can you not let go of the matter? You must marry for money, and she has none!"

"You could settle her dowry on me privately at the time of the marriage. She need never know."

"Never know? You would ask me to go behind her back, against her explicit wishes?"

"It could be a gentleman's agreement. Wives leave matters of money to their husbands. I am sure that, with a bit of gentle persuasion, I could win her hand."

"Do you think her daft? She knows you have little fortune. You made it clear to her last year at Rosings. Do you now believe she has lost her memory? It is insupportable. I will discuss it no further."

"You will regret this, Darcy. She will marry some pretty boy who worms his way into her heart, and he will take her God knows where. They may settle in Scotland, for all you know, and you and Georgiana will never see her again."

"Oh, I will see her! No matter where she goes or whom she marries, I shall always be her cousin, and she will not be lost to me. Not ever."

"Indulge your foolish fancies, but you do not have a right to deny mine. I shall at least ask Miss Bennet if she will be my wife."

"Without a suitable dowry?"

"If she says yes, I know you will not let her live in need. You cannot. It is written all over your face. You care too much for her, and you will provide for her one way or the other."

I felt a hand on my arm. "Elizabeth?"

I looked up to see Georgiana holding the requested music. I took it quickly and asked her to accompany me to my sitting room where we might memorize the words together. I feared she had overheard too much of the conversation between her brother and cousin, but if so, she did not mention it.

After that, time passed quickly, and the date of the ball soon arrived. I had little opportunity for a thorough inspection of the crocus beds on said day, but I was pleased to snatch a few moments and note their emergence in my journal before my maid claimed me for the obligatory perfumed ablutions, the donning of my gown, and the tedious but expert attention to my hair. Georgiana glowed in a pale-pink gown of moiré silk, and suddenly, I had a moment of regret that I had not graciously accepted Mr. Darcy's offer, for my ivory gown felt somewhat shabby next to hers.

Oh, 'tis too late now, I told myself with a sigh as I joined her in the hall.

We descended the staircase together, whereupon Colonel Fitzwilliam stepped forward and offered an arm to each of us. He escorted us toward the open door, through which I could see Mr. Darcy's large carriage standing ready.

"With two such lovely ladies in tow, I shall be the envy of every man at the ball tonight."

"Oh, Richard, are you certain I look acceptable?" Georgiana asked.

We both assured the girl of her loveliness as we walked across the wide hallway. The servants stood at attention, smiles on the maids' faces, and Mrs. Reynolds bade us a pleasant evening. I looked around, wondering at Mr. Darcy's absence, when he stepped out of the shadows just outside the door. He bowed slightly but remained silent as Georgiana and I climbed into the carriage. The colonel entered next and sat beside me. Mr. Darcy sat beside Georgiana, but his expression appeared as grim as ever. I hoped he had not already made liberal use of his newfound companionate bottle of brandy. He continued to remain mute unless directly addressed. I felt uncomfortable, as though the carriage had diminished in size. Colonel Fitzwilliam seemed to sit far too close beside me, and even though I shrank into the corner, I felt smothered. I was greatly relieved when the ride ended and we disembarked at the Whitbys' front door.

Lights bedecked the house, and music and gaiety signalled that the festivities had already commenced. Mr. Whitby introduced me to Admiral and Mrs. Denison, and they, in turn, brought forth their children: Andrew, Maurice, Marianne, and Fanny. Maurice was by far the more handsome of the two brothers, but it was Andrew who asked me to dance.

"Miss Bennet will be glad to honour you with her company, I am sure," said Colonel Fitzwilliam, "but she has promised the first two dances to me."

I smiled as Mr. Denison, with an understanding glance, bowed and turned away while the colonel took my hand and led me to the floor. I had hoped at least to make my way among the crowd and acknowledge those Derbyshire folk of my acquaintance before joining the dancers, but the colonel had other plans. The first piece was a stately tune, and the colonel proved an engaging partner, maintaining a steady patter of conversation. By the end of the first set, I found myself at ease and actually enjoying the ball. I had always loved dancing, and although my partner was not as expert at the art as one I recalled, he did prove agreeable.

At completion of the first hour, I allowed Colonel Fitzwilliam to escort me to the punch bowl where Miss Denison and her elder brother soon joined us. Marianne was a lovely girl with an animated spirit. I thought we might easily become friends, for she possessed that ability not only to poke gentle fun at her brother but to laugh at herself as well. I wished to know her better, but the colonel hovered about, frequently interrupting our conversation. I had never seen him so determined to put himself forward. When the music began for the next set, I welcomed Mr. Andrew Denison's hand as he led me to the line of dancers.

"So, you are a cousin of Mr. Darcy and his sister. Is that correct?" he asked as we circled the couple next to us.

"In truth, I dare not call myself a cousin, sir. It is a somewhat complicated interrelation, but family ties oft times are, would you not agree?"

"Ah yes. I have cousins I have never seen and probably never shall unless someone dies and leaves a great inheritance. Greed has a way of uniting long-lost relations, if only until the will is read."

"I would not have you think I visit Pemberley for that cause, sir. I am a poor relation and shall remain so."

"Indeed? I would think Darcy would right that wrong."

"Mr. Darcy is all kindness and generosity."

He raised his eyebrows at my remark, and we danced several steps without further conversation. I hoped to change the subject as his questions made me irritable. Must every man I meet inquire as to my fortune or lack thereof? *Of course, silly girl! What is the purpose of a ball other than to pair up possible marriage partners?*

"Have you enjoyed successful sport since your move to Derbyshire, Mr. Denison?"

He held my hand as we joined the promenade. "I confess I have had little time. My father has assigned me the onerous task of supervising the removal of rubbish from Bridesgate's attics."

I smiled. "A delightful task I am sure."

"Indeed. You would not believe the collection of personal mementos left by the Willoughby family. Deciding what to keep or discard has driven me to distraction. I am tempted to direct the servants to throw out the entire lot, but my father insists I retain any item that might be valuable, if only for sentimentality, until Sir Linton Willoughby arrives next week."

"Shall you have time to complete your chore before the owner visits Bridesgate?"

"Only if I devote myself to the assignment. You see before you a harried man, Miss Bennet. That is why you must honour me with another dance this evening. 'Tis the only pleasant activity I have enjoyed since arriving in the county."

I laughed at his exaggeration but agreed to be his partner later in the evening. With the musicians' final note, I felt flushed from the exercise, but not without pleasure. Mr. Denison led me from the floor, bowed, and assured me he would return to claim his dance.

I looked around, hoping to find Miss Denison. With surprise—no, astonishment—I watched Mr. Darcy escort her to the head of the line of dancers. He must have found her exceedingly charming to ask her to dance, for I knew he had not honoured any other lady the entirety of the evening. I watched as he took her hand, stepped close, and inclined his head. Evidently, he did not find conversation with her as trying as he had with me last year at Netherfield. Growing uncomfortably warm, I wished I had brought a fan. The Whitbys' fires were entirely too well tended that late in the year. I thought of having another cup of punch, but for some reason, I could not tear my eyes from the dancers and one couple in particular.

"Miss Bennet?"

I startled, as though someone had read my thoughts, and looked up to find Colonel Fitzwilliam at my side extending a refreshing cup toward me. I acknowledged his gift with gratitude, and when he suggested we step out on the balcony for a bit of air, I agreed.

"Your colour is high. I fear you have danced too close to the fireplace," he said as he led me through the double doors.

"The night breeze is a welcome change."

We stood next to the railing, whereupon he leaned forward and rested his forearms. "It is a beautiful night."

I agreed and lifted my head to gaze at the multitude of stars littering the heavens.

"You are quite beautiful in that position, Miss Bennet. The fairness of your throat is luminous in the starlight. That and the turn of your countenance prove a striking combination."

I immediately lowered my gaze and protested his remarks.

"No, I am serious. You are a lovely woman. Surely, you have been told that by numerous suitors."

"I do not collect suitors, sir. With my lack of fortune, they hardly stand in line."

"Mr. Denison appears smitten."

"He simply asked me to dance."

"Has he not requested your hand a second time?"

"That does not signify anything of consequence. If you asked me, I would dance with you a second time."

"Indeed? And…what if I ask for your hand a third time? Now, tell me, does that signify something of consequence?"

My heart beat faster, and I was grateful for the cool air, for I could feel my cheeks burn. What was the colonel suggesting? Surely, he was not asking for my hand in marriage here at the ball. I turned toward the French doors, anxious to retreat to the safety of the throng within.

"I am sufficiently refreshed. I think we should return, sir."

He caught my hand before I could reach the door. "Will you do me the honour of being my partner for the last dance, Elizabeth?"

"I...do not think—" I could not conjure up a reason to refuse him. "Yes ...if it is your desire, sir. Thank you."

"It is most assuredly my desire," he murmured as he brought my hand to his lips. The look in his eyes filled me with dread, and I quickly excused myself and hurried into the ballroom.

I SAT BETWEEN MARIANNE AND Andrew Denison at dinner. Mr. Darcy sat on Marianne's left, and Colonel Fitzwilliam sat directly across from me. I was relieved that the colonel did not act with any peculiarity or pay particular attention to me during the meal. There were no stares or long, meaningful looks into my eyes. One would never guess we had engaged in a significant moment earlier in the evening. He proved an engaging guest and entertained Mrs. Whitby with tales of his military exploits. From the vacant stare in her eyes, I doubt she knew much of the exotic places he mentioned, but he spoke with such animation that he amused everyone at the table within hearing.

Mr. Whitby asked Georgiana to play for us near the close of the meal, and although she was nervous, she agreed and performed in an excellent manner. After Marianne performed and two sisters played a duet, Mr. Whitby extended the invitation for me to play and sing, but I demurred. Obviously, I did not possess the talent already exhibited. I would not think of shaming myself or the Darcys as my sister Mary had done at the Netherfield Ball.

Mr. Darcy said little during the entirety of the feast, but I noted he kept the waiter busy refilling his wine glass. Without a doubt, I thought, he would not drink more than he could handle. I had never seen him lose control in a public assembly and could not fathom why he took such chances that evening.

Mr. Andrew Denison requested the first dance after dinner, during which he said our discussion of the Bridesgate attics caused him to recall a certain painting. He asked whether he might call upon me the following day and bring the picture, for he thought I would find it of great interest. I agreed, of course, but when I asked why, he refused to reveal his reasons.

"You must wait and see for yourself, Miss Bennet," he said with a sly smile. His blue eyes twinkled, and I decided that, although he might not be as handsome as his brother, Maurice, I did not find his appearance unappealing by any means.

After that, I danced with several other gentlemen; indeed, I seldom sat the entire evening. Once I did find myself without a partner, I witnessed Mr. Darcy ask Marianne to dance a second time. I decided I had made a mistake earlier, thinking she and I might be friends. Of a sudden, I decided that she smiled too much. It became clear we would not suit each other at all.

As the evening drew to a close, Colonel Fitzwilliam arrived to claim the last dance. Andrew Denison accompanied him and reminded me that he would call on the morrow. We had just concluded our conversation, and when he turned to leave, I saw Mr. Darcy approach.

"The last dance, is it not?" he said. "Will you do me the honour, Elizabeth?"

"Darcy!" Colonel Fitzwilliam hissed in a low voice. "Miss Bennet has already promised me."

"You have presumed upon her time more than enough this night. Elizabeth?"

He brushed past the colonel and took my hand firmly in his, steering me toward the dance floor without a backward glance.

"Sir…it is not done!" I whispered. "I…I beg you, do not make a scene."

He drew closer and spoke in my ear. "It is not I who would make the scene, Elizabeth. No one but you and I know our true connection. Will it not appear unnatural if I do not ask my *cousin* to dance at least once? Take your place in line."

The first notes sounded, and I recognized the song as a newer romantic air that called for greater contact among partners than any previous dance of the evening. I held my breath as Mr. Darcy stepped forward and encircled my waist with his arm. The position thrust our faces close, and he met my gaze with a dark, piercing stare. Was it my imagination, or did his hand linger longer than necessary about my body? Did he step nearer than he should when we clasped hands and danced forward? And why did my hand tremble so when I placed it upon his shoulder?

I cleared my throat and attempted to lighten the mood with conversation. His only response to my remark was a steady reading of my face. I saw his eyes travel down to my mouth, and I found myself blushing. Frantically, I searched for something harmless of which to speak.

"Are not the musicians talented? I have rarely heard such able completion of—"

"Elizabeth." He twirled me around and stepped away.

I took Mr. Whitby's hand and bowed in time to the rhythm before turning back to face Mr. Darcy. "Sir?"

"In your lifetime, have you ever, just once, danced without speaking?"

I glared at him as we clasped hands and stepped down the line. "Naturally. I simply—"

"Then, I pray you, bestow that favour upon me. Let us do nothing more than dance."

We circled the last couple in line and faced each other. Oh! The man was impossible! Very well. I would not tell him if the house caught fire. I gritted my teeth and determined to complete the set, but only because I refused to call attention to myself by leaving the floor abruptly. But I would not enjoy it. Oh no, I would not enjoy one moment.

And then Mr. Darcy took my hands and whirled me around and around. I inhaled sharply as the tempo increased, but I matched him step for step. He stared into my eyes with a ferocity I recalled from our first dance together at Netherfield. I refused to cower but met his gaze fully. But why…why must he incline his head so near? The scent of his skin intoxicated me. And he must not allow his hands to caress my shoulders when we clasped each other to descend the line. Was it my imagination? No, I knew his hands lingered longer, much longer, than needed.

This would never do. The melody enchanted me, and I felt myself caught up in the fascination of dancing with him. All those feelings I had earlier confessed to God now flooded my heart, and I knew I was lost. I had not forgotten the spell he could weave over me. In spite of all my declarations and determination, I had not overcome the delight I experienced at his slightest touch. I loved him, but not with a sister's love. And I never wanted our dance to end.

THAT NIGHT, I DID NOT close my eyes. Before dawn, I determined to leave Pemberley posthaste and return to Longbourn. I knew I could no longer stay in the same house with Mr. Darcy.

Chapter Seven

The post rumbled along the road outside Lambton with such jarring jolts that it set my teeth on edge. The driver seemed to possess innate knowledge of where each stone lay in our path, and I wondered whether he took mischievous delight in bouncing us up and down. How quickly I had accustomed myself to the comfort of Mr. Darcy's carriage! The public conveyance possessed neither the luxurious padding nor spaciousness of his vehicle. Three fellow passengers—a woman and two older men—shared the coach, forcing an intimacy I found oppressive. One of them, evidently, had not bathed for some time, and I kept my nose as close to the open window as permitted. The bleak, overcast skies without matched the grimness of the interior as well as my frame of mind.

I had slipped out of the house without notice in the pre-dawn darkness. Knowing that the family would rise late because of the previous evening's ball, I hoped the servants would be too busy to observe my departure. They had orders not to awaken any of us early, so I felt assured that I might make my escape without detection.

The five-mile walk to Lambton proved much more arduous than I expected, for the countryside possessed numerous inclines. I had packed my essentials in one small, light valise, but it grew heavy before I reached the town. In a brief note addressed to Mr. Darcy and Georgiana that I had left on my pillow, I told them I was leaving because I missed my family and Longbourn too much to remain at Pemberley.

While awaiting the arrival of the post in Lambton, I could not sit still. Fortunately, it ran on an early schedule that day, so we departed before ten in the morning. My head pounded by the time the horses worked themselves into a good speed. I took a deep breath and leaned back on the seat, realizing for the first time that I had clenched my teeth until my jaw ached. My nerves felt ready to crumble, and I struggled not to show my emotion. It would not do to expose myself in public, for I needed no offers of assistance that, naturally, would involve questions.

Misery possessed me. Why had I ever entertained the thought that I might visit Pemberley? It had all been a mistake, an impossible endeavour, a foolish, foolish dream. I would never be able to think of Mr. Darcy as my brother. Dancing one dance with him had dashed that illusion. I knew I must return to Longbourn and avoid ever seeing him again. I would never be Miss Darcy; I had no right. I would never have a place at my true father's table. I would be forced to make a new life with someone else and in some other home.

Although my friend Charlotte had in the past accused me of being romantic, I did possess a practical side. I acknowledged that I must marry, and since I could never marry the man I loved, I would return to Longbourn and make myself agreeable to any man I could respect. As long as he proved honourable and kind, I would endure the union.

Why had I not remained at Pemberley then and allowed Colonel Fitzwilliam to propose? I closed my eyes at the thought. Yes, he possessed excellent qualifications, but there was his connection with Mr. Darcy. I could not bear to think I would enter into a marriage where I was certain to be cast into his company. The idea was intolerable! 'Twould be better even to marry a farmer, and after all, was that not a more suitable match for one born as the result of a dishonourable situation?

My girlish dreams of a loving union had tumbled to the ground as quickly as the mist now falling outside the coach. I leaned my head against the side of the carriage and closed my eyes, hoping I might sleep and never waken.

I know not how long I slept, but I did awaken with abruptness. Amid shouts from without, the coach halted quickly.

"What's happenin'?" The woman beside me grabbed her basket and clutched it to her chest. "It's not the highwaymen, is it? Oh, pray, don't let it be highwaymen!"

Our two male companions rose and peered out each window of the coach. I drew back from the man nearest me, for my nose identified him as the person in need of a bath. Within moments, we heard the driver shout again and the distinct tone of a gentleman contradict him. I closed my eyes in dismay, for I could not fail to recognize the voice.

"I tell you she is my cousin," Mr. Darcy said. "Whether she purchased her fare under the name Bennet is immaterial. The lady is a guest at Pemberley, and I would never allow her to travel unattended in a public coach. I demand you release her to my care without delay."

"She never said she was from Pemberley, sir," the coachman answered. He opened the door and pushed back the man who hung halfway out the window. I shrank back when he offered his hand to assist me. "Come on, miss. Your cousin's here to take you home."

"No, I shall not go with him. I bought a pass for Hertfordshire. It is paid for, and I have the right to travel on this coach."

He looked back at Mr. Darcy, who dismounted and strode toward the carriage with a determined step. "Come, Elizabeth. Do not delay this good man's journey."

"I shall not. I am returning to Longbourn."

"Sir," the driver said. "If she don't want to go with you, perhaps it's best to let her be. I'll see she gets to her destination safely."

Mr. Darcy's brows knit together into a single, fierce line as he turned upon the driver and informed him what he could do to his coach, his career, and his liberty if he persisted in abducting his cousin.

"Abductin'? I ain't about nothin' like that, sir. The lady paid her money."

"If you do not release her to my care, I shall see you charged with seizure. My cousin is under my protection, and I have not relinquished it to you or anyone else."

The man yielded under Mr. Darcy's severity and drew back while my companions looked aghast. I knew no one would take my side against a man of his stature. He held out his hand, but instead of taking it, I shoved my valise at him. I then climbed out of the coach without his assistance, flinging myself away when he reached out to me.

"Do you want us to wait, miss?" the coachman asked.

"I told you she is under my protection." Mr. Darcy's tone was rigid and insistent.

"But the mist, sir. I fear the weather's 'bout to turn nasty."

"I shall see to her. Be on your way."

With a final hesitant look in my direction, the driver slammed the passenger door shut and climbed aboard to his seat. Within moments, I watched my only means of escape lumber down the road.

I turned and glared at Mr. Darcy. "I hope you are satisfied." Seizing my valise, I gripped it close to my chest like a shield and whirled around, taking resolute steps to follow the post.

"Do you propose to walk to Hertfordshire, Elizabeth?"

"You leave me no other choice."

"I have a horse, or are you so blinded with anger you cannot see it?"

"You know I am no horsewoman, and do not suggest I ride with you because I refuse."

"Very well. I shall walk and lead the horse while you ride."

I shook my head and continued on, taking pains to lengthen my stride.

"You are behaving like a child."

"Am I? Does that entitle you to assert yourself like a father? Never have I been so publicly shamed. I shall not forgive you."

"Publicly? In front of those common folk?" He snorted his disdain. "And if we are to speak of shame, how do you think I appeared before my servants, much less my cousin and sister, when I was told you had run off in the night?"

I stopped and faced him. "I did not run off in the night. It was morning. Am I not a free woman? Do I not possess control over my own person? Am I not permitted to come and go as I please? Evidently not in your house, sir. I would never have travelled to Pemberley with you if I had known I would be held there against my will!"

"No one is holding you against your will."

"Come now, Mr. Darcy, any fool can see you have just removed me from the only means I possessed to return home. If that is not holding me against my will, what is?"

"Travelling by post is not the only way you may return to Longbourn. It is an unthinking, dangerous choice. You are well aware that young ladies of breeding do not travel alone. All you had to do was tell me you wished to leave. My carriage would have been at your disposal. If you had considered this indefensible decision carefully, you would see that I carry the point."

Thunder rumbled nearby, and the mist suddenly turned into fully developed raindrops. I glanced at the sky, lowered my head, and left him standing in the road. I had not walked a few steps before the rain grew even heavier and began to pelt my head and shoulders severely.

"Elizabeth, you cannot walk to the next town. Let me put you on the horse, for we must take cover from this storm."

"No." I refused to slow my pace or look back at him. I knew my actions were senseless, but I no longer cared. I only wished to escape his presence.

A flash of lightning bolted across the sky, and thunder bellowed so loudly that I ducked my head. Rain increased without pity, and I felt water trickle down inside my gown. Another lightning strike proved near enough that I cried aloud in fear.

"Come, we must find shelter," Mr. Darcy commanded. He placed both hands on my waist and steered me across the road toward the woods. "Look, there is a bit of a shed before us."

I could see nothing for the vehemence of the storm. Water streamed down my face and clouded my vision. Where was he taking me? We began to run until we reached a ditch already filling with water. Before I knew it, Mr. Darcy lifted me up into his arms and jumped the ditch, the horse following close behind. He climbed the slight incline and carried me into what appeared to be the remains of a hut. It had but three walls standing. The roof, however, hung over enough to provide some measure of protection.

"This is not substantial, I admit," Mr. Darcy said.

Of a sudden, we both seemed aware that he still held me. I was clinging to his neck, and the look that passed between his eyes and mine said more than words. Immediately, he released me to a standing position, and I averted my face. With one hand, I straightened my gown and pelisse while still clutching the valise close to my breast. He removed his hat and shook off the water. Glancing around, he pulled an old bench forward, dusted it off with his hand, and indicated I should sit.

"I shall stand," I said. "The storm cannot last long."

"And then what? Shall you persist in this stubborn pattern of yours?"

"I have no other recourse. You have seen to that."

"You can return to Pemberley with me, change into dry clothing before you become ill, and if you insist, I will take you back to Longbourn first thing on the morrow."

"No."

"No? Is that the only reply I am to have? Why must you drive me to distraction with your ill behaviour?"

My ill behaviour? How the man provoked me! I turned my back on him and walked to the far edge of the shelter, staring out as the wind arose and stirred the trees. We said nothing more for some time, but I heard him begin to pace back and forth like a wild animal longing to be loosed. I thought of our coupling in the dance the night before and how my senses quickened when he touched me. For all his elegance, his upright demeanour, his superior, gentlemanly composure, I knew...I knew there was a primitive, untamed side to Mr. Darcy that he kept hidden from the world. *He will unleash it someday*, I thought. Chills ran up my spine at the idea, and a fire welled up from deep within me.

But not with me. I would never have more than the glimpse I had witnessed last night. He could never reveal that wild, passionate nature to me. It would be reserved for the woman he loved, if not the one he eventually took in marriage. It could not be me. Our father had seen to that. Suddenly, I hated George Darcy. *Why? Why had life conspired against us in this unthinkable manner?*

"Elizabeth, you are trembling."

I felt his hands on my shoulders as he turned me around to face him. I kept my eyes lowered, and I hoped he thought the tears that spilled down my cheeks were nothing more than the remains of the rain. He took off his jacket and placed it around my shoulders. "Come and sit down. Pray, do not weep. The storm is moving past."

I did as he said while he sat beside me holding my hand. "I want to go home, sir," I said softly.

"First thing tomorrow."

I shook my head. "I want to go today."

"Elizabeth, you cannot go in this condition. Let us return to Pemberley, and I promise I shall take you back in the morning."

"No. I wish to go today...alone."

"I cannot allow you to travel alone. You know the journey will require you to stay overnight at roadside inns. It is not safe."

"Send a maid along with your manservant. That will be sufficient."

I kept my face turned away from his, but he lifted my chin so that he might see into my eyes, and I trembled again at the tenderness of his touch.

"Why do you insist that I not accompany you?"

Slowly, I raised my eyes to meet his. "Pray, do not ask me."

His eyes held mine much longer than they should, and then they travelled down to my lips, and I watched him struggle to conquer the yearning that seemed to possess him. He tore his eyes from me, closing them as though he were in pain, and I saw him press his lips together while a great sigh escaped his guarded restraint. When he opened his eyes, he appeared as one haunted. Bowing his head in agreement, he released my hand and rose from the bench.

Within three-quarters of an hour, the storm stilled, and Mr. Darcy's carriage arrived. Upon departing Pemberley, he had ordered his coachmen to follow, but he had raced ahead of them from Lambton once he learned I had boarded the post. He had even thought to bring my maid, and she hastened to cover my shoulders with a dry shawl once I climbed into the carriage.

"There has been a change in plans," Mr. Darcy instructed his driver. "Do not return to Pemberley. Take Miss Bennet to her home in Hertfordshire."

He went on to give his servant sufficient funds to cover expenses for several days of travel and explicit instructions for my care and protection during the trip. When finished, he directed the maid to withdraw from the coach while he bade me farewell. Sitting on the seat across from me, he leaned forward and took my hands in his once again, smiling slightly.

"All is arranged. Stratton is to be trusted as well as the footmen. You may rely upon them with confidence."

"Thank you."

"Will you write to me?"

I shook my head.

"To Georgiana?"

"Of course, if she wishes."

"You know she will."

I looked away, unwilling to meet his eyes.

"Elizabeth, I..."

"Sir, I pray you say nothing more."

He turned his eyes to the window, and in doing so, he sighed deeply. "Then let us say farewell, and God bless you, Elizabeth." He raised my hands to his lips, and I caught my breath at the tenderness of his kiss.

"And you, sir," I murmured.

With that, he bounded from the coach, the maid climbed aboard, and we set off. Although I tried not to look back, I could not keep myself from turning and waving to him from the window. He stood in the road, his hat in his hand, but he did not wave in return.

As long as I live and memory survives, that image endures.

I RESUMED LIFE AT LONGBOURN almost as though I had never left. I told my parents Pemberley was a lovely place for a brief visit, but I could not remain longer. Mamá fretted and fumed as I expected, but my father simply patted my shoulder. Neither of them asked why I returned so quickly. Mamá was too busy complaining about my ingratitude, but I oftentimes looked up to see my father gaze upon me with a puzzled expression in his eyes. I did not seek him out to make further explanations, and he was not the type of father who made an effort to look into matters that might require more attention than he wished to give.

Fortunately, I had gained control over my emotions by the time I arrived home. I had wept during much of the first leg of the journey. Upon first observation of my discomfort, my maid asked whether she could be of assistance. When I refused and directed her to let me be, she followed my bidding and allowed me to indulge my grief while she shopped for our necessities at the first town we reached that proved large enough to contain suitable shops. On that first night back at Longbourn, I laid my head upon the pillow on which I had slept most of my life and knew my tears were done. I would no longer cry for what I could never have. I would content myself with the life before me.

As chance would have it, Mr. and Mrs. Bingley had returned from their wedding tour only a week before my return. Jane and I clung to each other upon our first visit. Our joyful reunion reminded me how much I missed her and how I longed to confide in my childhood companion and dearest sister. I did not, however. I told no one the true reason I left Pemberley. For that matter, I had never told anyone—not even Jane—that I loved Mr. Darcy. Now that all hope was gone, what reason remained to do so? I could not think of destroying her happiness by letting her know I could never hope for true marital felicity. 'Twas more prudent to keep some sorrows buried.

"And what are your plans now, Jane?" I sat across from her at our dining table upon which Hill, at Mamá's orders, had placed more dishes of food than we could ever consume.

"Caroline, Louisa, and Mr. Hurst join us next week."

"But after their arrival, we will stay at Netherfield only a short while," Mr. Bingley added before attacking a large helping of roast lamb.

"Oh no," my mother began to whine. "Why, Mr. Bingley, when you have just returned, must you take my daughter from the county again so soon?"

"We shall travel to London for the Season, Mamá," Jane said.

Her words greatly pleased my mother, and she ceased her complaints, choosing instead to rave about the balls and parties to which they would be invited—the opera, music recitals, plays, and art exhibits that were sure to fill their social calendar.

"Oh, Mr. Bingley, Jane is so beautiful that I am certain she will capture all of London's attention."

He readily agreed, grinning widely.

"Now, my dear, you must be diligent in returning calls and planning your first dinner party. Oh, I am all aflutter at the vision of your success. Have you ordered new gowns yet? You must allow me to advise you of the best warehouses in Town, for it will not do to purchase less than the finest materials."

Jane assured her that all would be well, and I smiled, thinking that much had altered in our lives, and yet, much would never change.

A week or so after the arrival of Mr. Bingley's sisters, we received an invitation to dinner at Netherfield. It was to be Jane's first entertainment over which she would preside as mistress of the great house. My mother and sisters were alive with excitement. Kitty changed her gown three times that evening before making a final selection. Mary collected her best music so that she might play for us on Mr. Bingley's pianoforte. I sighed at the thought of the opinion her performance would elicit from Caroline Bingley and Louisa Hurst. *Oh well*, I thought, *it is Jane's home now, and they might as well accept us, for we have no intention of going away.*

That night, the table was lovely, and we doubtless complimented Jane to excess, but she seemed grateful for our remarks. I gathered that a prolonged visit from Mr. Bingley's sisters would not prove easy for my sister to endure. Mr. Bingley, however, remained as attentive to her as he had before they married. I was glad to see that the familiarity of marriage had not dampened his affection.

After dinner, we suffered through Mary's recital and appreciated Mrs. Hurst's talent as she exhibited herself with a spirited rondo by Haydn. Mr. Hurst woke up once cards were suggested, and my parents joined Mr. Bingley and him at the table.

"Miss Eliza," Miss Bingley called to me as I walked across the room to sit beside Jane. "Shall you also spend the Season in Town, or do you prefer country solitude? I hear you remained but a short while at Pemberley. I do hope that grand house did not cause you to feel out of place."

"Not at all, Miss Bingley. The family could not have made me more welcome."

"Indeed? Did Mr. Darcy introduce you to Derbyshire society? And what did they make of his recent discovery that you were a distant relative? Were they much intrigued?"

I felt my colour begin to rise and steeled myself to remain calm at her needling. "On the contrary, everyone I met displayed the utmost civility and graciousness. At a neighbour's ball, I believe I danced every dance but one, and I sat down then only because I begged to rest for a moment."

A discontented look caused her nostrils to flare as she pinched her lips together in a tight, false smile. "And shall you join Mr. Darcy at Rosings for Easter?"

"I…have not made plans that far in advance."

"Really? My social calendar already overflows. However, I have made time to answer Lady Catherine's invitation to spend the Easter season with her. Louisa and I furthered our acquaintance with the dear lady the last time she stayed in Town. We dined with her on more than one occasion, and I took every opportunity to please her, for I think her the most elegant, proper lady. And, naturally, my intimate friendship with Mr. Darcy and his sister only endeared me to her ever so much. I do hope dear Georgiana will accompany her brother to Kent, for I long to spend a fortnight with her."

"No doubt she will," I said. "Jane, shall we take a turn about the room. I fear I am in need of activity after that delicious dinner you served."

Jane joined me, and we walked to the farthest corner.

"Lizzy, why not travel to London with Charles and me?" Jane asked.

"I would not wish to intrude upon your first Season as a married woman."

"You could never intrude. In truth, I would feel much more confident with you by my side."

"Jane, you do not need me. You will have your husband's support. He will make all the introductions, and I agree with Mamá that you will be a great success."

"Charles is the dearest and best husband, but I would so enjoy your company. Shall you not consider it?"

"I will think about it."

"Well, do not take too long to make up your mind. We depart at the end of the month."

I assured her I would give the thought my highest consideration. I had little desire to go to Town, but at least it would prove diverting, and I would enjoy seeing Mr. and Mrs. Gardiner. Even though they lived in a less fashionable part of Town than Mr. Bingley, I knew Jane would welcome them in her home. The only drawback to visiting London remained the possibility that I might meet with Mr. Darcy.

I led my sister back around the room where we sat down across from Caroline and Mrs. Hurst.

"Miss Bingley, is Miss Darcy going to London before she travels to Kent for Easter?" I asked.

"Mr. Darcy usually brings his sister to Town when he comes for the Season."

"You cannot depend upon Darcy even to come for the Season," Mr. Bingley said from the card table. "You certainly cannot expect him to be present at all the events on your calendar, Caroline. He dislikes the social scene and sometimes attends only enough to maintain his standing. I am not certain we will see either Darcy or Georgiana in Town at all."

"I would think, Miss Bennet, that you were privy to their plans more than we are," Mrs. Hurst added.

"They did not mention the subject while I was at Pemberley."

"Surely, you have heard from Georgiana since then, have you not?" Caroline asked.

"She has," my mother said unexpectedly. "Lizzy, you know a letter came for you from Pemberley in today's post."

"You did not tell me, Mamá."

"Did I not? Well, we were all in uproar preparing for this evening's outing. It must have slipped my mind."

I DELAYED READING GEORGIANA'S LETTER until morning. We returned from Netherfield quite late, and by the time I had dressed for bed and brushed out my hair, I felt somewhat weary. Although it pained me to admit it, Caroline Bingley's careless remarks had caused more strain than I realized. Both my head and neck ached. I felt as though all my muscles were tied up in knots.

After bathing my face with water, I carried the damp cloth to the open window in my bedchamber, continuing to rub its coolness across the back of my neck. The letter lay silently on the settee upon which I sank down. I picked it up and turned it over, observing Pemberley's seal.

That will never be my seal, I mused.

I closed my eyes at the thought and willed it from my mind. I might as well accept what could not be changed. I could never make public the fact that I was George Darcy's daughter. I would remain Miss Bennet until I agreed to exchange my name for that of the man I would marry.

The thought of Georgiana's reproaches within the unopened letter filled me with dread. What would I reply? What reason could I offer for my sudden flight from Pemberley? I certainly could not tell the truth. I could hardly admit it to myself. I wondered what Mr. Darcy had told his young sister. For that matter, what had he told Colonel Fitzwilliam? He, too, could not reveal the real reason for my unexpected departure.

I thought back to the last time I had seen Mr. Darcy. I saw his hair dripping with water from the rainstorm; I felt the tenderness of his touch, and my heart ached at the haunted sadness in his eyes. Not once had he asked me why I left Pemberley with such haste. Not even once. Why should he when we both knew the answer?

THE NEXT DAY, I SENT a note to Jane accepting her invitation to travel to London. Georgiana's letter made my decision. She and Mr. Darcy planned to spend Easter at Kent without stopping in Town. From Rosings, they intended to travel to Bath and avoid the city entirely. I would be safe at Mr. Bingley's house in Grosvenor Square—safe to start a new life under my new brother's protection. With any luck, I might attract the attentions of a good and honourable man who would help me bury the past for all time.

Mamá did not protest my leave-taking in the least. Indeed, she grew excited at the thought I might meet her future son-in-law in Town.

"Now, Lizzy, be agreeable when you meet eligible young gentlemen. Smile more. You have always smiled easily and often, but lately, your countenance has taken on an ill-favoured expression. You are growing more and more like an embittered spinster, and that is no way to catch a husband. Mark my words."

I sighed and shook my head. What could I answer? She would have me carry on like Lydia if the truth be known. But had I acquired a bitter spirit? I hardly knew.

"Do not mind your mother, Lizzy," Papá said. "You know her thoughts travel in one direction. But do not stay away too long, for you will be sorely missed, my dear."

I did not reply. Even when he kissed my hair, I did not respond in kind. Resentment toward him had taken hold in my heart, and I could not relinquish it. If only he had told me from the beginning that I was fostered, that I was not truly his daughter, then perchance my heart would not ache as it did today. Perhaps I would not possess this empty hole within me that I knew could never be filled.

Chapter Eight

The social whirl of London, with its assemblies, concerts, and balls, was in full swing by the time we arrived. Jane and I barely had time to order new gowns before attending the first affairs. Jane made a lovely debut, and her natural charm and grace caused even the harshest of society ladies to soften in her company. Mr. Bingley beamed with pride at her accomplishments and seemed to grow in stature when standing by her side.

As her *sister*, I was included in the invitations. With dismay, however, I soon learned that most of London knew of my connection with the Darcy family. Evidently, someone had spread the news that I was a poor relation of the Darcys who had been taken in by Mr. Bennet as an infant. I doubted that Miss Bingley would promote the story, seeing that she already regretted her brother's new connections and would not wish to call attention to them, so perhaps she was not the source. In a society that thrives on gossip, it takes but a word to spread a tale hither and yon. Colonel Fitzwilliam's parents may have shared their knowledge, or it may even have come from the mouth of Sir William Lucas during one of his frequent visits to Town.

And so, although I did not own the honour of bearing the name Bingley or Darcy, I enjoyed the affiliation with both families, thus creating measured acceptance mixed with disdain. Without a fortune, however, I was a poor match. As in Hertfordshire, my situation remained somewhat murky. I often wondered who I was and where I belonged.

I soon tired of the insincerity prevalent among the majority of London society that I met. I also grew weary of the disappointed expression gentlemen exhibited once they learned that my relationship to the Darcys had not afforded me pecuniary benefits. After Easter, I began refusing to accompany my sister and her husband to most invitations of the *ton*. I preferred spending time on the other side of Town with Mr. and Mrs. Gardiner, where things were somewhat duller but much more pleasant.

I had spent a fortnight with my aunt and uncle when their servant announced one morning that I had a gentleman caller. None of Mr. Bingley's friends knew the Gardiners, so I wondered who my visitor might be. After a questioning glance in my direction, my aunt instructed the servant to show him into the parlour.

"Miss Bennet," the man said in greeting, as he bowed.

"Mr. Denison!" I was overcome with surprise and hastened to introduce my former dancing partner from Derbyshire to Mrs. Gardiner, whereupon she bade him be seated. He carried a large, wrapped parcel in his hand and gingerly propped it against the side of the chair before he sat down.

"You are not easy to find," he said. "If I had not met Mrs. Bingley last night and overheard her tell someone that her maiden name was Bennet, I fear I never would have discovered your whereabouts."

"I had no idea you were in search of me, sir."

"You must admit that you departed Derbyshire somewhat abruptly, and no amount of inquiries would extract your destination from Mr. Darcy. He absolutely refused to share with me where you had gone. I confess the gentleman's conduct appeared strange to say the least."

"Strange?"

"Each time I broached the subject with him, his manner proved so fierce that I confess I sometimes wondered whether some dire misfortune had befallen you."

I laughed lightly in an attempt to put his mind at ease. "Oh, Mr. Darcy's manners can be infuriating at times, but I suppose we must allow that in a man of his standing."

My aunt took that moment to offer tea, an interruption for which I was grateful. She went on to engage Mr. Denison in the usual social chatter, asking how long he had been in Town, how he liked the warm weather, and so on. After a sufficient length of time had passed for which a proper social call should last, she rose, expressing how much we had enjoyed his visit.

He, of course, stood also, but looking somewhat distressed, he picked up the package beside his chair. "Miss Bennet, before I leave, I must ask whether you recall that I told you of a discovery I had made while clearing out the attics at Bridesgate Manor?"

"Why, yes, I do."

"I have brought the treasure today, and with your leave, Mrs. Gardiner, I should like to show it to Miss Bennet."

My aunt and I sat down and waited while he removed the string and paper from the large square shape.

"Now pray examine this painting, and tell me, do you detect the same remarkable distinction that I do?"

He placed the portrait before me, and I heard my aunt's quick intake of breath. "Why, Lizzy, she looks like you!"

A girl, who appeared a few years younger than I, sat beneath a huge, spreading chestnut tree. She wore a white gown with a yellow ribbon around her waist and a pale yellow rose tucked in her dark, flowing hair. Her bare toes peeked out from below her skirt, and her lips turned up in an arch smile, much like one I had oft times seen in the mirror.

"She has your hair, your nose, the turn of your countenance," Mrs. Gardiner declared. "Only her eyes are different. Otherwise, she could be your twin."

"That was exactly my impression the first time I saw you," Mr. Denison said. "When I met you at the ball, I knew I must show you the painting."

I was so overcome by the likeness that I remained silent, knowing not how to answer.

"The moment you walked into the Whitbys' ballroom, I assumed there must be some connection. You can imagine my disappointment when I arrived at Pemberley the following day and found you gone."

"Who...who is the woman?" I asked, my voice trembling.

"I do not know. I would guess that she is either a member of the Willoughby family or a friend. I thought you might tell me."

I shook my head, unable to take my eyes from the girl in the portrait.

"Last month," Mr. Denison said, "we expected Sir Linton Willoughby to travel to Bridesgate Manor to collect the items from the attic that my father deemed valuable to the family. Instead, he sent his steward along with a servant and cart. Therefore, I could not question the gentleman about the portrait. Rather than part with it to his servants, I confess I hid it under my bed."

"Hid it?" Mrs. Gardiner exclaimed. "But why?"

"I wished to share it with Miss Bennet. That is why I pressed Mr. Darcy as to her situation until he lost all patience with me. At last, I was forced to travel to London with my family, and giving up on my quest, I resolved to return the painting to Sir Linton. We arrived a fortnight before Easter, and I consider it my good fortune to have met Mrs. Bingley last night and ascertained where you were staying. Otherwise, I might never have been able to show you my discovery. Have you any idea what your relation to the woman in the portrait might be?"

"No, sir, I do not," I murmured. "Tell me, did you show the painting to Mr. Darcy?"

"I did."

"And what was his reaction?"

"He wanted to purchase it. When I told him it was not mine to sell and refused to give in, we exchanged strong words. We were at loggerheads. I would not part with the painting, and he would not reveal where you lived. Was I wrong to have persisted?"

I picked up the portrait and carried it to the window's light. "It is of no consequence, but I thank you for bringing it to me before taking it to the Willoughby house."

"I suppose you must return it," Mrs. Gardiner said. "Do you not agree, Lizzy?"

"What? Oh yes, I suppose you must."

Mr. Denison crossed the room and stood beside me. "Is Mr. Gardiner in London? If so, would you and he care to accompany me when I call on Sir Linton?"

"Accompany you?" I could not comprehend his meaning.

"Are you not curious as to the girl's identity and her close resemblance to you? Perhaps she is in residence at the Willoughbys' house."

My aunt answered for me, indicating that there could be any manner of explanation. "I have heard it said that everyone has a double somewhere in the world. You may have stumbled upon our Lizzy's, Mr. Denison."

"I see. So you are not interested in going with me?"

"I have never been introduced to Sir Linton Willoughby," I said. "I would feel out of place calling upon him."

"I have a letter of introduction from my father. He was angry when I told him I had held back the painting, and he insists that I face Sir Linton and return it myself. I shall be glad to introduce you."

I glanced at my aunt and shrugged. Truly, my shock at the likeness of the girl to myself was such that I knew not what I should do.

"Mr. Denison," my aunt began, "would you consider leaving the portrait with us tonight so that we might show it to Mr. Gardiner and seek his counsel? If he feels it is appropriate for Lizzy to go with you, I am certain he will lend his presence."

Andrew Denison agreed to the suggestion, and we made plans to meet the next afternoon.

As I HAVE COME TO expect, my plans for the next day went astray.

Mr. Gardiner awaited Mr. Denison's arrival in the parlour while I completed my toilette above stairs. Mrs. Gardiner said I looked lovely and squeezed my hand before I walked out the door of my bedchamber.

"I like Mr. Denison, Lizzy," she said. "And I think he may care for you."

I raised my eyebrows in question. "Aunt, this is a call of necessity. He must return the painting to its owner, and I am simply curious as to the model. I have not seen any undue interest upon the part of the gentleman toward me."

"All the same, smile often, dear, when in his company. It is one of your best features."

I sighed and took my cape and bonnet from the maid on the way to the stairwell. Must my every acquaintance with a gentleman warrant speculations of marriage? I heard the deep rumble of masculine voices from below and hoped I had not kept my uncle and Mr. Denison waiting long. Midway down the stairs, I stopped short. I saw my uncle standing at the foot of the staircase, but Mr. Denison did not stand beside him. I caught my breath at the sight of Mr. Darcy watching my descent.

After greetings were exchanged, my uncle explained that Mr. Darcy would go with us to Sir Linton Willoughby's house in place of Mr. Denison.

"I do not understand," I said, my voice somewhat uneasy. "I thought you were in Kent, sir, for Easter."

"I was, but now that Easter is past, I am here." His dark eyes searched mine as though he questioned his welcome.

"Mr. Darcy called on Admiral Denison this morning," Mr. Gardiner said. "And learning that you held the painting belonging to the Willoughbys, he requested and was granted leave to replace young Mr. Denison in this morning's call."

"Why would you do that, sir?"

"I am slightly acquainted with Sir Linton, and both the admiral and I thought it would be simpler than Andrew Denison having to obtain an audience with the man through a letter of introduction."

Mr. Darcy went on to explain that he had met up with the Denisons in Town through a mutual acquaintance at a party the night before. Jane and Mr. Bingley attended the same occasion, and she had told Mr. Darcy that I was in London staying with the Gardiners.

My, Jane has been busy, I thought. *First, she tells Mr. Andrew Denison where I am staying and then proceeds to inform Mr. Darcy.*

"I do not see that you need to concern yourself in this matter," I said. "After all, Mr. Denison is the one who kept back the piece of art, and as his father said, is it not his place to return it?"

"Perhaps, but the admiral was only too pleased to have me intervene. Sir Linton is...not an easy man with whom to deal."

"Of what deal do we speak? I thought we were simply returning the property to its owner."

"If so, Miss Bennet, then why must you attend?" Mr. Darcy raised one eyebrow and pressed his lips together.

"Because of the subject of the painting, naturally. One would have to be blind not to see the resemblance."

"Indeed, quite blind. I find the work fascinating and hope to make Sir Linton an offer for its purchase. That is my purpose for travel to Town. Once I heard in Kent from Miss Bingley that the Denisons were in residence here, I hoped to discover what they had done with the painting so that I might further my quest to own the work."

"I did not know that Caroline Bingley was acquainted with Mr. Denison."

"Before Easter, they met through mutual acquaintances here in Town."

"Lizzy," my uncle added, drawing near so that our words would not be heard by the servants. "I have informed Mr. Darcy that your aunt and I know the truth about your relationship with each other. I think it perfectly natural and fitting that he accompanies us to Sir Linton's residence."

The carriage stood waiting at the front door, and my uncle indicated that we should leave. I did not find the ride comfortable, for while I sat beside Mr. Gardiner, Mr. Darcy sat directly across from me, and I felt the burden of his constant gaze. As we drew near the house, he warned us not to expect accommodations customary to those of a baronet.

"The Willoughby fortune is greatly diminished, and they have been forced to retrench several times over," my uncle added. I was surprised that he knew of their circumstances until he explained that he had transacted business with their steward through the years. "Sir Linton has sold off more than just his family's land. I have come across their paintings, china, silver, and even draperies often enough. From my limited viewpoint, I would say the gentleman manages his family's assets poorly."

"To say the least," Mr. Darcy added.

I soon discovered the truth of those statements when we entered the house. Although a large, spacious, old townhouse, obviously beautiful at one time, it now reeked of disrepair and neglect. From the shabby livery worn by the servant to the lack of lighting in the hall, the dark, gloomy place possessed an abandoned air. We were shown into a drawing room bereft of furniture save for an old settee, a small table, and two worn and faded chairs. Mr. Gardiner indicated that I should be seated, but I preferred to stand beside him. Mr. Darcy walked to the window and stared at the overgrown garden without.

Some half hour later, our host finally appeared. He was tall and gaunt, both his silver hair and beard in need of a trim. He wore a faded suit of clothing bearing food stains spilled down the front of his waistcoat. A strong smell of spirits announced his coming.

"Gardiner," he said, "what brings you here?"

My uncle acknowledged him and turned to indicate Mr. Darcy at the window. Sir Linton knit his brows together, squinting at the light streaming in from outside.

"Darcy? What business do you have with me?"

Mr. Darcy advanced toward the man and bowed slightly. "May I introduce Miss Elizabeth Bennet?"

For the first time, his eyes fell upon me, and he blinked, seeming almost dazed. "Miss who?" he demanded.

"Miss Bennet," Mr. Gardiner said. "She is my niece."

I curtseyed, never taking my eyes from the man. It was obvious he did not like what he saw. He neither bowed nor greeted me in any manner.

"State your business," he said.

"Admiral Denison asked me to return a painting discovered in the attics of Bridesgate Manor," Mr. Darcy said.

"Another painting. Of what use are they? Is this one worth anything, Gardiner?"

"See for yourself," my uncle replied, as he handed him the wrapped parcel.

Sir Linton grumbled as he clumsily tore off the paper and threw it on the floor. "Do not see why it took all three of you to return my property."

"Perhaps you will when you examine it," Mr. Darcy said quietly.

The baronet held it up, blinked his eyes as though he could not focus them, and uttered an oath. "Cannot see what it is in this dim room. Why is no candle lit?"

"There is sufficient light by the window," Mr. Darcy said, leading him across the length of the room. "Now, sir, do you not find it of interest?"

Sir Linton stretched out his arms full length and held the painting aloft. Consternation crept across his face, and he uttered another oath. "I do not want this rubbish. You have come on a fool's errand to bring this to me. I will not have it in the house!"

He threw it on the floor and staggered backward. Mr. Darcy immediately retrieved the painting and held it up before him once more.

"Take another look, sir. Does not this painting bear a striking resemblance to one in this room?"

Sir Linton wiped his hand across his mouth in disgust, but recognition dawned in his expression as he eyed the painting and then turned his gaze upon me.

I walked toward him so that he might see my face more clearly. "May I ask, sir, who posed for the work?"

Again, he stared back and forth between the portrait and myself. "I shall tell you who she is. I shall tell you, all right. One who is dead to me and to this family!"

"She may be deceased, but Miss Bennet and I have a great interest in knowing her identity," Mr. Darcy said.

"You do not need to know, Darcy, and neither does she."

Sir Linton walked away from the window and slumped down in one of the chairs, but Mr. Darcy followed close behind him.

"I think we do, sir. I will make it worth your while to give us the information."

His eyes opened wide at the suggestion, and he sat up straighter. "What do you mean?"

"You know perfectly well what I mean. Not only will I pay to know the identity of the girl, but I should like to buy the painting."

He clambered to his feet. "How much?"

"More than sufficient, I assure you. First, tell us who she is."

Sir Linton swore once again, walked to the cold fireplace, and leaned his forehead against the mantel. "The girl was my sister—Elizabeth Willoughby. She is dead. Lost to my family and lost to this world."

My heart jumped into my throat, and I began to tremble. "How...how did she die, Sir Linton?"

He turned a withering eye upon me, and I trembled even more at the hatred I saw therein. "In childbirth."

"If you have lost your sister, do you not want her likeness?" Mr. Gardiner asked. "I would think you would treasure it for its memories."

"I want no memories of her!" Sir Linton began to pace back and forth. "She is dead to me, I tell you. She betrayed her family, and I will not have her image in my house."

"Pray, sir, will you tell me when she died?" I asked, my voice shaking.

He stopped and turned his fierce glare upon me. "Most likely, you know the date well—the sixth of December 1791. From the looks of you, you could pass for her brat."

I reached out for my uncle's arm, and he immediately led me to the settee. Mr. Darcy crossed the room to my side. "Are you ill, Elizabeth?"

I shook my head slightly, but my heart had jumped into my throat, and I felt my head begin to throb. Mr. Gardiner exchanged looks with Mr. Darcy and then returned his attention to Sir Linton.

"The date of your sister's death is the birth date of my niece. She was born in Derbyshire to a woman named Elizabeth and then taken to a distant county—Hertfordshire—whereupon my brother and sister took her in and raised her as their own. Could that make her your niece as well, sir?"

Sir Linton rose and swore again. "I am not saying it could, and nothing you say will force me to do so. I am saying I want nothing to do with Miss Bennet." He turned his eyes upon me. "If you think you come here to claim kinship with a noble family, think again. I shall never name you as a Willoughby, and there is no inheritance to share. So forget any thoughts of getting rich off me, girl!"

"Sir!" Mr. Darcy drew himself up and roared with such anger that he may as well have struck the man. "I will not tolerate any further offensive behaviour toward Miss Bennet."

The baronet seemed taken aback and actually sank back onto his chair.

"Miss Bennet came here seeking knowledge of the girl in the painting. She makes no claims upon your name or your fortune."

Sir Linton muttered something under his breath and wiped his mouth with the back of his hand once again. Suddenly, he yelled out a man's name, and when the servant who had admitted us appeared, he barked orders for a bottle of whiskey. Almost immediately, the servant returned with a tarnished brass tray containing a bottle and glass. Before the man could pour the drink, Sir Linton grabbed the glass and bottle from him and ordered the servant from the room. He then filled his glass and downed the contents with no attempt to offer refreshment to his guests.

"I have nothing more to say about Elizabeth Willoughby. She is dead and buried, along with the past. Let it remain that way."

"But, sir," I said softly, "will you not tell me something about her? I would be grateful for any information you might share."

He poured another glass and drained it before raising his eyes toward me. "I have nothing good to say about her. So what would you have me tell you?"

"What was her age when she died?"

"Age? Huh…could not have been more than seventeen. Just a slip of a girl…but wild at heart, always wild."

"What do you mean, 'wild'?" I stood and took a step closer so that I might hear him more clearly.

"Always running about the countryside, climbing trees, wading in the streams after she was long past the age for such things. She never cared for parlours or sitting rooms. If she could be out in the glens and dales or even on the moors, she was content. My mother despaired of settling her down —said she was like something untamed. My father did not care and said let her be. He spoilt her—him and my grandmother. You can blame them for petting her and allowing her to come to ruin."

"Were you there…the night I was born?"

"No! Not any of us were in Derbyshire when it happened. I had moved my mother and two sisters to London before we learned of Elizabeth's condition. When my father died the year before, I had become head of the family. My grandmother was a stubborn old woman. She refused to leave the county and insisted on remaining behind. Three months later, when my mother discovered that my sister was with child, the plan was to send her to a house in Dorsett so we could avoid questions and gossip, but my grandmother would not have it. She refused to let us hide Elizabeth with strangers and insisted that the girl stay with her. I returned my sister to Bridesgate Manor, and neither my mother, nor my youngest sister, nor I ever saw her again."

He stared into the bottom of his glass as though he could see the event taking place all over again. When he spoke at last, his voice had lowered to such a degree that I strained to hear him. "My grandmother wrote us about Elizabeth's death. Not long after that, she died herself."

Tears welled up in my eyes. Not only was I rejected, but my mother was as well. She had been abandoned with naught but a grandmother to love her.

Suddenly, Sir Linton rose from his chair and thrust his face close to mine. "If you are her child, your birth cursed us! From that day on, our fortunes reversed. I was forced to sell off my land, my holdings, and my belongings because of you! My other sister could not make a suitable match with such a pitiable dowry. My wife left me childless. My mother died a bitter old woman. It is all because of you—you, the secret that brought ruin on our entire house!"

Mr. Darcy stepped between Sir Linton and me. "Mr. Gardiner, please take Elizabeth to the carriage."

Tears streamed down my cheeks, and it is with difficulty to this day that I even recall my uncle leading me from that terrible house. We waited in the carriage for some time before Mr. Darcy proceeded from the baronet's house, carrying the portrait.

Immediately upon boarding the carriage, he sat down and leaned forward, taking my hand in his. "Elizabeth, are you well?"

I nodded. Misery possessed me to such a measure that I was unable to speak.

"I can see you are not."

He stepped outside the coach and directed the driver to hasten back to Mr. Gardiner's house immediately. After he returned to his seat, my uncle asked him whether Sir Linton had given him any further information. He sighed and looked out the window before answering but one word.

"Yes."

Chapter Nine

Mr. Darcy did not speak again during the return carriage ride to Gracechurch Street. His silence reigned with such authority that neither my uncle nor I dared question it. My spirits had fallen so low that I no longer had the energy to pose a question. That is not to say my mind was at rest, for it was beset not only with numerous queries but with the pain of humiliation as well.

Why had Sir Linton treated me with such cruelty? And if my birth was hidden, why should the event have caused his family's fortunes to fail? I could not understand the connection, and yet, he cast the fault and subsequent shame for a noble family's downfall upon my shoulders. How could that be?

By the time Mr. Darcy's carriage pulled up in front of Mr. Gardiner's house, I felt as though I could no longer breathe. I longed to run far from London, out into the countryside, away from houses or people, so that I might fill my lungs with air and conquer the suffocation that threatened me.

As my uncle assisted me down from the conveyance, I caught sight of the park across the street. With only a brief word, I stepped from the walk and darted through the passing carriages. Once safely on the other side, I hurried into the leafy arbour without a backward glance. I cared not whether I behaved unseemly; I could no longer bear the company of others. I needed to walk alone and silence the noises swirling about in my head.

I had rounded the first bend in the path that shielded me from view of the street when I heard rapid footsteps overtaking me. A scant glance over my shoulder revealed Mr. Darcy's long legs covering the distance in half the time it had taken me. I began to run. Thankfully, the park was deserted and I did not make a spectacle of myself before others, for I ran even faster when I heard him cry out my name. I felt my bonnet loosen and fall to the ground, but I paid it little notice. Erelong, however, I felt his hand catch mine, and even though I struggled, he would not release it.

"Elizabeth!" He pulled me into his embrace and sheltered my head against his warm, heaving chest. I could hear his heart beating wildly in my ear, and we both gasped to catch our breath. "Hush now; be still," he murmured, stroking my hair.

At the tenderness in his voice, my heart melted, and tears flowed down my cheeks unchecked. I allowed him to hold me thus for some moments.

If only I could stay here the rest of my life, I thought, *safe and protected within his arms.*

Perhaps I could. Had I not seen him hold Georgiana in a similar manner? Perhaps I protested his brotherly love in vain. Perhaps this was how a brother comforted a sister. Perhaps...

And then, he stepped back, and with one hand, lifted my face to meet his. As I raised my eyes, I felt naked, my need for him laid bare. His eyes searched mine, and the line between his brows increased in an expression of deep concern. I turned my face away, knowing I must conceal my feelings. I could not reveal the love I felt for him. I must not let him know how desperately I needed him.

He led me toward a stone bench a few feet away. There, he gently eased me down and sat close beside me, never letting go of my hand.

"You have wept enough; now speak to me."

"I feel such shame."

"Never! You have done nothing of which to be ashamed."

"My birth caused the ruin of the Willoughby family."

"Insupportable nonsense! Sir Linton's excessive consumption of spirits and dissipated lifestyle ruined his family's fortunes. It had nothing to do with you."

"But he said—"

"He did not speak the truth. The man is a profligate libertine and has been all his life. He blames others for his own trespasses, and he heaps most of his abuse on those he believes unable to defend themselves. Elizabeth, you have not brought shame on anyone." His voice softened. "It is not in your nature."

"But the circumstances of my birth—are they not cause for disgrace?"

"And I suppose you selected those circumstances? Out of the entire world, you chose to be the offspring of an unmarried girl and a reckless gentleman? Come now, I know you better than that. Your judgment is much more prudent than to make a choice so unseemly."

I looked up at his mocking tone and could not help but smile slightly at his raised eyebrows. "No, I should have chosen a wise, caring set of parents who provided well for their children. And while I am handpicking my family, I might as well have made them wealthy."

He shrugged. "Might as well. Why not select the best?"

"If only—"

"Yes, if only." He rose and walked back and forth several times, and then stopping abruptly, he turned and faced me. "Elizabeth, it seems we have solved part of the mystery of your birth."

"Part of the mystery?"

"We have found your mother."

"And we know my father. What more is there to solve?"

He sat down beside me. "I want to know why. Why would my father indulge in an act fraught with danger and dishonour and with a mere girl? I have made some calculations since learning Elizabeth Willoughby's age when she died. My father must have been more than ten years her senior."

"Evidently, age did not bring wisdom."

"But from all other accounts, it did. And from what I remember, my father was the most excellent of men—prudent, discerning, cautious, and moral. I cannot grasp why he would take such a chance."

"I would hope because he loved Elizabeth Willoughby. Today has proved a bitter, personal disappointment. Leave me with some semblance of faith that I was conceived in love."

"If I do, that destroys my belief in his devotion to my mother."

We both looked away at that moment. I closed my eyes, saddened that my only consolation brought grief to Mr. Darcy. Oh, why had my parents not considered the possible consequences when they engaged in such unacceptable behaviour?

I turned back to face him. "I must ask you: did Sir Linton enlighten you any further about my mother and father's relationship?"

Mr. Darcy sighed. "He professed to know little about it. Said by the time he learned of the connection, the deed was done. He blustered about, declaring he did everything in his power to protect his sister, even so far as locking her in her room." He shook his head, uttering a brief, disgusted sigh. "I have no idea why I did this, but I asked Sir Linton whether he knew the name of your natural father."

I held my breath. *Why would he ask that question? Do we not know?* "What …what did he say?"

"Something like, 'You know the answer to that, Darcy, as well as I do! If I were younger and in better health, I would tell you exactly what I think of him, but you are the hot-blooded type who would call me out, and I am no longer fit to fight a duel.' Then, he changed the subject and once again asked whether you were a fortune hunter preying upon my family. Do not be alarmed, for I was quick to rid him of that impression."

"Did you tell him you remembered a break between the Willoughbys and your family when you were a child and that your father instructed you to stay away from Bridesgate Manor?"

"I did. Sir Linton is a wretched scoundrel! He spoke ill of his own grand-mother—your great-grandmother. When he could not persuade her to move to Town and agree to send your mother away, he left them little on which to live. From then on, Lady Margaret lived a solitary life. She must have cut off all communication with surrounding society, or at least I assume she did. As I told you, sometime during my childhood my parents no longer called upon her, and Lady Margaret ceased attending either church on Sundays or any social gathering."

"Do you believe my birth caused her to become a recluse?"

He turned his eyes to meet mine. "Whether it did or not, the breach between my parents and Bridesgate must have happened once Lady Margaret learned of my father's part in her granddaughter's predicament. Elizabeth, there are so many unanswered questions. I long to know what truly happened!"

"I believe we know what happened, sir. What more is there to discover?"

"I cannot rid myself of this desire to know more. Why would my father do this? What would make him forsake my mother and enter an affair fraught with peril?" He rose and slapped his hat against the shrubs of holly lining the path. "I must speak with someone in my father's family. I know that somehow I can find the answers."

"But who? Is not your uncle deceased?"

"Uncle Henry is, but his widow lives."

"In Bath?"

He nodded. "She might have knowledge of the incident. My uncle may have told her of it."

"And your other uncle…Peter, is it?"

Mr. Darcy stared into the distance before answering. "He would be harder to find, but it is possible. Anything is possible if one searches long enough."

"You said you would tell me about him, but—"

He lowered his eyes to the ground. "It is not something of which our family speaks."

I rose, and we began to walk down the path side by side. We happened upon my discarded bonnet, and after Mr. Darcy retrieved it, he handed it to me. Even today, I recall that the scent of jasmine lay heavy in the air. Numerous vines wove their way through the shrubs, lighting the greenery with their delicate, yellow blossoms.

"Shall you tell me now? After all, Peter Darcy is my uncle as well."

He smiled slightly. "True. I do not know why I had not considered that. I shall tell you, but it is not something the family wants commonly known."

In the space of a half hour, Mr. Darcy laid forth the story that corresponded with the account Mrs. Reynolds had given me. Peter, the quietest of my grandparents' three sons, had always been his mother's favourite. I could imagine Siobhan Darcy's indulgent coddling of her little boy. Even when grown, he remained close to his mother, so close that he accompanied her to her clandestine worship services at the Papist church hidden in Pemberley's wood. Unknown to his father, young Peter's faith in the Catholic religion grew until he wished to join the church. His desires remained a secret between his mother and him until after her husband's death.

A few years thereafter, by the time he was at Cambridge, Siobhan had evidently laid aside funds in the event Peter wished to depart England and sail for Ireland without his older brother's knowledge. There, he could practice his faith without causing his family to suffer. Once he made his choice, all connection with his family at Pemberley was severed. Eventually, however, George Darcy and, subsequently, Mr. Darcy himself kept apprised of his general location through the priest at the church in the wood.

"Is that why you spoke privately with the priest on the day you took Georgiana and me to the chapel?"

"It is. He receives letters from another priest who lives near the Irish village where Peter Darcy resides. He told me my uncle is in poor health and may not live to see another spring."

"Do you think he knows of the events surrounding my birth? Did he leave for Ireland before it happened, or was he still in residence at Pemberley?"

"I do not know. As a child, I recall my father's anger when he learned Peter had gone away without a word to any of us, but I am unaware of the order of events. It was a period of tumult in our house, for Henry was frequently found in some disgraceful scrape or other misbehaviour. I think he joined the Navy that same year. I do remember how I missed both of my uncles and how much quieter and lonelier the house grew when they left, but as to when it happened, I cannot say. It all runs together in memories of my childhood."

We walked in silence for some time, and I was much engaged in reflecting over all that Mr. Darcy had told me when he spoke again.

"Elizabeth, I would caution you once more not to tell anyone of Peter Darcy other than your uncle and aunt."

"You do not need to remind me, sir. I would not reveal your family's secrets to anyone. If you prefer, I need not mention it to my aunt and uncle."

"I trust Mr. Gardiner. He has proven himself a man of discretion, and I have no quarrel with his knowing the truth. As you said earlier, Peter Darcy is your uncle as well as mine, and if you care to confide in Mr. and Mrs. Gardiner, you have my permission."

I smiled at him. How lovely that he shared my good opinion of my favourite relations. "Since you still have questions, might you write to your uncle in Ireland and make inquiries? Perchance he could provide the answers."

Mr. Darcy shook his head. We had returned to Gracechurch Street by that time, and we halted to allow the carriages to pass. "I cannot ask a man I have not seen since I was a boy to discuss such serious matters in a letter."

He took my arm and guided me across the street to the steps of the house. There, he stopped and turned to face me. "I have made plans to visit Henry Darcy's widow."

"Indeed? When might you go?"

"As soon as I can travel to Kent and fetch Georgiana. I cannot leave her under Lady Catherine's oppression any longer. Elizabeth, will you go with me to Bath?"

My eyes widened at the thought, and I felt my pulse begin to quicken. "I…I do not think that a good idea, sir."

I turned away and hurried up the steps. He followed close behind and opened the door for me. We stepped into the vestibule, and Mr. Darcy handed his hat to the waiting servant. He informed us that Mr. Gardiner had gone above stairs to greet his wife but would be down shortly. I walked toward the parlour and asked the servant to bring tea for Mr. Darcy and myself.

I settled myself upon the sofa and straightened my skirt, all the while averting my face. Oh, how I wished my aunt or uncle would soon join us or at least that the gentleman would refrain from any more discussion of his trip to Bath. Instead, he seated himself in the chair nearest me and leaned forward, forcing me to look directly at him.

"Why not, Elizabeth? I shall take Mrs. Annesley with my sister. Why should you not accompany us?"

"I do not see the need, sir. You are well acquainted with your aunt. I would find myself ill at ease meeting yet another relation with whom I must explain my birth. Besides, you are the one with questions...not me."

"I do not believe you."

"Sir?"

"You cannot be satisfied with today's resolution. Surely, you want to know why your mother and my father ever—" He broke off and placed his hand to his mouth in a movement I had witnessed oft times when Mr. Darcy was troubled. "Their involvement is simply insupportable! There must be more to the story, and I cannot believe you are not as curious as I."

"Believe it! I want no more details of this unfortunate affair. I have no desire to claim either the name Willoughby or Darcy."

"You are content to remain a Bennet?"

"I am not a Bennet, am I? That is the truth. I am...no one. I am just Elizabeth, and I do not know where I belong or to whom." I fought the bleakness welling up within me, but I could not hide my sorrow from him.

Mr. Darcy rose to sit beside me, taking both my hands in his. I turned my face away, but he commanded me to look at him. "You belong to me, Elizabeth"—my heart turned over—"and to Georgiana. We are your family. Why must you continue to fight it? We want you near us. You will always be welcome at Pemberley. You may come for long visits whenever my sister is home, and wherever you choose to live, I will protect you, provide for you. I will care for you."

I finally turned and met his eyes. "The way you did at the Whitbys' ball?"

He stiffened and released my hands. Rising, he took a step toward the window and then turned back. "Elizabeth, that will never happen again. I promise you."

"I believe you made a similar promise in the church at Longbourn, sir. I believed you then, but you did not keep your word."

"I behaved badly, I know. It was the brandy."

"And what will keep you from returning to the comfort of drink?"

Just then, Mr. and Mrs. Gardiner entered the room, and our private conversation ended. Mr. Darcy remained but a short while and soon made his departure. Later, my aunt gently questioned me about the day's events. Evidently, Mr. Gardiner had warned her of my fragile emotions, and when I began to hesitate, she tempered her inquiries and encouraged me to retire to my chamber.

Above stairs, I fell upon the soft bed and buried my face in the pillows.

A WEEK LATER, JANE PERSUADED me to return to Mr. Bingley's townhouse in Grosvenor Square. She had visited Gracechurch Street often during my stay with the Gardiners, but I had refrained from calling upon her. Now, she insisted I spend the remainder of my time in Town in her company.

"I shall miss you when you return to Longbourn, Lizzy. You must grant me this request, and if you do, I shall tell you a very great secret." She would not say another word or give me the slightest hint until I agreed to pack my trunk.

Once I had settled into my former chamber and directed the maid as to my belongings, I joined my sister in her favourite sitting room, where she told me she was with child. The news filled me with joy as nothing else had since Mr. Bingley had proposed to Jane. She bloomed with radiant happiness and informed me that Charles was over the moon at the news. Thus far, she had not been plagued with sickness of any kind, and her appetite had soared.

"I shall burst the seams of my gowns if I continue to eat in this manner!" she declared.

We laughed together at the thought, and I assured her she could order as many larger frocks as she desired. It was so good to laugh together, to direct my thoughts toward a thrilling, happy event. We spent no little time planning the nursery, wondering whether it would be a boy or girl, and pondering the choice of names.

"If it is a girl, I hope Charles will allow me to name her Frances Elizabeth after you and Mamá."

"I would imagine Charles will allow you to call her by any name you like, for if it is possible, he appears more besotted with you upon each occasion we meet. Oh, my dearest Jane, your news has made me so happy!"

This relief from my own troubles lasted but a few days, however, for by the end of the week, Jane informed me they were having guests for dinner on Wednesday next: Miss Bingley, who had just returned from Rosings, Mr. and Mrs. Hurst, and Mr. Darcy. I cautioned her not to strain herself, but she assured me she was quite well enough to preside over her table.

The night of the event, I attempted to come down with a headache as best I could, but I unfortunately remained in excellent health. There was nothing for it but to grit my teeth and join my sister's guests. I fussed with my hair and studied my choice of gowns in the wardrobe for some time, but at length, I could no longer find an excuse to remain in my chamber. With great reluctance, I abandoned my sanctuary and made my way to the drawing room.

Mrs. Hurst was the first to greet me with her insincere smile and veiled slights. Miss Bingley, likewise, looked me up and down as though I had walked in from the streets. Mr. Hurst's affair with the bottle had progressed nicely, and he hardly noticed my entrance. Mr. Bingley, however, crossed the room and escorted me to Jane's side. I loved Charles, for he was truly dear. I avoided glancing in Mr. Darcy's direction as long as possible, but, eventually, when Charles included him in the conversation, I was forced to raise my eyes to his and acknowledge his presence.

"Miss Bennet," he said with the briefest of bows. "I trust you are well."

"Perfectly," I said with a sigh, curtsied, and immediately turned away to ask Jane a question about the selection of flowers she had chosen for the table.

The evening progressed in much the same manner throughout dinner. With the absence of the men afterwards, Miss Bingley regaled us with how she had flattered and charmed Lady Catherine during her visit to Rosings. She seemed to take particular pleasure in stressing how she also took great pains to cultivate a friendship with Miss de Bourgh, although she feared that the poor woman would not live a long life because of her ill health.

"I would not be at all surprised if, when she weds, it will be a marriage of short duration, for I doubt—God forbid—that she would survive childbirth."

"Is Miss de Bourgh engaged to be married?" Jane asked.

"Not officially, but Lady Catherine says it will not be long before an announcement shall be made." She fixed a stare in my direction, smugness conspicuous upon her face. "Throughout the Easter holiday, she has worked behind the scenes to secure the alliance. And I have assured Lady Catherine that I have done all in my power to assist her and shall continue my efforts since I am intimately acquainted with the gentleman in question and his family. I promised her that I would keep my eyes and ears open. Thus, I have every hope of becoming as essential to the de Bourgh family as a daughter. I cannot fail to see how advantageous our connection might prove in the future."

I considered Miss Bingley's words decidedly distasteful, and I was relieved when, shortly thereafter, we were reunited with the gentlemen in the music room. Mrs. Hurst entertained us on the pianoforte longer than necessary, and once she rose from the bench, Miss Bingley took her place. She persuaded Mr. Darcy to turn the pages of the music for her and took every opportunity to flatter his command of the art.

For pity's sake, I thought, *any simpleton can turn pages.*

When the Bingley sisters' performance concluded at last, Mr. Hurst insisted they join the whist table. I had picked up my book and tried to lose myself therein when Caroline Bingley announced they simply must hear me sing and play. I protested strongly, but she would not have it. Signalling her sister to join the chorus, they both pushed and prodded until I could do nothing more than rise and walk reluctantly toward the instrument. I knew full well the cause of their persistence. They both possessed superior talent to mine and took great delight in exhibiting my ineptitude, all the while declaring their fervent desire to hear my efforts.

I sighed as I reached the pianoforte and rifled through a stack of music. What could I possibly find to play without making a fool of myself?

"Sing the song you performed the first time you visited Pemberley," Mr. Darcy said in a low voice.

I startled, unaware that he stood close behind me. I had last seen him near the card table and assumed he would join the players.

"I shall never forget the clarity of your soprano. It rivalled any I had ever heard before."

"Surely, you jest, sir."

"I do not. I pray you will sing it again, Elizabeth…for me." He spoke the last words so quietly that I had to strain to hear him.

I looked up to meet his eyes and saw no sign of mockery. He made the request in all earnestness. I fumbled through the music, mumbling that I did not know the song by heart. He took the stack from my hands, pulled out the required piece, and bade me be seated. My hands trembled as I spread open the pages.

"Oh!" Miss Bingley exclaimed. "I have drawn the most impossible hand. Will you not come and advise me, Mr. Darcy?"

He waited a moment or two before answering and then looked up with a serious expression. "Forgive me. I must remain constant at my appointed task. After all, I am the accomplished page turner in the room, am I not?"

I could not hide the smile that lit up my face, especially when I saw an expression of dismay pull Miss Bingley's mouth down at the corners. With sudden confidence, I played the first notes and began to sing. Oh, I misfingered many of the chords, but I sang out with all that was in me, and at the conclusion, I was rewarded with extraordinary applause from at least three people in the room and beaming approval on Mr. Darcy's face.

We took a turn about the room thereafter, and I was grateful that he kept the conversation light and pleasant. Mr. Darcy told me that, instead of returning to Kent to retrieve his sister, he had sent a trusted manservant in his place. His sister had endured Lady Catherine's company longer than necessary. Georgiana and Mrs. Annesley were en route from Kent to the Earl of Matlock's residence on the edge of London, where he planned to join them the following week. He told me of the earl's fondness for his niece and how she would be spoilt from the moment she arrived. We agreed that Georgiana possessed such an agreeable, loving nature that no amount of attention would ever ruin her. Our young sister was one subject on which we remained in perfect agreement.

Later that evening, however, Mr. Darcy took me aside privately once again to attempt to persuade me to accompany Georgiana, her companion, and him to Bath to visit Mr. Henry Darcy's widow. Although he uttered many favourable arguments, I remained implacable in my refusal. Consequently, we parted much less positively than we spent the earlier portion of the evening.

A FEW DAYS LATER, CHARLES and Jane left the house to call upon friends, and I found myself alone at last. I selected my favourite novel, had the maid fetch me a cup of tea, and proceeded to curl up in a comfortable chair beside the window in the library. It afforded me excellent light by which to read, and I looked forward to a long, quiet afternoon in my own company.

Unfortunately, I had read less than a chapter when the servant announced I had a visitor. A visitor? Who could it be—Aunt Gardiner? Surely not Mr. Darcy. I knew I had displeased him when last we spoke and hoped he had gone to join Georgiana at Eden Park by then.

"Miss Eleanor Willoughby," the servant said.

Willoughby!

I rose, smoothed my skirt, and composed myself. A few moments later, a woman entered, and I curtsied. Tall and thin with a pinched look about her mouth, I judged her to be younger than she looked. Her dress was perfectly sufficient but lacked the finery associated with the aristocracy. Her hair was already streaked with grey, and it was evident her complexion had lost its bloom some time ago.

"Elizabeth, is it?" she asked, her tone soft and undemanding.

"Yes, Miss Willoughby, Elizabeth Bennet."

She advanced into the room and examined me with great interest, her eyes poring over my face as though she searched for something or someone lost.

"You look so much like my sister," she said at last.

I bade her be seated in a chair close to mine and rang for more tea.

"You are her child—Elizabeth's child—no matter what my brother says. The evidence is shockingly apparent."

I coloured, and neither of us spoke for several moments. At last, I said, "Will you tell me about her? I long to know anything you are willing to share."

The servant entered with the tea service, and Miss Willoughby waited to speak while I poured a cup for her. As I picked it up to give to her, she reached out and held onto my hand.

"Your fingers are like hers, your hair, your countenance, especially your mouth. The only difference is in your eyes. They came from your father."

I bowed my head, suddenly ashamed of the circumstances of my birth all over again. Would she now denounce me as her brother had done? When she said nothing more, I ventured to meet her gaze and found a tenderness about her mouth, causing it to appear less severe, almost pleasant.

"I regret...very much that my birth caused the decline of your family's fortunes."

Miss Willoughby sighed and cast her eyes to the ceiling. "Is that what

Linton told you? Pay it no mind, my dear. He simply seeks someone other than himself on whom to pin the blame. It is true; Elizabeth was all set to make an opportune marriage, or rather, my mother and Linton had arranged that she would, when they learned that my sister had chosen another path. But let me assure you, our family's fortunes were already in great disarray due to my brother's obsession with gaming and his fondness for spirits."

"He said my birth kept you from making a successful alliance as well."

"Me? I was but eleven years old when you were born—hardly of an age to be sold to the highest bidder. No, by the time I reached the brink of courtship, Linton had long spent our fortune and blackened our name so that any man of consequence would never think of asking for my hand. You had nothing to do with it."

I felt as though a heavy sack of bricks had been lifted from my shoulders, and I breathed a great sigh. "You do not know with what relief I hear your words, Miss Willoughby."

"Will you not call me 'Eleanor'? I am your aunt, after all."

"I…I could not be that familiar."

"May I hope that someday you will feel differently?" When my only answer was to lower my eyes, she continued. "Tell me what you wish to know about your mother."

"Everything!"

She laughed lightly, rose, and walked to the window, fingering the drapery shielding us from the sunshine.

"You must remember that I was but a child when she died, so my memories are vague. Sometimes, I am not certain whether things happened as I recall or whether I dreamed them."

"If you were eleven when I was born, you must be old enough to have known her quite well."

"Oh yes, I knew her. I loved her. She was the dearest person on earth to me, and I would have done anything for her. It broke my heart when my mother and brother forced me to remain in London with the governess while they returned Elizabeth to Derbyshire and left her at Bridesgate with our grandmother. I remember how I cried and begged my governess to tell me where my sister had gone. Once she did, I demanded that she take me to Bridesgate as well, but she would not give over, for she had her orders."

Her voice had grown soft and tremulous, and I feared she might weep. I determined to guide the conversation onto a more cheerful subject.

"Tell me what she loved to do. Was my mother musical or artistic? Did she like to read or sew?"

Miss Willoughby laughed. "Read? Yes, at night, when it was dark and she was forced to remain indoors. Her sewing was hopeless, even worse than mine, and remember, I was but a child. I do not recall her spending much time at the pianoforte or at the easel, thus I suppose she was not particularly proficient at either art. What Elizabeth loved was nature—the wood and forest, trees and streams, anywhere outdoors where she could breathe. She often complained that she could not catch her breath inside. And she was beautiful, of course. In truth, she possessed all the beauty in the family. If Linton was ever handsome, I do not remember it, and you can see for yourself, the gods did not bother to bless me in that regard."

I offered to refill her cup, and she returned to her place across from me.

"Was she—Sir Linton said my mother was…wild. Is that true?"

She raised her eyebrows as she lifted the cup to her mouth. "I did not consider her wild; I thought her wonderful. She and I ran through the woods, climbed trees together, waded in the pond, and she discovered the most exciting places to hide. I considered it all a great lark, and even though she was six years my senior, I felt blessed to have her attention. That is why I kept her secret."

I looked up from my cup. "Her secret?"

"When he began coming around and they spent more and more time together, she made me swear I would not tell. I was flattered that she confided in me and, naturally, would not have told on her if my life depended upon it."

"I assume you refer to my father. So you knew him."

"Not truly. When they began to meet, it was always deep in the wood between our house and Pemberley. At the beginning, they simply laughed and talked, and they allowed me to tag along. Later, I served as lookout to warn them if anyone approached. I, of course, was innocent and knew nothing of the deep bond between them or that it would possibly end in my sister's death. All I knew was that she loved him, and in my childish eyes, he loved her. Elizabeth, I truly believe your parents cared deeply for each other."

Now it was my turn to rise. I had to turn my back to keep her from seeing the depth of emotion her words stirred within me. I thought my heart might burst from the need to weep. Several moments passed before I could speak, during which I walked to the fireplace and ran my fingers across the edge of the mantle. At last, I took a deep breath and faced her.

"Did you ever hear his name spoken, Miss Willoughby?"

The words that tumbled from my mouth shocked me! Did I—did Mr. Darcy, for that matter—still entertain the foolish hope that someone would announce that I was not the daughter of George Darcy?

She shook her head. "She simply called him 'Darcy.'"

"But surely you knew who he was. The Darcys were acquainted with your family. Did you not see him when they called upon your grandmother or mother?"

"I must have, but because I was a child, they were unimportant to me. I cannot say I ever recall seeing him but for his meetings with Elizabeth in the wood."

She rose then and indicated she must take her leave.

I expressed my pleasure for her call and asked that she call again. "I dare not visit you…Sir Linton—"

Miss Willoughby nodded and took my hand. "He was not always that way, my dear. Although he is many years my senior, I recall the affectionate brother he was before his vices and greed took over his life. I understand your reluctance to call, however, and if I am able, I will visit you again with pleasure. Next time, you must do the talking and tell me all about yourself."

We parted with a smile, and I returned to my former place by the window. The novel that had attracted me earlier could not begin to claim my attention though, for I had a treasure load of things to think about and feelings to sort.

Suddenly, I had a great desire to see Mr. Darcy and tell him all that I had learned.

Chapter Ten

Two weeks later, I received yet another letter from my father. He took me to task for my failure to acknowledge his last two messages. I could not help but smirk—this from a man who prided himself upon indolent replies to correspondence. I cannot say why I had not answered other than I could not think of anything to say. It was a sad fact that, in my mind, the bond between us had weakened until only the most delicate thread held it together. I could not help but remain angry with him for not revealing the circumstances of my birth earlier in my life. All reason argued in favour of his charity, yet I clung stubbornly to the pain and detriment I suffered upon learning the truth.

But I knew I must write him. Reading the whole of the letter, however, saved me from the task. He would travel to London on business within two days and call upon Jane and me as soon as he reached Town. He hoped to persuade me to return to Longbourn upon conclusion of his business.

I have not heard two words of sense spoken in this house since you went away, Lizzy, he declared.

My first thought was to refuse, but I had tired of London society, and now that summer was upon us, I longed for the fresh air and green fields of Hertfordshire. When Mr. Bingley announced that he and Jane would repair to Netherfield within a fortnight, I decided to comply with my father's request.

My only hesitation stemmed from the fact that I would no longer entertain any chance of seeing Mr. Darcy. I had not been within his presence since he joined his sister at the Earl of Matlock's residence. Surely, he had travelled on to Bath—or had he? If he remained in Town, I could not help but harbour the hope of an accidental meeting at one of the various social affairs that I attended with Jane and Mr. Bingley.

It is just as well that I leave, I told myself. Wisdom counselled me to remove myself from seeing Mr. Darcy again, for our encounter could serve neither of us well. I felt certain my face was simply a reminder of his family's guilt, and each time I gazed upon him, my heart continued to ache with sadness and longing for what could never be.

I had changed my mind about sharing Miss Willoughby's information with Mr. Darcy, for I sensed the pain it would cause him to learn that, evidently, his father loved someone other than his mother.

The return carriage ride to Longbourn proved an uneasy experience. My father attempted to entertain me with passages from books he had recently read, but when I failed to add anything to the conversation and answered his questions with brief, indifferent replies, he soon gave up and turned his attention to the landscape outside the window. Before long, his head began to nod, and I could hear the gentle swishing sound of his snore.

I examined his face in repose and saw age descending upon him. The lines on his forehead and around his mouth had deepened, and for a moment, I felt somewhat guilty about my coldness toward him, but only for a moment. No matter how I loved him, I refused to forgive his unwise decision. I could not relinquish the grief that afflicted my spirit. If only I had known from childhood that I was sister to Mr. Darcy…if only I had never met him…if only.

I found all at Longbourn much as it had ever been, except that Kitty had grown an inch taller and Mary's complexion appeared even more sallow than before. She had applied herself to the pianoforte, however, and had actually improved her skills. Her attempts to sing remained much the same.

Mamá's curiosity about London society dwindled once I assured her I had neither managed to secure a betrothal during my stay nor even entertained the idea. Her conversation turned to news of Lydia, who was with child. Upon learning of Jane's condition, she immediately ordered the carriage so that she might share the news with Mrs. Philips and Lady Lucas. Kitty followed me above stairs to my bedchamber, wishing to hear more of the balls I had attended while away. After a half hour, I shooed her from the room and sank down upon the window seat.

I gazed out at the lawn. The roses were in bloom; their reds and pinks mingled in perfect harmony with snatches of yellow sprinkled throughout. How many times had Jane and I cut roses, daisies, and marguerites, filling our baskets with their sweet perfumes, all the while talking and dreaming of young men we would someday love and marry? Jane's dream came true, but mine…would never happen. I knew that if and when I married, it would not be for love.

Within a fortnight, I found myself growing more and more restless. Unless I spent the day at Netherfield with Jane, I felt as though I would jump out of my skin. I knew my life would never be as it was before I went away, but I did not expect the growing dissatisfaction that coloured my moods.

I could not find a pastime within the house that held my interest. I read and re-read my favourite books and newer editions Papá recommended. I found them dull. My sewing skills had never been celebrated, but now I had even less patience for the task than before. Kitty often sought my opinion on the latest bonnet she had refashioned, but I could find little to admire about it. After enjoying Georgiana's musical talent, I found it ever more difficult to abide Mary's unrelenting practice. Mamá's constant chatter or complaints drove me to distraction while my father, naturally, hid in his study much of the day. Repeatedly, I sought release from my agitation outdoors. I walked for miles throughout the countryside and wood, but peace eluded me.

Had Pemberley robbed me of contentment?

Over and over, my mind strayed to that beautiful house. I wondered what colourful arrays of flowers and plants now filled the gardens there. I imagined the green of the woods and hills in summer and the carp feeding in the lake. I even saw the huge, sleek horses trotting out from the stable, eager to run in the steady warmth of the summer sun. And I thought of him…

Without fail, Mr. Darcy intruded on my thoughts each day no matter my attempts to banish him. I could see his dark curls fall across his forehead and the dimple in his cheek when he smiled, and try as I might, I could not rid myself of the memory of the light in his eyes when he turned in my direction. Would I never be free of those feelings?

One day, when despair overtook my spirit, I wandered deeper and deeper into the wood some distance from Longbourn. Before I knew it, I came upon the pond hidden within the leafy glade where I had happened upon Mr. Darcy all those months before. I could still see him pacing to and fro, all the while muttering angry oaths—oaths that I knew were brought about by knowledge of my birth. I wondered whether Lady Catherine had any idea of the horror her revelation caused her nephew. She cared naught whether her words tore my world apart, but did she not regret the anguish she brought upon Mr. Darcy?

Of course not! She accomplished what she set out to do.

I sighed at the remembrance of her superior indignation and felt my cheeks burn anew as her accusations rang in my ears. Suddenly, the summer heat seemed oppressive. I untied the ribbons of my bonnet and flung it down beside a group of rocks at the water's edge. I stepped lightly across the flatter stones and settled into my familiar place on the largest rock. The creek appeared cool and inviting. I looked over my shoulder and canvassed the surrounding trees and heavy foliage. Alone and hidden from the world, I slipped off my shoes and stockings.

How refreshing the cold water felt as I dipped my toes therein. I closed my eyes in pleasure and imagined myself bathing in such pleasant surroundings. Another look backward assured me that no one would discover my private Eden, and so I slipped down from the rock, being careful to lift my skirts to my knees so that I could wade in the shallow water close by the shore.

The stone-lined creek bottom proved slippery, but I enjoyed the feeling of the mud in between the slates as it crept between my toes. I lifted my head to the green branches above. The trees over the pond had grown tall and full so that their branches met overhead, providing a natural veil against the summer sun. My mood lightened as I ventured further from the rock on which I had sat.

Ah, I thought, closing my eyes, *what heavenly bliss!*

I stood with my face lifted to the sun and then shifted slightly to the right to feel its warmth on my cheeks. I was at peace with the world for the first time in many days…until out of the corner of my eye, I thought I detected a sudden movement in the wooded area. My pulse began to race. Was it a deer, or had I been discovered? As I turned to investigate, my feet slipped out from under me, and with a great, noisy splash, I sat down in the water. Hard.

"Oh!" I floundered about, awkwardly trying to stand. In dismay, I heard a twig snap in two.

Looking up, I saw Mr. Darcy on the bank, hands on hips and an inquisitive expression upon his face. "Elizabeth?"

Oh no, not him! Not now!

I struggled to find a way to compose myself and, in doing so, succeeded in splashing a great amount of water in my face. "Sir, I…I did not hear you approach."

"Obviously."

With difficulty, I managed to rise to my knees. "How long—that is —when did you arrive in Hertfordshire?"

A lock of wet hair fell across one eye. *Where had that come from?* I fumed as I tucked it behind my ear. Then I cringed as I realized that several long tresses had worked their way loose from the knot I wore. *What a fright I must appear!*

"Late last night. I am staying with Bingley, of course."

"Of course." At last, I managed to secure my feet beneath me, and I stood up, but I wondered how I would ever return to the bank with any semblance of dignity.

"I confess this scene fills me with surprise. I wonder: did you enter the water willingly, or did you possibly slip off this big rock as easily as you fell down in the pond?"

I glared at him.

"Do you often come here to wade, and if so, did you not think to bring along a towel?"

"No, sir, I have never waded here. I simply…found myself in the water."

"You *found* yourself in the water. I see. And…precisely how did that happen? It seems exceedingly fortunate that before you slipped—I assume you slipped—you had opportunity to remove not only your slippers, but your stockings as well." He gestured toward the evidence lying conspicuously upon the rock.

Once again, I glared at him. "In truth, I…well, I was already in the water before I fell."

"In the water…so you did not fall after all?"

"Not off the rock, but I said I fell, and I did…after I was in the water." *Is he deliberately being tiresome?* "Surely, you saw it yourself, for it was the shock of your appearance that startled me and caused me to stumble."

"Ah, I see. It is all *my* fault. Do forgive me." To my utter consternation, he seated himself on the rock, folded his arms, and smiled as though he thoroughly enjoyed my discomposure. "Tell me, Elizabeth, can you swim?"

I frowned and looked away. "A bit."

"So, I need not concern myself with saving you if you should, say, step into a deeper hole out there?"

"You need not concern yourself with saving me at all, sir." I began to wade back toward the rocks.

He chuckled and stood up. "'Tis a pity, for that water tempts me. Is it as cool and refreshing as it appears?"

I stopped short. *Oh no, surely not!*

"It is much too cold, sir," I said quickly. "I fear you would find it most displeasing."

He raised one eyebrow. "I think the lady would keep her charming pleasure all to herself." Kneeling, he cupped his hand into the stream. "Ah, I see why you gave in to such an impulse. The water is truly delightful." He straightened and resumed his seat on the rock.

Oh, how I wished he would go! At length, I had to speak. "Sir, are you not ready to leave?"

"Leave? Not in the least. I find this a shady reprieve from the summer sun. Besides, you may need my assistance. Crawling up the riverbank may not be as easy as crawling in."

He leaned over and held out his hand to me, favouring me with a broad smile. I felt my vexation begin to fade, for I found it impossible to remain peevish with him.

Once I had planted my feet on dry ground, Mr. Darcy took off his jacket and placed it about my shoulders. When I protested, saying the garment would become damp, he would not hear of it. Declaring it of little inconvenience if it kept me from having a chill, he turned his back and walked a short distance away. He feigned interest in surveying the surrounding scenery while I wrung the water from my skirts. With nothing to dry my feet, I forcibly pulled on my stockings and shoes.

Oh, why did I ever give in to such foolishness and step into that creek?

I looked up to see Mr. Darcy pick up a handful of stones and begin skipping them across the top of the water as he had done on the previous occasion when we met at the pond.

"I would think you must allow time for your frock to dry before you return to Longbourn," he said. "Do you not agree?" Still embarrassed, I did not answer. "Elizabeth? Are you respectable, or must we converse back to back from now on?"

I could not help but smile. "I hardly consider myself respectable, but we may speak face to face."

He turned around. "Good. I do not practice the art of skipping stones well when forced to do so with my left hand."

"I would say you do exceptionally well, sir."

He walked toward me. "Have you ever tried it?"

"Skipping stones? No, sir."

"It is very simple. I should be pleased to teach you." When I demurred, stating it was a man's sport, he shrugged and stepped up on the large rock before sailing another stone across the body of the pond. A whisper of a tap echoed three times as it skimmed the surface before vanishing into the creek with a single plop.

"If you had grown up at Pemberley, I should have taught you. After all, we are brother and sister, are we not?" When I did not answer, he turned his eyes upon me. "Elizabeth?"

"Yes, of course, but still—" I felt uncomfortable in his presence, and I shuddered to think of my appearance. I had no intention of attempting to learn how to skip stones when I resembled a half-drowned cat whose hair sticks out in every direction. I preferred to sit turned partly aside from him.

"Oh, I see. You did not grow up with a brother. Be assured that, if you had, I would have taught you many skills just as I did Georgiana."

"Like skipping stones across the lake. My, my, your sister is most compassionate. She has never once pointed out my deficiency in that area or the severe social disadvantages I shall suffer for lack thereof."

In the midst of taking aim, Mr. Darcy lowered his arm and cocked his eyebrow, as he fixed his eyes upon me. "You mock, but there are advantages to having an older brother."

"I do not doubt it, sir," I said, attempting an innocent tone.

"I believe you do. I believe you doubt that I could teach you anything."

"Not at all," I said softly. "I believe you could teach me a great number of things."

I raised my eyes to his and saw them darken. He took a deep breath before we both looked away. He sat down on the rock, leaving ample room between us, and simply tossed the stones into the pond one by one. We said nothing more for a while. The gentle play of water lapping against the bank proved somehow comforting as the heat of the sun warmed my skin. I was surprised at the peace that flowed into my spirit. It was as though no one else existed in the world. At length, I ventured to turn and catch a glimpse of him only to find his eyes upon me.

"Do you wish you had grown up at Pemberley, Elizabeth?"

His question caught me off guard. "Hardly, sir. My position would have been precarious, to say the least. Besides, it never would have transpired."

"It might have if my father had remained true to his principles. If he had acknowledged his role as your father, he could have reared you as his daughter. Men of much higher status frequently do so in like situations."

"I beg to differ. A gentleman may allow his natural daughter a place in his household, but she would never enjoy an equal position with his lawful daughter. I would not wish for that experience."

He sighed. "I would not wish it for you. It is just that I wonder how it might have been between us if we had shared a childhood."

"You doubtless would have resented me. I cannot imagine you enjoying the interruptions that a sister eight years your junior would have caused, especially one like me—curious, saucy, meddlesome."

He smiled. "True. Your impertinence would have tried my patience. Still …I wish I had seen what you looked like as a little girl."

"Snaggle-toothed and freckled. Not a pretty sight."

"Ah, then I am most fortunate to have been spared such an onslaught upon my senses since I, of course, have been handsome from birth."

"Undoubtedly. And modest as well—a model child," I declared, laughing aloud, although silently I imagined that he most likely had never been anything but beautiful.

Again, we enjoyed a compatible silence. It was as though we were at such ease with each other that we had no need for words. It was just enough to be together in that beautiful retreat.

"I wonder," he said at length, "where you would be today if you had grown up as my sister."

"Certainly not here."

"Why not? Bingley is my friend; thus, you would have met him. He would have purchased Netherfield, and we would have visited him. Of course, Bingley might have engaged himself to you by that time." He looked up and fixed a stare upon me as though he wished to see how I would take to the suggestion.

"If he did, I should have been cast aside once he met Jane at the assembly ball."

"You think that, do you?"

I sighed. "Why should we discuss this, sir? You know as well as I do that Mr. Bingley would never have married me, considering the unfortunate circumstance of my birth. No gentleman could."

"Would it surprise you to know that Fitzwilliam seriously considered asking for your hand?"

I closed my eyes in dismay. Must we return to the situation that had caused both of us such pain?

"When last at Pemberley, he appeared smitten by your charms."

"If he was smitten by anything, it was the prospect of persuading you to grant me an ample dowry."

"I do not need persuasion, Elizabeth. I told you I am more than willing to settle a dowry upon you if you will accept it."

I frowned. "Are you so eager to see me marry?"

"Of course not, and certainly not to Fitzwilliam!" He picked up another rock and hurled it far out into the pond. The noisy splash caused the jays in the cypress trees to flutter from the branches.

"I do not understand why we are having this conversation, sir. Colonel Fitzwilliam's attentions to me were dependent upon the belief that we are cousins. If he or any other gentleman learns the truth, marriage proposals will no longer be forthcoming."

I rose, wishing to change the subject. I murmured something about my skirt beginning to dry and my need to return to Longbourn. He stood and held out his hand, guiding me down from the rocks until we reached the soft grass below, whereupon I returned his jacket.

"I am surprised to learn of your visit to Netherfield, sir, for Jane failed to mention that you were coming."

"I confess I arrived without notice, a boorish action on my part now that Bingley is married. I must mend my manners and write for an invitation from now on."

"I trust Georgiana is well. Did you leave her at Eden Park?"

"No, I brought her with me."

I smiled with delight. "I shall take pleasure in seeing her once more."

"She is impatient for your company as well, and she wishes to become better acquainted with your younger sisters."

"I know they will be glad to visit with her."

"Shall I bring her tomorrow? Would that be convenient?"

"Certainly. I cannot help but wonder, however, what brings you to the country. Surely, it is not just for Georgiana's sake."

"We will stay at Netherfield but a week or so and then depart for Bath to visit my aunt. I still hope to persuade you to join us and make the trip, too."

"Sir, I—"

"Do not answer today. Just think on it, Elizabeth. That is all I ask. Have you ever been to Bath?" I shook my head. "It is a lovely place but fifteen miles from Bristol. I think you would find it diverting, and perchance my aunt may shed light on some of our questions."

Oh, why must we speak of that again?

"You forget. I have no more questions. *You* are the one who remains dissatisfied."

"If you had known our father, perhaps your curiosity would not yet be appeased. I tell you, Elizabeth, I must know why a man of his standing, who obviously adored my mother, would stoop to such degradation."

I stopped short. "Degradation!" *After the pleasant afternoon we have enjoyed together, will you actually use that term?* "You forget yourself, sir, for my mother was of more noble birth than your father."

"You misunderstand. I chose the wrong word."

"You did indeed. Excuse me, I must return to Longbourn at once."

I whirled around and walked swiftly into the wood. I heard him call my name, but I paid no attention, never slowing my pace in the slightest. So it was true; in spite of all his fine words and protestations to the contrary, Mr. Darcy did consider me a humiliation and reproach upon his family's name. I almost reached the edge of the wood before he caught my hand.

"Must you twist what I say and accuse me of offence so often? I meant no slur upon your mother."

I struggled to free my hand, but he held my wrist firmly and refused to let go.

"No, Elizabeth, I shall not release you until we settle this."

"It can never be settled!"

"It can if you will remove the blinders from your eyes and see the truth."

"I see perfectly well, sir. My vision is without fault, and for that matter, so is my hearing."

"But your understanding is not! How can I make you grasp that I would not intentionally do or say anything to hurt you?"

"Not referring to my mother as a degradation upon your father would be as good a place to start as any."

He stepped closer and fixed an angry stare upon me. "I told you that is not what I meant! Are you so thick that you cannot comprehend my words, or do you look for any reason you can find to dismiss me from your presence? What is it truly, Elizabeth? Do you dislike me with such fervour that you must make up transgressions I supposedly cause?"

"Why should I make up anything? You provide excellent cause without assistance!"

Our eyes locked together, his darkening once again—this time with anger. His jaw tightened, and the vein stood out along his temple. Our breath came quick and hard. My heart raced, and I supposed his did the same. His eyes moved to my hair, my cheeks, and down to my lips, and then...he blinked several times, looked away, and stepped back, releasing my hand. He turned his back, but I could see his laboured breathing as he struggled to calm himself.

What had just happened? How could an argument erupt between us with such passion? I turned away and engaged myself by donning my bonnet and straightening the ribbons. When I looked up, he still had not turned to face me.

"Sir, I..."

He lifted his hand in dismissal. "Pray, Elizabeth, not another word. We are both too angry right now. I fear we will utter words that neither of us can forgive."

What had I done? I swallowed, opened my mouth to speak, but said nothing. I deliberately walked slowly through the trees, out of the wood, and into the lane, hoping he would stop me once again, but he did not. Further down the road, I turned twice to see whether he followed, but I saw no one. I returned to Longbourn, sick at heart, grieved that I had wounded him so. How could a time of joy turn to sorrow in a single moment?

Why did an ordinary day once again become a day of anguish?

Mr. Darcy did not bring Georgiana to visit Longbourn on the morrow. She arrived with Jane and without mention of a reason for her brother's absence. My parents welcomed her. Mamá was obviously in awe of her fine clothes, and Mary and Kitty seemed pleased to renew their acquaintance with her. Jane persuaded her to play for us, and all were suitably impressed with her talent. When Mary took over at the instrument, Kitty drew Georgiana aside to view the trimmings on her latest bonnet. She seemed overwhelmed at first with all the attention, but after tea, she joined Kitty for a stroll in the garden and appeared at ease in her company. It was good to hear the sound of their laughter float through the open window.

Jane wore a weary expression as she answered our mother's constant questions regarding her health and plans for the nursery. After she explained the same things for the third time, I rescued my sister by requesting her able assistance in the stillroom.

"Oh, Lizzy, your sister is far too busy now to putter around that musty old place with you. She has servants to arrange her flowers, a service you might enjoy if you would take advantage of your connections with the Darcys and encourage the men you might meet through them."

"Mamá, if I had fifty servants to arrange my flowers, I would still prefer to do them myself as I quite enjoy it," I replied. "Come, Jane, you must see the blue hydrangeas. They shall make excellent dried arrangements for autumn."

She was only too eager to join me, and we spent an hour of contentment secluded in our refuge. We talked of Mr. Bingley's excitement over the coming babe, how she had caught the upstairs maid pilfering her perfume, the fact that Mr. Bingley's favourite horse had to be put down, and the upcoming ball he wished to hold before she progressed too far in her confinement.

Never once did she mention Mr. Darcy, and I began to despair of gleaning any intelligence of him. I could not help but worry that he remained too angry with me to bring Georgiana to Longbourn himself, and yet, I knew not how I might broach the subject without revealing our quarrel.

"You must have been surprised when Mr. Darcy and Georgiana arrived on your doorstep unexpectedly," I said at last.

"Surprised, but not displeased. Charles enjoys his company, and I find his sister delightful. With such pleasant cousins, Lizzy, I wonder that you do not wish to return to Pemberley."

"It is tempting at times, particularly when Mary practices the same song for half the day. Tell me, do they plan a long visit?"

"No. In fact, Mr. Darcy announced at breakfast they would leave within three days. Charles is disheartened, but thus far, none of his arguments have dissuaded his friend."

"Will he not even stay for the ball?"

"You said yourself, Lizzy, that Mr. Darcy does not like to dance. Perchance that is the reason for his sudden removal."

"Perchance," I murmured, although I knew the answer all too well. He could not wait to place miles between us. I must have wounded him even more than I feared.

That night, I could not sleep. *Three days* pounded in my ears like a relentless throbbing headache. He would leave Hertfordshire, and I might never see him again. Is that not what I wanted? Had I not repeatedly told myself that it would be better if we forgot all about each other? And yet, my heart ached at the realization that we would part in anger.

What if he were killed in some accident along the way? I could never tell him that I was sorry I had spoken harshly. He was wrong to disparage my mother, and yet, it seemed insignificant in comparison to the possibility that the last words Mr. Darcy heard me utter were filled with bitterness and ill feeling. If only he would call upon me before he left Netherfield Park.

But he did not come.

Early on the morning of the third day, I arose, sipped a cup of coffee, and slipped out the door. I determined to walk to Netherfield, hoping to see Mr. Darcy before he departed or, even better, chance to meet him before I reached my destination. I knew he enjoyed an early morning walk before the world awakened, as did I, and I prayed he would take one last tramp through the wood before setting out on his journey. I hurried to Oakham Mount, but found it solitary. From there, I ploughed through the wood until it opened upon the secluded pond where we had last seen each other. I heard no sound other than frogs croaking and an occasional fish surfacing to feed.

Sick with disappointment, I returned to the road and turned in the direction of Mr. Bingley's estate. Within moments, I heard the sound of a carriage approaching. Although I stood well out of its path, I made certain I was clearly visible to all riding within. My heart jumped into my throat when I recognized that the vehicle belonged to Mr. Darcy. Surely, he would direct the driver to halt when he saw me. I began to breathe easier when I saw the horses slow down as they approached, but to my utter dismay, the carriage did not stop.

Mr. Darcy sat at the open window, his arm resting on the sill. He stared into my eyes as he passed by, but he did not lift his hand in any semblance of a wave. I followed him with my own eyes, turning around completely to watch him disappear around the bend. A cold chill crept up my spine at the expression I had seen on his face.

Nothing remained on his countenance other than bleak resignation and a sadness I cannot describe.

Chapter Eleven

After the scene on the roadway, days crawled by with unreasonable tediousness. I sometimes thought daylight stretched into twenty-four hours before evening fell. I longed to be alone with my thoughts, to avoid my family's questions as to why I suffered such discomposure and what had become of my former lively self. While spending the required hours in their company following supper, I counted the minutes until I could flee to my chamber. Why, I do not know, because sleep deserted me.

For hours, I sat by the window, gazing at the stars and wondering where Mr. Darcy was. *What is he doing? Does he still think of me with anger?*

I tortured myself with the possibility that my hasty accusations had severed all regard he might have felt for me. If only I could see him once more and make things right between us. When I did sleep, troublesome dreams disturbed me. I constantly chased after something, but what or who it was I knew not.

After a miserable week had passed, Jane drew me aside one day at Netherfield. At her invitation, I had come for dinner, along with Mamá and my younger sisters. After we dined and my mother began to doze in the parlour, Jane suggested the girls and I join her for exercise in the park. She cleverly led me down a separate path from Mary and Kitty, thus securing our privacy.

"Now, Lizzy, I insist you tell me what causes this unvarying dark temper to linger about you," she said firmly, linking her arm within mine. "Your countenance is as downcast as it was during the days following Lady Catherine's unfortunate visit. Has something else befallen you?"

I coloured and turned my attention to the summer daisies. "I do not know what you mean."

"Yes, you do. Tell the truth, and face me when you speak. Your eyes have always revealed when you attempt to deceive."

"Do not be silly, Jane. I have no reason to lie. I am simply weary with life."

"Weary? You? Why, Lizzy, you have always found stimulation in everything around you. Your wit and intelligence have served you well in the past. Why should you find life wearisome now? What circumstance has altered? Do I dare say you have changed your mind and now wish you had tarried longer at Pemberley?"

"Perhaps. I do not know. I just feel as though I am smothering at Long-bourn. I cannot find one reason to anticipate the future other than the birth of your baby."

"There has been a scarcity of social activities this summer, perhaps because of the unusual heat. But lest you forget, our ball is set for Thursday night. There should be a full moon, and Charles has planned every last particular. He refuses me licence to participate at all for fear of plaguing my well-being."

I smiled. "Your husband is very attentive."

"To a fault! If he had his way, I would lie in bed all day and be waited on hand and foot, but enough about me. You shall not escape my inquiries by changing the subject. Is the lack of suitable admirers in Hertfordshire cause for your dissatisfaction?"

"No, Jane, I am resolved to remain an old maid most likely and become a favourite aunt to your children because I shall spoil them excessively. Do not worry so."

"An old maid! Not you, Lizzy, not with your romantic nature. No, I know there is someone, a man as perfect for you as Charles is for me. And with any luck, he is coming to Netherfield for the ball."

I laughed lightly. "What makes you think that?"

"Charles told me that a stranger is coming, a single man of modest fortune, someone neither you nor I have ever seen."

"Oh? And does he have a name?"

"Mr. Hayden Hurst."

"Hurst? Not—"

"Yes, he is Mr. Hurst's younger brother, and he arrives with Louisa, Caroline, and Mr. Hurst tomorrow."

I could not help it. My mouth dropped open. "Surely, you would not wish me married to Mr. Hurst's brother! Why, that would make me sister to Louisa."

"You can bear it if I must. I prefer to imagine him an exceedingly agreeable man whom you may highly esteem in many respects. Besides, he may not resemble his brother at all. With any luck, he will be as handsome as Charles."

"With my luck, he will favour the reading material of Mr. Collins!"

We both commenced to giggle, which brought Mary and Kitty running around the shrubbery to hear the joke. The afternoon succeeded in lightening my spirit for a while, but I entertained few hopes for the Netherfield ball.

My fears were not unwarranted, for Mr. Hayden Hurst proved to be as I expected—a younger version of his brother. Although not yet quite as rotund, his affinity for food and drink foretold a future in his brother's image. Even had he been handsome enough to tempt me, his disinterest was evident. He danced only two dances, choosing Caroline Bingley for his partner. Afterward, he sat beside his brother, sharing his attachment to the wine bottle.

Ah well, it mattered not to me. Observation of the younger Mr. Hurst's foibles provided passing amusement. I danced sufficiently with the few eligible men among our company, dined on delicious food, and enjoyed watching Jane bask in the light of Hertfordshire society as well as the loving looks of her husband. All in all, it was a pleasant enough diversion, but nothing more.

The days thereafter provided little variation, and the blackness descended upon my spirit once again. No matter how I tried, I could not rid myself of thoughts of Mr. Darcy.

The next week, however, the arrival of the post made my heart beat faster. I received a letter postmarked from Bath. My hands trembled as I unfolded it. Had he possibly written to me? How disappointed I was to see Georgiana's signature signed neatly at the bottom.

Oh! I said to myself, but at least I would have some news. I flew up the stairs, closed the door to my chamber, and settled myself in the window seat to read in peace.

Dearest Elizabeth,

How I wish you were here with us!

One can never tire of Bath. The honest relish of balls and plays and everyday sights would fascinate you, my dear cousin. And I must tell you of the Pump Room. The natural spring waters are said to provide excellent medicinal properties. Mrs. Annesley and I visit the place almost every day. I find myself in awe when Lady Dalrymple arrives with her following. She deigned to speak to me on Tuesday and said she recalled my parents from summers she spent in Derbyshire.

Still, I am lonely much of the time. Wills spends the majority of the day cooped up in our uncle's library with our aunt. She is a hawkish sort of woman, spare and rather dried up, but pleasant enough, especially in comparison with Lady Catherine. I know not why they search through old journals, ship logs, and records that belonged to my uncle. When I ask Wills, he says he is researching our family history, but he did the same thing at Eden Park. And at Rosings, he questioned Lady Catherine until she became even more peevish than usual. I ask you, how much family history can one search for?

I did make a lovely friend at last night's ball in the Upper Rooms. Her name is Maria Simpson, and she is but two years older than me. Her older sister, Emily, is magnificent, and she was surrounded by beaus the entire evening. I do not think she sat out one single dance. Even Wills asked her to dance more than once, which I found amusing as he so rarely puts himself out for anyone. I am to meet Maria at the Pump Room this afternoon.

Oh, I must tell you this. Wills and I (and Mrs. Annesley, of course) leave Bath for Ireland within a fortnight! It will be my first sea voyage, and I am excited and frightened at the same time. I do wish you were going with us. I should not be nearly so afraid with you beside me.

Do write, and tell me the news at Longbourn. Till then, I remain Your affectionate cousin,
Georgiana

Ireland! Why would Mr. Darcy sail for Ireland? The only reason I could think of would be to seek his uncle Peter Darcy. Had he discovered something new, something of importance that would cause him to undertake the journey? And yes, I wished I could also make the trip—how exciting that would be—but I knew it was out of the question.

I re-read the letter, hoping I had overlooked some message from him. Not one word. He had not even extended his regards to me. Surely, he knew to whom Georgiana wrote, and yet, he remained locked in that stony silence my angry words had provoked. Oh, why had I not held my tongue?

Resentment settled upon me when I read the part about Mr. Darcy dancing with Miss Simpson. I could imagine his attentions directed toward her, for I knew how exciting it was to dance with him. Two dances…she must be truly handsome to claim his time to that degree. He would surely call upon her, or perhaps he would join Georgiana for tea with the younger sister, and Miss Simpson would attend as well. Suddenly, I became aware that my breath was coming hard and fast.

What are you doing? You have no right to be jealous. He is your brother.

I knew he would find someone eventually and marry. I just always thought it far in the future—that *someday* we often speak of that never actually arrives. I allowed my mind to wander once more. I could see their marriage in the chapel in Derbyshire, her installation as mistress of Pemberley, even the birth of a son who inherited Mr. Darcy's dimples.

I jumped up, pulled open a drawer to my desk, threw the letter therein, and slammed it shut. Grabbing my bonnet, I tripped down the stairs and invited Kitty to walk to Meryton with me. I told her I was in the mood to buy a new bonnet. She hastened to join me, alive with anticipation at the thought of shopping and so grateful for my attention that it shamed me. I had neglected her and Mary, but at the moment, I craved distraction, company, anything that would erase those dreadful images from my mind.

Two days later, the Gardiners and their children arrived at Longbourn. The entire week before, Mamá had complained because her brother had written and asked whether they might leave my young cousins in our keeping while they travelled on to their destination. Yet, naturally, she agreed to their request.

"My sister has no idea how the noise and confusion tries my nerves," she said repeatedly. I sighed, as I knew full well that my sisters and I would be the ones who entertained the children.

I assumed Mr. and Mrs. Gardiner would stay for a long visit, so I was surprised to learn they planned to depart Longbourn within four days.

"Pleasure bent again, I assume," Mamá said with a disapproving eye.

"A bit of pleasure and work, Fanny," my uncle answered. "Madeline is due a holiday, and since I have business in Bath, we decided to make an expedition of it."

My eyes opened wide! "Bath? You are going to Bath, Uncle?"

"Yes, my dear. It will be an agreeable trip, I am sure. Since your mother has generously agreed to allow the children to remain at Longbourn, it promises to be a true excursion. 'Twill bring back fond memories, for your aunt and I spent our wedding journey there many years ago."

He turned a loving eye upon his wife, who turned a delightful shade of pink. I rose and took a chair closer to them.

"I have always longed to see Bath."

"Hmph," Mamá snorted. "You have never mentioned Bath in my hearing, Lizzy. If you wish to visit near the sea, you had much better travel to Brighton where the militia is quartered. You might have a chance at securing a husband there as Lydia did. I cannot see any reason for you to go to Bath."

My aunt gave me a look that we both understood perfectly. "But, Fanny," she said. "Bath has many scenes of interest to engage Lizzy's fine mind."

"Yes, Mamá, I should so love to visit the city."

"Lizzy is in need of a husband, not more curiosities with which to clutter her mind. She is of an age to marry, and I fear if she does not settle down and choose someone soon…well, I declare I do not know what shall become of her! We cannot all live off Mr. Bingley when her father dies and we are thrown out of Longbourn and left to starve in the hedgerows."

My uncle cleared his throat. "I have heard there are excellent families who either live in Bath or travel there on holiday. It would not be unusual for at least a goodly portion of them to possess sons of marriageable age. I would say Lizzy's chances for a prosperous marriage bode much better at Bath than Brighton."

Mamá's expression changed instantly. The thought of a prosperous husband demanded her immediate attention. Within the hour, she had plagued my father until he agreed I might make the trip. All I had to do was pack and banish the quaking within. Would we arrive before Mr. Darcy embarked for Ireland, and, if so, might I meet him by chance? Even more important, how would he receive me?

IT RAINED STEADILY THE DAY we rode into Bath, a state of affairs that I soon learned would be a frequent occurrence. The downpour did not last long, however, and left the air hot and damp. My aunt and I made frequent use of our fans as we settled into our lodgings in Pulteney Street. Even with the humidity, I felt revived by the bustling sounds of the city. I leaned out the spacious window of my chamber to observe the feast of colour without. My eyes went here, there, everywhere. Up and down the avenue, a constant parade of people passed by, some dressed in ordinary attire, but many clad in fine clothing and expensive bonnets and hats. Evidently, the rich did populate Bath or at least spent their holiday in residence.

We dined in the hotel the first evening although I longed to go out. My attempts to unobtrusively search the dining room with my eyes failed to disclose a familiar face. My efforts, however, did attract my aunt's attention.

"Lizzy, do you look for someone in particular?"

I immediately issued a denial and turned my consideration to my plate.

"Madeline, you and Elizabeth must tour the city tomorrow while I conduct my business," my uncle said.

"Would you not rather we waited for you?"

"No, my dear. I shall join you when I finish. Lizzy is young and cannot be expected to while away the days cooped up inside."

I made the appropriate protests, but not strongly, for I longed not only to see the city but also to discover a way to meet with Mr. Darcy. As yet, I had not told the Gardiners of his possible presence in Bath, hoping we might simply happen upon him instead.

As it came about, we dwelt in the city three days without chancing upon either Mr. Darcy or Georgiana. Mrs. Gardiner did look up an old acquaintance, a Mrs. Parry, and we spent the afternoon of the third day in her stuffy, hot parlour on Gay Street. A lady of some age, she inquired as to my marriage expectations and then proceeded to discuss suitable partners for me with my aunt as though I no longer sat within their presence. By the end of the visit, my patience had grown as thin as wet parchment. Were the prospects of single women the only topic of conversation available when older ladies assembled?

That night, I re-read Georgiana's letter. Noting the date she wrote it, I quickly calculated the time that had passed. Ten days—ten days had gone by. *Wills and I (and Mrs. Annesley, of course) leave for Ireland within a fortnight.* They would depart Bath within four days! Desperation seized me, and I determined I would do all in my power to find Mr. Darcy before he left the country.

Having concluded the major portion of his business obligations for the week, the next morning, Mr. Gardiner offered my aunt and me a carriage ride through the city. He wished to show us the port area along the River Avon as well as the more fashionable portion of Bath. That was exactly what I hoped to see.

"I would love to, Uncle, if my aunt agrees and if you will consent to visit the Pump Room with us sometime during the day. We insist you taste the spring waters."

"Oh yes, my dear," my aunt said. "You must drink some. I have never tasted water like it."

He acquiesced, and we soon left our rooms for the sidewalks below. We entered the Pump Room first, whereupon my uncle pulled a face when asked to judge the quality of the water. We walked up and down speaking to no one until Mr. Gardiner happened upon a business acquaintance who engaged him in a lengthy conversation—so lengthy that I despaired of having time to tour much of the city by carriage. The man's wife took an interest in my aunt, and they spent no little time becoming acquainted.

Unsatisfied and concerned that we would never leave, I wandered a short distance away from them to gaze through the window at the shops across the street. I became engrossed in watching people as they passed by. So intent was my concentration that I failed to notice the gentleman who appeared at my side.

"Miss Bennet?"

I turned in amazement to see Colonel Fitzwilliam beaming down upon me. "Colonel, I...am surprised to meet you here."

"As am I to see you. How did you come to visit Bath?"

"I travelled with my aunt and uncle." I gestured back in their direction, but their attention continued to be held by their acquaintances. "Are you here on duty?"

"No, I had leave available and came with my brother. He is engaged to a resident of Bath, Miss Julia Allen. By the bye, did you know Darcy and Georgiana are also in residence?"

"I did receive a letter from Georgiana telling me they were to visit their aunt, I believe. Are they still here? I understood they planned to travel on to Ireland."

"Yes, to both your questions. They travel to Holyhead to catch a ship within—let me think—less than four days now. You must visit them in Camden Place. I am certain they would not wish to leave without seeing you, and I cannot tell you how enchanted I am to find you here. I was quite disconcerted when you left Pemberley with such haste. You did not even say farewell."

I heard the censure in his voice. "I…left a note, but no matter, I agree that it was rude on my part. I pray you will forgive my lack of manners. A sudden wave of pining for home overtook me without warning."

"I understand the longing to see those for whom we care." He smiled and drew closer. "Since those days in Derbyshire, I have longed to see you again. Shall you introduce me to your aunt and uncle?"

"Of course." I turned quickly while realizing my heart had begun to race. Time evidently had not lessened the colonel's speculation at securing my hand.

We joined the Gardiners and their friends, and I made the appropriate introductions. The colonel charmed both couples with his agreeable nature and asked us to luncheon with him. My uncle's business associate declined, and he and his wife bade their farewells, but my aunt accepted Colonel Fitzwilliam's invitation. As we walked down the street, the colonel repeated his insistence that we contact Mr. Darcy and his sister while we were in Bath. My aunt and I walked behind the men, and she began to slow her steps until we were far enough back that the men could not hear her soft conversation.

"Lizzy, did you know the Darcys were in Bath?"

"Why, yes, Aunt. I received a letter from Miss Darcy a few days before we left Longbourn."

She looked at me curiously. "I see. Tell me, dear, does Colonel Fitzwilliam know of your true relationship with his cousins?"

"No," I whispered, "and Georgiana does not know either, so we must not speak of it. Papá and Mr. Darcy agree that the fewer people who know the truth, the safer my reputation."

"A wise decision. You may depend upon our discretion. Neither your uncle nor I will ever make any revelation."

"That is why I told you. I trust you both without question."

During the meal, Mr. Gardiner mentioned our plans to tour Bath by carriage, whereupon the colonel offered not only his carriage but also his services as our guide. I did not relish spending the afternoon in his company, but I knew he was the connection to seeing Mr. Darcy. I bestowed my brightest smile upon him as he took my elbow and ushered me out into the sunlight.

Since the morning rains had ceased, the colonel ordered his brother's landau that he had borrowed to be opened. He proceeded to point out various sites of interest throughout the city. We rode down Bond Street and then over to the Circus area and reached the Royal Crescent at last. The beauty of the architecture and shape of the buildings proved stunning. We surveyed the impressive design for no little time. At length, Mr. Gardiner suggested we travel on to the River Avon, but Mrs. Gardiner expressed a desire for refreshment.

"I know just the place," Colonel Fitzwilliam announced.

Within a short time, the carriage turned into Milsom Street and drew up at Molland's, where we dined with such pleasure that my aunt declared Molland's marzipan the best she had ever tasted. Sitting by the window, I watched the rain return. The place began to fill with people wishing to avoid the shower. I observed the door's frequent openings with little interest until, suddenly, my heart beat faster, for I recognized a familiar face and figure. Mr. Darcy removed his hat and shook the water from it before he raised his head and looked over the room. Within moments, his gaze met mine.

If my presence surprised him, he hid it well. Naught but a quick blink of his eyes betrayed him. About the same time, Colonel Fitzwilliam looked up and noticed his cousin. He stood and beckoned to him.

"Darcy, over here."

My hands turned icy cold as I wondered what effect my presence would merit from him. He made his way through the crowd. After speaking to Mr. and Mrs. Gardiner, he bowed slightly in my direction and sat down next to my aunt. His manner was cordial as he expressed surprise at our visit to Bath. He directed every remark to either my aunt or uncle, but not one to me.

"And how did you happen upon the Gardiners and Miss Bennet, Fitzwilliam?" he asked, turning toward his cousin, who sat beside me.

The colonel explained our chance meeting, and my aunt told him of the day's tour of the city. My uncle added that the river would be our next destination. When the colonel asked Mr. Darcy whether he might go with us, he declined, stating a former promise to his aunt laid claim to his afternoon. Light conversation ensued for a good half hour; at the conclusion of which, he rose and made his farewells. He still had not directed any word toward me or even allowed his eyes to be fixed upon me. Not only did I feel cut by his behaviour, but I was truly alarmed that he might never speak to me again. I watched him walk to the counter to purchase a package of sweets.

"Pray, excuse me, I will fetch another glass of water," I said, quickly rising. I refused the colonel's offer to retrieve it for me and crossed the room with great haste. Mr. Darcy had just received his change and turned to leave. I darted in front of him blocking his path to the door, and he halted abruptly.

"Miss Bennet?"

"Sir, I would ask you to extend my regards and apologies to Georgiana. I received her letter a day or so before we departed Longbourn, but I did not have time to reply."

"Very well."

"I wonder…shall you escort your sister to the ball in the Upper Rooms tomorrow night?"

"I had not given it much thought."

"I would love to see her."

"Shall I ask her to call on you? Where did you say you are staying?"

"In Pulteney Street. I shall be at home in the morning if she is able to come."

"I shall tell her." He bowed slightly and began walking toward the door. I found myself following him, attempting to delay his leaving.

"Georgiana wrote to me how much she enjoys watching you dance—with a Miss Simpson, is it not?"

He stopped and turned to face me. "I did not know my sister reported my dancing partners to you."

I shook my head slightly. "Oh no, sir, she did nothing like that. She simply mentioned it in passing, and I thought you had perhaps at last found someone with whom you enjoyed dancing."

His eyes pierced mine with their severity. "Good day, Miss Bennet."

With dismay, I watched him walk through the door and down the sidewalk. *That did not go well*, I thought. *You made a fool of yourself, an utter fool!*

GEORGIANA DID CALL THE NEXT day, and I was thrilled to see her again. Until I saw her familiar smile, I had not realized how my affection had grown for the girl. We spent an hour in conversation, during which I am afraid my aunt did not have a chance to say more than a few words. Once more, she told me how preoccupied Mr. Darcy was in his search through his uncle's old records. She failed to understand why they attracted his interest, but she spent little time considering the matter. We talked of Bath and the various attractions she had visited, how welcome her cousin's company had been on several excursions, and the new dresses she had made by a seamstress in the city whom she highly recommended.

When I asked her whether she would attend the assembly that night, she replied that her brother had agreed to take her. Since she was not out yet, Georgiana explained how Mr. Darcy allowed her to go to the balls if she remained in the background and simply observed the dancing. I gently prodded her for information on whether the Simpson sisters would be in attendance, and she happily informed me that they would.

"You must meet them, Elizabeth, for I know you shall like them as I do."

I smiled in agreement, all the while biting my tongue. I then directed the subject to their upcoming journey to Ireland. Georgiana said that the departure had been delayed a week due to some complications with the passenger ship. When I inquired as to the reason for the trip, she said only that Mr. Darcy had important business with someone in the country, and that it must be conducted as soon as possible. I thought it unusual that she should accompany her brother on a business trip, but she said Mr. Darcy thought it would be good for his young sister to see the ancestral home of their grandmother.

"Did you know my grandmother was from County Cork?" she asked.

"I did. Your brother shared a bit of family history with me when I visited Pemberley."

"How odd. He did not tell me until we came to Bath and he determined to make this trip. I found it somewhat shocking, did you not?"

"When one examines any family's roots, one is bound to uncover surprises."

She smiled and rose to leave, vowing to look for Mrs. Gardiner and me that night at the Upper Rooms.

As I dressed for the evening, I thought of Georgiana's new dresses, and I regretted not paying more attention to the wardrobe I had packed. Why had I not included the new gowns I had made in London when visiting Jane? Once again, Mr. Darcy would see me in the same gown I had worn at the Netherfield Ball.

What difference does it make? He will most likely have eyes only for Miss Emily Simpson, I thought.

I would be fortunate to warrant a glance from him, much less a civil word. It was obvious that he was still angry with me. I simply had to make an opportunity to speak with him privately and make things right between us.

I did not wish to imagine him crossing the Irish Sea with its rough currents when he still thought ill of me.

The season was full, so the room was crowded when we arrived. Mr. Gardiner repaired directly to the card-room, and my aunt and I were left to squeeze through the mob alone. She eventually spied the wife of my uncle's business acquaintance, who claimed her attentions. I was left to fend for myself. I looked over the busy room, hoping to see Georgiana, but to no avail. I drew close to the edge of the throng to observe the dancers. I was relieved not to find Mr. Darcy among them, an emotion for which I silently scolded myself. I simply must stop caring with whom he danced.

I was about to turn back and rejoin my aunt when I looked up to see Colonel Fitzwilliam by my side. He asked me to dance, and I agreed. I preferred dancing any day to being an observer. As soon as the music began again, we took our place in the line.

"Did your cousins accompany you, sir?" I asked after the first turn.

"They did. I placed Georgiana in a suitable position to have a good view of the floor."

"I suppose Mr. Darcy remained by her side."

"For a while, at least. Have you met the Misses Simpson?"

I shook my head.

"The younger, Miss Maria, has become a favourite of Georgiana, and I saw her making her way through the crowd to join her. That will free Darcy from tending his sister."

"You said the *Misses* Simpson. Thus, I assume there are two?"

"Right you are. My young cousin has the wild idea that her brother is smitten with Miss Emily Simpson. I have yet to meet her, but I hear she is quite the beauty."

"Ah." I could think of nothing further to say, but evidently, my dissatisfaction was reflected in my expression.

"Why the frown, Miss Bennet? Does this air displease you?"

I instantly placed a smile upon my face. "Oh no, sir, simply a momentary pang. I am quite enjoying myself."

At the conclusion of the reel, Colonel Fitzwilliam introduced me to Captain Allen, a fellow officer from his unit who was brother to Miss Julia Allen, soon to become the colonel's sister-in-law. He promptly asked for my hand, and we spent the next half hour on the dance floor. When the music ended and we bowed in closing, the captain escorted me to the punch bowl, where he secured a cup for both of us. I had taken but a sip when I looked up to see Mr. Darcy approaching with a woman on his arm who was surely one of the most beautiful God ever made.

He introduced Miss Emily Simpson, and I, in turn, presented Captain Allen. My former partner immediately asked Miss Simpson for the next, and she smiled sweetly and accepted. We passed a few moments in light conversation until the instruments sounded. I watched Mr. Darcy's eyes follow the couple as they proceeded to the floor.

"Miss Simpson is a handsome woman," I said.

"She is." He continued to gaze at her, watching her graceful movements in the dance.

Of a sudden, the heat in the room became oppressive, and I opened my fan and began to use it.

"Pardon me, sir." I curtseyed briefly and turned to make my exit.

"Where do you go?"

"To join my aunt."

"Would you not rather step outside for some fresh air? I find it much too close in here."

"As you wish." I allowed him to lead me through the crowd toward the open doorway. Once we found a quiet area away from the others enjoying the breeze on the balcony, he turned directly toward me.

"It is time we talked. Do you agree?"

"Yes, sir, I do. I most certainly do."

Silently, I prayed, *Oh, God, temper my words with discretion. Do not let Mr. Darcy leave for Ireland if we remain at cross-purposes.*

Chapter Twelve

The moon was but a sliver that night. The stars, however, littered the dark sky in a profusion of light. I closed my fan, basking in the cool air as it gently ruffled my curls. I might have given myself up to the wonder of that beautiful night had not a pressing task beset me. I knew I must swallow my pride and apologize to Mr. Darcy. Taking a deep breath, I turned to face him.

"Sir, when we parted in Hertfordshire, I fear I spoke in anger. I did not mean to give offence."

"And I meant no slur upon your mother. You must believe me."

"You used the term 'degradation.' Surely, you know that I am somewhat sensitive because of the circumstances of my birth."

"Of course, I understand. Truly, I do. But you must perceive that I did not refer to your mother."

"Then to whom?"

"I referred to my father's behaviour—how a gentleman of his character could take advantage of a young girl. I consider *his* conduct degrading —degrading toward my mother, toward your mother, and toward himself. I cannot conceive of the father I knew acting in such a manner."

He braced his hands on the railing and raised his face to the sky as though the answer lay hidden somewhere in the heavens.

"I have not told you of the visit Miss Eleanor Willoughby paid me."

"Willoughby?" Mr. Darcy took a step closer. "Elizabeth, did she come to abuse you as her brother did?"

I raised my hand in protest. "No, no, nothing of the sort. She was entirely

the opposite: compassionate, gentle, and caring. She told me of my mother
—the kind of girl she was, her interests, her joys, and—"

"And what?"

"Oh, I do not know…other things. When our visit ended, I felt as though
I had a glimpse of my mother's spirit."

"Of what other things did she speak?" he insisted. "Did she tell you of
her relationship with my father?"

I met his gaze. He had turned just enough that the starlight revealed the
concern in his eyes. "She told me of how they met in the wood, how they
spent much time together, and how Miss Willoughby kept watch to warn
them if anyone approached."

Mr. Darcy slammed his fist down on the railing and let forth an oath.
He then asked my forgiveness for his language.

"Are you telling me my father not only seduced a young girl, but he used
her child of a sister to shield him from discovery? That is utterly reprehensible!"

He began to pace back and forth, possessed by anger. Instead of making
things better, I had wounded him even more. At length, he stilled and turned
back to me. "Is that all, or is there more you would tell me?"

It was now my turn to look away. I played with the tassel of my fan and
peered out into the darkness, up at the moon…anywhere rather than look
into his eyes.

"Elizabeth, tell me now. Delay will only postpone the effect."

"I cannot, sir."

"Why?"

"To do so will bring you even more pain while it eases mine."

I heard his sudden intake of breath. "He loved her."

I could do nothing other than bow my head.

Sleep was not my friend that night. Over and over, I played out the
conversation between Mr. Darcy and myself. I hated the suffering that Miss
Willoughby's words brought him and that I had been the one to reveal the
painful truth. In my memory, I saw him return me to Mrs. Gardiner's side
in the ballroom and then make his way to Colonel Fitzwilliam. With but
a few words in his ear, which I assumed secured the colonel's agreement to
tend Georgiana and return her home at the end of the evening, Mr. Darcy
stormed out the door of the Upper Rooms and into the night.

Of what good had been my apology? I had hoped to soothe the anguish I had inflicted upon him by my previous misunderstanding and our harsh exchange. Instead, I had cut him to the heart with the account of our parents. What would he do? Where would he go for comfort?

I heard not a word from either the Darcys or Colonel Fitzwilliam for three days. Mrs. Gardiner asked me whether Mr. Darcy and I had quarrelled at the ball, for she had noticed his swift departure after our return from the balcony. I told her the truth: we had not quarrelled. I refrained, however, from sharing what had transpired between us, although her curiosity was evident.

On the evening of that third day, after my aunt and uncle and I returned from dining, we were surprised when Mr. Darcy knocked at our door. It was rather late, and he apologized for calling at that hour, but I was so relieved to see him seemingly recovered from his ill spirits that I did not need an apology. Mrs. Gardiner offered him a glass of sherry, and we passed a few moments in idle conversation.

Upon the servant's removal from the room, Mr. Darcy asked whether he might speak to us concerning an important matter. My aunt offered to excuse herself from the discussion, but he requested that she remain. I was surprised and attempted to obtain some clue as to what he was about by searching his expression, but I remained ignorant.

He beckoned us to gather around the table, whereupon he drew out papers from his coat pocket. He then explained to the Gardiners how he and I had embarked upon a search through old journals, records, and correspondence at Pemberley, seeking further knowledge of my mother's identity. Now that we knew she was Elizabeth Willoughby, he had continued the quest about my birth without my aid at the homes of Lady Catherine, the Earl of Matlock, and Mrs. Harriet Darcy in Bath.

"And did you learn anything of interest at Rosings or Eden Park?" I asked.

"I learned to trust my instincts that we do not know the entire story. For some reason, Lady Catherine grew angrier the longer I questioned her, and at last, she openly refused to answer any more inquiries. At the Earl of Matlock's home, my uncle gave me free rein over letters from my father that he had saved through the years, but I found nothing of significance. I feel quite certain that my uncle remains uninformed in regard to the matter. In fact, he is curious as to your exact connection with the family."

Unfolding an obviously aged letter, he laid it on the table for us to examine.

"However, when I reached Bath, I found this among Henry Darcy's papers. He was my uncle, Mr. Gardiner, my father's youngest brother, and I am residing at his widow's house in Camden Place."

"What is the significance of these papers?" Mr. Gardiner asked.

"It is a letter written by my father to his brother Henry in which he mentions *the trouble*. It is dated but a fortnight before Elizabeth's birth."

"And you think *the trouble* refers to Lizzy's birth?"

"I do. Here, read it for yourself." He handed the letter to Mr. Gardiner, and his wife urged him to read it aloud.

22 November 1791
Pemberley
Dear Henry,

I am glad to hear you are making progress in your new undertaking. I feel certain you can make a new life and discover a fine future in the Navy if you will forget the past and apply yourself with all diligence. If you continue in your pursuit of the nearest pretty ankle as you did in Derbyshire, you will find…

"Well, perhaps I should skip that part," my uncle said.

"Yes, yes," Mr. Darcy agreed. "It is nothing more than brotherly advice. Begin with the third paragraph from the bottom, if you will, Mr. Gardiner."

Have you heard any news from Peter? I refuse to believe he has met with foul play, even though the authorities deem it most likely since we neither have seen nor heard from him since March. Unfortunately, here at Pemberley, hope dwindles as the days pass. Anne, in particular, has taken his disappearance with great affliction. She, along with our mother, always favoured him. I am thankful, now, that Mother has passed on. If the chill had not taken her in January, I fear the loss of Peter would. Even young Fitzwilliam seems to miss him. Of course, having both you and Peter depart within a few months of each other has proved difficult for the boy. He misses the sport with which you entertained him.

As to the urgent matter that presses upon me, Lady Margaret sent a message last evening. Time is growing nigh, and I fear I will be unable to keep the trouble from soon becoming evident to all. I must think of some way to conceal it from Anne. How I wish you were here. I miss your cockeyed assumption that all will turn out well, however misguided it might be, and of course, Peter—oh, Peter! With his steadfast faith, he could always give me hope and provide the answers, especially in this instance. Do you not recall days gone by when together, the three of us—the Darcy brothers—could solve any problem that beset one of us! I understand your absence. We agreed it was best—but I, as well as others, suffer Peter's desertion most acutely. The burden of secrecy regarding the trouble weighs upon me, but I shall persevere. Whatever she decides, I shall attempt to do what I think is best.

If you have any word from Peter, alert me immediately, I pray you.

"It is signed, *your brother, George Darcy.*"

"What do you make of it, Mr. Gardiner?" Mr. Darcy asked.

"I hardly know. I agree that *the trouble* apparently refers to Lizzy's impending birth, but it appears your father did not keep his parentage hidden from his brothers."

"Nor did he keep it secret from Sir Lewis de Bourgh," I added. "Is that all? Did you find any added reference among the admiral's papers?"

"I did. Look at this journal entry written in my uncle's hand."

He extended a worn, leather-bound book to me. I read it and handed it to Mr. Gardiner, who shared it with my aunt.

"It would seem Admiral Darcy is the one who eventually found Peter," Mr. Darcy said.

"The entry states he located his brother when he harboured in County Cork, Ireland on 2 June 1805," my uncle said, continuing to read aloud.

"The port is Co...what is the name?" Mrs. Gardiner said. "I cannot make it out."

"Cobh," Mr. Darcy said. "Elizabeth, I have scoured my uncle's maps and learned that Cobh is not all that far from the town in which our grandmother, Siobhan Darcy, was born and reared."

Mr. Gardiner handed the book to Mr. Darcy. "Then, at the time this was written, Mr. Peter Darcy had returned to an area near his mother's home."

"Exactly. This discovery affirms my decision to travel to Ireland and find Uncle Peter."

I turned away from the table and took a few steps toward the settee on which I had previously sat.

"Elizabeth, are you not pleased with my find?"

"Yes, of course. I just fail to understand the necessity of your making a difficult trip to Ireland to visit your uncle. What good will it do to question him after all these years?"

"Where does your uncle live now, Mr. Darcy?" Mr. Gardiner asked.

"According to a Derbyshire clergyman—to be honest, a Catholic priest —who corresponds with a fellow priest in that area of Ireland, Peter Darcy still dwells in County Cork. He lives in my grandmother's birthplace, a small village called Ballymeghan. To answer your question, Elizabeth, this letter from my father to Uncle Henry proves, as we considered earlier tonight, that he shared knowledge of your birth with him. Doubtless, by now, Uncle Peter knows as well and can enlighten me on the matter."

"Are you settled that Mr. Peter Darcy knows?" I asked. "From the date of that entry in the journal, Admiral Darcy did not find his brother until I had reached the age of fourteen. After all those years, do you think the admiral would have spent their brief time together speaking of your father's disgrace that had been disposed of long before? I do not. I think they would much rather have spoken of lawful family events: Georgiana's birth, your mother's passing, and the admiral's own marriage. From all accounts, I think the Darcy family forgot me as easily as one forgets the rubbish tossed out at the end of the day."

"Lizzy!" Mrs. Gardiner exclaimed, rushing to my side. Anxiety descended upon Mr. Darcy's face, and he, too, started toward me.

My uncle, however, detained him. "Mr. Darcy, was there no correspond- ence from your father to the admiral after that journal entry, perhaps seeking an address for his brother in Ireland?"

"I did not find one, sir, but I do recall receiving a letter from my father when I was at Cambridge, informing me that Uncle Peter had been found alive and well in Ireland. That was the first time I learned of my uncle's conversion to Catholicism and how my grandmother helped him to leave England. Other than being grateful my uncle was well, I thought little of the matter at the time. Unfortunately, my father died the next year, and Uncle Henry's death occurred only three years later."

He turned back and crossed the room until he stood before me. "Eliza- beth, I do not know why, but I cannot cast off the feeling that we might find the answers we seek in Ireland."

"Sir, you take a severe measure upon yourself in order to satisfy your curiosity. Most likely, it will all come to naught. I pray you will let this go."

"I cannot. And I cannot believe that my entire family *forgot you* as you say, but I must know for my own peace of mind. If there is more information out there, I shall have it."

He walked to the fireplace, placed his arm upon the mantel, and fixed a gaze upon me of such tender concern that I felt my heart beat faster.

"And if it turns out that your fears are correct," Mr. Darcy said, "that the previous Darcy generation did simply put you out of their minds, then I assure you...the present one shall never do so."

"Pray, excuse me," I murmured. Turning, I fled above stairs to my bedchamber.

I sank down upon the window seat and pushed open the panes, gasping in the night air. My chest ached, and I could not seem to get enough air. I raised my eyes to the heavens. I had to accept the truth that my existence caused pain to the person I loved most in the world, and now he would even travel to another country because of me.

Why must Mr. Darcy persist in this endless quest for answers he most likely would never find? When would he not acknowledge that his father was not the man he thought him to be? Why must he spend his days searching for God knows what? George Darcy callously committed adultery with a seventeen-year-old girl, and I was the consequence. Avoidance of the truth brought nothing but anguish. Acceptance of it brought misery. There could be no happy ending.

I began to weep. I know not how long I sat at the window until a knock at the door startled me. My aunt entered the room and hurried to my side when she saw my tears. She pulled me into her embrace and laid my head on her shoulder, all the while patting my back and murmuring soothing phrases. At length, I drew back, wiping my eyes.

"Has he gone?" I whispered.

"Yes, Lizzy." She rose, walked to the bed, and straightened the pillow. Beckoning to me, she gestured toward the sofa. We settled ourselves against the cushions before she spoke again. "Now, my dear, I believe a serious talk between us has been long delayed."

"What do you mean?"

"I mean what exactly is Mr. Darcy about?"

"I do not understand."

"Do not feign ignorance, Lizzy. We are both too intelligent to fool each other."

"I would never attempt to fool you, Aunt."

She sighed. "Not intentionally, of course, but, dearest, we both know Mr. Darcy's passion to determine the circumstances of your natural father and mother's relationship has gone too far. He is like a man obsessed!"

"I asked him not to undertake it on my behalf."

"He no longer acts on your behalf, Lizzy. Mr. Darcy seeks to satisfy himself, and I can think of only one reason why he remains steadfast in his pursuit."

I said not a word, for I feared what she would say next.

"My dear, ever since we met Mr. Darcy at Pemberley last year and witnessed his attentions to you, your uncle and I have suspected he was in love with you. Then, when he took it upon himself to rescue poor Lydia from Mr. Wickham, we felt certain that our suspicions were correct. I even hinted as much in my letter to you at the time. Do I speak the truth? Is he in love with you?"

I looked away, unwilling to face her. "Mr. Darcy has vowed that his affection for me is that of a brother."

"And has he been able to keep that vow?"

I closed my eyes and laid my head against the back of the sofa. "Do not ask me that. Only he can answer that question."

"As I thought," she murmured.

I sat up quickly. "Pray, do not think that he has acted in an untoward manner. Mr. Darcy is every bit a gentleman."

"I never doubted that. What I wonder is how you feel in return."

"What difference does it make how I feel? The situation is immovable. We masquerade as cousins, but, in truth, we are brother and sister. Whatever we may have felt in the past—or even now—must be repressed. To do otherwise is unthinkable."

Mrs. Gardiner rose and closed the window, securing the latch. "I thank you for your honesty. It confirms my decision tonight."

"What decision is that?"

"Mr. Darcy has spent the last half-hour in an attempt to persuade your uncle and me to allow you to accompany Georgiana and him to Ireland. My instincts forbade it, and now I know they were correct. It would be far too dangerous for you to spend that much time in his company."

"I never agreed to go to Ireland. I wonder why he is so insistent."

"He *said* he wanted you to meet your uncle Peter Darcy, for he is your father's only living brother. I, however, wonder whether he has admitted the true reason even to himself."

I looked away again. "You suspect him of some improper purpose, Aunt?"

"I suspect he would do anything to keep you beside him. I suspect he thinks he acts from only the highest and most noble motives, but I do not believe he knows himself. He is either unwilling or unable to face the truth. One does not banish feelings of love by a simple stroke of will."

"I know that better than anyone," I whispered.

"The only saving grace for both of you lies in placing distance between you. We must leave Bath. We must return you to Longbourn, or if that will not suffice, you may travel on to London with us. You must find someone else, Lizzy, and so must Mr. Darcy."

THE NEXT MORNING, THE RAINS began in earnest. The weather suited my mood, for my spirits remained as dark as the clouds hovering over the city. After breakfast, my aunt and I began the task of packing. We directed the maid in her duties, but since we had come prepared for several weeks' visit, too many tasks existed for one person to complete quickly. I sent her to Mrs. Gardiner's chamber and undertook the job of filling the trunk with my belongings. It felt good to stay busy. Even though I was weary from a sleepless night, my greatest fear was time to sit idle and think.

When we ceased our duties for tea, I noticed that my aunt had carried her bonnet and shawl into the parlour.

"Are you going out in this weather?" I asked.

"I have exhausted my supply of tonic, Lizzy. I cannot think of enduring that journey to Hertfordshire without it."

"Why not send the maid?"

"With all she has to do? She cannot spare the time if we are to depart on the morrow."

"Then, allow me to go for you. I need fresh air, even if it is damp, and it is but a short walk to the apothecary."

The rain continued as I opened my umbrella and set out. My skirts were mussed by the time I reached the shop, and I hurried inside, relieved to reach shelter. Several people shopped within, and thus, I was forced to wait for my purchase.

I sighed as I thought of our leave-taking. Mrs. Gardiner did not think I should meet with Mr. Darcy before we left. I had written a note to Georgiana and instructed the servant to deliver it after we had gone. I felt guilty as though, once again, I was stealing away, but my good sense agreed that it was a prudent decision. Mr. Darcy would have exerted all efforts to change my mind. But, oh, I hated to think of him travelling such a great distance.

At last, my turn at the counter arrived, and I quickly paid for my purchase. Just as I reached the door, who should open it for me but Colonel Fitzwilliam!

Oh no, I thought, *not him again!*

"Miss Bennet, what a fortunate meeting! I was on my way to call upon your aunt, and I hoped to see you. There is something important that I would speak to you about."

"'Tis too bad that you should call today, Colonel."

"And why is that?"

"My aunt is not receiving visitors this afternoon."

"Is she ill? I see that you have been to the apothecary."

"I purchased a remedy for her. Pardon my haste, sir, but I must return to the house directly."

"I hope Mrs. Gardiner recovers quickly. I—"

"I shall relate your greetings. I bid you farewell, sir."

I hurried up the street, leaving him standing alone, his hat in his hand. *That was not quite a lie,* I told myself, *but less than the truth.* Aunt Gardiner said I must marry, and perhaps I should reconsider Colonel Fitzwilliam, but not now. I was in no mood to make a choice that day.

Upon entering the house, I heard my aunt's and uncle's voices coming from the parlour. I was surprised that Mr. Gardiner had returned so early, for at the breakfast table, he had declared that our sudden departure would force him to spend the entire day completing his final business obligations. I handed my bonnet and umbrella to the servant and walked into the room.

"Then, Edward, you must allow Lizzy and me to return to Hertfordshire without you."

"I shall not. You know I had to return Bonner to London to take over for Jensen. We no longer have a man-servant to accompany you, and I cannot have my wife and niece travel without escort."

"Is there not some way you might delay your business trip? Could you not take us home first?"

I cleared my throat. "Should I excuse myself, Uncle? Do I intrude?"

"Of course not, Lizzy. Come in," Mr. Gardiner said. "Since you will learn of this soon enough, you may as well hear it now."

I could not imagine of what he spoke, but my aunt wore a crestfallen expression.

"You will never believe this, Lizzy," she said, throwing her hands up in the air.

"Goodness! Tell me what has happened."

"An important shipment I expected today has been lost," my uncle said.

"And where—of all places?" my aunt added, shaking her head. "Off the Irish coast!"

"Due to rank incompetence! The entire operation in Ireland must be looked into and corrected if I am to continue trading with that company."

"That is not all," my aunt said. "Your uncle insists he must travel to Ireland to personally rectify the situation. Immediately!"

"Madeline, I have explained repeatedly that I shall lose a great amount of money if I do not take care of the matter. Attempting to certify by post that business is done correctly obviously does not work. The merchandise is essential. I have promised large orders of fine Irish linen and glass to my best customers. If I do not deliver, my competitors will gobble them up before my eyes. And, in addition, I am sorry to admit that a substantial portion of my business is dependent upon the consignment of wool alone and the assurance that I receive subsequent shipments from the area in an appropriate manner. It requires my personal attention. I trust no one else to complete the task."

I sank down upon the settee. "What does this mean, Uncle? Shall my aunt and I remain here in Bath while you make the trip?"

He picked up his cup of tea and took a sip. "I cannot feel right about leaving you here alone for that long a time."

"Then, what shall we do?"

My aunt sat down in the chair across from me. "Lizzy, Edward says we must accompany him to Ireland."

My eyes widened. "Uncle, could you not send for your man-servant to return? Surely, my aunt and I might remain here until he arrives from

London, and then he could take us to Longbourn."

"Bonner returned to Town this morning to take the place of my steward, Jensen. I must have someone I trust in charge of the house while we are gone. I received word from Jensen last week that his widowed sister died, leaving orphaned children. There is no one else in his family who can step in and take care of the matter. Since we were travelling and our youngsters are with your parents, I gave him a month's leave to see them settled. I can hardly go back on my word and take him from such a demanding responsibility simply to escort you home. As for your father, well, we all know he hates to travel more than any man I know."

"I doubt that Thomas would put himself out to fetch us," Mrs. Gardiner said, "for Fanny writes that he is gouty again."

"All the more reason for Papá to come to Bath. Are not the hot springs the perfect antidote?"

My aunt shook her head. "Not for your father."

"Oh yes," I said with a sigh. "I forgot that he considers the baths nothing more than the remedy of charlatans."

"Your mother says his humour is ill, indeed, and you know how he detests travel. He made his yearly trip to Town when he brought you home last month. I cannot see him leaving the comfort of his library so soon to embark on a long trip to and from Bath when he is ailing. Besides, Fanny will be cross if he leaves her at home with a houseful of children, even though we both know he provides little help. Still, she must have someone to whom she may complain."

I sighed, knowing my aunt spoke the truth. "Well, this cannot be an impossible dilemma. Surely, we can discover some solution to the problem other than a difficult journey across the Irish Sea. Why, that would take a long time, indeed. May we not sleep on the matter? An answer may come to one of us by the morrow."

"I cannot put off the trip, Lizzy," Mr. Gardiner chided, "for us to bide our time, conjuring up an answer out of nowhere!"

"I did not mean to offend you. I simply—"

"I know, I know, my dear. Forgive my short temper. This entire predicament has sorely tried my patience. I simply must reach Ireland without delay!"

None of us said anything more for a good quarter hour. My uncle opened his file and began to rummage through his papers. Spreading the purchase orders, bills, and correspondence across the table, he sighed more than once as he pored over them. The longer he studied the records, the more agitated his expression grew. My aunt refilled his cup of tea, but he waved it away with an air of vexation. She turned a questioning gaze toward me, but all I could do was shrug my shoulders. It appeared that we did not have a choice if Mr. Gardiner was to save his business.

At last, he straightened up and faced us. Removing his glasses, he rubbed his eyes. "There simply is no other answer. I must set off immediately, and both of you must go with me, for I shall not leave you unprotected in this large city. I met with Mr. Darcy an hour ago, and he says he can secure passage for us on the ship upon which he will sail."

"Mr. Darcy!" I exclaimed.

My uncle walked across the room, sat down in the chair across from me, and leaned forward.

"Now, Lizzy, I know your aunt discussed with you our belief that you should avoid his company, but in this matter, I am afraid we must avail ourselves of the gentleman's assistance. It is not the ideal solution, but as long as Madeline and I accompany you, we shall lessen your chances of being alone with him."

"I do not like it, Edward," my aunt said.

"If there were any other solution, my dear, do you not think I would seize hold of it?"

"Do not alarm yourselves on my account, I pray you," I said, rising. "I have dwelt in Mr. Darcy's presence much of this year. I am not afraid of him. I know he will keep his sentiments under good regulation."

"Of course," Mr. Gardiner agreed. "And with all of us making the journey, along with his sister and her companion, all should go well. Let us put aside our fears and make the best of it. I suggest you both write to Fanny tonight and console her with the happy thought that our children shall be hers for the duration."

FOUR DAYS LATER, WE BOARDED Mr. Darcy's carriages for the long trip to Holyhead. It was a tiring journey in itself, taking many days on difficult roads, and by the time we reached our destination, my aunt and Mrs. Annesley both suffered from the experience.

We recovered at the inn at Holyhead for two days and, at last, walked onto the deck of *The Falcon*, a passenger ship embarking for Dublin.

I could not help but be excited at the prospect before us. I had little experience with the sea, for I had never been aboard any boat other than a ferry. The brisk ocean breeze seemed to dispel my dark mood. Since childhood, I had possessed a cheerful perspective, and by that time, I wearied of the continuous ill temper that had plagued me for so long. If I had to make the trip, I might as well attempt to enjoy it. Thus, I began to anticipate visiting a different country with some degree of keenness. After all, what did I have to return home to?

Once, during the expedition across Wales, I wondered why I had not suggested that my uncle ask Colonel Fitzwilliam to take us back to Longbourn. He would have provided the perfect escort and saved my aunt and me from the voyage. An argument might be that I did not want to encourage the colonel in his pursuit of my hand. However, if I was honest, I had to admit that I was selfish, for I dreaded the long absence from Mr. Darcy even more than I wished to spare him my company.

I still could not see a favourable resolution to our situation, but simply being in his presence and that of Georgiana made me feel better. He was obviously pleased that I was making the journey, no matter the reason why. At each stop along the way to Holyhead, whenever we had met, his optimism seemed to spill over onto me. I could not see any sensible hope in his quest, but then, hope sometimes has a mind of its own.

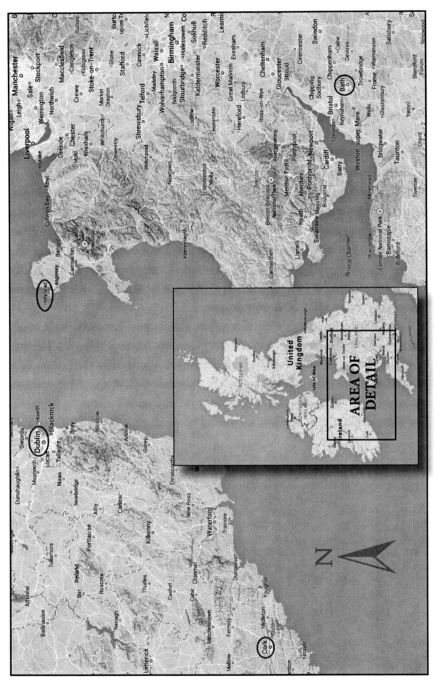

Trip to Ireland: map of significant locations

Chapter Thirteen

The infamously rough crossing of the Irish Sea meant that *mal de mer* beset some of the men and most of the ladies on board *The Falcon*, including Mrs. Gardiner, Georgiana, and Mrs. Annesley. Miraculously, I escaped, as did my uncle and Mr. Darcy. I kept busy by directing the maid in tending my aunt for much of the voyage and prayed for deliverance from the treacherous waves. Our passage had surely proved to be a challenge thus far.

At last, however, the storms abated, and we enjoyed smooth sailing. I had been confined below deck for so long that when we were told we might emerge to take the air, I could not wait to climb the stairs. My aunt remained too weak to rise from her bed but for short periods, as did Mrs. Annesley. Georgiana, however, recovered more quickly, and she was as eager as I to distance herself from the detention we had been forced to endure.

The fresh sea air enticed us, and we hastened to the railing to breathe deeply and watch the waves. The ocean appeared much calmer. One found it hard to reconcile the idea that it was the same sea that had tossed us about with such recklessness only the day before. Unexpected, infrequent wind gusts still occurred, however, causing me to catch my breath when the ship pitched sharply.

Georgiana exclaimed when we caught glimpses of the creatures beneath the surface of the water. A number of basking sharks lurked within sight, a fearsome spectacle that covered my arms in gooseflesh.

"Those great, voracious fish are an awesome sight," Mr. Darcy said, having joined us without my notice.

"Oh, Wills, would it not be dreadful to fall into the sea?"

"All the more reason you must take care and not venture too near the edge. Shall you and Elizabeth join me in a stroll? I could benefit from the exercise."

"An excellent suggestion," I said, "for I have been longing for a walk to restore my energy."

"As well as your spirit, I would wager." He smiled and offered one arm to his younger sister and one to me.

Several times, we walked the length of the deck as far as passengers were allowed. Before making the final return, we stopped to watch the busy seamen alternating sails and stowing ropes. I craned my neck and shaded my eyes with my hand in order to follow a sailor as he scrambled up the rigging to the mast and climbed into the crow's nest. What a view he must have had from that lofty perch!

At that moment, the man cupped his hand to his mouth and cried, "Land ho!"

Immediately, all eyes turned westward, where he was pointing. We hurried toward the bow and searched the horizon. Neither my sister nor I could see it, but Mr. Darcy fixed on a faint outline. Georgiana declared she must share the news with Mrs. Annesley, for she felt certain it would aid her companion's recovery to know our deliverance was nigh. She hastened toward the hatch and soon disappeared below stairs.

Aware that Mr. Darcy and I were alone, I started to withdraw my hand from his arm when, suddenly, the ship lurched upward and then immediately downward, having encountered a particularly large swell. I felt myself sway and lose my balance. I could not refrain from falling against Mr. Darcy. Instinctively, his arms encircled me. Within moments, he had steadied us both, but not before we had been thrust against each other. The scent of his skin enveloped me. I could feel the powerful strength in his arms, and I began to tremble.

"Do not fear, Elizabeth, you are safe with me," he said into my ear.

I stepped back, knowing that I was not. Yes, he might protect me from the sea, but who would shield me from the forbidden emotions he unleashed within my heart?

"I...should return to my aunt and see to her needs."

"If you wish. Allow me to escort you to the stairs."

"No, I am now quite well, sir. I can make my way unaided."

Without meeting his gaze, I turned and fled below. Hearing steps behind me, I turned to see that Mr. Gardiner had followed from above deck. He wore a decided frown.

"Uncle, is something wrong?"

"A moment with you, Lizzy, if you please." He led me into the empty dining hall. "My dear, I question the wisdom of the scene I just witnessed."

"What scene do you speak of?"

"Finding you within Mr. Darcy's embrace."

I felt the heat of a blush rise up my neck and burn my cheeks. "It...happened in all innocence, sir. The sudden movement of the ship almost caused me to fall, and it forced me against the gentleman. He meant no untoward behaviour. He simply attempted to assist me in securing my balance."

"Yes, I saw it all, Lizzy. He, however, did not release you as quickly as he might have. As we discussed before, I think it best if you avoid his presence as much as possible."

"That will prove difficult in these confined quarters."

"Still, I counsel you not to be alone with him." He patted my shoulder somewhat awkwardly. "I do not accuse Mr. Darcy of impropriety. I simply remind you of the concern your aunt and I expressed in Bath. You must neither encourage nor tempt the gentleman in any manner."

Tempt him!

I bit my tongue to refrain from making a sharp retort. He said no more and signified that we should return to our cabins. Once my door closed behind me, I sank down upon the narrow bed. For some time, I fumed silently at the suggestion that I had purposely led Mr. Darcy astray or that he had done anything amiss. Eventually, after I calmed myself and took time to examine the situation, I could see the wisdom in my uncle's words. If Mr. Darcy had not truly renounced his romantic feelings toward me, and if I were honest, I doubted that he had, I should do all in my power to help him accomplish the feat. The question remained: Who would assist *me* in conquering my own love for him?

Oh, why had Mr. Gardiner insisted that I make this trip? We would be thrown together constantly, and I trembled anew at the thrill I had felt when held within Mr. Darcy's warm embrace. My aunt and uncle were correct. No matter how I would miss him, 'twas more prudent for us to be apart.

The sensible side of me acknowledged that things would be easier once we left the ship, for after we reached Dublin, Mr. Darcy and Georgiana would travel on to Cork.

As I HAVE COME TO learn, what I expected did not happen.

After Mr. Gardiner met with several of his business connections in Dublin, he determined that the majority of the goods my uncle had ordered were literally manufactured in County Cork, and the entire shipment had set sail from the nearby harbour at Cobh. From the intelligence he was given, Mr. Gardiner learned that, if negligence had occurred, it would have transpired in Cork City. Thus, we would be forced to travel south in a hired carriage to the same county where my grandmother had been born and very near the place to which Mr. Darcy journeyed. The moment I heard the name of our destination, my mouth fell open.

"Impossible," I murmured when Mr. Gardiner told me. *Are Mr. Darcy and I destined to be thrown together?*

"We have been invited to dine with Mr. Darcy and his sister tonight, Lizzy," my aunt said. "But I fear I do not feel well enough to go out." She had not regained her strength from the sea voyage and had remained inside our lodgings the entire week we had been in Dublin.

"Then I shall stay with you."

"Oh no, my dear, for you have been confined inside these rooms far too long. You must accompany your uncle this evening."

"I have been out now and then. Do you not recall that I took a long walk this morning? I watched the traffic on the River Liffey."

"That is not the same as engaging in good conversation with someone other than me, Lizzy. I insist that you go along with Edward and visit with Miss Darcy. I am certain she longs for your company. She seems to come alive in your presence."

"As does her brother," my uncle added.

"That is why I shall remain here, sir," I announced. "I shall not have you fretting over my being in Mr. Darcy's company all evening."

He smiled. "I shall not fret, Lizzy. Mr. Darcy and I have travel plans to discuss. You will not be alone together, so I see no reason for you to decline the invitation."

Thus, a few hours later, I changed my gown, fussed with my hair, pinched my cheeks, and bade Aunt Gardiner good night, for she said that she would be abed by the time we returned. The carriage transported us from the Norfolk Hotel on the north side of the city into the centre of town. The Darcys were in residence at the exclusive Gresham Hotel on Sackville Street, Dublin's main thoroughfare.

Inside, candles glowed throughout, casting a shimmering glow over the sumptuous room, accenting its modern splendour. Crystal, fine bone china, and well-polished silver sparkled on every table. I was surprised to find the accommodations rivalled any I had seen in London, for I possessed the English prejudice that Ireland remained a poor, backward nation. Perhaps we would find that to be true in the countryside but certainly not in that area of the capital city.

Mr. Darcy and Georgiana descended the magnificent staircase, and her eyes lit up when she saw us approach from across the room. After greetings were exchanged, we were immediately shown to our table in the main dining room. Mr. Gardiner explained his wife's absence, and Georgiana sympathized, saying that Mrs. Annesley also still suffered the effects of the trip. The evening passed pleasantly enough, and I noticed that Mr. Darcy seemed in exceptionally good spirits. He was completely at ease with my uncle, and oft times when I looked up, he bestowed a smile upon me.

"Is this not good fortune that we shall travel to Cork together?" he said.

"It will prove beneficial for us," Mr. Gardiner said, "for now I shall not have to navigate the route alone. I confess I sometimes feel that the Irish do not even speak English. Their brogue garbles the language something fierce, and they appear to use an excessive number of words to convey a single thought. I often feel as if they speak to me in riddles."

"They do speak their own version of our mother tongue," Mr. Darcy agreed with a smile. Just then, a hotel porter appeared with a note for him, which he read quickly. "Have the package delivered to my apartment." The porter bowed and disappeared.

Our meal was drawing to a close when Mr. Darcy asked whether my uncle and I might visit with him in his private rooms above stairs.

"Well, sir, the hour grows late," Mr. Gardiner answered.

"It will not take long. I wish to show you something that I consider important."

"Splendid!" Georgiana said. "Elizabeth and I shall not yet be forced to part."

Mr. Darcy, however, thwarted his young sister's plans. "You, my dear, must retire for the evening. You have kept far too late hours ever since we arrived. I insist that you rest up for the journey ahead."

Even though she protested, he remained firm in his decision, and so it was that Mr. Gardiner and I joined Mr. Darcy in the parlour of his lodgings while Georgiana went to her chambers.

After my uncle accepted his offer of sherry and I declined, Mr. Darcy had the servant retrieve a thick packet that had obviously just arrived by post. Placing it upon the table, he opened it quickly. "Perfect! My steward sent precisely what I requested."

I turned to Mr. Gardiner, who sat beside me on the sofa with a questioning look, but he appeared no more knowledgeable than I.

Mr. Darcy took several bound books from the package and brought them with him as he sat down on the chair nearest the sofa. "These books are what I wished you to see."

My uncle put down his glass. "Atlases we may use in our travels?"

"No, nothing like that. These, sir, are several of my father's diaries."

"Diaries!" I said. "I thought our search at Pemberley proved fruitless."

"We found no additional books that I had not previously canvassed. I did not show you these, Elizabeth, because I did not think they held anything of note concerning your birth. However—"

"You have had second thoughts, sir?" my uncle prodded.

"I have. I read these books for the first time in the year following my father's funeral. My mood was dark with grief for months after I lost him, and I found solace reading the ordinary jottings my father had made note of through the years. Most entries pertained to management of the estate and his other holdings, but now and then, I was delighted to find lengthy, personal notations about my mother and myself, and in later volumes, he wrote of Georgiana as she grew up. He did not write on a daily basis; he often allowed weeks between posts. But if one reads carefully, one finds a consistent testimony of his life contained therein."

"And yet, you say that he never mentioned my birth. Then why, sir, have you now changed your mind? Why should these books be of interest to us?"

"Before we left Bath, I began to ponder that question. Why had my father never marked such an important occurrence?"

"Well, naturally, because he wished to keep it hidden."

"A pertinent conclusion, and one I shared…until I remembered—"

"Remembered what, sir?"

"Pages are missing from these books."

"Missing? How do you know?"

"See for yourself." He held a book open for us to see. "Look closely. Can you not see that pages have been torn out? And not just in this book. In several volumes, there are remnants of torn pages left behind."

Mr. Gardiner took the book from his outstretched hand and examined it closely. "Why should that signify anything of importance, Mr. Darcy? Perchance your father simply made an ink blot and wished to begin anew."

"A possibility, sir, but as I considered making this journey to Ireland, I also wondered why my father had not told me more about finding his brother after all those years. For that matter, why had he not written more about it in the diaries? Here, observe this one." He rummaged through the stack until he found a volume marked 1805. "There is but one entry made about Peter Darcy this entire year. Pray, read it aloud, Elizabeth."

I smoothed the page open and followed his finger to the appointed place.

14 July 1805

Received letter from Henry this date. Peter is alive! He has found him near, of all places, Mother's birthplace in Ireland. Says he is well. After all these years, I rejoice. My brother, who was dead, is alive. If only he could return to Pemberley, we would kill the fatted calf, put a ring upon his finger, invite the neighbours, and hold a feast. Alas...

"And that is where the next page is removed," Mr. Darcy interrupted. "See!"

"I do," I answered. "But what significance does it hold?"

"From then on, my father never makes mention of Peter again. Not any-where—not in a single diary he kept thereafter. Does that not seem strange?"

"And it appears he either did not finish his thoughts in this entry," Mr. Gardiner added, "or—"

"Or, for some reason, he thought it best to remove what he had written," Mr. Darcy finished. "And that is not all." He picked up another book. "The year of your birth, Elizabeth, Father writes about Peter's disappearance in March. He tells of his distress and the anguish it causes my mother. Here, listen to this.

24 March 1791

Returned to Pemberley from London this night. What Wickham (Mr. Wickham, Sr., was his steward at the time) *wrote in his letter to me is true—Peter is nowhere to be found and has been missing ten days. Anne is growing ill with worry. Tomorrow, I will begin the search with visits to the neighbours, and I pray I must not call in the detectives. Oh, merciful God, let this be some foolish prank he is playing. If it is, however, I shall have his hide!*

"That year, over and over again, from March until the middle of June, my father writes of his unsuccessful search for his brother, and then…evidence of discarded pages begins. Throughout the book, pages have been removed."

Mr. Gardiner rose and refilled his glass from the decanter of sherry. "I think a simple explanation may exist for the volume written in 1791. By the time the summer months arrived, your father's despair over finding your uncle gave way to the dilemma facing him over Lizzy's birth. He could have noted her expected arrival but then discarded his observations so that no evidence remained to connect him to her in any way."

"Except that Sir Lewis de Bourgh failed to destroy the one letter Mr. George Darcy wrote about my birth," I said.

"One would draw those conclusions," Mr. Darcy said, "if our suppositions are correct."

I sighed and leaned back against the sofa. "How are we ever to discover any other answer, sir?"

Mr. Darcy rose and returned the diaries to the table. "That is why I have come to Ireland. If Peter Darcy does not hold the key, then I have nowhere else to turn."

"Key to what?" I asked, irritation in my voice. "Surely, you do not hope to have your father's name cleared, do you? Have we not seen proof enough of his participation in the deed?"

"What *proof* have we seen? Lady Catherine has produced a letter—"

"Written by Mr. George Darcy," Mr. Gardiner said.

"True, but examine it again, if you will." He withdrew the letter from his coat pocket and handed it to my uncle. I rose and stood beside him, looking on while he read. "Not once does my father say that the child in question is his."

"But Lady Catherine said—"

"Yes, yes, I know." He waved his hand as though to dismiss my words. "My aunt most definitely had her say."

My uncle looked up from his reading. "Are you saying that you doubt the veracity of Lady Catherine?"

"No...no, I would not disparage her in that manner. Oh, I do not know what I am saying, except for one thing."

I held my breath, wondering what he could mean and what he might say next.

"Lady Catherine is concealing something. She would brook no questions concerning the details of what Sir Lewis told her about the night he carried Elizabeth to Hertfordshire. Repeatedly, she said it was none of my affair." His voice rose in volume. "None of my affair! I ask you, if it is none of my affair, then whose?"

Mr. Gardiner and I exchanged looks, and I could see the concern on my uncle's face. "Mr. Darcy, the hour does grow late," he said. "I believe we must depart."

"I apologize for keeping you," he replied, looking somewhat surprised that we should wish to leave.

We made our farewells, and the two men agreed to meet on the morrow to discuss the final details of our travel plans. Mr. Darcy appeared preoccupied and proved quite hasty in his final remarks. I descended the stairs, my mind in a muddle.

In the carriage, my uncle remained silent for some time. I wondered what he was thinking, but in some ways, I did not care to know.

"Lizzy," he said at last. "Do you think that you are George Darcy's daughter?"

What?

"I...well, yes, of course. Lady Catherine said I was, and I have not seen any evidence to dispute her word. Why do you ask me that?"

"Because I strongly suspect that Mr. Darcy no longer believes you are his sister."

THAT NIGHT, I SLEPT LITTLE. My uncle's statement whirled around and around in my head. Could it possibly be? Might I be the daughter of someone other than George Darcy? No. I had not seen one thing to make me think that. Yet, I had seen much to support the fact that I was his daughter. Lady Catherine stated it as fact most assuredly. The letter that George Darcy wrote to Sir Lewis would certainly lead one to believe that I was his child. Mr. Fawcett said I was the natural child of a gentleman from the North Country. Eleanor Willoughby said my father was called Darcy, and I bore a distinct resemblance to George Darcy's mother, Siobhan.

If George Darcy was not my father, who could it be? I allowed my mind to wander freely. What if Lady Catherine had tried to mask her husband's infidelity? Perhaps while visiting Derbyshire long ago, Sir Lewis met my mother and lied, telling her his name was Darcy. He evidently had relied upon George Darcy for help in the past. Was it because he had been faithless in his marriage vows? Could I have been his mistake? I shuddered at the thought. I had never met Sir Lewis, but I could not imagine that young girl I had seen in the portrait attaching herself to a man married to Lady Catherine. If so, why would George Darcy have worded his letter in the manner that he did? *Tonight, I must beg leave to call in all favours you owe me.* No, that did not make sense, and Eleanor Willoughby never mentioned that her sister even knew Sir Lewis. It could not be him.

Siobhan had two other sons besides George: Henry and Peter. I knew nothing really of Peter, other than he converted to the Catholic religion, and he wished to live in his mother's homeland so much so that he ran away rather than risk his brother's disapproval. I doubted that he was responsible for my birth, for it appeared that he cared little for anyone in Derbyshire. He did not even write to his family once he settled himself in his new home. I had the impression that he must have been a serious-minded, solitary man, not one who would trifle with a neighbour's young daughter.

Henry, however, was handsome, headstrong, and had an eye for the ladies. Could he have been the Darcy my mother met secretly in the wood at Pemberley? And if so, did his widow know of my existence? Perhaps she feared that, if she revealed the truth, it would damage her late husband's good name. Had she encouraged her nephew to travel to Ireland on an endless quest only to prevent his discovery of the truth in Bath?

My head ached at the possibilities, and I punched my pillow with all the confusion that possessed me. What good would come from hoping for what could never be? Why dare to contemplate the idea that George Darcy was not my father, only to have it snatched away from me? The girl I had been a year ago might have dreamed such a dream, but I no longer possessed that girl's faith. It had died in the garden at Longbourn when Lady Catherine came to call.

We departed Dublin three days later. Mrs. Gardiner had regained a bit of her strength by that time, and I hoped that the subsequent journey would not assign her to bed once again. Our carriage followed behind that of Mr. Darcy, but oft times, Georgiana and Mrs. Annesley exchanged places with Mr. Gardiner. It proved a merry exchange when four women travelled without men to overhear the conversation. I was surprised, but not displeased, that Mrs. Annesley entered into the dialogue much more freely at those times.

"And how do you like Ireland?" my aunt asked her.

"Much more than that sea voyage. I was never so glad to feel firm ground beneath my feet in all my days!"

That provoked a spirited discussion between the two older women of the ills they had experienced aboard ship.

Georgiana took the opportunity to speak to me about how charming she found the country. I marvelled at the changes I had seen come over her since first we met last year. That shy, quiet young girl had blossomed, becoming much more confident and animated. She spoke of her future debut the next spring and insisted that I go to London and accompany her to teas, balls, and other social gatherings.

"Would you not rather have someone by your side who is more accustomed to such events? What about Miss Bingley? She is well acquainted with the public life of London, and I know that she desires your company, for I have heard her remark upon it more than once."

"Miss Bingley desires my company for one reason only, Elizabeth: she wishes to marry my brother."

"Georgiana!" Mrs. Annesley exclaimed, interrupting her discussion of rheumatism with Mrs. Gardiner, even breaking off in mid-sentence to reprove her young charge.

"Well, she does. You know it as well as I!"

"One must not disrespect an older lady, my dear. She may not be your equal in some matters, but she is an accomplished lady."

"Yes," I added, lifting my chin. "It cannot be denied. Miss Bingley does possess a certain air."

Georgiana began to giggle, and Miss Annesley's attempts to calm her failed utterly. Her laughter was infectious, and I could not suppress my own amusement. It was obvious that we behaved in an unseemly manner, but it was not long before both older ladies could not refrain from bursting forth in mirth as well. We laughed until we were forced to hold our sides in pain, and Mrs. Gardiner begged us to desist, for she was quite uncomfortable. I wondered whether the shepherd in the field that we passed could actually see our carriage shaking from the hilarity within.

It was good to laugh. It reminded me of growing up in a house filled with five girls. Suddenly, I longed to see all of them once again. I missed Jane in particular, and I knew that my aunt yearned to hold her children. Ireland seemed like the other side of the world from Longbourn. And yet, I did enjoy Georgiana's company. Sweet and unassuming, she brought joy to my life, and I thought how much I would miss her when we returned to England and resumed our separate lives. For that matter, I would miss her when we separated in Cork.

"Georgiana, has Mr. Darcy told you much of the city to which you travel?" I asked later.

"Wills says Ballymeghan is more of a village than a city. That is the only information I have been told since I learned my grandmother was born there. I wish I had known her, but she died long before I was born. My brother remembers her, but not well. Evidently, she had been in poor health for some years, and she kept to her chambers most of the day."

"Do you remember this uncle whom you plan to visit?" Mrs. Gardiner asked.

"Oh no. He left Pemberley as a young man and never returned. I do recall visits from Uncle Henry, the one who lived in Bath."

That statement aroused my interest. "What was he like?"

"Tall and handsome in his uniform and always happy. His beard tickled when he kissed my cheek, and he was forever taking sweets from the kitchen and giving them to me when no one was watching. I thought him absolutely wonderful!"

"I have only seen his portrait at Pemberley, and I agree that he was handsome," I said. "I did not see much resemblance between Mr. Henry Darcy and your father."

"They might have looked more alike if Uncle Henry had shaved his beard. I do remember that his eyes were different from Father's." She leaned forward and peered closely at me. "In truth, Elizabeth, your eyes are much like my uncle's. Perhaps it is a family trait that both of you inherited even though you are not closely related."

I straightened and turned my attention to the window.

"I wonder whether Wills ever determined the exact connection between our family and that of Elizabeth."

"He has certainly devoted himself to the quest," Mrs. Annesley said. "He spent countless hours upon the task at Rosings, Eden Park, and especially Bath. Do you share his curiosity, Miss Bennet?"

"I—"

"Lizzy has never been one to shut herself up inside for too long, no matter the pursuit," my aunt interjected. "Give her a good, long tramp in the woods though, and she considers it a perfect day."

I breathed out with relief as my aunt's statement renewed Mrs. Annesley's discussion of her various ailments occasioned by the last lengthy walk she had attempted.

An expression of disinterestedness settled upon Georgiana's countenance, and she devoted herself to the passing scenery for a while. We remarked on the many shades of green that coloured the island, but eventually, she grew drowsy, removed her bonnet, and leaned back against the seat. I, too, wearied of the long journey and hoped we would stop soon to spend the night. The carriage rocked on as consistently as the ladies' conversation. I was left to allow my mind to wander at will. Without fail, it returned to questions of my parentage.

I thought of Henry Darcy and the native similarity we shared. Had Mr. Darcy ever noticed it, and if so, had he shared the news with the admiral's widow? I wondered what kind of man Peter Darcy would turn out to be and whether my presumptions of his character rang true. The only portrait I had seen of him was with his brothers, and he was but a young child at the time. Mr. Darcy had said he was now ill. Oh, I hoped we did not arrive too late for Peter Darcy to answer his nephew's questions.

AT LENGTH, THE CARRIAGE PULLED into the small village of Cashel, and we clambered out, ready to stretch our limbs from the forced confinement. My uncle informed us that we would spend the night there at an inn. We followed him into the whitewashed, thatched house that bore the name

"Fitzgerald's" above the door. Our lodgings were somewhat simple but clean and tidy. Neither Mr. and Mrs. Gardiner nor I found the accommodations unsuitable, but I wondered how Mr. Darcy and his sister would feel. I doubted that either of them had ever stayed the night in such a humble dwelling.

My aunt wished to lie down before our meal, and Mr. Gardiner sought a drink in the local pub. After making certain that I was not needed, I slipped outdoors for a short walk. The few shops across the street had closed, but I did not need to make a purchase. I simply yearned for exercise, so I strolled several blocks without any destination in mind. Suddenly, I heard someone call my name, and when I turned, I saw Mr. Darcy advancing upon me.

"Elizabeth, where do you go?"

"Nowhere, sir. I am simply taking the air."

"The sun goes down soon. You must not wander about alone. After all, this is not Hertfordshire. Shall I keep you company?"

I nodded, and he smiled as we fell into step. After discussing my aunt's health, we remained silent for a block or two. Mr. Darcy then pointed out the Catholic church around the corner, and we watched as the black-robed priest hurried inside. The man had not acknowledged us in any manner.

"Do we trespass, sir? The priest does not appear friendly."

"He may fear our notice since we are clearly strangers in these parts, and the Papist church is no longer the religion of the ruling class. Besides that, we are English." He spoke as though we had committed a crime.

"I do not understand. Ireland is now united with England, is it not? Are not both countries under one parliament?"

"They are in name, but this country has little representation in London. Besides, the conflict between our nations goes back centuries, and the Irish people's struggle continues. I have been told that the place to which we travel, County Cork, is a stronghold of resistance to the English. In fact, it is known as 'the Rebel County' with no small amount of pride among the natives."

"Do you think Mr. Peter Darcy will welcome your visit?"

"Yes. No matter the years past, the difference in religion, politics, or country, we are the same blood, and in Ireland, blood relations trump all else. He is my uncle, and I cannot imagine him refusing to see me."

"Is he accepted here?"

We had crossed the footpath and begun to retrace our steps back to the inn. "I would surely think so, else why should he stay all this great time?"

I took a deep breath. "If Peter Darcy knows nothing of me or the circumstances surrounding my birth, will you put this search of yours to rest at last?"

He turned and looked directly at me. "I think he does, Elizabeth. I feel in my heart that Uncle Peter will answer my questions."

"But why?"

"I cannot explain it. Do you recall that I once told you how Bridesgate, the Willoughby house, seemed to call out to me as a boy?"

I nodded. "Even though your father instructed you to stay away from it."

"Exactly. I have that same feeling about this country and about Peter Darcy. I think he knows the circumstances surrounding your birth."

"But if he does not, sir, what then?"

We had reached the inn, and he stopped short before entering. "Do not say that."

"But you must consider it."

"No, I must not!" Although he had not raised his voice, his tone was as unyielding as though he had done so. We stared into each other's eyes until, at last, I turned and walked into the house.

Chapter Fourteen

After spending yet another night in another inn and a long, hard day of travel on country roads, we reached our destination at last. Although not as large as Dublin, Cork was a fine, bustling city, exceedingly more populous than any of the villages we had encountered along the way.

As we drove through the streets to the Imperial Hotel on the South Mall, we admired the sunset reflected off the handsome limestone buildings lining the banks of the River Lee. Seagulls greeted us with their screeching cries as they followed the ferryboats carrying passengers upriver from the town of Cobh to Merchants Quay. The surroundings were rich with sounds and smells from the nearby Grand Parade Market, with its abundance of fresh fish, and the local brewery, famous for its dark stout. The odours penetrated my senses, but I, unlike Mrs. Annesley, did not find them unpleasant.

"Oh, Georgiana, I fear your appetite will suffer if we remain outdoors. Come, we must hurry and escape this dreadful air," she said.

"It is not so very bad. May we not watch the sun go down?" Her companion would not be dissuaded, however, so the young girl reluctantly followed all of us inside.

Our apartment was the most superior by far since we left Dublin. My uncle's time would be much occupied by business, including travelling down to Cobh at the mouth of Cork Harbour. Thus, he expended the additional funds necessary to secure our lodgings in the same establishment as that of the Darcys so that my aunt and I would not be left alone during the day.

During the course of our meal together that evening, however, Mr. Darcy announced that he would depart on the morrow for a short visit with the Earl of Killaine at Castelaine and wished to leave Georgiana and Mrs. Annesley in Mr. Gardiner's care while he was gone. Both gentlemen then insisted that we were not to venture far from the hotel until my uncle returned each evening.

"Oh, Wills, must you go so soon?"

"It is only proper that I call upon the earl as his family and ours have been acquainted for many years. I have written to inform him of our coming, and he has secured a cottage for us in Ballymeghan. I must see that all is in order for our arrival."

"I do not understand the connection between our family and this Irish earl you call upon. I do not recall hearing of him before."

"He is the son of our grandfather's friend from Cambridge. It is due to his father that our grandparents met. If he had not invited James Darcy to visit during that summer, we would not be alive today."

When she asked where he lived, Mr. Darcy said it was about three miles outside the village of Ballymeghan.

"And is that where you hope to find your uncle?" Mr. Gardiner asked.

He nodded. "My source in Derbyshire corresponds with a priest in Ardfield, which I understand lies but a short distance from there. The priest says that Peter Darcy has made his home in the village. Before I begin my search, Lord Killaine, most likely, can tell me precisely where Uncle Peter dwells."

"I wish you good luck, Mr. Darcy," Mrs. Gardiner said, and my uncle echoed her sentiments.

I felt Mr. Darcy's eyes upon me. "And you, Elizabeth? Do you not wish me luck?"

I raised my eyes to meet his. "Of course, sir, and even more, I hope that what you find will grant you peace."

Three days later, my aunt and I had joined Georgiana and Mrs. Annesley in their parlour after dinner. While attempting to teach me a simpler method by which I might master a difficult embroidery stitch, the older ladies burst into laughter at my pitiful struggles and subsequent display of temper when I succeeded in repeatedly knotting my thread. I made such havoc of it that they were forced to take turns trying to work it loose; however, all their efforts were in vain. At last, Georgiana solved the matter by cutting the thread.

"Elizabeth, you had better begin all over again."

"I think I should give up," I said, laughing with the others, "and admit that my fingers were not created for sewing. Look at the bloodstains I have left on this scarf."

"Perhaps you might dye it a soft rose colour when the task is completed," Mrs. Annesley offered.

Just then, we heard the outer door open and slam shut. Subsequent rapid footsteps echoed directly into a bedchamber, followed by another slammed door. We looked at each other in wonder.

"Goodness, could that be Wills?"

"If it is, something must be amiss," Mrs. Annesley said.

"Perhaps we should go," my aunt said.

Georgiana rose. "No, it is still early. I shall see what is abroad."

We all prevailed upon her to remain with us and give her brother time to recover from his trip. She had just sat down again and picked up her needlework when, once more, we heard doors slam and the same rapid footsteps departing the apartment.

I looked at Mrs. Gardiner, and we both folded our work and put it away. "I really do believe we should make our departure," she said. "It has been a lovely evening."

We made our farewells and returned down the hall to our quarters. My uncle sat snoring in his chair, his book lying open upon his chest. My aunt woke him, and shortly thereafter, they retired to their chamber for the night.

I walked about the room and picked at the daisies in the pitcher upon the table. Looking through a small stack of books lying beside my uncle's chair, I found nothing that interested me. I spied the full moon through the window and thus pulled the curtain aside. Below in the moonlight, I saw Mr. Darcy pacing back and forth on the footpath outside the hotel. He carried his hat in his hand, and several times, he raked his hand through his hair.

Something is terribly wrong, I feared.

Turning back to the room, I tiptoed near the door of the Gardiners' room, from which I heard nothing but silence. Quietly, I gathered my shawl around my shoulders and slipped out the door. I made it down the stairs and to the lobby without meeting anyone, but just as I reached the outer door, the alarmed porter asked whether he could assist me. I could think of no reason to account for my actions, for I knew that a single woman would not normally leave the hotel alone at that late hour. So I simply lifted my head, assumed my best imitation of Miss Bingley, and waved him away.

I hurried out the door, whereupon I found Mr. Darcy still madly pacing.

"Elizabeth!"

"I…saw you from the window above."

"You should not be out here."

"I must know what ails you, sir. You are obviously angry…upset. What is it?"

"Nothing. Nothing you can make right."

"What do you mean?"

He made a helpless gesture and hit his hat against the side of his leg.

"Tell me what has happened! Is it your uncle? Are you too late?"

He took my elbow. "Come, I must return you to Mr. Gardiner."

"He and my aunt have retired. Will you not take but a moment and tell me?"

A man passing by stared at us.

"Not here. Let us cross the street."

He led me out of sight of the hotel to where we had a clear view of the river. We strolled in silence, the moon glistening on the rippling surface. The water lapped against the pier, and I knew I should have loved being there in that setting if not for the anguish on Mr. Darcy's face.

We sat down on a bench looking out towards the mouth of the harbour and remained silent for several moments before I spoke. "Did your visit with Lord Killaine not go well? Is that what troubles you?"

"The earl was cordial. He said his father had spoken often of his friendship with my grandfather, and what a scandal it caused when Siobhan MacAnally sailed off to England with James Darcy."

"Did he seem angry?"

He shook his head. "Not at all. His father actually aided their escape. Of course, he was a young man back then. He had no idea how dangerous their decision truly was or what serious consequences it would yield."

"If the past does not anger Lord Killaine, then what causes your present distress?"

Mr. Darcy rose and stared up at the sky. I stood up and gently touched his arm. "Sir, may I not share your troubles as you have often shared mine?"

When he turned to me, I held my breath at the pain I saw reflected in his eyes. "Elizabeth, I have made this trip in vain. Peter Darcy will not give me the answers I wish for."

"Why not?"

"Because he cannot."

"He has died?"

"No."

"Then why ever not?"

He lowered his head and took a step toward the wharf. I walked with him, refusing to let up. He gave a great sigh.

"I began this search with you for your mother, and once we discovered Elizabeth Willoughby, I should have been content. You seemed to be, while I simply could not."

"You want to know why."

"I want more than that." He turned and faced me. "I want—oh, my dearest girl! I need someone—anyone—to tell me that my father is not your father."

My heart rose into my throat. I swallowed and looked away then walked back and sank down on the bench.

What had he done? Had he actually spoken the very hope that lived deep inside me—the same dream I attempted to bury daily, but which refused to remain hidden?

I was conscious of his return and that he sat beside me, but I could not face him.

"I know I promised that I would look upon you as my sister, and I intend to keep that promise. But I must be honest and confess that is not my heart's desire. I want—"

"No, do not say it! You must not say it, sir." I jumped up to return to the Imperial.

"Wait," he said, catching my hand. "Wait. Forgive me. You are right. I... do not know what possessed me. It is just that I have received such disappointing news this day."

"If it concerns me, do I not have a right to know?"

He sighed again. "I have searched everywhere for a hint, a clue, some revelation that you were fathered by someone other than George Darcy. I have combed through every document I could find at Pemberley. I sought out the vicar at the church for a record of your birth. There is none. Your mother's death is recorded, but that is all. I have told you how Lady Catherine provided no answers. Eden Park was the same. I even called upon Sir Linton Willoughby again, but he refused to see me. And Bath...I thought surely I would find more than I did among Uncle Henry's many journals and correspondence. I even dared to insult my aunt by asking whether her husband could possibly be your father. Her answer is what drove me to Ireland."

"Her answer? What do you mean?"

"Aunt Harriet said Admiral Darcy was close-mouthed about your birth and spoke of the occasion only once. He said that his brother had chosen to forsake a woman and child in Derbyshire, and that after the woman died, the child had been taken to a far county to be fostered by an unknown family. She assumed the brother was George, for he was the sole brother she had met. For years they thought that Peter was dead. I could not accept her assumption, and that is why I am here. I hoped to find Uncle Peter and confront him. I had this insupportable notion that he might— In truth, I had determined to force him to take responsibility for your birth...until today."

I sank down upon the bench once again. "What happened today?"

He sat down beside me and leaned forward, holding his hat between his legs. "I learned from Lord Killaine that Peter Darcy could not be your father, for he is a Catholic priest."

"A priest!"

"That is why he ran off without telling his family. He travelled directly to this country and began his studies to join the priesthood. He had always been meant for the church, but not that of the Papists. Evidently, his mother's influence truly shaped his life. After her death, there was nothing to keep him at Pemberley. Lord Killaine said he has served the poorest parishes in Ireland, devoting his life to good works. That hardly sounds like a man who would desert a woman and child, does it?"

"No," I whispered.

We said nothing more for a long while. The sadness rose up between us like a deep chasm over which no one crosses. Rising at last, he said, "Come, I must return you to your rooms."

As we crossed the street, I felt as though heavy weights pulled at my legs. My shoulders drooped, and weariness settled upon me. When we reached the door to the hotel, I stopped.

"What will you do now? Shall you return to England without seeing your uncle?"

"No, I shall see him. The earl confirmed the fact that he has not long to live. It is only right that I visit him, and I wish to introduce Georgiana to him."

I nodded.

"I still would like for you to meet him."

"Why? Would it not be shameful for a man of God to witness the result of his brother's sin?"

"If Peter Darcy is the same man I remember as a boy, he will not hold you responsible for another's misdeeds. I hope you will go with me to Ballymeghan."

FOUR DAYS LATER, MY AUNT and I departed Cork City with the Darcys for Siobhan Darcy's birthplace. Business concerns forced Mr. Gardiner to remain behind. He would make numerous trips between the city and the harbour at Cobh either by ferry or by hiring one of the local jingles, little horse-drawn cabs that provided transport each day. Not wishing to leave my aunt and me alone all day, and since his wife had rallied from the stresses of travel, he allowed us to go to Ballymeghan without him.

I saw little of Mr. Darcy during those four days before we left, and when I did, he kept his distance. Depressed and brooding, he said little to any of us. I noticed that he did accompany my uncle to the local pub down the street every evening, and they often stayed until closing time. I prayed that my brother visited the establishment for Mr. Gardiner's company alone and did not seek refuge from his sorrows in a bottle of Irish whisky. If Mr. Darcy drank to excess, my uncle never made mention of it, but then, he had always possessed a modest affinity for spirits himself.

Ballymeghan was situated about forty miles from Cork City, and the day's journey proved excessively diverting, for it took us along the picturesque coastline with its magnificent views. I was content to stare out the windows the entire trip. The only sights that marred the scene were the obviously poverty-stricken tenant farmers attempting to scrape out a living in the fields. Many of their dwellings were little more than hovels, and numerous children littered the yards while the fine houses of the landowners contrasted sharply in their affluence. Mr. Darcy had told us that, with the English occupation, native owners who formerly owned much of the land now made up little more than five percent. Most had been reduced to the status of tenant farmers working the land for the benefit of the oft-absent English landlord.

As we drove into the village of Ballymeghan, I noted its tranquil setting.

The whitewashed, thatched cottages were well tended. Set against the lush, green hills in the background, they made a charming, typically Irish scene.

I was pleased to see the fine, spacious house Mr. Darcy had rented for all of us to share. He had brought his own servants and sent one ahead to secure local help. Thus, we were ushered into a lovely, limestone house with everything made ready to receive us.

"What a charming little place," Mrs. Gardiner exclaimed. She was relieved to be free from the bumps and jolts of the carriage ride but did not protest when I urged her to rest in her chamber. I supervised the maid unpacking my aunt's belongings before seeking my own room.

"That will do, Lizzy. Go along, and arrange your things as you like. I shall lie down for a bit before dinner."

After setting my possessions in their proper places, I returned to the parlour, where I found Mr. Darcy pouring a glass of brandy. He offered me a sherry, which I declined.

"Do you find the lodgings to your liking, sir?"

He shrugged. "As long as Georgiana is content, they will do. And, of course, I trust that you and Mrs. Gardiner are satisfied."

"Very much so."

I noticed that his voice had not the slightest inflection. It was as though a man devoid of emotion—of life—had spoken. I walked to the window covered in fine Irish lace and pulled aside the curtain.

"What a beautiful little village this is. I have not seen its equal during our entire journey. I wonder whose fine mansion that is far up on the hill." I hoped to prick Mr. Darcy's interest and lift his dark mood.

He joined me at the window. "That is Castelaine."

"Where the Earl of Killaine lives?"

He nodded. "His presence affords this village more prosperity than most we have seen, for it enjoys his protection."

"Tell me, sir, why was he able to retain ownership of Castelaine when so many landowners have been disenfranchised?"

"He is a clever man and enjoys the benefits of his connections." Mr. Darcy returned to the brandy decanter, and I frowned, not only at his words but also at his actions.

"I do not understand," I said, crossing the room to the nearest chair.

"Lord Killaine's younger brother, Pádraig, married Maíra McKenna, a wealthy widow who possesses a treasure even more valuable than riches."

"What could that be, sir?"

"She is Anglican. Not particular about his religion, it was a simple thing for Pádraig Killaine to renounce Catholicism and become Anglican in order to secure her hand. Lord Killaine's wife also has a prominent Anglican cousin —the Bishop of Shrewsbury, in fact. He is a close colleague and friend to the Bishop of Canterbury and, hence, the Crown. Such family associations have assured the earl's continued preservation of Castlelaine."

"A fortunate man."

He looked disinterested. "A prudent man. Maintaining goodwill toward his Anglican relations provides him the power to protect his community and, doubtless, my uncle as well."

"Why should your uncle need protection?"

"According to Lord Killaine, *Father* Peter Darcy does not always play inside the law. He scorns the dictates designed to subdue the Catholic faith, and he has done whatever was needed to assist his parishioners to practice their *true* faith."

"And does that distress you, sir?"

"It means little to me. He chose this life. What he does with it is up to him."

Another resigned answer, I thought. "All the same, though, he sounds like an interesting man, but then, I have yet to meet an uninteresting Darcy."

My impertinent remark failed to provoke any rejoinder from him as it would have in the past. A chill raised gooseflesh on my arms when I examined his face. Expressionless, the light had vanished from his eyes as surely as if one had doused a candle.

The NEXT MORNING, I AWOKE to what promised to be a day of perfect weather. A gentle breeze wafted in through the open window of my chamber, stirring the starched linen curtains. Although white clouds scattered across the blue sky, the sun shone through in abundance. We had encountered rain almost every day we had visited the country, and I welcomed a brighter interval.

Smelling the delightful aroma of rashers and sausages from below, I hastened to dress, unwilling to await the maid's assistance. When I entered the dining room, I was surprised to see Georgiana and Mr. Darcy finishing their meal. Their well-dressed appearance gave every sign that they were obviously going out.

"I see that you do not delay in meeting your uncle," I said after morning greetings were exchanged and I sat down across from Georgiana.

"We do not go to meet Uncle Peter," she announced. "Wills is taking me to meet Lord Killaine at Castelaine."

"Oh?" I looked in his direction.

"Lady Killaine expressed a desire to know my sister, and we made arrangements to meet at one o'clock."

"Tell me, have you learned whether your grandmother's relations yet dwell in these parts?"

"She has two nephews and their families living in the area."

"And shall you visit them while you are in Ballymeghan?"

"I do not see the need or have the inclination." He rose from the table and strode from the room without another word.

My spirits had dampened upon seeing that Mr. Darcy's mood had not lifted. He appeared much like a man uninterested in anything or anyone. I knew only too well that severe disappointment ruled his outlook. He was drowning in final acceptance of what could never be changed.

After the Darcys left the cottage, I visited with Aunt Gardiner at her bedside for some time. Once again, yesterday's journey had robbed her strength, but she assured me that a day in bed would put her to rights soon enough. I told her of our companions' expedition for the day, never hinting that anything was wrong. Fortunately, she was too tired to see through my cheerful performance as she would have had she been herself.

When she had finished her breakfast and the maid had taken the tray below stairs, she was ready for a nap.

"Why not take a stroll, Lizzy? The village seems safe enough, and I know that you are yearning to free yourself from walls. Do not stray too far, though. None of your three-mile rambles, mind you."

I smiled and agreed, promising to return within an hour or so. Although I remained worried about Mr. Darcy, once I stepped out into the sunshine, the quaint little village lifted my spirits, and I looked forward to discovering its charms. Not much larger than Meryton, it contained a small public house with a store on one side. A limited collection of bonnets had been placed behind the glass, and I noticed several women entering the shop while two men loitered outside the pub. As I passed by, I stopped short when the publican swept dirt out the entryway. He bobbed his head and begged my pardon, but I gave him a smile to signify no harm had occurred.

I walked down to the end of the street, having seen most of what there was to offer in the village other than the church sitting prominently at the opposite end of the main road. The bridge we had crossed upon reaching Ballymeghan lay in the other direction, and I set off to examine the River Bandon below. I was delighted to find the water as clear as any I had ever seen in Hertfordshire and, even more splendid, a well-worn path that ran alongside for some distance.

I trotted across the bridge and scrambled down the bank. On the path, I stopped to watch the trout jump. Perhaps my uncle and Mr. Darcy might enjoy fishing there once Mr. Gardiner concluded his business and joined us. The thought of Mr. Darcy's dark temper rose before me, and I feared that it would take more than fishing to brighten his perspective. *I shall not think about him*, I told myself and continued to follow the path.

Around the bend, the walk widened. A part of it diverted off, leading up an incline to a small cottage. I smiled, thinking how lovely it would be to live there and awaken to the mist rising on the river as the morn dawned over the mountains. I spied a patch of wild daisies a short distance ahead, closer to the river's edge, and spent no little time choosing the yellow and white blooms to make a bouquet I might take back to my aunt. At length, I sat down in the soft, green grass and felt content to watch the reflection of the clouds on the surface of the water.

I allowed my mind to drift, insensible either to time passing or to the sky darkening. Thus, I was taken by surprise when the heavy Irish rain began to fall. I jumped up and looked about for the nearest shelter. There was nothing under which to hide, for the trees had been cleared well back from the river. I shaded my eyes from the merciless downpour and saw the small overhang of the thatched roof on the cottage I had passed. Within moments, I ran up the slope and huddled beneath the tiny bit of protection, stretching my shawl over my bonnet to shield my face. With dismay, I watched the rain increase and drops collect on the ends of the straw roof above me before splashing down onto my dress.

"Good morning."

I startled at the voice behind me and turned quickly to see an older man dressed in black standing at the door he had opened. Obviously frail, he leaned on a rough cane. I blinked when I realized he was a priest.

"I…beg your pardon, Father."

"You had best come in, lass, before you catch your death."

He opened the door wider and took a few steps back into the room. I hesitated, but he urged me to enter with a welcoming gesture.

"Sure, these summer showers catch us all out, even those of us who have lived here all our lives, much less a stranger in our midst. I am correct, am I not? You are not from around here at all."

"I was picking blossoms down by the water."

"Ah yes, the flowers never fail to tempt us away from the path we are on, as well they should. Come in and sit down until the damp chill dispels."

He walked slowly to a chair beside the large fireplace in which a turf fire burned, warming the whole parlour. In truth, it could not be called a proper parlour. It was more like a single, large room with a bed at one end and a small table and chairs next to the window. Although sparsely filled, it was neat and clean, and I saw that the furnishings were worn but comfortable.

"Forgive the place, my child," he said as he watched me look around his home. "I do little these days, but Father Rafferty will come along later to tidy up a bit and cook me a meal."

He eased himself down upon the chair, and I saw that the bed had not been made, as though he had just risen.

"I am sorry to intrude. I had not anticipated the brunt of the rain."

"Sure, my dear, but the stoop offers slight protection when water from Heaven truly falls. You had much better sit in here and tell me all about yourself. From your speech, I sense you have travelled a long way."

"I have, from England."

"England? My, my, that is a great distance. I was born in England, you know."

"Oh? In what part, Father?"

"What part? Why, the prettiest part, of course—Derbyshire. Oh, forgive me, for I have not introduced myself—Father Darcy."

Darcy? Had I stumbled upon my uncle all on my own?

Amazement rendered me unable to observe the slightest civility and tell him my name. With the black clouds blocking the sun and dimming the already scarce light coming through the tiny windows, he rose to stoke the turf fire and to light a candle on the table next to his chair.

"Pray, sir, could you be Father Peter Darcy?"

"I am. Sure, and has someone told you of me? Step closer, child, into the light."

I removed my bonnet and smoothed my frock before crossing the room. The priest held up the candle as though his sight had dimmed. He squinted at me, blinked several times, shook his head, and peered closer.

"Ah, if me eyes are not playing tricks again, or is it me feeble mind? I never know these days." He inclined his head in my direction, and then, his mouth gaped open. He clutched at the arm of the chair and sank down upon it. "Eliz...Elizabeth? Is it you? No! She is dead. Do I see a vision?"

"I...am Elizabeth, Father. How did you know my name?"

"You cannot be! Child, who are you?" His hand shook with such violence that I stepped forward and took the candle from him. "But it is you, my... my own Elizabeth."

His words frightened me. His ill health evident, I wondered whether the priest might collapse before me. What should I do? Whom could I call upon for assistance?

"Sir, I am Elizabeth Bennet."

"No, not Bennet...Willoughby. You are Elizabeth Willoughby...Darcy."

Elizabeth Willoughby Darcy! The old man does not make sense. I have no right to the name Darcy.

I took a step backwards. "I...I fear that you are confused, Father. My name is Elizabeth Bennet."

He shook his head, and a tear slid down his cheek. "You are my Elizabeth, returned to me after all these years. You are come back from the grave."

"Sir, you do not know what you say. You must be ill. May I fetch something for your distress?" I scanned the room, wondering where he might keep medicine.

"No, stay before me, I beg of you. Do not leave. I must know from where you have come."

I glanced over my shoulder, hoping the rain had ceased. I had the strongest urge to flee the cottage, for I doubted this man was in his right mind. "I...I—"

"Lass, tell me!"

He had evidently known Elizabeth Willoughby in the past, but I had to make him understand that he was mistaken. Did I dare tell him I was her daughter? Oh, why was Mr. Darcy not with me at that moment? I took a deep breath.

"Father, pray listen carefully. I am not Elizabeth Willoughby, for you spoke the truth. She died long ago."

He leaned forward and tugged at my hand until I knelt before him. Reaching for the candle once again, he searched my face. "You have her face, her smile, her beautiful curls, but the eyes—no, the eyes are not hers. The eyes are those of my mother."

I swallowed. "I have been told that I am the natural daughter of your neighbour in Derbyshire, Elizabeth Willoughby."

"*Natural* dau— What are you saying? That is not possible. You are mistaken, for Elizabeth had no child. And yet…your every expression is hers. I cannot comprehend it! This could not have happened as you say."

Shame washed over me, and I felt the heat of a blush overtaking my cheeks. "It grieves me to bring you alarm, sir. I assumed that you knew of your brother's connection with my mother and of her death in childbirth."

At my words, he sank back against the chair, his face turned deadly white. "What do you say such things? My brother? Which brother? I do not understand."

"Your oldest brother, Father: George Darcy."

"George? Insupportable! What would make you utter such a falsehood?"

Now, my mouth gaped, and I felt the room begin to spin. "George… George Darcy is my natural father. Lady Catherine said— She gave me his note. Why should you doubt it, Father?"

"Catherine? Catherine presumed to say that you are George's daughter! I cannot take it in. Why? It defies all reason."

I sat back on my heels. "What are you saying, sir? Am I not George Darcy's daughter?"

"Of course not! Some monstrous trick has been played. You must be Eleanor's daughter and…perhaps Henry's. Did he return to Pemberley when little Eleanor grew up?" His voice quavered. "Tell me, child, when were you born? The date…the year…when?"

"1791—the sixth of December."

He looked away as if he was counting. "The same year. Nine months later." His face turned ashen, and his breathing grew shallow. "No, no, it cannot be. Oh, dear God, she must have been with child when I left Pemberley… with child when I was told she was dead!"

I began to tremble. "Father, what are you saying? Forgive me, but I care not when you left Pemberley. Have mercy and tell me, who is my natural father? Could it be Henry Darcy?"

He lifted his clouded, green eyes from the floor to meet mine, and I felt a chill of recognition.

"No, not Henry... No, it can only be me. You must be my daughter, Elizabeth. And I am not your *natural* father. I am your father. I married Elizabeth Willoughby before you were conceived."

My stomach lurched violently, and I feared that I would be ill. Frantic that I would disgrace myself, I jumped to my feet and looked for an escape. Without another word, without explanation, reason, or regard for either manners or the priest, I bolted from the room and out into the rain.

I cannot tell you what happened thereafter, for all reason left me. I must have run down the path along the river a great distance. Hours later, I came to myself sitting beneath a tree, staring out at the rippling stream, not knowing where I was or how I came to be there.

Two phrases echoed round and round my head. *I am* not *a bastard! I am* not *his sister!*

Chapter Fifteen

When at last I regained my wits on the banks of the River Bandon, I realized that the rain had evidently ceased sometime earlier, for my clothes were but slightly damp. I shivered, aware that the sun sat low in the sky. Rising to my feet, I glanced at my surroundings, thankful to see that, although I had run far from the cottage in my disturbed state, I had not strayed from the river.

I must return. Aunt Gardiner will worry, I thought, taking several steps toward the path, but then, the realization of what I had learned in the priest's cottage flooded my mind once more, and I stopped. I stood absolutely still.

I am not *a bastard! I am* not *Mr. Darcy's sister!*

The loveliest feeling I could imagine swept over me, and I began to smile. I smiled and smiled and smiled. *I am* not *his sister!* The words swirled around me like snowflakes, and I stared in wonder. Instead of feeling chilled, a delicious warmth filled my heart.

I looked about for my bonnet but then realized I must have lost it somewhere along the way. I examined the place where I had sat, making sure I had not left my reticule behind. No, it hung from my wrist. I turned back to the path and raised my head, determined to return, but I did not take a step. Instead, I caught my breath.

Mr. Darcy stood before me, his hat in his hand. "Elizabeth!"

"Sir," I whispered, for my voice had somehow vanished.

He did not move toward me nor I toward him. We simply gazed at each other as though we might never drink our fill.

He swallowed. "I am not—we are not—brother and sister."

"I know."

And then, he dropped his hat. Before I had time to blink, he crossed the distance between us, clasped my face between his hands, and covered my mouth with his! Hungrily, he kissed me, greedily prodding my lips until they parted. I felt a heat well up from deep within that I had never known before.

Just as suddenly, he released me and stepped back. I watched his chest heave as he struggled for breath. I underwent my own struggle, attempting to grasp what had just passed between us. He lowered his chin and raised his eyes to stare at me from under his dark brows, as though he dared me to lash out at him in rebuke.

"What I did was improper." He took a breath. "Was it not?"

I nodded, frowning a bit. *Is that all he can think of—impropriety?*

He closed his eyes, a tortured look about his countenance. "I suppose you expect me to beg your forgiveness."

Do I dare speak honestly? I swallowed. "No."

His eyes flew open, incredulity therein. "No?"

"No." I took a step toward him, hoping he could see the light in my eyes.

"Elizabeth, may I dare to hope?"

"You may." I pressed my lips together to keep from smiling.

He turned his face away to the river, and then with a great sigh, he turned again as though he would gaze at the trees. Instead, he lowered his head to the ground below. Finally, he allowed himself to meet my eyes as though he could not believe the words I had spoken. He shook his head.

"You are too generous to trifle with me. If your feelings are still what they were in April a year ago, tell me so at once. *My* affections and wishes have only multiplied, but one word from you will silence me on this subject forever."

I closed my eyes and looked away, struggling not to weep, but he misunderstood my actions.

"I would not have you under obligation to me because of what just transpired between us," he said quickly. "There are no witnesses, and I swear that no one shall ever know of my transgression."

I turned back to meet his gaze. "I do feel under obligation."

"You do? But why?"

"Be...because I wanted it to happen."

The nerve in his forehead twitched. He opened his mouth and then closed it. Inclining his head, he repeated, "You...wanted it to happen?"

I could not help but smile. "I did."

"Dearest Elizabeth, I have loved you for so long, and I hope—I pray—that you will be mine, for I simply cannot go on without you."

I took another step toward him. "William, I will."

Delight overspread his face. He gathered me into his arms and gently touched his mouth to mine. Soft, undemanding, caressing, his kiss awakened my desire even more. My arms reached up to encircle his neck, and I could not keep from entangling my fingers in his curls. My body yielded to his with a need so fervent that it overwhelmed me. The fires we had banked for so long would not be denied.

His lips moved across my forehead and my cheek as he pulled my head onto his shoulder. "Oh, my lovely, loveliest Elizabeth…I cannot breathe without you."

Fortunately, or unfortunately—however one chooses to look at it—our good sense eventually returned before we gave in to our passion there by the river. The sun had almost disappeared over the wood behind us by the time we returned to the bridge and, consequently, to the house where our companions awaited.

While passing Father Darcy's cottage, I asked whether we should make certain he was well. William ran up the slight hill while I waited below. He spoke briefly to a priest at the door but did not go in. It took but a few moments before he returned to my side.

"The priest was Father Rafferty. He had come shortly before I concluded my earlier visit. I asked him to tell Uncle Peter that I had found you and that you are well. The priest said he insisted that my uncle retire, but he has not yet fallen asleep, so Father Rafferty will inform him. I fear Father Darcy was quite overcome with the day's revelations. He expects us on the morrow, though, for he has much to say, and I have questions to be answered."

"As do I."

We had talked without ceasing during the walk back to the village. William told me that he and Georgiana had returned to the house from Castelaine mid-afternoon to find Mrs. Gardiner alarmed at my lengthy absence. She feared that I had been caught in the heavy downpour.

Immediately, William had gone to search the village, eventually learning at the pub that someone had seen me walking in the direction of the river.

He followed the path, discovered the priest's cottage, and inquired therein, whereupon he found his uncle and heard the shocking news. They had spent no little time attempting to grasp what had happened before Father Rafferty arrived and saw that his friend and advisor was ailing. Leaving the younger priest to see to his uncle, William had resumed his search for me.

I was amazed that I had run so far, obviously in a stupor.

"If I had not found you, Elizabeth," he said right before we reached the house, "I could not have rallied."

"You must not say such things."

"Perhaps not, but it is true. I have never feared any man, but my need for you—" He broke off and took my hands in his. "Oh, my darling girl, the strength of my need for you is so great that it frightens me! Promise that you will never leave me."

"I will not leave," I whispered just before the servant opened the door for us.

Inside, we struggled to conceal our emotions, but my aunt's curious expression upon greeting us showed that we failed. While walking, we had decided to refrain from informing Georgiana of what we had learned until after we had spoken to Father Darcy again. After all, the story was not just mine but his as well, and we knew that it would affect not only his standing in the church and the parish but also his very life. I feared for his fragile health and prayed that the shock would not cause him serious harm.

Before our meal, I enjoyed a warm bath and washed my hair. I chose my brightest gown, and the maid nodded in approval when she finished my hair.

"You look particularly well tonight, Miss Bennet."

I smiled. In truth, I could not yet keep from smiling. All the joy I thought I had lost and all the love I had repressed for almost a year now coursed through me without restraint. I simply could not constrain my elation. My aunt walked into the room just as the maid carried the wet towels out the door.

As simply as possible, I told her of what had happened at Peter Darcy's cottage and how I had responded, how Mr. Darcy found me, and that we had professed our love for each other. She, in turn, was not only relieved but also exceedingly pleased that I was to be happy at last with the man I loved. The moment we had returned, she had guessed, of course, that something momentous had occurred to provoke the felicity that neither Mr. Darcy nor I could mask.

Throughout the meal, I felt William's eyes upon me like a gentle caress, and I am certain that my love for him shone forth each time I looked up and met his gaze. Georgiana had not failed to notice the change in her brother's spirits, but fortunately, she did not recognize the connection between us as the cause.

"I think that walk in the rain did you good, Wills."

"Indeed?"

"Yes, your temper has lightened. I declare that I have not seen you this pleased in months."

"I believe you are right, my sweet sister. I must walk in the rain more often."

She smiled innocently, and I clutched my napkin to my face to hide my amusement.

Following dinner, Georgiana played on the small pianoforte Lord Killaine had installed before we arrived. Although she deemed it inferior to the one her brother had given her at Pemberley, she was able to coax one lilting tune after another from its keys.

Suddenly, Mr. Darcy rose. "I am in serious need of dancing a reel!"

"A reel!" Georgiana cried, clapping her hands. "Oh yes, I know the perfect Irish air."

"Come, everyone," he demanded. "We must all join in."

Shock evident upon their faces, Mrs. Annesley and Mrs. Gardiner laid their needlework aside. Mr. Darcy called the servants and assisted them in quickly shoving the settee, chairs, tables, and chaise back against the walls.

"Now, let us participate. Yes, all of you. Ladies, come now. Mrs. Gardiner, you may partner with Mrs. Annesley, and Elizabeth…you shall dance with me."

Mr. Darcy graced me with a most tender look. It took all my strength not to run into his arms.

The older ladies protested at first, but the gentleman would not be dissuaded. He signalled Georgiana to begin and then held out his hands, indicating that all four of us should join hands in a circle. Upon commencement of the first notes, much hilarity ensued as we skipped and bounced our way around the room. Mr. Darcy called out encouragement with each change in pattern. Never had I seen him behave with such disinterested abandon. We laughed until, after three dances, Mrs. Gardiner begged to be seated, complaining that the merriment had caused a stitch in her side.

To quench our thirst, we sipped sherry. We continued to laugh and talk for some time. Conversation sparkled, for Mr. Darcy treated us to one amusing anecdote after another. Where had this man been hiding all my life? Discarding the burden from his heart had freed him in more ways than I ever imagined. I knew he possessed a reserved nature, and I doubted that night's excess of spirits signalled a permanent alteration in his character. Nevertheless, such knowledge did not prohibit me from thoroughly enjoying the pleasure he allowed himself to exhibit that particular evening.

At length, the ladies began to yawn, and they and Georgiana soon bade their good nights. I lingered a bit, hoping to snatch a moment alone with William.

"Are you coming, Lizzy?" my aunt asked, walking toward the door.

"In a moment, Aunt."

She cocked her head. "Be sure to look in on me before you retire, my dear."

"I shall."

"And do not be long."

I nodded, knowing she would not sleep until I had done as she wished. Once the door closed behind her, however, William caught my hand and pulled me to him.

"She knows, does she not?"

"She does, and she is more than pleased for us. I could not keep from telling her."

"I am happy that you did. I long to step outside the door and shout to the entire world, 'Elizabeth Bennet loves me!'"

I laughed and leaned my head back to gaze up at him.

"Do you know how much I love you?" he said softly.

"I think so, but I should dearly love to hear you tell me all the same."

"I would rather show you," he whispered, gathering me close.

I lifted my face to his and felt myself surrender as his lips covered mine. Softly, he caressed my lips, nibbling and teasing until they parted. He then captured my mouth, provoking delicious waves of desire to flood over me. Unknowingly, I spread my hands over his chest, stroking repeatedly until I reached his face. His arms had encircled my waist, and he pulled me nearer and nearer.

"I cannot hold you close enough," he whispered in my hair.

"You shall. Never fear, William, you shall."

He smiled, softly tracing his thumb along my chin. "Such a long time to wait." He groaned. "How shall I survive until we return to Longbourn? Think of that sea voyage that awaits us!"

"I have every confidence in you. Once you set your mind to something, your will is unrelenting." My tone was gently mocking.

"Except when it comes to you. My love, you will always be my weakness."

"I cannot picture you with any weakness."

"Now that you are privy to my confession, you must be merciful."

I smiled. "Then, for mercy's sake, I shall leave you now."

"And in what manner can your leaving me be considered mercy?" he cried, reaching for me as I stepped out of his arms. "Your absence certainly will not relieve my suffering."

"Still, it is prudent, for if I do not, I fear that my aunt will soon walk through the door to fetch me."

He sighed. "If you must." As I took another step from him, he pulled me back. "One more kiss before parting."

Reclaiming my lips, he proceeded to take my breath away once again, and it was with the greatest difficulty that, at length, I managed to loosen myself from his embrace. As I began to climb the stairs, he watched me ascend, but when I reached halfway, he covered the distance between us in two long strides. Holding my face in his hands, he kissed me quickly, released me, and then kissed me again.

I have never taken longer to reach my chamber than I did on that glorious night.

THE NEXT MORNING, I AWAKENED late. I had slept more soundly than I had in over a year. Consequently, I walked into an empty breakfast room. As the servant set steaming coffee and muffins emitting an exquisite aroma before me, he said that Master Darcy had gone out, and the ladies were assembled in the parlour.

Surely, William has not left for Peter Darcy's cottage without me, I hoped.

"Please ask Mrs. Gardiner to join me," I directed the servant. Within moments, she walked into the sun-lit room, dressed to go out, but for her pelisse.

"You are up at last, Lizzy."

"Forgive me. I did not know it was so late."

She waved her hand to dismiss my apology and then hastened to announce that all of us were to call upon Father Darcy that afternoon. She also explained that Mr. Darcy had gone on some errands but would return within the hour to escort us.

"All of us? What do you mean, Aunt? Has Mr. Darcy informed Georgiana of what transpired yesterday?"

She assured me that he had not but stated that he thought it proper to introduce his sister to his uncle directly. He had arranged with Mrs. Gardiner that, after a suitably short visit, she would suggest that Georgiana and her companion join her for a walk along the river. Mr. Darcy and I would remain behind so that we might talk with the priest alone.

"Will Georgiana not question why I fail to accompany you, for she knows I am fond of walking?"

"You are to say that you are tired from your long sojourn in the rain the day before and that you prefer to wait in the priest's cottage until we return."

Mrs. Gardiner smiled as though she enjoyed this small attempt at artifice. She also said she longed for Mr. Gardiner to join us so that Mr. Darcy could formally ask his blessings upon our union. In Papá's absence, he would serve as my guardian.

Perhaps, I thought, *William ought to ask my true father for his permission*, but I did not give voice to my reflection.

Our scheme for the afternoon succeeded without impediment. I was relieved to find that Father Darcy had survived the night after receiving such a shock. It was distressing, however, to see that he was unable to rise from his bed. Father Rafferty ushered us in and explained that the older priest's strength had failed him that morning. Father Darcy, however, was pleased to meet his niece, and he was cordial to her companion and my aunt, but I noticed that his eyes rarely wandered from my person.

The younger priest cautioned us not to prolong our visit, which aided in my aunt's design to remove Georgiana, her companion, and herself after only a brief visit. Father Rafferty also departed at the same time after assuring his friend that he would return later that evening.

Once they had safely withdrawn from the house, Mr. Darcy questioned his uncle as to the true state of his health and whether he wished us to leave also. The priest dismissed his nephew's concern.

"I must talk to Elizabeth. I must tell her how it all took place. You may stay, Fitzwilliam, for you should hear this also, especially since you have suffered from Catherine's tale about George."

Mr. Darcy sat in a chair at the foot of his uncle's bed while I settled myself on a stool nearest my father. I leaned forward so that I might hear every word he wished to say and gazed into a pair of eyes that matched mine, but for their age.

"Dearest child, you truly are my daughter. Although you are the image of your mother, I can see bits of myself in you as well. What must you think of me, leaving you to be reared by another?"

"Let us not speak of that now, Father. I so long to understand what happened all those years ago."

He reached out his hand and patted my cheek before closing his eyes. Seeming to travel back in time, my father began his tale.

"I fell in love with Elizabeth Willoughby during the summer of 1790. I had returned home from Cambridge and found myself restless, accepting at last the bitter truth that I could not be an Anglican vicar as my father had planned before his death and as my older brother, George, presumed I would do. After spending countless hours at my ailing mother's bedside, listening to her urge me to remain true to my Catholic faith, I, at last, tired of the emotional struggle and sought refuge on the back of my favourite horse. Several times a week, we roamed the trails that led us throughout the hills and woods of Derbyshire.

"One day, after a particularly long, hot ride, I dismounted some distance from the grounds at Pemberley and threw myself down in a grassy meadow. I allowed my horse to nibble at the tender, green shoots while I rested. I had almost fallen asleep when I heard a rustling in the trees some distance away and the distinct musical tone of a girl's laughter. I rose to follow the sound. I crept into the wood, whereupon I heard footsteps retreating through the bush. A twinkling of colour appeared before my eyes, and I darted after it in full pursuit.

"She led me on a merry chase before I caught her, but I was well rewarded with what I had snared. For there before me stood a barefoot girl with laughing eyes, a wild tangle of dark curls streaming down her back, and an arch smile upon her lips that proved enchanting.

"When she identified herself as Elizabeth Willoughby, I could not believe the beautiful creature standing before me was our neighbour's little girl from Bridesgate Manor whom I had seen now and then through the years. When had she grown up? And why had I never before noticed how lovely she was?

"From that moment, we became inseparable. She was as natural as the forest she loved and yet foreign to every woman I had ever known before in my one and twenty years. A freedom possessed her—freedom from drawing rooms, parlour conversation, pretence, and formality. It was as though she and the earth were one, and outdoors, under God's benevolent eye, hidden deep in the wood that adjoined Pemberley and Bridesgate, she thrived as a healthy rosebud blossoms when given generous servings of rain and golden sunlight.

"I found everything she did and said fascinating, and she, in turn, encouraged my company. She shared her favourite haunts with me while I entertained her with tales of my life at Cambridge and of my family's plans for me to inherit the living at Kympton.

"'That means you are to be a vicar,' she said.

"'And therein dwells the dilemma.'

"'I do not understand,' she said. 'Do you not wish for a career in the church?'

"'Not the Anglican church.'

"I then explained to her about my mother's Irish heritage, about her elopement with my father, her subsequent break with her family, and of her living a lie throughout her marriage. I described how she had attended Anglican services all those years with her husband and sons and allowed her children to be baptized in the Protestant religion. All the while, she yearned in her heart for George, Henry, and me to someday become members of the true church. Elizabeth, of course, had no idea of what *true church* I spoke, but she was as open and innocent as a child when I began to teach her Catholic doctrine.

"At length, we visited the small chapel in the wood at Pemberley that my father had allowed to be built for my mother. There, Elizabeth accepted further instruction in the faith from the priest, Father Ayden. It was not long before she professed a desire to become baptized. After doing so, she received Our Lord in Holy Communion and completed the necessary studies for Confirmation. All this was done in secret, of course, and our growing relationship remained hidden.

"Elizabeth's younger sister, Eleanor, often accompanied us on our rambles in the wood, but she feared the priest and would not enter the church with us. She did keep watch without, however, to make certain we were not discovered. We made it into a sort of game, which she found highly entertaining, and she was only too pleased to play at what she considered an adventure. Eleanor had no idea of the gravity of her sister's decision or the growing strength of our feelings for one another.

"My mother's illness advanced that autumn, and I delayed my return to Cambridge because of it. I had always been particularly close to her, and she sought my presence even more as her health declined. She became possessed with the idea that I move to Ireland, her homeland, where I might practice my faith without the consequences affecting the futures of my brothers. My father had died some years earlier, and George, who was eight years my senior, had assumed his place as head of the family. He had married Anne, a titled lady, whose connections could assist George in any future ambitions he might entertain.

"'Once I am dead,' my mother said, 'George will be free of what this country considers the Catholic taint. If you go to Ireland, Peter, there will be no one to hold George back. And you might also re-establish contact with my family in County Cork. I trust that my brothers' hearts have softened and that they will take you in. When you reach the shores, call upon Lord Killaine. He will aid you once he learns you are my son and that you have embraced the church.'

"Of course, my mother knew nothing of my affection for Elizabeth or my horror at the thought of leaving the girl behind. Upon good days, which grew ever less frequent as the months passed, Mother made particular plans for supporting my leave-taking. She urged me to keep it our secret, for she and I both knew that George would not approve.

"Sadly, three weeks after Christmas, she died. It was a bitter, cold day in January, and I felt the loss deeply. I sought refuge at the chapel in the wood, and it was not long before Elizabeth found me weeping there. She shared my grief, not because she knew Mother well, but because she loved me. Any emotion either of us felt ruled the other, for our spirits were bound to each other.

"The day after my brothers and I buried Mother, Elizabeth and I made plans to marry. We engaged the support of the parish priest, and then I travelled to London to secure a special licence, having told my brothers I was calling upon a friend from school. We could tell the truth to neither of our families, for her brother would have forbidden it and never given his consent, especially when he learned that I had influenced his sister to change her religion. I also knew that George and Lady Anne would not understand. After all, I had not completed my education nor did I possess much of a future, for now that I was Catholic, I could never accept the living at Kympton.

"Elizabeth's brother, Sir Linton Willoughby, was an ambitious but indolent scoundrel."

Mr. Darcy gave a disgusted grunt of agreement and rose from his chair.

"I see you have discovered that for yourself, Fitzwilliam." Father Darcy asked for water, which I quickly brought to his bedside. "Thank you, my dear." He sipped from the glass before returning it to me.

"Having assumed leadership of his family after his father's death, Willoughby had already wasted much of his fortune. He was his mother's favourite, however, and she would deny him nothing. Together, they had determined to marry Elizabeth to Lord Dudley Haversham, a balding, stout, old widower twice Elizabeth's age. Plans to secure the alliance during the approaching Season in Town were already underway, for Sir Dudley's appetite for young women was well known. Thus, it was essential that I married Elizabeth before she was forced to depart Derbyshire.

"To comply with the legalities of the Crown, we married on the first of March 1791 in the Anglican Church in which the vicar had baptised us and in the faith he assumed we yet professed. I secured his pledge and that of the witnesses, his wife and daughter, to keep the union secret until we informed our families.

"Afterwards, we proceeded to the Catholic chapel where Father Ayden married us before God. Two Irish labourers working temporarily in the country, whom Father Ayden had given shelter for the night, witnessed our vows. They made their marks, and on the morrow, they went on their way. We planned to announce our marriage to both of our families a fortnight later just before the Willoughbys were to leave for Town. That gave me sufficient time to confirm our passage to Ireland from the funds my mother had quietly hidden away for me in a distant county with a banker unknown to George.

"I shall not share with you how and where Elizabeth and I managed to be together during those two weeks, but be assured that I was as resourceful as any man violently in love. We determined to tell our news to Elizabeth's family before we confessed the marriage to George and Lady Anne. Our plans, however, went astray at Bridesgate, and I never told George that I had married.

"Sir Linton erupted into a rage the likes of which I had never witnessed before. He vowed that he would annul the marriage! He declared that our wedding was invalid because Elizabeth was not of age when she married and when she converted to what he called the *Papist* religion. He said he would see me in hell before he ever allowed me near his sister again. He announced that Elizabeth *would* marry Lord Haversham and that, if I made any attempt to change his plans, he would discredit my family's reputation. After ordering Elizabeth confined to her room, he drove me from Bridesgate."

By that time in his uncle's narrative, Mr. Darcy had risen from his chair and begun to pace back and forth.

"My first thought was to employ George's aid, but he and Lady Anne had not yet returned from Town. They had travelled there with Henry to commence plans for his enlistment in His Majesty's service. I was wild with anger, fear, and frustration. I had no one at Pemberley to call upon for help, and I knew that the Willoughbys planned to leave Derbyshire the following day.

"At last, I raced through the wood to the chapel and sought Father Ayden's counsel. We reviewed my options at length, and he advised me to return to Bridesgate that night after Sir Linton's temper had cooled. He could not believe the man would not listen to reason once he settled down, and the priest assured me that Elizabeth's brother would not annul our marriage.

"That night, I hastened to see Sir Linton. A frightful storm broke just as I climbed the stone steps to the entrance of the house. I recall how the butler refused me entry, evidently upon his master's orders, and I stood out in the rain, waiting. At length, Sir Linton appeared and that is when…the inconceivable happened."

Father Darcy's voice broke, and I watched tears fill his eyes. He clutched at his chest and inhaled sharply. I rose and ran to fetch the powder Father Rafferty had shown me earlier. I stirred it into another glass of water. Mr. Darcy assisted him in sitting up, and the priest sipped the draught for some time before resuming his account. As I turned to sit once more on the stool, he caught my hand.

"Stay close beside me, lass. Sit on the bed, pray, for my strength falters."

I eased myself down beside him, for I, too, had noticed the weakness of his voice. "Perchance you have said enough for today, Father."

He made a feeble gesture in protest. "No...no, I must tell you before I am no longer able to do so. You, of all people, have the right to know."

He swallowed visibly and then fixed his eyes on some unseen object in the distance. He remained silent for so long that I feared he was lapsing into some sort of vision, but just as I despaired of his return to the story, he rallied and began again.

"That night, at the commencement of that terrible storm, Willoughby told me that my Elizabeth was dead. Dead...even after all these years, I still find it difficult to say the word."

"A bold-faced lie!" Mr. Darcy exclaimed, balling his hands into fists.

"Yes, Fitzwilliam," Father Darcy agreed, "but I did not know it until yesterday. Willoughby said Elizabeth had fallen down the stairs from the second floor and broken her neck. Shock and outrage coursed through me. I wanted to throttle him, but he slammed the door in my face with a hatred I shall never forget. I cannot recall much of what happened after that. I must have wandered through the wood like a madman all night, for at dawn, I came to myself on the steps of the chapel, soaked and chilled from the rain.

"Inside, I threw myself before the altar and cried out my despair. The next thing I remember was Father Ayden's endless questions as to the cause of my sorrow. I grasped little of what he said, other than something about allowing God to work in my life.

"Out of my mind with grief, I fell into a raging fever. Father Ayden put me to bed in his quarters and tended to my needs. I remember begging him to return to Bridesgate and give Elizabeth the last rites before her brother had her buried. When he suggested returning me to Pemberley or at least going there to inform George, I insisted that he do as I ask and go to Bridesgate instead. I assured him that all my family was in London, so a visit to Pemberley would be useless.

"I remained with him for several days, eventually growing stronger. Upon my recovery, Father Ayden told me of what had transpired at Bridesgate. Armed men hired by Willoughby met him at the entrance to the grounds. The steward informed the priest he was not welcome and that neither he nor Peter Darcy would be admitted under any circumstances. Father Ayden asked to see Elizabeth's body, but he was told that she had already been buried in an unmarked grave in a secluded place unknown to anyone but Sir Linton. Not even buried in consecrated ground!

"A burly footman made a menacing gesture with his weapon, lending force to the words of Willoughby's steward. 'Sir Linton says to tell Mr. Peter Darcy he is not welcome at Bridesgate. If he or anyone from that Papist church trespasses, our orders are to treat him as any common intruder.'

"I did not return to Pemberley. I did not write to George or Henry in Town. Within the week, I recovered enough to depart for Holyhead, where I booked passage on a ship sailing for Dublin and made my way to my mother's home county. The banker my mother had trusted gave me his pledge of secrecy. I also secured Father Ayden's vow of silence about the matter before leaving, for I now feared for his safety as well as that of my family. To my way of thinking, Willoughby had become insane."

"But why?" Mr. Darcy cried. "Why did you not go to Father and ask for his aid?"

The old priest closed his eyes. "To this day, my boy, I do not know why I failed to inform my family of my whereabouts. Perhaps I was simply too undone with my own misery to think clearly. When Henry found me fourteen years later, that, too, was his first question, but I did not have an answer, and I still do not. By that time, I wore the cassock I wear today. Perhaps I knew George would never approve my decision to join the priesthood, and I did not wish to endure the aggravation of his censure. I freely admit that is not an adequate reason, and I regret having caused Lady Anne and George, as well as Henry, anguish over my disappearance.

"I never told any of them about my marriage to Elizabeth. After all, she was gone, and the entire union had existed no longer than a fortnight. When Henry found me and yet did not mention the Willoughbys, I assumed Sir Linton's wrath had faded and he had kept it quiet, wishing to hide the news of what he considered his sister's disgrace from even my family.

"Now, you tell me Elizabeth did not die as her brother falsely declared. Rather, that she died some nine months later in childbirth. How deserted she must have felt! What must she have thought of my forsaking her? A coward …surely, she must have considered me the lowliest of cowards. I cannot forgive myself for having left her." Tears trickled down his worn, lined cheeks.

"Sir Linton is the one I shall not forgive," Mr. Darcy declared, and I murmured my agreement. He walked across the room to the window. He stood there some time before turning to face us. "What I wonder is exactly how much my father knew of this matter."

"What do you mean?" I asked.

"Did he know that Elizabeth Willoughby had married Uncle Peter, or did he believe her child was born out of wedlock?"

"According to Lady Catherine, he believed the latter," I said.

"But…did Lady Catherine tell us the truth?"

Father Darcy sighed. "If I know Catherine, she told as much truth as she needed to satisfy her demands."

"She demanded that I never engage myself to Mr. Darcy," I said.

"Precisely," Mr. Darcy said. "And she professed to believe that Elizabeth was the *natural* daughter of George Darcy. Surely, my father would never have told such a lie, even to protect you, Uncle Peter. I say that a call upon my aunt is in order as soon as we return to England."

"And I shall write to Miss Willoughby this evening," I added. "I would be interested in knowing how much of the story she assumed that we knew, but did not."

"Is Eleanor happy?" Father Darcy asked. "She was such a lively little girl. Her laugh was delightful. One could not keep from smiling upon hearing her."

I sighed. "She has not had an easy life living with her brother, but I am thankful to report that she bears a pleasant expression and a kind manner. She has never married, but she seems content."

A light tap on the door signalled the ladies' return. They waited without as we made our farewells.

"Shall you visit me tomorrow, my dear?" the priest asked, clinging to my hand. I assured him that I would. "Then, God give me strength so I may begin to beg your forgiveness on the morrow."

"There is nothing to forgive, Father. You have been sinned against as much as I."

Chapter Sixteen

That evening, Mr. Darcy and I remained much subdued. Fortunately, Georgiana chattered happily about her upcoming visit with Lord Killaine's daughter on the morrow. Being nearly the same age, they had taken an immediate liking to each other's company, and Miss Niamh Killaine had invited her to spend the day. They planned to ride horses selected from her father's highly regarded stable and enjoy a picnic with their older companions. Miss Annesley, regrettably, did not share her young charge's enthusiasm for horses, but she did her best to remain cheerful.

When Georgiana took her place at the pianoforte, I sat down at the desk and began my letter to Miss Willoughby. I hardly knew what to say, for my father's story had stunned me. The need for answers, however, drove me to find the words.

"Wills, shall we repeat last evening's entertainment? I have discovered another reel among my music."

"Not tonight."

"Oh, why not? We all had such fun last evening."

Mrs. Gardiner intervened, stating that she remained tired from their walk, and Mrs. Annesley agreed, especially in light of the forthcoming day that awaited her.

Georgiana brooded a bit. "I do not see why everyone should be dismal tonight."

I looked up to see Mr. Darcy's gaze upon me as he filled his glass with sherry. 'Twas true; our mood was low, but how could it be otherwise? The tragic story of Peter Darcy and Elizabeth Willoughby hung over us. I felt guilty for my personal joy. Mr. Darcy and I were free to confess our love for each other, when my parents' happiness had been cruelly snatched away.

Before long, Mrs. Annesley suggested that she and Georgiana retire. Since our company lacked the previous evening's sparkle, Mr. Darcy's sister did not resist. Bidding us good night, my aunt soon followed. In private, before dinner, I had informed her of what we learned from Father Darcy. Thus, she did not need to wait up for me, but I was well aware that she would not sleep until she knew I was safely above stairs. I assured Mrs. Gardiner that I would join her shortly upon completion of my correspondence.

The moment the door closed behind her, I felt William's presence beside me. It took but one look to pass between us for me to lay down my pen and step into his embrace. Gently, he kissed me and held me close, wrapped securely in his strong arms.

"I love you," he whispered in my ear.

"And I love you." I buried my face in his neck, delighting in how his scent never failed to stir my senses. He led me to the sofa where we sat together, my head upon his shoulder.

"Did you accomplish your letter?"

"Almost. I found it difficult to compose."

"Understandably."

I raised my head so that I might see his face. "Do you feel guilty, William?" When he frowned, I said, "Because we are happy and my parents were denied the right to their life together?"

"Your father would wish you to be neither guilty nor unhappy."

"Sometimes I fear that this will not last. That from out of nowhere, some demon will appear and steal away our pleasure."

He laid my head back onto his shoulder. His touch was gentle and comforting. "No, no, my love, no one shall take away our contentment. I will not allow it. Why should you fear the future?"

My eyes filled with tears. "Because it happened before. I thought my life was my own. I knew who I was and where I came from, and just when I discovered that I loved you, it all dissipated before my eyes. One word from Lady Catherine destroyed my faith that I would ever delight in life again. If it happened once, could it not do so again?"

I felt the muscles in his arms tighten. "If I find that she did this out of spite, someone had better restrain me!"

"At times, I think it is best that she told us. Papá would never have revealed it."

"And why should he? True, we are cousins, but that connection will not impede our marriage. When I think of the anguish you and I suffered all those months thinking you were my sister…" He placed his lips on my forehead and drew me closer.

"It enabled me to discover my true father."

"And encumbered Uncle Peter with a profound burden of guilt."

"I grieve for him. I fear he will never regain his health."

He kissed my hair. "I share that fear, but the fragility of his health existed before we arrived."

"Shall I lose him just when I have found him?" A tear slid down my cheek. William stopped its descent with his lips.

"Come now," he said, rising to his feet. "No more tears tonight. God willing, you shall spend much time with your father."

"When do we sail for England?"

"I am in no hurry, and Mr. Gardiner must conclude his business before we book passage. I sent him a post this morning, urging him to join us as soon as possible." He smiled, pulling me to my feet. "I have something important to ask him."

"Oh?" I gave him an arch smile.

"I assume I should ask your uncle's blessing on our engagement since he stands in for Mr. Bennet on this sojourn."

"Yes, but I would have you ask another as well." He raised his eyebrows in question. "My father, Peter Darcy."

William nodded in agreement and smiled before touching his lips to mine. We kissed several times before he pulled me into a closer, warmer embrace, deepening his search until I succumbed and parted my lips. I melted into his arms and yielded my mouth, allowing him free rein, feeling my desire quicken and begin to flare. When I laboured to breathe, he, at length, withdrew, burying his face in my neck, his lips continuing to nibble my ear and the tender spot below. We parted for the night with great difficulty, repeating the previous evening's farewells.

Oh, how I loved him and longed to be his wife!

In the weeks that followed, I spent much of every day in my father's company, often beside his bed. On a good day, Mr. Darcy and I assisted him down the slope so that he might sit by the river on a chair that William had transported down the hill. I covered him with a light blanket and felt cheered that he was able to enjoy the warmth of the sun and fresh air for a short while.

We talked of everything. He wished to know all about me, my life at Longbourn, my sisters, and of course, my parents. He seemed particularly interested in Mr. Bennet, inquiring how he had treated me, whether he had been kind or harsh. I grew quiet and said little other than he had provided for me and never treated me unkindly. Father Darcy, however, sensed that my reserve did not exist without reason. Gently, he continued to search until I confessed my anger that Papá had allowed me to grow up ignorant of the truth. I had always believed him to be my father, and because that fact had been disguised, I doubted that I would ever trust him again.

"You have not forgiven Mr. Bennet, have you?" he asked. "Why not?"

I shrugged. "I cannot say, Father. We were always close. In truth, he favoured me above my sisters. I cannot seem to overcome the shock that he would conceal such an important truth about my life from me."

"Has he ever acted toward you in an unloving manner?"

"No," I said softly.

"Then, is it not possible that he simply acted out of love? What child would wish to grow up thinking she did not belong? I suspect Mr. Bennet followed his conscience, wishing to spare you pain."

"But the manner in which I was told caused me great pain."

"True, but the man who reared you did not bring it about. From what I have learned of Mr. Bennet, he has been a good father to you. He gave you a home, a family, and his name." When I did not answer, he said, "Consider my counsel, Elizabeth, and deal tenderly with this fine man who obviously loves you. He simply did what he thought best, and is that not all we can expect from a man?"

I bowed my head, unable to meet his eyes, but I did not promise to follow his admonition.

Of course, Father Darcy was also interested to learn under what circumstances I had met his nephew. It had not taken long before he suspected that we were in love, and he gave us his blessing without reserve.

"Fitzwilliam is my only nephew. Even if I had others, he would remain my favourite. I cannot think of a better man to be your husband, my child."

His eyes misted over as he spoke to us. In truth, he often struggled not to weep. I fear that he truly suffered from the revelation of my existence coming upon him without warning.

That is not to say he had not lived a good and an exciting life. He confided some of his exploits on behalf of his parishioners that had oft times resulted in narrow escapes from penal confinement. If not for Lord Killaine's friendship and influence over the local magistrate, Father Darcy might not have evaded arrest. Being an Englishman also proved advantageous when he argued his case and disguised his fervent support for the rights of the Irish people. All in all, he had lived a remarkable life, and I did not tire of hearing his tales.

At the conclusion of each visit, Father Darcy continued to cling to my hand, for he knew the time would soon arrive when I must return to my homeland. I felt torn in half. I could not wait to marry William, but I did not want to leave this father I had grown to love so easily.

Within a month, Mr. Gardiner joined us at Ballymeghan, his business affairs settled at last. Mr. Darcy had written to him a second time, informing him of our discoveries and telling him of our love for each other. I knew full well that he would not find the latter surprising. The first evening my uncle spent in the village, he was more than willing to grant his approval of our engagement.

After dinner, at the conclusion of his talk with Mr. Darcy, they walked into the parlour, and Mr. Gardiner announced the happy news to our companions. My aunt, of course, simply smiled, but Georgiana was shocked. I am pleased to report, however, that the coming marriage filled her with delight. She declared she was glad that we were to be sisters, and I answered in kind. Little did she know how relieved I was not to be her sister by birth!

In the days that followed, Mr. Gardiner met Father Darcy. The two of them discussed with Mr. Darcy the consequences of revealing locally that the priest had a daughter. While the Irish loved their priest, they also had a hearty regard for any and all scandal, and such news would be the talk of the parish and neighbouring parishes for some time. He, of course, had told his confessor, who did not think it necessary to enlighten the people. The bishop was informed, and he agreed, largely out of respect for his friend and benefactor, Lord Killaine, but coupled with the fact that he did not want a scandal on his hands. My father accepted the bishop's decision, although he declared that he was willing to tell the world, for he was proud of me, a fact that filled my heart with peace. Shame had been my companion for so long. I often had to pinch myself to realize no cause for it had ever existed.

Mr. Darcy asked the priest for his counsel as to whom we should tell in England and, also, whether we should inform Georgiana that I was Peter Darcy's daughter. He asked them to bring his niece to visit him once more, whereupon he told her a love story. At the conclusion, she wept.

"That is the saddest tale I have ever heard, Father," she said.

"It is true," he responded.

"True? Do you know the couple involved?"

"Intimately." He then explained that it was his story and that of his wife, Elizabeth.

Georgiana's eyes grew wide. "But you are a priest, Father. I do not understand."

"It happened before you were born, my child, when I was very young and before I made the decision to join the priesthood. I was the young man who fled Pemberley, thinking my bride had died, never knowing she was with child. I made a new life for myself in this country, for I could not bear to remain without her in the place where she had lived."

"And the baby, Father. What happened to her?"

"The baby will soon become your sister."

"My sister? I do not understand. Elizabeth will be my sister when she is wedded to Wills."

Father Darcy nodded. Slowly, recognition registered on Georgiana's face. I held my breath, wondering what her rejoinder would be. She rose from the chair on which she sat, and after running around the bed, she embraced me. We clung to each other, unable to speak until she, at last, turned toward her brother. "Wills, why did you never tell me before?"

"I did not learn the truth until we came to this village. When I did, I thought the revelation belonged to our uncle and to Elizabeth."

"How long have you loved her?"

"A long time."

"No wonder you discouraged me from matchmaking when she last visited Pemberley!"

"No wonder, indeed," he said, hugging her close. His eyes met mine, and I rejoiced to know that we no longer were required to keep the circumstances of my birth secret.

AT LAST, THE TIME ARRIVED for us to leave Ballymeghan. Only the evening before, a letter from Miss Willoughby had arrived with the post. I shared it with Mr. Darcy and the Gardiners and then set out to show it to my father. Mr. Darcy accompanied me, for he also wished to bid his uncle farewell. Fortunately, it was a fair day for the priest. He sat by the fire in his favourite chair and called for us to enter when he heard the knock on the door.

"I have heard from Miss Eleanor Willoughby, Father," I said after we had greeted each other. "Would you like to read the letter?"

"My eyesight is dim, my dear. Shall you read it for me?"

I pulled my chair close to his so that he might hear every word.

London

My dearest Elizabeth,

I received your letter with alacrity, but I confess I am shocked that Linton did not share the entire truth of the matter concerning your mother. I rejoice that you have found your father after all these years. I remember him with pleasure, for I thought him the most agreeable of men. Naturally, from my tender perspective, I had few with whom to compare. Still, he always treated me with kindness.

I had no idea that you were unaware of your parents' marriage. Linton certainly knew, as did my mother and grandmother. I remember the morning your father came to call after they had been married some two weeks earlier. We were all present in the drawing room—my brother, sister, mother, and grandmother—but when your father made the announcement of his marriage to Elizabeth, I was quickly dispatched to the schoolroom. I confess, however, that I did not remain there once my governess began to doze in her chair. I crept down to the landing, where the uproar brewing within the drawing room could be heard quite clearly.

Linton vowed to annul your parents' marriage. He threatened your father with direful warnings that I did not understand at the time. Once he drove him from the house, he assured Elizabeth that she would carry out his plans and marry Lord Haversham, and if she refused or ever told anyone of this prior marriage, he would commit bodily harm upon Mr. Darcy. Mother then called the servants and told them to finish packing for our immediate removal to London.

I shrank back into the shadows and watched maids scurry to and fro like mice running from a tomcat. Linton personally escorted Elizabeth up the stairs and forced her into her chamber. When I witnessed her pitiful pleading and cries for his understanding, I could not remain hidden. Running out into the open, I grabbed my brother's hand and attempted to disengage his grip from my sister's arm. My efforts were as ineffectual as a tiny insect waging war upon a wild boar. He thrust her into the room and locked the door behind her.

I did not know your father returned to our house that night. I do recall the terrible storm, for its roar was the only sound that muffled my sister's weeping. At that time, I knew nothing of the lie Linton told your father.

All of us left for Town the next day, save my grandmother. Elizabeth and I were kept apart most of the time or governed by either Mother or the governess. I remember that, during the journey, my sister attempted to run away more than once, but she was recovered each time.

In London, Elizabeth was kept under lock and key for what seemed like ages to a child, but could not have been more than two or three months. Of a sudden, one day she was gone—returned to Bridesgate without explanation. I suppose I was considered too young to be told why. I never saw her again.

In December, a few weeks before Christmas, I was told that my sister had died. I was heartbroken, undone with sorrow. When I asked the cause of her death, no one answered me. I suppose my mother grieved, but if so, she kept it hidden from me. Linton continued on his descent into personal destruction. My grandmother passed away the following month, and when we travelled to Derbyshire to close up the house, I stole away one afternoon and discovered Elizabeth's grave. There were no blossoms to be found in January, and I grieved that I could not cover her grave with the yellow daffodils she loved so well.

I looked up to see my father sobbing. Tears filled my eyes, and my throat constricted so that I could not continue. William saw my distress and took the letter from me. Father Darcy beckoned, and I knelt on the floor at his feet, holding his hand while William finished reading.

I did not learn that my sister died in childbirth for seven years. Upon her deathbed, my mother revealed the truth to me. She was terrified of dying, afraid that she would be held accountable in the next life for her part in Elizabeth's tragic story.

You ask whether my sister knew that Mr. Darcy believed her dead. I cannot answer that. As I said, I was prevented from being in her presence alone, for Linton and Mother blamed me for knowing of your parents' friendship and keeping it secret. I do know that I never saw her smile again or any trace of that lively spirit she had always possessed. I saw nothing but grief and hopeless resignation in her eyes. We snatched but a moment to speak alone the day before she disappeared from our house in Town.

"I shall always love him, Ellie," she whispered.

"Surely, Darcy will come for you," I said.

"Yes, he will come if he can, but I fear something dreadful has happened to him, for I know he would never forsake me. No matter what happens or what they do to me, they cannot destroy what I feel in my heart. Linton may annul my marriage, but I shall never marry Lord Haversham. I shall die first, for Darcy will always be my husband."

Those were the last words I heard Elizabeth utter.

I am sorry, my dear, that I cannot shed more light on your questions or give you more agreeable news. I do know this: Your mother loved your father, and if she had lived, I know she would have loved you more than life itself. She would not have you grieve for her. She would wish for you to live life to its fullest. Be happy, Elizabeth, for your mother's sake and for your own.

With deepest regards,

Eleanor Willoughby

I heard Mr. Darcy fold the paper and slip it into his coat pocket. I had laid my head upon my father's knee, and he gently smoothed back my hair. All three of us remained silent, save for the sounds of my father's weeping. At length, I looked up at his lined face, and he reached out, clutching me to his breast.

"I love you, Father," I whispered over and over.

"And I love you more than you will ever know, my own dearest child."

I could hear Mr. Darcy begin to pace, as he did when greatly disturbed. "What has happened is monstrous! Someone must pay for this. I shall call out Willoughby as soon as I reach London!"

"No!" I cried. "William, you must not."

"Stand still, Fitzwilliam. You tire me out with all that walking about. Come, and listen to reason."

Mr. Darcy looked as though he wished he might utter an oath, but he ceased pacing and sat in the chair I had vacated.

"It is not right, Uncle! Willoughby should not go free without suffering some consequence for this heinous deed."

"From what you and Elizabeth have told me, Linton has not gone free. His life is ruined, and he has no future. Do not seek revenge, for it will not undo the past. Leave him to God."

"I shall never forgive him!" Mr. Darcy muttered.

"You must. Both of you must forgive the man. Your hatred will do him no harm, but it will kill your souls. Forgiveness is the only answer, my children."

"You ask too much, Uncle."

"All things are possible with God, my son." He patted my hair again and stared off in the distance. "The only obstacle I cannot overcome…is how to forgive myself."

"But, Father," I said, "you have no guilt in this matter."

He tenderly placed his hand upon my cheek. "Tell that to my heart, my child."

WE SAILED FROM IRELAND ON the twenty-sixth day of September, taking advantage of the last calm seas before the harsh tides of winter set in. Leaving Father Darcy had proved painful, for we both knew it was most likely that we should never meet again. Before we parted, I asked him whether he regretted learning of my birth.

"Never, my child, for knowing that Elizabeth and I will live on in you and your children is a blessing I never anticipated. I thought that dream had died in England, and now I rejoice that it has come true."

William and I had discussed the possibility of my father returning to Pemberley with us, but we feared that he could not survive the journey. When we raised the subject with Father, he declined as we expected, stating that Ireland was his home. It had been so far too long for him to leave it now. I promised to write often, and he assured me that Father Rafferty would read the letters to him and copy his answers as he dictated. A generous flood of tears was shed between us, but we parted with a smile. Although I was sad, I longed to go home, and thus, my feelings were conflicted as we rode out of Ballymeghan.

I shall not relate the tedious and often boring detail of our journey. Suffice it to say that it was as tiring as one might expect, by both carriage and ship. My heart, however, gradually began to grow lighter with the passing of each mile, for I looked forward to the future with expectations that I had not dared to entertain before. I knew that, God willing, Mr. Darcy and I would wed at Longbourn Church as soon as he was able to secure a special licence. That thought sustained me through all the discomfort of travelling.

It seems somewhat silly, but I recall that the most difficult aspect of the journey was the fact that William and I were unable to find a moment of privacy together. During the confinement of the long carriage ride, either Georgiana and Mrs. Annesley shared the coach or Mr. and Mrs. Gardiner did. William was forced to content himself with simply gazing upon me as the miles crept by. We found the inns crowded along the route to Dublin, so finding a hidden setting proved impossible. Even when we took a walk in the evening, Georgiana wished to keep us company. We loved her, but oh, how we hoped she felt too tired for exercise at the end of each day. Alas, God blessed the young girl with an unpardonable amount of energy!

We spent a week in Dublin awaiting our ship, during which Mr. Darcy secured tickets for a box at the theatre on Wednesday night. Neither Mrs. Gardiner nor Mrs. Annesley felt up to the evening, so my uncle and Georgiana accompanied us. Believe me when I say that Mr. Darcy took every opportunity to hold my hand each time the audience turned their attention to the stage. Softly, he traced circles in my palm or caressed my wrist with such tenderness that I confess I could not tell you what the play was about. I could feel his eyes upon me, and consequently, I spent most of the evening returning his loving gaze rather than watching the actors' performance. Not a word was spoken between us, but we did not need words.

Once aboard ship, our attempts to be alone were impeded even more. The cramped quarters below deck threw us together with our companions and the other passengers, and on deck, of course, we were in open view of the captain and his crew. Our separation began to play on Mr. Darcy's temper. More than once, he answered Georgiana with a tone of irritation or refused her requests, whatever they were, a behaviour I had not witnessed before and one that puzzled his young sister.

At length, one evening at the close of the meal, as he withdrew from the table to join the gentlemen for a drink, he stopped beside my chair.

"Your shawl, Miss Bennet," he said quietly as he picked it up from the floor.

Evidently, it had slipped from my shoulders and dropped from the chair. Placing it in my hands, he also enclosed a tiny scrap of paper. I looked up to meet his eyes and read the message therein. As soon as possible, I unfolded the note.

Meet me on deck after the others retire.

My heart beat faster at the thought. Might I possibly slip away without alerting Mr. and Mrs. Gardiner or being heard by anyone else? The thought filled me with adventure. I feared the evening would never end. The captain and ship's doctor entertained us with a duet on cello and violin. Their performance was quite proficient, but it would go on and on. Georgiana was entranced and wished for a pianoforte so that she might join them. I began to think they should play all night.

Finally, the company dispersed, and we bade each other good night before we settled in our cabins. I did not undress. Instead, I repeatedly checked my appearance in the small mirror. One would think I was to attend my first ball from the glow on my cheeks.

While tapping my foot impatiently, I placed my head against the wall, hoping to hear nothing but silence from the next room. When all was quiet, I proceeded to the door and leaned against it to detect noises from without. Imagine my surprise when someone rapped on the door precisely on the spot next to my ear!

"Oh!" I cried aloud, but opened the door forthwith to find my aunt asking to come in.

"Why, Lizzy, you have not even begun to prepare for bed. Are you not tired?"

"I…I am. I was just…looking for a favourite book before I turn in. What brings you, Aunt? Are you unwell again? May I be of service?"

She smiled, her complexion turning slightly pink. "No, I just hoped for a quick word. I have news that I wish to share with you. I am with child again."

"With child? How wonderful! Are you certain?"

"All the signs are evident. That is why I have suffered illness so often on the journey. I tell you, Lizzy, I am much relieved, for I feared these aches and pains were a sign of age. Now, I see that I am not so old after all."

"Of course not! I am thrilled. What does Uncle Edward say?"

"He is pleased. He hopes for another boy so that, eventually, when he changes the name of his business to *Gardiner and Sons*, there will be one more to add to the company." We laughed merrily and discussed the upcoming event no little time before she, at last, rose from the bed to leave.

"On another note, Lizzy, I must ask you whether you have noticed how abrupt Mr. Darcy has been with his sister today. Is something amiss?"

I shrugged. "Perhaps he simply tires of the voyage."

"Hmm...it seems so out of character, for he is the soul of patience with her most days."

"Everyone has a disagreeable day, even Mr. Darcy, it seems."

"Yes, even Mr. Darcy. You are quite certain he has not mentioned anything to you, Lizzy?"

"No," I said honestly, for he truly had not spoken of his ill humour, although I knew perfectly well its cause.

My answer seemed to satisfy Mrs. Gardiner. She withdrew shortly thereafter, cautioning me not to sit up too late. Thus, I was forced to blow out the candle and remain quiet for some time, awaiting the cessation of sound that signalled her eventual retirement for the night.

I heard the bell tolling the midnight hour when I cautiously opened my door, slipped out, and tiptoed up the stairs. My efforts were rewarded with the smile on Mr. Darcy's face as he waited beside the stairway.

"At last," he said. "I began to think you would not come."

"My aunt came calling." We walked to the railing and then crossed to the starboard side of the ship. "I confess I found your note surprising."

"Surprising? And why is that? When a man is as starved as I am for time alone with the woman he loves, why should he not resort to any and all pursuits?"

I laughed lightly. "It has been a long time since we have enjoyed a solitary meeting."

"Long? It has been an eternity. Do you have any idea how I yearn to kiss you and hold you close?"

"We still cannot do so, sir, for we are hardly free of company. I feel the eyes of the seamen upon us this very moment."

"True, but at least we may speak without restraint."

We had reached the bow and stood at the railing, leaning into the wind.

The night was beautiful, filled with stars that seemed to stretch to the ends of the earth. The splash and churn of waves below us muffled our speech, so even if a crewmember walked past, we could not be heard. Mr. Darcy leaned with his elbows against the rail, extending his arms over the water. We stood in silence for some time, simply content to be together.

At last, I decided to speak. "Mrs. Gardiner noticed your short temper with Georgiana today. She wished to know whether something was wrong."

"And did you tell her?"

"What should I have told her?"

"That I am in a horrid mood because I cannot take you in my arms. That I find it more and more difficult to pass each day so near and yet so far from you."

"Naturally, sir. That is exactly what I told her."

He smiled. "None of your impertinence, miss, or I may kiss you right here in front of everyone."

"William!"

"I am in pain, Elizabeth."

"Pain?"

"For want of you."

I looked up at him, wishing I could assuage his yearning. "You simply must not."

"Have no fear. I will not touch you. See, my hands are before me. I do not even brush against you when you stand there as tempting as a goddess. But I can feel you…your warmth, your softness…every lovely bit of you."

I could not speak, for his words of love caused that heat deep within to rise up and flood my senses. The way he looked at me and the ragged tone of his voice were so tender that he may as well have placed his hands upon me.

"Do you wonder how I know what you feel like?"

"I dare not ask."

"Dreams…endless dreams. I have dreamt of you for nigh on to two years."

"William…"

"I knew just how you would fit in my embrace—as though you were made for it—how the warmth of your silky skin would set me on fire and how the essence of your scent would remind me of everything good in this life. I have known these things since long before I could admit that I loved you, for you have haunted my dreams without mercy."

I swallowed. "When did you first know that you loved me?"

He smiled. "I hardly know. I was in the middle before I had even begun."

I could feel his eyes upon me as they moved from my hair, over my face, my lips, and down to my neck like a loving caress.

"How...how do you do that?"

"Do what?" he asked, smiling again.

"Make love to me with your eyes?"

"As easily as drawing breath." He groaned and turned his back to the rail. "Oh, why does this blasted ship not give a sudden lurch and throw you into my arms again?"

"I found it very difficult being in your presence when we thought we were brother and sister."

"Difficult! It was a wretched nightmare! And it went on and on and on. I thought I should never find the truth."

"When did you doubt our relationship? What made you persist in this long, endless quest?"

"When did I doubt that I was your brother? Almost from the beginning. Oh, I tried to accept it. I struggled with everything in me, but I found it impossible."

"Because of your father's character?"

"Because I knew God could not play such a monstrous trick on us." He indicated that we should walk, and we ambled slowly up and down the deck. "And yes, I refused to accept that my father could have been guilty of such dishonour, but even more, my stubborn will refused to believe I could never have you. My greatest fear was that Fitzwilliam or some other man would win your hand in marriage before I could find the truth."

"So you were jealous?"

"What do you think?" He smiled down at me.

"I feared that you were seeking a wife, first at the Whitbys' ball when you danced with Miss Denison and then when I saw Miss Simpson on your arm in Bath."

"Diversions...nothing but diversions."

"Poor Miss Simpson, to be called nothing more than a diversion. I fear you broke her heart."

"Save your sympathy for someone else. Miss Simpson has a string of suitors, and she has broken more hearts than any other woman in Bath.

She cared little more for me than I did for her, for she had set her cap on a titled conquest. If you wish to feel sorry for someone, you should feel sorry for me. I was forced to watch you dance with every man in the house at those blasted balls!"

That remark made me laugh. "I did not dance with every man, sir, but you certainly selected the most beautiful ladies."

"I beg to differ, for at each ball, I desired most ardently to dance with the most beautiful woman there, but it was forbidden."

He inclined his head so near, and the expression in his eyes was so filled with passion that it was all I could do not to lift my lips to his.

Suddenly, he placed his hand at my elbow and steered me toward the hatch. "Hang this ship and these seamen. I must kiss you, Elizabeth!"

As we reached the stairs, he told me to go below and step into the dining room. We could not descend at the same time lest it appear unseemly. I started to protest, but the look in his eye silenced me. That night, he was a man who would not be refused.

Inside the dining hall, I wondered at Mr. Darcy's reasoning, for the wall adjoining the passageway contained four large windows. How might we find privacy therein? Some minutes passed before I saw him making his way down the hallway.

"Come," he said. "Surely there is some hidden alcove in this room."

I watched in wonder as, in the dark, he began to open doors to closets filled with supplies. At last, he pushed open a door and motioned to me. I joined him in the galley. I marvelled at how the ship's cook managed to prepare meals in such tight quarters. Mr. Darcy bade me wait just inside the door while he scoured the area. I wondered how he could see his way without a candle.

"At last," he said upon his return, "there is no one here. We are quite alone."

He pulled me into his arms, and I felt my skin begin to burn in anticipation. Gently, he kissed my cheek, my ear, and my neck before finding my mouth. Over and over, he stroked my lips in teasing nibbles until I took his face between my hands and stilled him, making him truly kiss me. I felt engulfed by love for him, filled with passionate desire to merge us somehow together for all time. I understood what he meant when he said he could not hold me close enough, for I clung to him, never wanting his kisses to cease.

They did, however, when we heard a strangled sort of noise within the room. We froze in each other's arms. He placed a finger to his lips and softly stepped away, shielding me with his body. It was nigh on to impossible to see any movement in the dark. After indicating that I should stay put, Mr. Darcy silently advanced further into the galley. The noise occurred again before he returned, and something about it sounded familiar. Within moments, he returned, placed his hand at my waist, and hurried us through the door back into the dining area.

"What was there?" I whispered. "It almost sounded like an animal."

"A human animal."

"Someone was there? Did he see us?"

Mr. Darcy shook his head. "He could not see anyone. It was the cook, sound asleep in a hammock at the end of the galley. The noise we heard was his snore."

I began to giggle, not only at the circumstances but also at the pained expression I could hear in Mr. Darcy's voice.

"I see nothing amusing about this, Elizabeth."

"Forgive me," I whispered, taking his hand. "It is just that you sound so disgusted."

"Indeed. Shall I tell you how I feel?"

"I think I know. Let us say good night, William, before we are discovered."

He sighed. "You are sensible, of course. Return to your cabin. I will wait until you have had time before I step into the passageway."

Wistfully, I smiled at him. "I love you," I whispered.

"That is my sole comfort." He kissed my forehead and sent me from the room.

Chapter Seventeen

U pon reaching Holyhead, I thought Mrs. Annesley might kiss the ground beneath her feet. Once more, she had suffered from sea-sickness almost the entire voyage.

Fortunately, my aunt was spared the affliction this time. She told me privately that she suspected her illness on the trip to Dublin had been due to expecting a child all along. Nonetheless, she was more than relieved to reach land.

After securing lodgings for us, Mr. Darcy paid a call upon the office containing the mail packets heading for Ireland. That evening after dinner, he asked Mr. Gardiner and me to join him.

"I have a letter from my aunt in Bath."

"Is something amiss?" Mr. Gardiner asked.

"Our former search through her husband's journals and correspondence caused her to undertake a thorough cleaning of the library after my sister and I departed. While directing her servants to clear away stacks of old cor-respondence and other papers, she discovered a letter written by my father to his brother tucked inside Admiral Darcy's prayer book. Mrs. Darcy said she never thought to look there, for her husband was not a religious man, and she rarely saw him open the book."

He handed the wrinkled pages to my uncle. "Why not read it for yourself?"

Mr. Gardiner held the letter near the candle and cleared his throat.

15 July 1805, Derbyshire
Dear Henry,

I rejoice that you have found Peter. How I long to see the dear boy and hold him close once again! Of course, he is no longer a boy. Evidently, he has grown away from all of us more than in the geographic sense, especially in light of the calling he has embraced. I cannot say I approve or that the news pleases me. I, however, wish him well. His choice will not lessen my love for him. I am surprised to learn that Mother aided him in going to Ireland by discreetly laying by her own funds for his use.

You must not regret your decision to withhold knowledge of the child from him. I agree that it was for the best. She would be fourteen years old by now, and what would a Catholic priest do with a girl of that age? Besides, it would interrupt his life, calling for full explanations among his peers, perhaps even cause scandal in his parish, and all for naught, for what could he do for the lass? From what you say, he lives a life of sacrificial poverty—hardly a suitable means by which to offer support.

Yes, perchance we do have a moral responsibility to inform him that he is a parent, but, in my opinion, it would serve neither him nor the child well. According to Lady Margaret, when Peter disappeared, he believed his wife was dead, and none of them knew he had left the girl with child until months later. Knowledge that Elizabeth had been, in fact, alive at the time would only grieve him and impose a burden of guilt from which he might never recover. Nine months later, his wife truly was dead, so it is preferable to let things remain as they are—hidden and buried for all time.

I believe the child is better off growing up where she is. She will never know her connection to our house or to a singular priest living in a secluded village in Ireland. And why should she? I cannot imagine any need arising for her to have such knowledge.

Listen to my counsel, and put your mind at ease. You have taken the correct action.
Affectionately,
George

"So the brothers Darcy acted from noble intentions," Mr. Gardiner said. "Fourteen years after the fact, they could see naught but harm resulting from their revelation of Elizabeth's birth to Father Peter Darcy."

"I find one sentence chilling," Mr. Darcy said. "'I cannot imagine any need arising for her to have such knowledge.' If my father had only known the turmoil his decision would cause years later." He turned to me. "Elizabeth, have you nothing to say on the matter?"

I had sat down when my uncle ceased reading. "I hardly know what to say. It is all so strange…hearing people I have never met speak of my life and arranging things that would result in such far-reaching consequences. I feel as though they speak of some other girl, someone I never knew."

"Lizzy, you are not going to be missish now, are you? I am sure neither Mr. Darcy nor I want this information to cause that."

William sat down beside me. "Forgive me. I should have been more considerate. I never meant to give you greater pain."

I shook my head. "Neither of you must fret over me. It is just that each time we uncover another piece of the puzzle, it—"

"It makes you sad," he said softly.

"Not sad, simply overcome. At times, this situation still seems imaginary to me. Can you understand what I mean? I feel as though I stand at a distance, watching it happen to someone else. Oh, I do not know how to explain it."

I rose and picked up the letter from the table where my uncle had placed it. I ran my hand over the lines on the paper, as though touching the words might make it real.

"I believe you are simply fatigued from the long journey, Lizzy," my uncle said. "I suggest you retire early tonight. Perchance sleeping on dry ground will give you sounder rest and renew your spirits."

He patted my arm and said he thought it time to join the ladies.

Mr. Darcy nodded, assuring him that we would be along in a few moments. As soon as Mr. Gardiner closed the door, William took my hand in his and lifted it to his lips.

"Dearest, it grieves me to see you like this. Would you rather that I refrain from sharing any further discovery with you?"

"What more is there to learn?"

"Once I deliver you safely to Longbourn, I plan to visit my barrister in London and then Lady Catherine. I shall also call upon Sir Linton Willoughby again and insist that he see me."

"Oh, William! You promised you would not challenge him."

"And I shall keep my word. That does not mean I shall not call him to account for his misdeeds."

"What can that possibly accomplish?"

"It will give me satisfaction, my dear."

"Is that so important? Should we not be grateful for the happiness we have found and let the past be?"

He led me back to the sofa and bade me sit beside him. "I am grateful. Believe me; no one is more grateful that you are mine and that we are to be married soon, but I shall deal with Willoughby. Do not attempt to dissuade me, for my mind is set on it."

"And Lady Catherine?"

He pressed his lips together, and a scowl extended over his face.

"William, tread carefully. She is your aunt, and I would not have you break close family bonds on my account."

"If I discover that she knew the truth and deliberately deceived us, she will be responsible for any rift it causes in our relationship. Elizabeth, you are everything to me. If my aunt cannot accept that, then she and I shall no longer meet."

AT LAST, WE REACHED LONGBOURN. I do not know who was happier to see us—the Gardiner children or Mamá. Relief covered my mother's countenance. Mary and Kitty seemed none the worse for the duties I knew she had fobbed off on them, but I doubted either of them would regret giving up their charges in favour of their own pursuits once again.

My parents seemed surprised that Mr. Darcy and Georgiana accepted their invitation for supper that evening before going to Netherfield, but once Mamá was assured that Hill could cover the extra company, she rallied to entertain such prominent guests. Her attitude toward Mr. Darcy had long since softened when she learned he and I were related, and she no longer railed against his proud, arrogant manners. Now, she professed they were his right as long as there was a chance he might procure a suitable husband for me.

Once dinner was over and the men repaired to Papá's study, I found myself growing uneasy. The three men seemed to tarry much longer than usual over their brandy. At last, they emerged. My uncle and Mr. Darcy smiled at me, and I saw the light in my betrothed's eyes. Papá, however, wore a downcast expression as he beckoned for me to join him.

I dreaded this private conversation between us but for the fact that it would secure my engagement to the man I loved. As soon as I closed the door, Papá fulfilled my apprehensions.

"Lizzy, are you out of your mind, accepting this man? Oh, I gave him my consent. One does not refuse such a man. We all know him to be a proud, disagreeable fellow, but if you like him, that does not signify. However, if you do not… Oh, my dear, let me not bear the burden of seeing you enter into a marriage with a man you cannot respect."

"Is that your only cause for disapproval?"

"Yes, of course. Now that we know the whole of the story, no impediment exists. If you truly like the man, well—"

"I do…I do like him. I love him. Indeed, he has no improper pride. If you only knew how generous he is. He is simply the best man I have ever known."

Papá blinked several times and patted my shoulder. "Well then, my dear, I am glad I was wrong. I could not bear to part with you to anyone less." He walked around the desk and sat down, sighing deeply. I rose to leave when he called me back.

"Mr. Darcy informed me that you found your father."

"Yes." I waited to see what else he might say.

"I trust he is a good man."

I looked him straight in the eye. "A very good man."

"I am glad, Lizzy."

"Is that all?"

He nodded and waved his hand to dismiss me. I turned to leave but not before I saw the sadness descend upon his countenance. *I should comfort him*, I thought, but I did not. I walked out the door without another word.

Why did I persist in that implacable resistance to forgive him? My head told me that Papá had acted in all good conscience, that he had rescued me from an unknown future. He had given me the home and name of a gentleman. Still, my heart remained bitter.

I thought of how close we had once been. I had known his thoughts before he spoke, for our minds were much alike. Our shared amusement at the foibles of others, our proclivity for the same books, and our like sense of humour had set us apart from Mamá and my sisters. Even the bond between Jane and me had never been the same as that between Papá and me. Perhaps that is why his silence resounded in my heart as betrayal. I had thought he would never keep the truth from me, especially about a matter as important as my birth.

Within a matter of moments, Papá left his study and followed me into the drawing room, where he shocked my mother with the announcement that Mr. Darcy and I were to be married. I shall not bore you with a recital of how she was stricken mute for at least a full five minutes and then proceeded to gush with enthusiasm over such a union. If one dismissed the merits of memory, one might have believed that she had favoured Mr. Darcy above all other men from the first night he appeared at the assembly ball in Meryton.

My sisters were alive with excitement and pressed us to name a wedding date.

"At least allow me leave to tell Jane first," I cried.

"Yes, yes, you must tell Jane!" Mamá said. "Oh, think of it! Three daughters married! I am the happiest mother in all of England."

THE GARDINERS DEPARTED FOR TOWN the next day, but not before Jane and Mr. Bingley arrived at Longbourn along with the Darcys. My sister and I embraced and clung to each other, or as well as anyone could cling to a woman six months into her confinement. I marvelled at her size, but the bloom on her cheeks assured me that all was well. We had so much to tell each other, and I longed for some time alone with her.

At length, we all followed my aunt and uncle and their children to the carriage, whereupon we bade our farewells, securing their promise to return for my wedding.

"Shall we take some air?" I asked Jane as the others returned to the house. Mr. Bingley and Mr. Darcy remained to escort us to the side yard where we seated Jane on a stone bench. Mr. Darcy and I had agreed earlier to share the news of Father Darcy with my sister and brother. At Netherfield, the night before, he had told them we were to be married, an announcement that gave them much satisfaction.

Relating our find in Ireland, naturally, shocked both of them. Telling them of the lie that had separated my parents before my birth rendered them almost speechless.

"How could one do that to a sister?" Jane asked at last.

"I know little of Sir Linton," Mr. Bingley said, "and none of it good."

"That is why I leave for London on the morrow," Mr. Darcy said. "I shall have it out with Willoughby and get to the bottom of this. I know my father. He would never have forsaken his brother's child without cause."

"But, Mr. Darcy, if he had not, I should never have had Lizzy for a sister, so it is not all so bad, is it?"

"Trust dear Jane to find some good in any situation." After sitting beside her, I patted her hand, and I was rewarded with a smile.

"Shall I come with you, Darcy?" Mr. Bingley asked. "I shall be glad to lend a hand."

"No, your place is here with your wife. I would not take you from her." He turned his eyes upon me. "I regret having to leave Elizabeth for any length of time. Once this is behind us, I shall never let her out of my sight."

We all smiled at his declaration, but I regretted that he was to go at all.

That evening, Mr. Darcy and I slipped out of the house, leaving Georgiana at the pianoforte and the others enjoying her performance. He led me back into the yard out of view from the parlour windows. There, he pulled me into his arms and kissed me gently.

"I must hold you as long as I can," he said. "Long enough so that I can still feel your softness and retain your sweet scent within my senses all the days we are parted."

"Must you go?"

"We have spoken of this, my love. You know the answer."

"Yes, but I do not care for it at all."

He smiled and kissed the tip of my nose. "That shall spur my return."

I HAD ANTICIPATED MR. DARCY's absence lasting but a week or less. As it happened, I did not hear from him for almost a fortnight. A short letter arrived then, a poor excuse for his return, but one I was thrilled to receive all the same. Therein, he stated that he had deposited Georgiana with the Earl of Matlock at Eden Park, met with Sir Linton, and then with Mr. Darcy's attorneys.

I found the missing pages from my father's diary. He promised to share them with me upon his return, which I hoped would prove imminent. Instead, he wrote that he would leave for Kent the next day. I was disappointed that I would not see him as soon as I wished. However, the remainder of his letter was filled with tender words that filled me with delight. My future husband certainly knew how to write a love letter.

I made valiant efforts to fill the days we were forced to be apart. Frequent visits to Netherfield occupied much of my time. Lady Lucas invited us to tea, and Mamá was pleased to see most of the Hertfordshire ladies in attendance, thus allowing her opportunity to crow over my successful alliance. We attended a card party at Mrs. Philips's house, and my aunt called at Longbourn every other day. Mamá carted me to the dressmaker several times. Not only was I fitted for my wedding gown, but I also ordered three more new dresses. Papá had agreed to fund whatever I needed, and naturally, Mamá wished me to select only the finest of materials.

"She must go to Mr. Darcy in gowns befitting her new position," she declared. "Oh, think of all our Lizzy shall have, married to a man with ten thousand a year!"

"I wager he will not spend the entire sum on Lizzy's clothes," Papá answered, a statement that made me smile, for I had just entertained the same thought.

I made time to assist Kitty with her latest addition to an old bonnet, and I even practiced the pianoforte enough to play a duet with Mary. It seemed that I wished to share my newfound joy with almost everyone. Such attentions were welcomed, and I realized how much I would miss my sisters, for soon, I would leave them for a new life. I hoped with all my heart that eventually each of them made happy unions with good men of their own.

Still, I found myself missing William more and more each day. I rambled through the Hertfordshire countryside, wishing I might happen upon him. Each time the post arrived, I raced to meet it. And every night, I sat at the window of my chamber, reliving each moment he had held me in his arms.

At last—at long last—the day came when Hill announced his name, and Mr. Darcy walked into the parlour. It was all that I could do to keep from running into his embrace. He bowed as he kissed my hand while Mamá welcomed him with excessive effusions. He spoke to her in a cordial manner, but his eyes never left mine. Papá joined us, and they spent no little time in general pleasantries. All the while, my arms ached to hold him, and my lips longed to be kissed.

We suffered through dinner, sitting across the table from one another. I was not surprised to find that, at the end of the meal, I had scarce touched the food on my plate. After having a drink with Papá and spending sufficient time thereafter within the company of my family, Mr. Darcy rose and bade us good night. I read the message in his eyes to follow him from the room.

"I shall see you to the door, sir," I said.

"Oh yes, let us all see you off, Mr. Darcy," Mamá said.

"There is no need," he protested. "I know the way perfectly well, ma'am, but, Elizabeth, I would speak to you a moment." He bowed in my mother's direction. "With your leave, of course, ma'am."

She nodded, still in awe of her new son-in-law to be, and I saw Papá smile. At the door, I took William's hat from the servant and dismissed him.

We closed the door behind us and walked out into the dark and into each other's arms. His mouth covered mine before a word was said. How could a man taste so sweet? I gave myself up to him in willing surrender. Again and again, he took my lips while his arms bound me closer to his warm body, his hands roaming up and down my back.

"Oh, how I have missed you," he whispered, "your lips, your skin, the scent of your hair, the way you feel in my arms."

"No more than I have missed you." I nestled into his neck.

"Oh yes, more, much more. No one could ever miss anyone as I have missed you. Dearest, at times, I found it hard to breathe for want of seeing your face. Tell me you will marry me without delay."

"I will, I will," I said, laughing. "But when?"

"By the end of the week?"

"This week?"

"Yes," he said, nodding vigorously. "I have the licence. Why should we wait?"

"Why, indeed?" I answered, laughing again.

"Shall you come to Netherfield tomorrow? Bingley will allow us time alone, and I have much to tell you."

"What happened at Kent?"

He shook his head. "Not tonight. I shall tell you all on the morrow. Tonight, I wish only to hold you."

IN THE BINGLEYS' DRAWING ROOM the next day, I visited with Jane for what seemed an impossible length of time. Most days, I should have welcomed a long span of time to talk to my sister, but that morning, my eyes kept straying to the doorway, hoping that Mr. Darcy and Mr. Bingley would soon return from shooting.

At length, they came. William strode to my side immediately and kissed my hand, his lips lingering and his hand pressing mine. Jane asked them how they had fared in their sport, and her husband was only too willing to enlighten us on each and every shot. Even when we sat down at the table, Charles continued on and on. I learned more about the exercise that day than I ever wished to know.

We tarried over the meal for some time, and I had to admit that it was most pleasant. There, with my favourite sister and brother, and my own dear love beside me, I could not have asked for more—other than the fact that I was anxious to be alone with William and to hear what he had learned on his journey.

"Shall we retire to the drawing room?" Jane asked at last. "Or perhaps you would enjoy a walk in the garden, Lizzy."

I saw a knowing look pass between William and Charles. "My dear, I must insist that you rest," Mr. Bingley said. "Come along, now. Our guests will understand."

"But, Charles, I do not wish to forsake Lizzy."

"Go, Jane," I said. "You should keep up your strength."

"Besides that," her husband said, "I am sure Darcy is more than willing to keep our sister company."

"Oh, of course." Jane blushed and allowed Mr. Bingley to help her rise from her chair.

"I shall go along to make certain the drapes are drawn so that you will not be disturbed." Charles turned and glanced over his shoulder, giving William another sly look as he escorted his wife from the room.

Mr. Darcy led me into the library and closed the doors behind us. He then proceeded to kiss me as any man ill with love would do. I certainly did not protest but responded to his lovemaking as I did each time his lips met mine, filled with wonder at how his mere touch could provoke such exquisite ripples of desire in me.

At length, however, we reluctantly drew apart so that he might share news of what he had learned while in London and Kent. He bade me be seated at the library table, where he had placed a packet containing the missing pages from his father's journals.

"Where and how did you find these?" I asked.

"As planned, I called upon my barristers. They were acquainted with my quest for information about your birth, for I had engaged them to begin the search on the same day last year that Lady Catherine produced the note my father had written to Sir Lewis. For most of these past months, their efforts have been in vain. However, while we were in Ireland, Mr. Barnesdale called upon his grandfather, who had been my father's attorney for many years. He retired to the country, and he is quite aged, but he remains interested in his grandson's cases. When Mr. Barnesdale began to discuss his fruitless labours on my behalf, the old gentleman produced this packet of papers."

"But why should they be in his possession?"

"My father had given them to him for safekeeping years ago. His orders had been to secure them in a place where no one else would find them. He had been told to relinquish them to no one other than my father's brothers or me. Unfortunately, when he departed the firm, the elder Mr. Barnesdale neglected to instruct his grandson to call upon him if there were any inquiries regarding George Darcy. Consequently, the pages from my father's diaries had been locked away in the old man's personal safe within his house for years, their existence known only to him. Just think: had he not lived to such an advanced age, I might never have found them."

William opened the packet and began placing page after page before me. They began, as we had suspected, in June of the year in which I was born. Sir Linton Willoughby had returned his sister to Bridesgate once he learned that she was with child. Since that knowledge had destroyed his plans to annul the marriage and marry his sister to Lord Haversham, his temper had flared out of control. He stormed into Pemberley, demanding that George Darcy inform him as to Peter's whereabouts. That was the first time George learned that his brother had secretly married Elizabeth Willoughby and that she was to bear his child. He was also shocked to discover that Peter's influence had persuaded Elizabeth to convert to Catholicism.

Over and over, I read of the anguish George endured because of his brother. He spent an extravagant amount of that year searching for Peter and dealing with Sir Linton's rage over the matter. George offered to take Elizabeth into his family, promising that she and her child would always have a home at Pemberley, but Willoughby refused. He was obdurate that no one ever learned that his sister's husband had deserted her or that she had embraced the Catholic religion. He would not tolerate Papist connections tarnishing his reputation or deflecting his ambitions.

Once Sir Linton saw that Peter Darcy was not returning and was perhaps dead, he determined to rid his family of any evidence that Peter and Elizabeth's union had existed. He threatened the vicar of the local church with the loss of his living if he or his family ever revealed that a wedding had taken place, for he would not brook the scandal caused by talk that his sister was with child and deserted by her husband. He would rather send her out of the country. Willoughby stood over the vicar, forcing him to expunge the record of their marriage from the church annals. At first, the clergyman balked, but when Sir Linton saw that there were no other entries on the page, he tore out the page himself.

Neither George nor Sir Linton possessed knowledge that Peter and Elizabeth had also married in a Catholic ceremony, for no one existed to bear record to the fact. Unfortunately, Father Ayden, who had married the couple, was killed in an accident not long after Peter disappeared and before George returned to Pemberley from Town.

Willoughby made certain his grandmother kept his sister locked in her chamber at Bridesgate during her entire confinement, refusing her leave to see anyone. All of George's efforts to speak with Elizabeth were denied, and Willoughby told him that, if he did not keep silent about the matter, he should fear for the safety of his family.

William picked up one of the pages and began to read aloud.

11 September 1791

Normally, I would disregard Sir Linton's threats, but Fitzwilliam is young and freely roams the woods between Bridesgate and Pemberley, although I have instructed him to stay away from the Willoughby house. The baronet's rage is not only beyond reason; it is demented. So far, I have kept Anne unaware of this wretched dilemma, but I shall be forced to tell her and curtail both her and Fitzwilliam's activities if I do not go along with Willoughby's demands. I fear for Anne's health. She is so delicate that the least distress puts her in bed and the doctor must be fetched.

What am I to do? And why, oh why, did Peter desert his young wife?

"The man dared to threaten my mother!" William said, balling his hand into a fist. "Here is another entry little more than a month later."

22 October 1791

I called upon Willoughby during my trip to Town. He remains unbending in his stubborn, insupportable mood. He refuses to claim the child if it lives, and he vows that it shall not be reared at Pemberley. He insists that, once delivered, his sister and her child must take up residence at a cottage he has secured in an obscure village in Scotland, far from either Derbyshire or London. I fear Willoughby plans to cast his sister from the family, for Lady Margaret says they have no relations in that country. She said it was all she could do to insist that her granddaughter be allowed to remain at Bridesgate until her confinement is over. If Sir Linton had done as he originally planned, he would have banished the girl to Scotland upon first knowledge that she was with child.

I shall do whatever I can for Peter's poor wife, but oh, how I wish my brother would return!

"Elizabeth, what if you had been born in Scotland? I should never have known you!"

The torment in William's eyes caused me to rise from my chair. I held out my arms, and he stepped into them, allowing me to comfort him for no little time.

When we returned to the writings, I picked up a page.

28 November 1791

Lewis has been here ten days. Once again, Catherine has learned of his misdeeds—this time with an actress in Town. I have written to her, attempting to intervene, but, thus far, she refuses to relent.

"So now we know why your father prevailed upon Lady Catherine's husband for assistance. He truly could call in the favours he had performed for Sir Lewis."

"As a lad, I wondered why my uncle oft times visited Pemberley or our house in London without Aunt Catherine," William said, a bemused expression upon his face.

I cut my eyes at him. "Shall you have an actress in Town after we are married?"

"Only if you take to the stage," he answered, bending over to kiss me. He pulled out a chair and seated himself beside me. "Let us continue."

7 December 1791

Peter's child was born last night—a girl—apparently healthy. She has her mother's colouring, but I can see my brother's imprint upon her face. Elizabeth Willoughby died an hour after giving birth. Poor girl! I suspect that despair robbed her of the will to live. Her brother should be shot!

Lady Margaret summoned me right after the birth. Her daughter and grandson remain in Town unaware that it has taken place. She pleaded with me to take the babe before Sir Linton comes and sends her to Scotland. I have sent the child to Rosings with Wickham and Sarah, as I trust them both without question. I pray that Lewis can find a suitable home for her, and that he keeps news of the birth from Catherine so that she never tells my dearest Anne.

What a sad ending to this tale! I fear I shall suffer guilt the rest of my days for the part I have played. If only I could find Peter, but I fear he must be dead, for he is not the kind of man who would leave his wife and child.

William laid the journal entry down and sat back in his chair, his face troubled. "I thought my father a stronger man than that. If he had possessed more courage, you might have enjoyed a much altered life."

"At least he kept me in England. That must have required a great deal of fortitude to resist Sir Linton's certain anger when he became privy to your father's interference."

"Why could he not have stood up to Sir Linton and insisted upon rearing you at Pemberley?"

"You must not judge him harshly. He had your mother and you to think of before all else. It was a difficult situation, and your father had great responsibilities, but he did what he thought best."

He gazed into my eyes. "You are generous with my father, and yet you cling to a grudge against the man who nurtured you."

I swallowed and turned away. "That is different. Papá should have told me long ago."

"Still, he, too, did what he thought best, did he not?"

Unease settled upon me, and I did not like the feeling. *Had I treated Papá less than fairly when he did so much for me?* I rose and freshened my cup of tea. I determined not to think on the matter, for I found it painful. I poured another cup for William and changed the subject.

"Shall you ever learn why your father removed those pages from his journals?"

"Barnesdale provided the answer. He said that, the year before he died, Father summoned the elder Barnesdale to Pemberley. My father had been told by the physician to put his affairs in order because he did not have long to live. Father trusted the senior Mr. Barnesdale more than any other attorney as he had retained him since inheriting Pemberley as a young man. He was the one whom Father had instructed to send support for your care all those years. Together, they went through my father's papers, and the barrister suggested that Father either dispose of anything that linked him to Peter's child or allow Mr. Barnesdale to provide safekeeping for the evidence. My father gave him correspondence from Henry and Sir Lewis before recalling that he had written about the birth in his journals. A thorough inspection of the volumes from the year 1791 onward caused him to remove the pages from the diaries. In doing so, he also decided to take out anything he had written about Peter becoming a priest."

"But why did Mr. Darcy not destroy his writings?"

"The elder Mr. Barnesdale stated that was Father's original intent, but something caused him to reconsider. He said perhaps he had been in error to keep all of it hidden all those years, and that someday someone might need to know the truth. The attorney thought his client referred to Peter Darcy, thinking he might eventually return to Pemberley."

I reached out and took William's hand. "Who would have thought your father's information essential for his son to know?"

He brought my hand to his lips. "Strange how life comes about."

"Did you call upon Sir Linton while in Town?"

He frowned and looked away. "I did. He refused to see me, but when I told the servant that I would not leave the premises until his master granted me an audience, Willoughby eventually consented."

"Will you tell me what happened?"

"I shall say only this: Sir Linton knows precisely what I think of him. He has been told that not only do you and I know the truth, but Peter Darcy does as well. He knows that, but for the unbelievable forbearance my uncle urged me to consider, I should have called him out then and there—and I should have prevailed. And finally, he knows that he shall never prevent his sister from seeing you whenever and wherever she chooses, or he will have me to contend with, and mercy on my part shall no longer exist."

"Excellent!" I clapped my hands together. "I wish I could have witnessed that meeting."

"I would not have had you there, for the language used would not have been fitting in the presence of a lady. Indeed, Elizabeth, I do not ever want you to see that man again."

He had risen by that time and crossed the room to the window. "I see that your sister has left her chamber, for she walks in the garden with Bingley." He glanced at the clock on the mantel. "I suppose we should join them, for we have spent a long time in seclusion."

I walked over to the window. "Not before you tell me what happened at Kent. Jane and Charles appear content in their stroll."

William slipped his arms around my waist. "What a determined little thing you are, for you must have it all."

I smiled as he nuzzled my neck. "Do not attempt to distract me. I wish to hear everything, and then, let that be an end to all things unpleasant, for we have a wedding to plan."

"Very well, if you insist."

He took my hand and led me back to the sofa facing the fireplace. There, he described his meeting with his aunt and all that he had learned.

As we had gleaned from George Darcy's journal, Lady Catherine had long been aware of her husband's attraction to other women. Shortly after I was born, she learned from the servants that he had taken a baby out of Kent, and she assumed it was his child. Like many wives, she preferred to know as little as possible about her husband's indiscretions. But, on Sir Lewis's deathbed, when he began confessing his sins, she brought up the baby and insisted he tell the truth, fearing that he was financially maintaining the child.

Sir Lewis told Lady Catherine that the baby was the daughter of Peter Darcy and his wife, Elizabeth Willoughby, that Peter, as she already knew, had disappeared, and that Elizabeth was dead. He told her of Sir Linton's demands, and since George thought Peter had either died or deserted his young wife for some unknown reason, he had sent the babe to Sir Lewis to secure a proper home, agreeing to furnish her support. George had sworn him to secrecy, so Sir Lewis took the child to Hertfordshire where he told Mr. Fawcett the child was simply the natural daughter of a gentleman from the North Country.

"When my aunt called at Longbourn, she knew very well who your parents were," William said. "And she knew that you were legitimate. Sifting through Sir Lewis's papers last year, she came upon the note my father wrote when he had you transported to Kent. She deduced that you were that baby, and all she had to do was travel to Hertfordshire and confirm it with Mr. Fawcett. Then, she used the ambiguity of my father's letter for her own purposes."

"Does she hate me to the extent that she would allow such a falsehood?"

"As you know, Elizabeth, Lady Catherine is not a person to be crossed. When she approached me with her demands that I officially engage myself to Anne, and I declined, she would not tolerate having her wishes scorned. She would destroy your reputation rather than see us marry."

When I asked William how he persuaded her to finally make that confession, he told me it was not as difficult as he anticipated. At first, of course, Lady Catherine professed ignorance of the truth. Shown the stack of evidence William had accrued, however, she could not deny who I was or who my parents were. She then attempted to claim that she had acted in good faith when she made her revelations to William and me.

"'Darcy,' she said to me, 'you know I desire only the best for you, and my Anne is by far the most suitable wife you could possibly have. For that matter, I wish the best for Elizabeth Bennet. It is a disservice to suggest that she rise above her station in life. Your father's decision was correct and should be honoured. After all, Miss Bennet is much better off as the daughter of an obscure country gentleman than she would have been had Sir Linton carried through on his threat to send her to Scotland.'

"That is where my aunt made her error," William said, "for I had made no mention of Sir Linton's threat during our visit. I knew then that she was not telling me the truth. If she knew of Willoughby's threats, she could only have learned it from her husband.

"I told Lady Catherine that all connection between her house and mine, including any contact with Georgiana, would be irrevocably severed if she did not tell me the truth immediately. When I received nothing more than indignation in response, I rose from my chair, left the room, and walked down the hallway directly to my waiting carriage. Before the footman closed the door behind me, a servant came running from the house, entreating me to return.

"I inquired whether that was Lady Catherine's only message," William said, "and the servant replied that she wished to speak further on the matter. I said, 'And this is my message in return. Tell Lady Catherine that I have said all I have to say and that I shall not discuss the matter with a servant.' I dismissed the man, who hurried back to his mistress. Her outraged roar resounded with such strength that I could even hear it as I stood beside the carriage! However, within a few moments, the lady herself emerged from the house and walked down the stone steps.

"'Shall we walk?' she asked, inclining her head in a direction away from the carriage. I nodded and fell into step with her. We walked into the garden, out of sight or hearing of the servants, before she spoke again.

"'Darcy, you impose heavily upon my affection for you with this insolent treatment,' she said. 'Take care that you do not trample underfoot my naturally agreeable disposition.'

"I did not reply but met her stare with one of my own. Both of us refusing to retreat, we glared at each other for some time, but I would not give over. Finally, I turned to leave. I took but a few steps before Lady Catherine threw up her hands and agreed to tell the truth. Acknowledging that she had actively sought to prevent our engagement by using my father's note in the manner that she did, she declared once more, 'I did it for your good, Fitzwilliam. Surely, you must see that.'

"'I see nothing of the kind, Aunt,' I said. 'You maliciously attempted to ruin Miss Bennet's reputation and destroy all chance for my happiness.'

"She disputed that statement by uttering some sort of nonsense, such as, 'You will never be happy with her, just as your mother was never happy with George.'

"Her statement bewildered me, for my parents were devoted to each other. When I refuted her words, she began to rant. 'George Darcy and his Papist Irish mother! But for the Darcy fortune, my father should never have agreed to his marriage to my sister. I even offered to marry George in her place, for I knew that I was a much more suitable match for him. Anne was too delicate, too soft. George needed a strong woman like me, a woman of great passion, yet great dignity. Together, he and I could have—'"

That part of the tale made me sit up straighter, and I placed my hand on William's arm to interrupt him. "Are you saying that Lady Catherine was in love with your father?"

He threw up his hands. "Heaven help him if she was! I cannot tell you with what fortitude I attempted to suppress the horror I felt listening to her words. Fortunately, she came to herself before revealing more than I should ever wish to hear."

"What did she say?"

"She resumed the tired old argument she has harped on since the beginning. 'Miss Bennet is an upstart. Your place is with Anne. It was decided long ago by your mother and me.' I told her that I did not believe her, for Mother never made the slightest suggestion that I should marry Anne, and neither did my father. I said that it had been Lady Catherine's doing from the beginning, and unless she admitted that she was in the wrong, all connection between her house and mine would be broken.

"She continued her attempts to convince me otherwise, but when I remained silent, she relented at last and reluctantly offered a brief, bitter apology."

William shook his head. "That is the only occasion upon which I have heard my aunt apologize or admit that she has done wrong. It should be recorded in the annals of history, for I doubt that anyone shall ever bear witness to such an event again."

I gave a sigh of relief, and we both remained silent for a while, attempting to absorb all that had transpired. At length, I leaned over to kiss William's cheek. "You, sir, are a true proficient in the art of persuasion."

"Am I, now?" He pulled me close and began to kiss my ear, his lips trailing down to my neck. "Does that mean you shall do whatever I say?"

I laughed. "Perhaps...with the proper inducement."

He pulled me onto his lap and continued to kiss my neck, my ear, my cheek, coming ever closer to my lips. "Is this proper inducement?"

"This, sir, is improper seduction."

But I allowed him to continue all the same.

Chapter Eighteen

William and I did not marry at the end of the week. Mamá protested lack of time to adequately prepare for the event. Even though we declared that we wanted naught but a simple ceremony with only close family in attendance, she insisted that we must have a proper celebration. Besides, it would afford us opportunity to send express posts to Town to invite the Gardiners and have Colonel Fitzwilliam escort Georgiana.

I rather dreaded facing the colonel. I was relieved that I had never granted him a private audience whereby he might actually have proposed. William had not the slightest sympathy for his cousin. Indeed, I think he looked forward to parading his prize before him. Mrs. Gardiner wrote that they could return to Longbourn by Wednesday next, and upon telling William, he pronounced Thursday morning as our wedding day and not a day later. His tone was so marked and the look in his eye so fierce that Mamá dared not suggest further delay.

The day before the event, William and I had escaped my mother's nerves and demands by retreating to the walled garden farthest from the house. There, we had used the opportunity to steal a few kisses and murmur words of love to each other. Unexpectedly, the wind came up, warning that winter would soon be upon us. I had neglected to bring my shawl, and I began to shiver in William's embrace.

"Shall we return to the house?" he asked.

"Oh, I do not wish to give up this rare privacy just yet."

"Then, I shall fetch your wrap."

I protested, but he would not be deterred, promising to return before I could miss him. But I did. How could I not? He had become as essential to me as the air I breathed.

I walked about, noting that the plants were most likely wearing their final blooms of the autumnal season. That part of the yard contained few plots of colour, providing a refuge for natural grasses and reeds instead. I recalled how Lady Catherine had called it *a prettyish kind of a little wilderness*. Only a year earlier, she had led me past the wall of stones into its seclusion before unleashing upon me her particular brand of torment. I shuddered anew, recalling the abyss into which I had fallen upon hearing her words.

"Lizzy?"

I whirled around, startled to find Papá standing behind me.

"I did not mean to frighten you. Mr. Darcy said I would find you here."

"Is he not returning?"

"In a moment. I hoped for this opportunity to speak to you, for the morrow will be upon us before we know it, and you...will be gone."

I looked away, uncomfortable at hearing how his voice trembled, for he rarely revealed himself in such a manner.

"I fear for you to begin a new life with this...distance between us." I made no answer. "Lizzy, once again, I must tell you how I regret causing the estrangement. You know me well. I normally can forego the guilt my frailty as a father causes, but this time, I am utterly ashamed of myself... and I find that I cannot overcome the deep sorrow caused by the gulf that separates you and me."

His grief was evident. Suddenly, the fact that he had suffered much too long because of my stubborn prejudice overtook me. My heart began to ache. My throat tightened, and I felt the quickening of tears.

"Papá, I am at fault. I have judged you harshly, and I was wrong. You have fathered me in a manner that belies the relationship of a man and his foster child, for I never felt less than your own. I knew that you loved me as much as you loved Jane or Kitty or any of my sisters."

"Or more," he whispered.

"Oh, Papá!" I threw my arms around him. "Will you forgive me for acting the ungrateful daughter?"

"If you will forgive me for being the foolish father who did not consider you brave enough to know the truth."

Some time later, William found us sitting on the stone bench, my hand resting in Papá's as we talked. William started to excuse himself, but my father rose, bidding him take his place beside me. After kissing my forehead, Papá walked back to the house.

William placed the shawl around my shoulders, and taking out his handkerchief, he wiped the tear from my cheek. "I take it all is well between you?"

I nodded. "You lingered in the house a long time. Did you do so to afford Papá time alone with me?"

He shrugged. "I could not find that pesky wrap of yours anywhere."

WE MARRIED IN LONGBOURN CHURCH on the first Thursday in November. The day was glorious—one of those beautiful autumn mornings lit with sunshine, hidden now and then by a few downy clouds, and with just a bite of cold weather in the air. All my sisters, save Lydia, were in attendance, including my newest, Georgiana. Mr. and Mrs. Gardiner had arrived as planned without their children, giving Mamá cause to rejoice. Colonel Fitzwilliam was William's only additional relation who came, and the colonel displayed not the slightest regret at having lost my hand, an affront to my spirit I bore as best I could.

As William and I spoke our vows, the sanctuary was flooded with radiant light. My heart overflowed with the warmth of love I felt within the church, love not only from the man who stood beside me but also from the family witnessing our vows. I realized how truly blessed I was to have grown up as Elizabeth Bennet. Leaving through the church entry to return to Longbourn, surrounded by our loved ones, I spied Mr. Fawcett standing just outside the door. I reached out and clasped his hand as he smiled his approval. Papá had told him the truth about my birth but a few days earlier, and I could see that he shared in my happiness.

After a clamorous, joyful breakfast and many congratulatory wishes, we at last kissed and hugged our families. Bidding them farewell, we departed in William's carriage. He had asked me whether I wished to honeymoon in Florence or Vienna, but I was as tired of travelling as he. All we truly longed for was to go home to Pemberley. Georgiana was to return to Eden Park with the colonel, so we found ourselves alone at last.

The moment the carriage rounded the bend and could no longer be seen by anyone at Longbourn, William removed his hat. After he untied my bonnet, he pulled me close. He kissed me with tender, lingering kisses that stirred my senses.

"Are you warm enough, Mrs. Darcy?" he asked, wrapping his arms around me even tighter.

"I am."

"Are you happy, Mrs. Darcy?"

"Exceptionally happy."

"Are you content to be called 'Mrs. Darcy'?"

"You know that I am, but at this moment I believe I would be content no matter what you called me."

"Even 'Bessie'?"

"Even 'Bessie'…dearest Fitzwilly."

WE SPENT OUR WEDDING NIGHT in a fine house outside Daventry in North-amptonshire. I was surprised to find the owners away until my husband announced that he had bought the house ten months earlier. It was a modest estate about the size of Netherfield, providing excellent sport, or so he assured me. William planned to let it out as soon as renovations were complete. Thus, we were not forced to spend our first night of marriage making do with inadequate facilities at a village inn.

Little remained to finish the place, and I found the house more comfortable and much grander than any I had expected to encounter on the road. A full staff of servants was in place for our visit. We arrived to fires lit in every room, well-polished floors and furniture, an abundance of light, and the promising aroma of a sumptuous wedding supper in preparation.

A lady's maid who met me in my chamber quickly unpacked and then helped me bathe and dress for the evening meal. She laid out my finest nightgown for later use, and I felt my heart quicken in anticipation of the night to come. I had preliminary knowledge of what to expect, but still, I felt nervous, hoping I would not disappoint my husband. Jane had assured me only the night before, when we had snatched a few moments alone in my room, that all I must do was follow Mr. Darcy's lead. She had blushed repeatedly while imparting her brief instructions concerning the wedding night, so much so that she had to sit down and fan herself.

William stood waiting at the foot of the staircase as I descended, and I hoped he approved of my dress. The light in his eyes told me that the simple green gown pleased him. At the table, neither of us seemed to have much appetite, although the meal was deliciously prepared and elegantly served. I found myself partaking of more wine than food to the point that, when we rose from the table at the close of supper, I had to reach for the back of the chair to steady myself.

"You should have eaten more," William whispered in my ear as he took my arm and guided me into the drawing room. My eyes widened when I heard myself giggle.

Where did that come from?

"Shall you play for me, dearest?" He gestured toward the instrument sitting prominently near the window.

"I fear that I should play even more poorly than usual tonight." My eyes beseeched him not to insist, and he did not.

"Then, sit here by the fire while I provide the music."

What? Has my husband kept his talent hidden from me all this time?

I could not believe Georgiana had failed to tell me that her brother was proficient on the pianoforte. Instead of walking toward the instrument, however, William rang the bell for the servant. Within moments, three men entered the room, walked to a far corner, and picked up a violin, bass fiddle, and cello. I smiled with delight when they began their serenade with the loveliest of songs.

William poured himself a snifter of brandy and then picked up the bottle of sherry with a questioning look in my direction. When I nodded, he smiled and brought me a glass before sitting close beside me on the sofa.

"Do you think of everything?" I asked, inclining my head toward the musicians.

"I want tonight to be perfect."

"'Tis more than I have dreamed of."

"I trust you will say that in the morning."

His statement and the piercing look in his eyes made me drink the sherry far too quickly, for I drained the tiny glass in one gulp.

"Another?"

I nodded my head more than I needed to. "Please."

He smiled again, rising to fetch me another drink. "I suggest you *sip* this one."

"I will." I nodded and took a sip, and from somewhere, another unfortunate giggle escaped.

William rose and held out his hands to me. "Will you do me the honour of dancing with me, Mrs. Darcy?"

"I...yes, of course." I could not help but smile. "But how shall we dance with just the two of us?"

"I wish to teach you something new called the waltz." He led me to the wide, open portion of the vast room, and after nodding at the musicians, he took me in his arms.

"William!" I was surprised at his boldness in front of others.

"This dance allows a somewhat shocking position, but one I consider perfect for dancing with my wife."

The most beautiful music I had heard in a long time began. The romantic nature of the waltz proved enchanting. It did not take me long to follow William's lead, and I loved how the three-quarter rhythm provided perfect timing for the steps of the dance. Secure in his strong arms, I felt like a princess in a fairy tale. Round and round he whirled me until I began to laugh aloud.

"Where did you learn this?" I asked at the end of the song.

"At a ball in Bath. A couple who had honeymooned in Vienna introduced it. Evidently, it is fashionable in Austria." He signalled the musicians to begin again, and they commenced into yet another song in the same tempo.

"Once upon a time, I do recall hearing you declare that you did not care for dancing." I gave him an arch smile. "Then, you surprise me with a reel in Ireland and now the newest of steps."

"It all depends upon my partner. I detested being forced to lead around every mother's daughter seeking a husband. But now that you are my own darling wife, I find I tolerate dancing fairly well."

Just then, I stepped wrong and fell against him. He caught me and helped me to regain my footing. When he suggested that we sit down, however, I did not object, for by that time, the room was spinning. I reached for my glass of sherry as he guided me to the sofa.

"I suggest, my dear, that you forego the sherry for water from now until we retire."

"If you wish, but sherry tastes better," I said, giggling again.

He smiled and whispered in my ear. "Elizabeth, if I drink because we cannot marry and you drink because we can, how shall we ever make this union work?"

I leaned my head back and smiled up at him. "Seems a hopeless task to me."

"Nothing is hopeless," he growled. "Come with me."

You must believe me when I tell you…my husband made it work.

As MUCH AS I FOUND myself swept away by the enchantment of the night before—as exciting, enlightening, and somewhat surprising I found the marriage bed to be—awaking within my husband's arms the following morning touched me so profoundly that I almost wept.

My head lay upon his chest. I took a breath and revelled anew in his delicious scent. My arm was thrown around his bare waist, and the warmth of his skin filled me with pleasure. He held me in a close embrace, his chin resting on my head. Oh, how I loved that man!

Stirring slightly, I raised my eyes to see whether he still slept. Instead, I was greeted with a smile.

"How long have you been awake?" I asked.

"Long enough to rejoice that I am not dreaming."

"This is not a dream, is it?"

"It cannot be, for no dream feels as good as you." He kissed my forehead, and I lowered my gaze, hoping he did not notice the mist in my eyes. Unfortunately, nothing escaped William.

He lifted my chin, and I saw his frown. "What is it, my love? What is wrong?"

"Nothing. I am simply overcome with happiness."

"But you must not weep. Happiness does not create tears."

"At times it does." I raised myself enough to lean upon my elbow. "I wakened this morning feeling so safe, so wanted, so loved that I cannot find the words to convey what I mean. All I can say is that for the first time in more than a year, I feel as though I have come home. In your arms, I feel as though, at last, I am truly where I should be."

"My only love, you are…you are exactly where you should be."

He pulled me down into his embrace. We were content simply to hold each other for the longest time, marvelling at the unbelievable gift we had been granted in becoming man and wife.

OUR ACCOMMODATIONS FOR THE SECOND night of our journey were not as fine by any means, but it mattered little to either of us. The food did not compare to our wedding night feast; no musicians with strings entertained us, and the bed was by no means as soft as the former night's. I tell you the truth—we could have slept in a barn as long as we slept together. I no longer needed the wine bottle to calm my nerves, for William had proved a patient and generous lover, and I found that I took to his guidance with exceptional speed. Now that I had been introduced to the delights of married love, my eagerness almost matched his.

We found that we were compatible not only in bed but out of it as well. Upon reaching Pemberley, I undertook my duties as mistress of that great house as though I had been born there. At times, I was astonished anew at the fact that, but for Sir Linton's interference, I might have come into the world in one of those bedchambers.

William fascinated me with all that he knew about the history of our home, and I spent countless hours listening and learning from him. Wishing me to be acquainted with an outline of his estate duties, he introduced the basic tasks he attended in running Pemberley.

In the weeks to come, I was surprised to learn that William not only owned the vast lands surrounding Pemberley and his townhouse in London, but he also possessed a home in Ramsgate.

"It is but a cottage," he said. "My father bought it so Mother could enjoy the benefits of summers by the sea. I should like to take you there if you have not had your fill of the ocean."

I smiled and kissed his cheek. "By the summer months, I am quite certain I shall be glad to visit the sea again."

"And would you welcome another ocean voyage?"

I was surprised he made that suggestion. "Perhaps."

"Do you recall how narrow the beds were onboard *The Falcon*?"

"I do," I said, wondering why he asked such a curious question.

He pulled me onto his lap and began running his finger along the neckline of my gown. "I rather think I would enjoy sharing one of those beds with you."

I laughed and played with his curls. "Would you now? For how long?"

"Oh, we could begin with at least a hundred years."

WE HAD RESIDED AT PEMBERLEY as husband and wife for a little over a fortnight when William called me into his study one day. He said the post had come, and several letters in the stack were addressed to me. I recognized

Jane's script and that of Aunt Gardiner, but the third hand belonged to a stranger. Intrigued, I opened it to see Father Darcy's signature, his writing obviously weak. He had dictated it to Father Rafferty as planned, but he made the effort to sign his name.

He hoped that we were married by the time his letter arrived, and his best wishes and prayers for our happiness made up most of the remainder.

You have filled my heart with joy that I never anticipated, Elizabeth. I am still amazed that I have fathered such a daughter.

Father Rafferty added a postscript wherein he stated that my father's health declined daily. He doubted that he would live to see the new year. That statement saddened me, and I hastened to answer the letter.

Chapter Nineteen

After spending Christmas with Georgiana in London, we were to take her home with us to Pemberley the third week in January. I looked forward to our return because, although I enjoyed being in Town now that I was married, I still preferred country life in Derbyshire. Before we left, however, I told my husband that I wished to call upon Miss Willoughby.

"I would prefer to send a message asking her to call upon you, instead," he said. "Have you any objection?"

I agreed, of course, for I had dreaded returning to that dreary house belonging to the baronet. My aunt replied soon after receiving the note, indicating that she accepted my invitation with pleasure. She was to call on Thursday next, but to our surprise, the visit occurred sooner than expected.

Late one night in the early part of that same week, we had been listening to Georgiana play for us when we heard a knock at the door. My husband rose, curious as to who might call at such an hour. Instead of a caller, he was surprised to see that a message had been delivered.

"Georgiana," William said, upon reading the note the servant had brought in. "Would you excuse Elizabeth and me? It is late, and I believe it is past time for you to retire."

I was surprised at William's statement, for he rarely directed his younger sister as to when to go to her chamber. Gradually, he had begun treating her more like the young woman she had become. She frowned but did not question him. Instead, she rose from her chair and bade us good night.

"William, whatever is the matter?" I asked upon Georgiana's removal from the room.

He took my hand, assisting me to rise from the sofa. "I did not wish for my sister to hear the contents of this note, for they are quite alarming."

My eyes widened, fearing that one of my family had fallen ill.

"It is from Miss Willoughby."

"Miss Willoughby! At this time of night?"

"Sir Linton is dead."

My mouth flew open, but I could not think of anything to say.

"Elizabeth, he fell from the second floor and broke his neck."

"Oh!" I leaned against him, for I suddenly felt faint. "We must go to her."

William shook his head, leading me back to the sofa. "I shall go alone. She requests my assistance."

"Do you not think that my presence would comfort her?"

He rang the bell for the servant. "I would not have you witness the scene. Naturally, the constable has been called, and there is much confusion. I prefer that you wait here. Are you well enough for me to leave you?"

I nodded. "I am well, but I would rather go with you. I do not like the idea of my aunt being alone at such a time."

"If she is willing, I shall bring her home with me." He kissed my forehead and then strode from the room.

Thus, it came about that my uncle died the same unspeakable death that he had proclaimed for my mother in the falsehood he told my father all those years ago. I shuddered at the thought that he fulfilled his own horrid prophecy.

Suffering from shock and grief, Miss Willoughby remained with us for more than a week while William made arrangements to bury Sir Linton. He also assisted her in meeting with her brother's attorneys. My husband's kindness increased my admiration of his fine character, for he was more than considerate of my aunt's state.

There were no male heirs to inherit the Willoughby property. In truth, none of the three Willoughby children had offspring other than my mother. Sir Linton's will directed that his property, such as it was, be left to his sister. William and I knew that Aunt Eleanor could not be content living in that decaying townhouse, so we encouraged her to visit us at Pemberley, which she agreed to do later in the year.

"I have so longed to see Bridesgate again," she said one day as we stirred our cups of tea while sitting in the small parlour.

"Then, you shall, for we are acquainted with its tenant, Admiral Denison."

"I have not lived there since I was but a child."

"I hope it will provoke memories of more pleasant times."

She reached out and took my hand. "Each time I look upon your face, my dear, I remember pleasant days, for I see my sister. Your presence lifts my spirits in a manner I thought had died long ago."

I was surprised at her words, for in my mind, I could still hear Sir Linton's accusations that I had ruined his family. My aunt had declared his charges untrue, and I had vowed to rid myself of that memory. Life had taught me, however, that some vows are difficult to keep. Hateful words linger with a pain that is not easily forgotten.

"You look positively lovely. May I be so bold as to suggest that marriage suits you?"

My aunt's statement startled me from my reflection, causing me to blush and smile. "I am more than content."

"Then, do I assume correctly that you and Mr. Darcy have made a love match?"

I nodded. "We have."

She reached for my hand. "Your mother would be so pleased!"

"Do you think so?"

"Without a doubt. At last, you wear the name to which you were born. May you enjoy a long life as mistress of Pemberley."

Although Eleanor Willoughby and I were still strangers in many respects, little by little, I was beginning to feel that we were truly related, that here was someone to whom I actually belonged. Would she one day be as close to me as my Aunt Gardiner?

WITHIN A WEEK OF AUNT Eleanor's departure from our townhouse, William announced that we would travel to Pemberley. I could not wait to return to Derbyshire. Although the mansion would be dressed in winter's white by that time, I anticipated the warmth and loveliness I would find waiting within. The beauty of my new home was not all that called to me. I desired the tranquillity that soothed my soul each time I walked by Pemberley's windows and viewed the prospect of the surrounding woods and groves. I could not grieve over Sir Linton's death, yet I longed to escape all memory of its horror. I was eager to leave London behind.

Unfortunately, upon returning to Derbyshire, we were met with greetings even more grievous.

While we were in Town, a letter from Ireland had arrived at Pemberley stating that Father Darcy had died on the sixth day of December.

His passing was easy and peaceful, Father Rafferty wrote. Within the packet containing the message, the priest had included my father's rosary. I held it in my hand, noting that most of the beads were worn thin from his years of prayers.

"He died on your birthday," William said softly.

I raised my eyes to his. "He died on the same day that my mother died."

We both grieved Peter Darcy's loss in our own way. William thrust himself into the management of his estate, keeping himself busy throughout the day. I took long walks all over Pemberley's extensive grounds. I longed to plunge into the wood, but it was still quite cold. Snowfall had been less than usual that winter, but a sharp wind often arose without warning. My husband had asked me not to wander off alone, and I obeyed.

I thought of my father's life. I thought of how events and people had conspired to rob him of the love of a wife and family, yet they provided him with a purpose he evidently found fulfilling. I thought of the good he had done, and I was proud of him. Then, I began to think how cheated I felt not to have known him longer. My spirits lagged, and I found the same melancholy creeping back into my moods that had beset me for so long during the past year. I had thought it all behind me, but once again, life had taken a bitter turn. And yet, for some strange reason, I could not weep over my father's passing.

William was as loving and compassionate as I knew he would be. That first night, upon reading the letter, he had held me in his strong, comforting arms all night long, for I could not sleep. He had gone out of his way to provide me with time alone so that I might grieve in private, cautioning Georgiana not to intrude when I departed the house for my sojourns in the garden. After the first few weeks, he offered distractions, such as rides through the countryside, visits with neighbours, or even an invitation for my family at Longbourn to come, but I refused all of his suggestions.

At length, one day, William walked into my sitting room, where I sat alone, staring out the window. He said nothing, but strode through the adjoining door into my chamber, returning within moments carrying my new fur-lined cloak and hat.

"Come, Elizabeth, let us go out."

"I do not wish to call on anyone."

"Then, we shall not see anyone, but you will leave the house. Look without; we are graced with one of those rare days in February. The sun shines, the snow melts, and, best of all, the wind has disappeared."

I protested, but he would have none of it, insisting that I rise from my chair while he fastened my cloak securely. He donned his long coat and hat and ushered me out the door. I was surprised to see the phaeton harnessed and waiting in the drive, its big yellow wheels still bright and shining. When I asked him our destination, he refused to say.

Once we were securely seated and the fur rug wrapped around us, he flicked the reins, and we drove away from Pemberley. I could not help but recall our previous ride in that conveyance a year before. Much had changed since that occasion but not Mr. Darcy's driving. Again, we careened down the road at a speed that robbed me of breath, and I was forced to cling to him for dear life. This time, however, I had not the slightest hesitation in hanging onto his arm.

When my husband turned up the path leading to Bridesgate Manor, I began to protest that I was in no mood to visit with Mrs. Denison or the admiral.

"That is good, for they are not at home. I have it on good authority that the family journeyed to Town on Tuesday last."

"Then why are we here?"

He refused to answer my query but drove around the circular path that led to the back of the house. Servants, who were obviously acquainted with the master of Pemberley, held the horse while we climbed down from the phaeton. Mr. Darcy spoke briefly with the steward, who nodded and led us through the back garden. He pointed toward a slight incline some distance from the grounds and left us to my husband's pursuit. I followed him quietly, having given up asking questions he would not answer. We walked through a stand of trees that opened upon a glade, containing a single gravestone.

I caught my breath. "William, is this where my mother is buried?"

"It is." He took my hand and guided me until I reached the stone bearing her name. *Elizabeth Willoughby Darcy.* I fell to my knees and traced the letters with my fingers.

"It was here all along," I said softly. "If only we had found this grave last year—"

"Yes." He knelt beside me, taking my hand in his.

For some reason, I felt peace descending upon my spirit. There, in that quiet haven, fixed evidence existed of the mother I never knew.

"How did you know to bring me here, that I needed to see her grave?"

"Because I know you."

I turned to see his eyes upon me…eyes filled with love and understanding. What had I ever done to deserve such a good man?

Once again reaching out to the stone, I retraced my mother's name. "William, *Darcy* was not always here, was it? Did you have it added?"

He stared into my eyes. "Why not? It was her name."

We sat there for some time until I was ready to go, thinking we would return home. Instead, William turned the horse off the road and onto the narrow path leading through the wood. Within a short time, we arrived at the Catholic chapel.

"Will you go in with me?" he asked before descending from the phaeton. When I nodded, he jumped down and then lifted his arms to assist me.

Inside the building, the familiar odours of incense and old wood greeted us. We were the only visitors, and after William saw me seated in a pew, he walked to the side of the sanctuary, knocked on the door, where he was met by the priest, and entered the sacristy.

I gazed at the altar and the statue of the Madonna and Child. My eyes lingered on the Celtic cross on the table. I could see my grandmother lighting candles, fingering her rosary, and praying for forgiveness for having worshipped in the Anglican Church. I saw a young Peter Darcy and then Elizabeth Willoughby as they embraced the Catholic religion. I saw the devoted couple as they stood before that altar and vowed to love each other forever. I saw my father prostrate on the floor, pounding his fist into the slate, pouring out his anguish when he thought my mother dead.

And finally, at long last, I began to weep. Great, painful sobs escaped from deep within as though they had been locked away for eternity. I wept for the past that had been stolen from me, for what had been, and for what could never be again. I mourned the loss not only of my parents, but of the childhood I might have known. I mourned the loss of the person I might have been. I mourned the loss of the person I had thought myself to be. I mourned the injustice that had caused these souls such pain, and I mourned for the loss of innocence and hope that I had suffered.

And when, at length, my weeping subsided, I mourned no longer.

I felt William's presence beside me, unaware as to when he had joined me. I looked down to see his dear, strong hand holding mine. Taking a handkerchief from his pocket, he gently wiped the tears from my face.

"I have something to show you," he said softly.

I rose and followed him to the sacristy, wondering why he should lead me there. Inside the small room, he introduced me to the priest and then indicated that I should sit at a table. Before leaving the room, the priest placed a large open book in front of me.

William pointed to the page containing writing, but I could not make it out. I attempted to decipher what he wished me to see before realizing it was not written in English.

"I cannot read Latin, William."

"Look closely. I believe you will see names that you recognize."

I questioned him with my expression but did as he instructed. There, among all the foreign words, I saw the names *Peter Darcy* and *Elizabeth Willoughby*.

"The answer we sought this past year was right here," William said. "For with many other words and phrases, this entry states that your parents were married by Father Timothy Ayden in this parish on the First day of March in the year of our Lord 1791. If I had only known last year that your mother had become Catholic, I would have found the answer right under my nose."

"Thank you for finding it now," I whispered. "It gives me a feeling of serenity to see it written down, much like touching my mother's gravestone."

I sat there no little time, gazing at the priest's handwriting from more than twenty years past. William waited patiently, and when I rose at last, he asked me whether I was ready to return home.

I shook my head. "Pray, take me somewhere new. I need to see a part of this country that I have never seen before."

WE RODE FOR MILES, MY William and I, down roads I had not yet travelled and through countryside I had never seen, and still, we remained in Derbyshire, according to my husband. At last, he reined in the horse, causing the phaeton to stop. I was amazed at our destination, for we had left the main road and struck out through paths not clearly marked. I had realized that we were climbing, but until I looked back, I had not the slightest idea that we had ascended to such a height.

"If we venture farther, we shall have to walk. Shall we?" he asked, and I agreed, of course.

The landscape had turned barren, without grass or trees nearby. Instead, we climbed up a portion of huge stones flat enough to walk on, yet leading higher and higher. At length, when I began struggling to catch my breath, William suggested that we content ourselves with the view. I turned to glance over my shoulder and was surprised at how far we had climbed. I walked to the jagged edge of the cliff upon which we stood and looked down.

"How deep the valley lies below us!"

William joined me and took my hand in his. "Do not stand too near the rim."

I found myself entranced by not only how tiny the stream below appeared, but by the absolute terror the thought of falling produced in me. I had never feared heights, but then, I doubted that I had ever before climbed to such an elevation. We stood there, each of us lost in our own thoughts.

At length, William spoke. "Where are you, dearest—wading in that stream below?"

I shook my head. "Nowhere near that pleasant."

He frowned. "Then where? I hoped to distract you from your grief."

"You have," I assured him. "It is just that—"

"Just what?"

"Standing on the edge of this precipice makes me think of life itself."

"Indeed? In what way?"

"It takes but a step to encounter disaster. A single event can change an ordinary day into a day of tragedy."

"I suppose," he said, removing his hat. "By the same reasoning, however, a single event can make a horrid day into one more lovely than can be imagined. It is all in how one chooses to look at it."

I released his hand and knelt down, continuing to gaze at the scene far below.

"I understand what you are saying. One must be hopeful in one's outlook, but William, what do I do with this fear that continues to beset me?"

"Of what fear do you speak?" He placed his strong hands upon my shoulders and brought me to my feet.

"The fear that I have lost my faith. The fear that no matter how much we love each other or how good our life together is or how much we try...out of nowhere, on a day that begins in all innocence, something may come along to make the life we know disappear as easily as a vapour dissolves into nothing."

He turned me around and took my face in his hands.

"Elizabeth, you have experienced a series of shocks in the past fourteen months that would fell the strongest of faiths."

"As you have."

William shook his head. "Mine does not compare with yours. I was never told that I am not who I thought I was, that my parents were not the parents who gave me birth, that the name I had worn all my life was not my own, or that my truth was altered through no fault of my own. And I did not discover my father only to lose him within a matter of months. You have endured more than you should have, Elizabeth, but you have survived. If your faith is weak, give it time. I believe it will grow strong again."

I turned away, gazing at the scene far below once more. "But how, William? How will my faith ever take root anew?"

"By looking up." Tenderly, he lifted my chin. "You have spent far too long staring at what lies below or looking over your shoulder, watching for what may or may not creep up from behind. Feast your eyes on all that lies ahead of us." Holding his arm aloft, he gestured toward the hills.

I did as he said and was amazed at the vistas I saw in the distance, at how far one might see from the peak on which we stood, and at the magnificence of the prospect before me. How had I missed such a sight?

He slipped his arms around my waist, and together we attempted to take in the wonder of all that we could see.

"What is it that the psalmist says?" he whispered in my ear. "I will lift up mine eyes unto the hills..."

"From whence cometh my help," I finished.

"I cannot promise you that each day will be perfect, Elizabeth, for, granted, life is fragile. There is one thing I do know: our love is not fragile. Our love is strong and enduring. Our love will stand when all else fails. As for the rest of it, what can I say? We are all in God's hands. Let us leave it to Him."

Epilogue

T en years have now passed since I married Mr. Darcy, and he still makes love to me with his eyes. In a crowded room, across a noisy, joyful dinner table, it takes but one certain glance, and I feel that rush of anticipation overtake me, knowing that he wants me. I have seen numerous days surprise me, for many events have transpired, but William remains constant.

Our family has been altered by marriages and births. Both Mary and Kitty married men from Hertfordshire. Thus, Mamá enjoys the frequent company of two of her daughters. Jane and Mr. Bingley left Netherfield within a year of my marriage, moving to a neighbouring county within thirty miles of Pemberley. That move has afforded my sister and me much joy now that we dwell within easy distance of one another. They are parents to three daughters and a young son, all sweet children possessing hearty constitutions.

Mr. and Mrs. Wickham remain in Newcastle and continue to reap what they have sown. Mamá writes to tell me each time my youngest sister visits Longbourn, but I have rarely had opportunity to be there at the same time. Thus, I must say I have only seen her twice since her marriage, and I have never encountered Mr. Wickham again, for he is much employed with his own pursuits.

Georgiana had a successful Season the first spring that William and I were married. Within two years, she wed Mr. Wentworth, the grandson of a prominent gentleman in Town. They have two daughters, one of whom is the image of Georgiana.

Six months after William and I married, a sad event transpired at

Bridesgate when Admiral Denison's wife fell ill and, within days, departed this earth. He appeared most cast down for much of the following year. However, as things happened, he remarried the next year.

Admiral Denison and Eleanor Willoughby were married eighteen months after her brother's death. The admiral took her home to live at Bridesgate, the house she had loved as a child. After Sir Linton's death, she had made frequent visits to Pemberley, and she and I had continued to grow closer. During those visits, we had called on the Denisons, never dreaming my aunt would one day become the admiral's bride and my neighbour.

THE DAY WILLIAM HAD BROUGHT me home to Pemberley as his bride, he had surprised me by an addition he had made to the gallery of family portraits in the great hall. Included on the wall hung the picture of my mother that Andrew Denison had discovered in the attics of Bridesgate.

"When did you order this placed at Pemberley?" I asked in wonder.

Standing behind me, he slipped his arms around my waist. "The day after you agreed to marry me. I wrote to Mrs. Reynolds that evening from Ireland and directed her to carry out my wishes."

"Thank you, William." I lay my head back on his shoulder and gazed up at the mother I had never known.

"The portrait hangs where it should have all along, for she was the proper wife of Peter Darcy and the mother of the mistress of this house."

"I wish we owned a likeness of my father as a grown man."

We walked a few paces to stand before the picture of the three young Darcy brothers.

"We shall simply have to see the future man reflected in the face of this young boy," William said. "And when your portrait is done, I believe we will see reminders of both your mother and him in your lovely face."

"I have never had my picture painted."

"You may do so with one qualification."

"Oh?" I cut my eyes at him. "And what might that be?"

"I shall sit in on each of your sessions with the artist."

"Indeed? I would think that should prove most tiresome."

"I never grow tired of gazing at you, my love."

"A pretty answer, but is it completely truthful?"

"What do you mean?"

"Surely, you would not prove jealous of the poor artist who is forced to draw my likeness."

"Hmph! How could I not grow jealous of a man who looks upon your beauty for hours at a time?"

"William! You have no reason for concern. Surely, you know that you alone own my heart."

He drew me into his arms. "I do. However, I alone also claim possession of your body, and no man shall spend hours in your presence without my company." He kissed me tenderly. "Indulge me, sweet one, for mercy's sake."

I kissed him back. "I do recall once upon a time promising you that I would have mercy."

"You did, and I always collect on promises."

RECENTLY, WE ADDED YET ANOTHER portrait to the gallery of Darcys, one I happen to consider as dear as the great image of my husband, for only a few inches from the likeness of my father and his brothers as children hangs the portrait of three more young Darcy brothers. George Fitzwilliam, Peter Thomas, and Henry Edward sit on a deep-green velvet couch, their dark curls brushed, their shining, pink cheeks scrubbed, and their starched white collars almost in place.

Our Georgie, named naturally for his grandfather and father, is the oldest at nine years of age. Henry Edward, our youngest, who is all of five years old, wears the names of our uncles. And our seven-year-old middle son, Peter Thomas, with the twinkle in his green eyes belying the serious demeanour about his mouth, is named for my fathers, Peter Darcy and Thomas Bennet.

Already an accomplished horseman at a tender age, Georgie does well at any sport. He dogs the steps of his father, and I know he will make an excellent master of Pemberley one day. Little Henry is, naturally, still my baby. His playful capers can make William and me laugh on the bleakest of days. And dearest Peter—inconceivably, he reminds me of both my fathers, for he has an excellent mind, already excels at his studies, and prefers his own company much of the time. I often find him with his head in a book while his brothers run and play outdoors. On the other hand, it is uncanny how his sharp wit makes one think that Papá has somehow passed down his gift to the boy.

AND NOW, AS I CLOSE this account and reflect upon the past ten years, I tend to dwell on the happiness I have been granted all because Mr. Darcy fell in love with me. I would not, however, have you believe that our marriage has always flowed smoothly or that we have not endured trials. I would like to say that the day Lady Catherine lied to me in the garden at Longbourn did not change me…but it did. It left me with a wariness that plagued me and worried William.

For some time—years, in fact—I confess that I struggled with periods of darkness. To most, I appeared much as I ever had. My disposition was amiable, and my wit remained impertinent. I seemed the woman upon whom fortune had smiled. I was the wife of Mr. Darcy, after all, and mistress of Pemberley. Nevertheless, at times, I found myself overwhelmed with fears of the future and even of the present day. I would forget my husband's admonition and feel that I was yet being pulled back into my past. I wish I could say I regained my faith as easily as William wanted me to…but I did not.

When my children were born, I determined they would never experience that same pain of uncertainty that dwelt within me. I set out to become the best of mothers, a proposition that, of course, is insupportable. I sought to protect them from everything. If not for their father, they never would have ridden horses or climbed trees. I blundered in other ways, but their tender hearts forgave me.

My prayer book became my constant companion. William bought me a new Bible with pristine white pages, unstained with tears or wrinkled from use. I, however, preferred his mother's old prayer book. I had discovered it hidden away at the back of a drawer in the desk she used to write her letters. The pages had been turned often, and I was somehow comforted to know that another wife and mother had evidently retreated to that same book to strengthen her faith. I kept my father's rosary near the book, for it consoled me because it had been his.

Slowly, my faith returned. Bad dreams ceased to disturb my sleep, and weeks would pass wherein my thoughts never strayed to the note, yellowed with age, that had altered my existence. I had no desire to live a life devoted to my suffering. I prayed to become whole again, and eventually, God granted me that desire.

I can now say that for the most part, I am recovered. I face each day, if not with optimism, at least with confidence that my loved ones and I are resting in God's hands.

Throughout these years, naught but one knew of my struggles, and that one, of course, was my dearest William. His strength supported me when I stumbled, and his faith sufficed when mine failed.

My husband continues to declare that our love will increase until the grave claims us and even beyond. I am unsure about the last part of that statement because I do not know what happens to love after death, and I recall that when it comes to declarations of love, my husband remains wildly extravagant. Still, I cling to that promise with all that is within me.

One thing I am sure of: I will not presume to enjoy this good life, or this good man, without thanking God. I shall be oh so grateful for the blessing each day brings.

I may not utter the words aloud, but they are ever present in my thoughts.

CPSIA information can be obtained at www.ICGtesting.com
Printed in the USA
BVOW03s1052180315

392253BV00002B/166/P